Other books by **Gary B. Boyd**

# Make
# Sure
## You're
# Right

## GARY B. BOYD

**author**HOUSE®

*AuthorHouse*™
*1663 Liberty Drive*
*Bloomington, IN 47403*
*www.authorhouse.com*
*Phone: 833-262-8899*

*Published by AuthorHouse   02/05/2021*

*ISBN: 978-1-6655-1626-6 (sc)*
*ISBN: 978-1-6655-1628-0 (e)*

*Library of Congress Control Number: 2021902479*

*Print information available on the last page.*

# CONTENTS

# DEDICATION

This novel is dedicated to America's police officers, men and women who selflessly put their lives on the line every day and night so I can write my books and my readers can enjoy my writings in safety. Special note to my grandson **Christopher** of Austin, TX PD, nephew **Ray (T.R.)** of Mayes County, OK Sheriff's Office, grandson **Clayton** of Austin, TX PD Forensics, cousin **Rick** of Jay, OK PD, cousin **Larry** of Fayetteville, AR PD Ret., friend **Matt** of Rogers, AR PD, friend **Clifford** of Texas DPS Ret., friend Bob of Oklahoma Highway Patrol Ret., friend **Ellis** of Benton County Sheriff's Office Ret.

None of my work would be worthy of publication without the help of my wife **Shirley** and my daughter **Tina**. They correct my mistakes and argue with me when my story strays.

# PREFACE

The saw "*The first liar doesn't stand a chance*" is only suited to besotted tale telling during episodes of questionable braggadocio. In fact, sober minds cling to first tellings as unshakable gospel. If you question the veracity of the previous statement, simply follow Social Media. In the blink of an eye, a mere moment in unmeasurable time, a cell phone video forms the unshakeable opinions of millions, provides vitriol to unsettled minds, and incites action where action is seldom necessary.

Law enforcement officers fight crime in a world filled with too often un-supporting politicians and public opinion that is too easily swayed by the blatherings of Mainstream Media that is influenced by Social Media. Like self-fulfilling prophecies, the circular arguments posed by the unusual alliance of Social Media and Mainstream Media feed upon themselves to create fictional, even mythical, realities – and that is plural. The Media is no longer a source of news for the sake of presenting facts to its customers. And customers they are beyond doubt. The Media is in the business to sell a product. Social Media is the marketing tool that tests the product for acceptability, to determine what the customers want, and the Media pushes that which sells.

Thus rumors are born. Once said, once seen, nothing short of a significant emotional event can shake the veracity of a well rooted rumor. Entire social movements are built around incomplete information – or well-planned lies. The politics of Man are replete with evidence that truth is not necessary to foment radical ideas. One only needs to present a grain of truth within a bushel of untruths to gain the attention of the malleable masses. Manipulation only requires that untruths be made to seem authentic. The rumor becomes perception, perception becomes reality, and public opinion is formed to inexorably change the lives of humans and the course of history.

Police Chief Sarah James only wants to fight crime. That is her job. That is what she is paid to do. She does not want to change public opinion – except to put her and the Devaney Police Department in a good light.

# CHAPTER 1

Monday 7:15

Things changed.

Sarah knew some things would change when *she* changed from Interim Police Chief to Police Chief. Change is the natural order of things. Change is inevitable. She did not expect everything to remain the same, comfy and cozy with developed familiarity. But - the newly minted Chief of the Devaney Police Department did not expect her whole world to change.

Keith was deeply involved with Zoey Kopechne. Not that Sarah did not see that coming. In fact, it was already there before the Council meeting that resulted in her change from Senior Detective to Interim Police Chief. She knew it would change; but when she most needed the intimate emotional support, there was none. She also knew it had to change. She and Sergeant Keith Locke could no longer be, not under the changed circumstances.

The uneasy peace that existed between Sarah and Mayor Kamen changed. There was no peace. Mayor Kamen's agenda did not allow peace between City Hall and the Police Department. *Citizen Friendly* and limited funding for law enforcement were what Jordon Kamen sought as her legacy. Mayor Kamen was more concerned about all things environmental than she was about the needs of City Departments, in particular the Police Department. The Mayor's vision did not change just because Sarah's title changed to Police Chief. Jordon Kamen wanted to fundamentally transform the staid city of Devaney into a modern, forward-looking example of what a city should be. Sarah James was not Mayor Jordon's first choice for Chief. As a matter of fact, Sarah James was not the Mayor's choice at all. *"Good Ol' Boy"* City Councilman Joseph Elsea, negotiated Sarah to be the Interim Chief while he tried to smooth the way for *"retired"* Police Chief Bill Keck to be reinstated.

Councilman Elsea was Sarah's lifeline, and Bill Keck's. That changed when Sarah arrested the long-time Councilman for feeding fentanyl and carfentanil tainted drugs into Devaney's illicit drug supply. As bad as it was, Joseph Elsea's intentions were good. The Councilman believed his approach to remove all the illegal drug users would rid his city of drugs forevermore. In his desperate mind, if he eliminated the drug customers, he would eliminate the need for drug sellers, and he would rid his city of the scourge forever. That arrest shoved Sarah into the limelight with a jolt. The public loved her. Her actions proved that no one was above the law. Interim Chief was no longer an option in the Public Mind. Mayor Jordon had no recourse but to hire Sarah as Devaney's first female Police Chief. A change Sarah had not bargained for - but she accepted it as necessary.

Lieutenant Tony Kendall, a stalwart law enforcement officer and stellar leader of a small but efficient group of undercover cops left Devaney Police Department. That change rocked Sarah. It shook her confidence in her ability to lead Devaney PD. If the key players in Devaney PD did not trust her leadership, there was no way she could succeed. In the beginning, she was sure that Tony was satisfied with her in the role of Interim Chief, even though he had more time-in-grade than her. When her role changed to something more permanent, she still thought that he was savvy enough to understand the politics of a small city. The fact that he left to accept an offer to be Police Chief in a Devaney-sized city in Missouri, a well-compensated career move for the man, did not lessen the sting to Sarah's ego. It did not remove her self-doubts. She could only wonder … and fear … that Tony's departure was a harbinger of further attrition. She had no desire to rebuild Devaney PD. She was sure that would entail more change than she could tolerate.

Sarah also discovered she had an ego. That was a change. She always envisioned herself as straight forward and faithfully dedicated to her spouse … law enforcement. She learned from her mistakes and grew.

That was her style. She was sure she had no personal agenda, no self-aggrandizing goals. She only had a motto, one not even of her own creation. One adopted from a networked acquaintance, Detective Daniel Sanders from a city in a neighboring state. He lived by Davy Crockett's motto, *"Make sure you're right then go ahead."* She adopted the same, a constant reminder that her first solo case almost resulted in a miscarriage of justice. A murder case where she jumped at the first circumstantial solution available, impatient to get her first solve and prove herself capable. That case taught her what every good detective knew - never get ahead of the evidence.

"Good morning, Darling."

Sarah's descent of the stairs from the second story office area was temporarily halted in reaction to a loud and cheerful voice. She gripped the handle of her motto inscribed coffee cup as she focused on Sergeant Maria Honeycutt's smiling face. The lifer was always in a good mood, unless circumstances dictated something different. Sergeant Honeycutt took life in stride. She did not get rattled by daily events. The slightly overweight, fifty-something woman with gray-streaked brown hair approached the stairs, her belt gear rattling the standard police rattle. She was the weekend, nighttime Shift Commander – by choice.

"Good morning, Maria," Sarah responded. She allowed herself to smile, even though her mind was filled with thoughts of the upcoming day's schedule – nothing to smile about. It was time to perform her morning rounds; to contact the on-coming shift and the overnight shift. She had received no middle-of-the-night calls over the weekend, but that did not mean Devaney was quiet. She liked the fact that Maria chose to work weekend nights. The experienced woman knew what merited an emergency for the Chief of Police. "How was your night?"

"Lonely without you," Honeycutt wriggled her heavy eyebrows as she replied with a suggestive grin.

Sarah knew the woman would lead with something like that, especially if there were no issues of note. An unashamed lesbian, Maria Honeycutt had made a game out of playfully teasing Sarah ever since Sarah's rookie debut with Devaney PD. Her comments were no worse than those made by male officers, and far less demeaning. Sergeant Honeycutt did not change. Sarah knew that the Sergeant would stand behind her and support her as

Chief, just as the veteran had done for other Chiefs in her storied career. Sarah grinned, "I'm sorry you were lonely – *not*. That must mean I have nothing to fear. No angry contact cards. No hot line calls to the Mayor's lackies."

"I can't answer to those. We did write a few speeding tickets and check on a few suspected prowlers. You know how people are. Nothing good happens after midnight. But - no reported bank robberies."

Sarah smiled appreciatively. The reference to bank robberies was an obscure code that dated back to a former Chief who often admonished his officers to not "leave the banks unguarded." In plain language, it reminded the officers to not be distracted from their duties. "I suppose your Relief is exhorting his officers to be *citizen friendly*?" The statement was a question, with a sarcastic emphasis on the Mayor's city motto.

"Of course," Maria chuckled. "They're in the squad room. Will you be entertaining the Mayor today?"

Maria's question did not require an answer. She was just "keeping her ear to the ground." Sarah answered anyway. Nothing to hide. "No. She's decided to entertain me. I have been *invited* to her inner sanctum." She shook her head. "Fun stuff, this Chief duty."

"Are you going to paint the squad cars green?" Sergeant Honeycutt, and most of the Devaney police force, knew that the Mayor wanted to change the squad car colors from black and white to two-toned green. Lieutenant Glasgow had let that become known; a tidbit thrown out to make it seem like he was still connected to the regular duty officers, willing to share secrets. A not so subtle way of feeding the Mayor's thoughts into the minds of individual police officers. The Mayor felt that the traditional, stark colors were intimidating. Green tones would make the police seem more accessible, more *citizen friendly*. And green vehicles would underscore her environmental agenda for the city.

"And that would be a solid *no*," Sarah responded between sips from her gray cup with Davy Crockett's words emblazoned in pink. Black coffee with one packet of sugar dumped into the bottom before filling, finally cool enough to drink. "But - I'm sure I will be asked to do something just as unpalatable."

Sergeant Honeycutt nodded. "Stand up for yourself, Chief. Kamen won't last past her interim status. She's not a survivor like you."

Sarah did not see a hint of a smile. The Sergeant was being sincere. "Thank you, Sergeant. I will stand up for the Department. We have good people here who are doing a good job. Someday, the Mayor will understand that."

"We can hope," Honeycutt added as Sarah left for the squad room and her morning rounds.

The morning routine for the employees of the Devaney Police Department, officers, and civilians alike, did not change ... much. The first few months were filled with anticipation and maybe some dread as everyone waited for Sarah to revamp the department to make her mark. Who was in, who was out, who was up, who was down? Of additional concern was the fact that everyone knew Chief Keck had been fired by Mayor Kamen within months of her assuming the role of Mayor, a first term Councilwoman selected by the City Council to replace deceased Mayor Clairmont. Everyone in the department knew how Sarah came into power as the Chief of Police. As much as they knew her and liked her as Senior Detective, they still had doubts about the changes she might make – or even if she was the right person to make those changes. No one knew whether Sarah was under the influence of Mayor Kamen or if she would stand on her own ... *could* stand on her own.

Those concerns gradually faded as it became apparent Sarah owed nothing to Jordon Kamen. Also, strong words from Sergeant Honeycutt and supporting words from Lieutenant Taylor McCuskey helped the transition. Even Lieutenant Tony Kendall encouraged the officers to accept Sarah as their leader before he left. Sarah's early morning greetings with personal contact helped smooth the transition. Sarah avoided dramatic changes. But changes happen as sure as time passes. As Police Chief, she had to be a change agent, assist the transitions.

Lieutenant Glasgow cautiously knocked on Sarah's open office door where she sat at her desk after finishing her morning rounds. She recognized the sound of his footsteps, grown tentative whenever he entered the Police Station after his promotion to head of Devaney's Public Outreach Department.

The Public Outreach Department, though defined as a division of Devaney PD, was funded by the Mayor's Office and reported to Mayor

Kamen – or her surrogate, Zoey Kopechne. That department was housed in City Hall, not the Police Station. Melvin Glasgow had accepted the role eagerly. It was a promotion. He and Corporal Keith Locke, promoted to Sergeant, thought the move would be good for their careers. Instead, both men found themselves on eggshells anytime they walked into the Police Station.

Sarah tried to hide her disappointment in Lieutenant Glasgow, even though it was not his fault. He was simply doing his job, what he was paid to do. No one could honestly blame him for that. "Come in, Melvin. How can I help you?" Keep it simple and friendly until some other reaction was required. Besides, she had preparatory work to do before her meeting with the Mayor.

"The Mayor asked me to bring the list of contact card comments from the weekend. She wants you to be prepared to respond to them when you come to her office." The Lieutenant's hand reached across Sarah's desk and offered a folder filled with sheets of paper.

Sarah smiled bemusedly. The same list could have been e-mailed, as it usually was. The contact list was not officially on the agenda for the meeting. "Is there something that requires immediate attention, Lieutenant?" She knew the reason the Mayor changed the delivery mode, and the urgency the change would imply. A distraction from the primary reason for their upcoming meeting. An attempt to take Sarah's mind off *"guarding the bank."*

"I'm not sure, Ma'am. The Mayor insisted that I personally hand this to you. I haven't really studied it."

Sarah saw the nervousness in Lieutenant Glasgow's body language. He was not being truthful. He had seen the complaints. He knew what the Mayor's message was. He was afraid to take sides, to openly demonstrate which side he was on. "Thank you, Melvin. I appreciate it." She opened the folder. The top piece of paper was typed in bold font. "CRITICAL" was its heading. She read the quotation typed below the heading. *"The officers held their hands on their guns the whole time. I don't appreciate armed threats around my children. Rein in your gestapo!"* Sarah looked through the other pages, searching for additional information. "Where is the contact card tracking number?"

Lieutenant Glasgow's eyes danced. "I don't think that one came from a contact card. I think it was from the hotline. Zoey tabulates those." His words contradicted his earlier denial of knowledge.

Sarah hated the contact cards, but they at least offered traceability. They were two-part and sequentially numbered to allow the tabulators to connect them to a particular officer-citizen contact. The officer attached one part to shift reports, and the citizen returned the other part via mail. That meant a delay of several days. The hotline calls were random and seldom provided a link back to a single incident, especially for traffic stops. Too anonymous. They were usually made spontaneously, within a few hours of the incident – by an angry citizen with a beef. "Okay. I will address the concerns." Sarah watched Glasgow's body relax. He had done his duty. "Have a good day, Melvin. Maybe I'll see you at City Hall later." There was no need to be rude.

Sarah called out to Liz Sweeney, her Administrative Assistant as soon as Lieutenant Glasgow's footsteps faded. Sarah was not yet comfortable asking someone else to do tasks that she used to do routinely, but that was why the Chief had an Administrative Assistant. "Liz, do you mind calling Zoey to get the time code on the citizen hotline call referencing Gestapo?"

"Not at all." Liz was loyal to Devaney PD, regardless of who occupied the Chief's office. "I will try to not rock the boat."

Sarah responded with a soft laugh, "Thank you, Liz." She knew the experienced woman would tactfully leave a mark on the young woman at the Mayor's office if Zoey offered any resistance.

# CHAPTER 2

## Monday 8:30 A.M.

The Mayor's two Administrative Assistants ran interference. For a woman who decorated every nook and cranny of City Hall with banners and posters sporting her *Citizen Friendly* motto, she shielded herself well from the public. Sarah was forced to wait in a recently added waiting office immediately outside Mayor Kamen's private office.

"The Mayor will see you now, Chief James," offered the inner Assistant, Missy.

Sarah smiled. No need to be rude to the young sycophant. The forty-something Mayor preferred to be surrounded by younger females. Probably because young women were easily influenced and were inclined to admire women in leadership roles. Sarah understood the attraction. She had very few female role models in her career. "Thank you, Missy." Sarah waited until the young woman opened the door to allow entry. The first thing she noticed in the Mayor's office was another door. She knew that door once led to a private restroom, but the area had been remodeled after Jordon Kamen was placed in the position of Mayor by the City Council. That door now offered an exit so incoming visitors could not see who was there before them. The Mayor limited public exposure to her activities, except those activities designed for public exposure.

Mayor Kamen forced a smile. "Come on in, Sarah. Have a seat." She motioned toward a pair of chairs close to the front of her wide desk.

"Thank you," Sarah smiled as sincerely as the Mayor did. She chose a chair and adjusted its position before she sat.

Without fanfare, Mayor Kamen scowled, "What are you going to do about your officers using force and intimidation during routine traffic stops? I thought that behavior would cease with Keck's dismissal."

Sarah did not take the bait. "I assume you are referencing the hotline message that you were kind enough to share with me. The one with the Gestapo comment."

"Yes. What are you going to do about those officers' behaviors? To wield a weapon during a routine traffic stop is abhorrent. And there were children present. No excuses."

"If it were true, I would agree," Sarah said while maintaining her composure.

"Are you saying the citizen lied?" the Mayor challenged, her disdain undisguised.

"Not lied. Exaggerated." Sarah opened one of several folders she carried with her and looked at it for a moment, as if refreshing her memory. "That call came in at approximately 2:00 A.M. this morning, so I had to do a little digging to sort through it. The closest traffic stop to that time was shortly after midnight. The vehicle stopped was a pickup truck with darkened windows and a lift kit."

"How do you know what time the call came in?"

"Those calls are public information." Sarah chose to not mention Zoey's reluctant role in the information gathering. "More than likely, the driver of the lifted pickup was the caller."

"What difference does that make? Your officers wielded their guns on a routine traffic stop. Like I said, no excuses."

Sarah suppressed a smile. She was unsure whether the Mayor received partial information, bad information, or was simply creating an incident to badger the police department, to weaken Sarah's resolve to resist demands for transformation to meet the Mayor's agenda. "I have the patrol video footage - if you care to see it later. I will tell you that the vehicle was traveling more than twenty miles per hour over the posted speed limit, and weaving. That is evidenced by the patrol unit camera," she paused for effect, "in case the officers' notations might be considered biased. The officers were required to use the siren to get the driver's attention because he appeared to be trying to elude them."

"How can you tell the driver's intent from a video? Sound like you are building an excuse for your officers' reckless behaviors."

"I deal in facts, Mayor. If you follow enough drunken speeders, you will learn to read the movements of vehicles, to understand what the drivers are intending. Not always right, but right more times than not. Only the resulting stop can clarify the reasons for the driver's behavior."

"So, pulling a gun is the response to suspected drunk driving?" the Mayor snapped.

"The officers did not pull their weapons at any time during the stop. I have video to prove it. As a matter of fact, in case I was incorrect on the particular traffic stop in question – which I'm sure I'm not, I have videos from all traffic stops for the last couple of months that we could review to see if any officers pulled their weapons during any traffic stop."

The Mayor softened slightly but continued her challenge. "So, what happened that upset this citizen? The officers did something to inspire that call."

"The officers approached the vehicle cautiously, according to protocol. It was night. The driver was speeding and driving erratically … evasively."

"The driver would not have made up wielded weapons," the Mayor insisted.

"Normally you wouldn't expect he would make up something like that. But because of his erratic behavior, he was administered a field sobriety test – which he passed. Turns out he was too sleepy to be driving. It made him angry when the officers made him take the test."

"So, they were wrong. He wasn't drunk, yet they pulled their weapons?"

"I already told you that they did *not* pull their weapons. They approached the vehicle cautiously, at night, with their hands close to their holsters. Standard protocol."

"There were children in the vehicle. Why would they even consider using their weapons?"

"The windows of the vehicle were darkly tinted. It was night. The officers had no idea who was inside it. Besides, the presence of children has never deterred a bad guy from violence. The officers have no way of knowing how the driver, or a passenger, will react. Patrol officers have no way of knowing which stop could be their last. They must be ready for anything, especially at night."

"I want it stopped."

Sarah leaned forward, glared at the Mayor, and said pointedly, "Do you want to tell Micha Michalski-Jensen that she should not be ready for the worst night of her life?"

The Mayor's mouth moved without sound for several seconds. "What's that supposed to mean?"

"Micha was the officer on that traffic stop. Passenger seat. The behavior of the driver made both officers suspicious of intent. Per protocol, they kept their weapons accessible."

"Maybe Officer Michalski-Jensen should not be allowed to be on patrol."

Sarah glared. "This is not about Officer Michalski-Jensen. She was cleared for full duty by the psychiatrist. Her actions during the stop are above reproach. Her caution was warranted regardless of her personal circumstances. Neither she nor her partner knew what the driver would do. The vehicle video shows a perfectly executed stop with a sobriety test, warranted because of the observed driver behavior. In addition, the body cameras that we added after Micha was shot show the real story of what occurred. It is clear that the driver was belligerent, but neither officer reacted out of protocol."

The Mayor relaxed. "Apparently, we are going to agree to disagree on this issue. But - we have more pressing matters to discuss. Your proposed budget is out of line."

Sarah settled her mind to the task at hand. The Mayor's attempt to rattle her with the hotline call did not work. She knew the budget requests were the real reason for the meeting. She knew budget battles were standard for the Chief of Police. There was never enough money in the city coffers for all the city's essential needs plus the pet projects of elected officials. Pet projects were seldom allowed to go unfunded. Chief Keck often lamented the aggravations of budget time. Now it was her turn. She was not overly surprised by Jordon Kamen's opening comment. She expected push back from the Mayor, an environmental activist who was on public record wanting to reduce funding for police activities.

Mayor Kamen pulled a small packet of papers from a stack to her left. "I see you want to add five patrol officers and two patrol cars to your budget. What makes you think the citizens want to pay for more Gestapo agents?"

Sarah refused to be goaded. Facts were her recourse. "The recent annexation added three thousand people and almost three square-miles of city. According to the county records, there are thirty-four miles of roads to patrol in that area."

"You're trying to justify officers because of road miles? That's ridiculous."

"Those roads lead to people's houses and property. The city annexed them. The city is required to provide police protection. To do that, we must patrol the roads. Patrols require resources, officers and vehicles."

"Sarah, I think you know my position on police presence. It's nothing more than intimidation. A constant reminder that *we are watching you*." Mayor Kamen emphasized her comment with sarcasm and air quotes. "We don't need the heavy hand of the law hovering over our citizens. Besides, the Sheriff has a responsibility for protecting the citizens of the county. It looks to me like you're trying to double-dip into the taxpayers' pockets."

"The Sheriff will lose funding because the taxes from that part of the county will be diverted to Devaney. It appears to me that the money is already available," Sarah paused for impact, "and allocated."

Mayor Kamen leaned back in her chair and laughed derisively. "And you think for one minute that Sheriff Herriman will reduce his force just because we annexed three square miles of the county? That is less than one percent of the county. See, Chief James, I have data too. You really don't know much about how things work, do you?"

Sarah gritted her teeth and held her tongue for a moment. The novice politician was trying to assume a position of experience based upon a few months difference in service. "Mayor Kamen, I *do* know how things work. That is why I am requesting five additional officers and an additional patrol unit. The national average for staffing in a city is more than twenty officers per ten thousand population. If I used that as my guide, I would be asking for seven officers plus supporting equipment just for the annexed area. Technically, we are operating with only one-hundred twenty-three uniformed personnel. Compared to national averages, we are understaffed by at least ten officers. I have already spoken with Sheriff Herriman regarding co-operative patrol of the new annex, at least until we can understand the needs as a city."

Mayor Kamen leaned forward suddenly. "There you have it! He can do it. Let the County take the brunt of the Gestapo complaints. I'm not going to approve a budget for more police spending when our citizens are demanding less police presence. It's not going to happen while *I'm* Mayor. That's why the citizens of this city put me in this office."

Sarah reacted. She did not mean to. She could not help herself. She blurted, "The citizens of Devaney *did not* put you in this office. The City Council did." She saw darkening anger on Jordon's face. All she could do was wait for the outburst.

"The citizens elected the Councilmembers, therefore the citizens put me in office!" The Mayor's red face quivered for a moment. "It is *best* that you remember that because I have the power to fire you. You know that's true, especially without your criminal friend to protect you. I will not approve your request. I've told every department head; we will use Zero Based Budgets. If you can't justify it, you won't get it. You're a smart girl. Figure out how to protect the citizens in a friendly way."

Sarah knew she had hit the wrong button. The meeting was over as far as the Mayor was concerned. Fortunately, budgeting was not a single day, one meeting process. They would meet again, hopefully on better terms. In the meantime, Sarah knew the Council had the final say. Even if the Mayor did not carry Sarah's entire request to the Council for approval, Councilmembers could easily question and amend the proposal. Nothing was final until it came to a vote. She already had plans to schedule meetings with Councilmen who were strong police supporters ... and friends of Bill Keck. She could only hope they did not harbor ill-will toward her for the arrest of one of their own. She rose to leave.

"Where are you going?" the Mayor snapped. "I didn't dismiss you."

Sarah scowled angrily and retorted. "I came here to have an honest discussion about budget, not to be threatened. If that's all you are going to do, I have more important work to do."

Jordon Kamen face froze between her anger and shock. Her expression finally settled on self-assured smugness. "Work like your arrest of Joseph Elsea?" she taunted. "No Miranda Rights and now he can walk free."

Sarah suppressed her urges. The first thing that came to mind was to wipe the crooked smile from the older woman's face. Instead, she calmed herself and replied, "Councilman Elsea's case is mine to resolve, not yours. He will be prosecuted in a court of law, not in the court of public opinion – or the Mayor's Office. Do you want to discuss budget further or waste time attacking me? Otherwise, I have a job to do." She clinched her jaw and waited for a response.

"My mind is made-up," Jordon responded curtly. "I will not approve any further excessive demands from the Police Department. You will learn how to run the department like it should be run, or not run it at all. It will not be a money pit sucking down taxpayer dollars anymore."

"Then we are through for today," Sarah said as she wheeled toward the exit door. On second thought, she abruptly turned to go out the entry door and smiled at a startled Missy on her way through the waiting office.

Sarah forced herself to breathe calmly as she walked across the large lobby of City Hall and down the steps toward the parking lot. She fully understood how Bill Keck felt after encounters with Mayor Jordon Kamen. Probably with all other novice politicians as they flexed their muscles in their early months. She wanted to kick the side of her car. She was angry with herself for allowing Jordon Kamen to get to her.

# CHAPTER 3

## Monday 9:15

Sarah's mind swirled with angry thoughts as she drove. The Mayor was still inside her head. A jolt from an unnoticed pothole brought her back to reality.

Sarah knew the Mayor would not budge on the budget. She knew that going in. She needed a plan to break through the impasse. That plan would involve a visit with former Chief Bill Keck, either on the golf course or at his favorite lunch café. Their friendship had grown from a professional boss-employee relationship to a respectful need for one another. Bill Keck became Sarah's mentor after Senior Detective Carl Franken died. After Mayor Kamen fired Bill Keck, Sarah became his connection to his past, to his history as a long-serving Chief of Police. She still hoped that he would be reinstated. She liked her life before the changes.

Sarah knew the Mayor was right. Her arrest of Joseph Elsea could have been done differently. Her focus was entirely on the evidence, not the process. Councilman Elsea had become a friend. Even something of a confidant and secondary mentor. Joseph Elsea was the one who invited Sarah to join a regular Saturday golf foursome that included Chief Keck and Planning Commissioner Harley Kosac. On the day of the arrest, it was all Sarah could do to retain her composure, to not allow her personal feelings to interfere with her job. It was tough. She simply allowed Joseph to talk before she cuffed him, before she placed him under arrest. Now, the homicide and drug distribution case against Joseph Elsea could be in jeopardy because she did not read him his Miranda Rights. At least, that was what the Mayor's accusation implied. She pointed her car toward the County Courthouse and District Attorney Charles Dunn's office.

Devaney was the county seat of its county. The county was heavily populated for a mid-American rural state. Almost two-hundred thousand people. Only sixty to seventy thousand of them lived inside Devaney city limits, a fact that was steadily changing. Most of those people lived in smaller towns that scrambled to keep Devaney from engulfing them. Annexation was the strategy of Mayor Kamen in her push for more stringent control over the surrounding areas. The environment was her agenda. For reasons shrouded in the mists of time, the County Court House was across town from City Hall. Sarah drove with a frustration releasing grip on the wheel.

DA Dunn was in court and unavailable. A setback for Sarah's troubled mind. Assistant DA Marcie Ignack was scurrying between her office and a courtroom, ferrying requested information to the DA. Her trademark loose lock of blonde hair bounced between her nose and her ear, partially obscuring one eye. The lock changed sides periodically to suggest an air of randomness to it. The errant tress coupled with a liberal application of rouge on her otherwise pale cheeks projected a busy, harried persona. It was a look that appealed to attentive jurors. "Sarah," she called out when she saw Sarah in the hallway. "You look down. What's up?"

Sarah smiled. She and Marcie were compatible as friends, one calm, the other hyper. Marcie knew the law. The Assistant DA was not handling Councilman Elsea's case, but she might know the DA's feelings regarding the possibility of a conviction. "I was hoping to talk with the DA, to get an idea of how the preparation was progressing on the Elsea case."

"Oh." Marcie seemed perplexed. "As far as I can tell, everything is progressing as it should. You did know Clara is representing him, didn't you?"

Sarah winced. Clara Taylor was a mature attorney, skills honed by years of experience as a defense lawyer. A winning lawyer. More often than not, Clara would find a legal loophole that would either get a favorable jury ruling or get reduced charges and sentencing. Clara Taylor would doggedly pursue any mistake by law enforcement or the Prosecutor and make it the focal point of her case. There was no doubt in Sarah's mind that it would be part of Clara's strategy to make Joseph Elsea's pre-Miranda confession inadmissible. The confession was not the primary evidence against the former Councilman, but Clara could taint the entire case against him with legal mumbo-jumbo. She was that good. "I knew that, and I'm not surprised. Like everyone else in this town, Joseph knows she's his best bet."

"I'm glad the DA has decided to handle that one," Marcie said as she brushed the blonde strand away from her eye, only to have it droop back into its designed position. She squeezed the folder she was carrying against her diaphragm, forcing her breasts higher into the deep V of her blouse. Another practiced move in a world dominated by men. She used any distraction to gain the advantage in the pursuit of justice.

Sarah proceeded cautiously. Even Marcie could not reveal everything to everyone. "Do you know if the evidence is solid enough for the DA to prosecute successfully? I really take this one personally."

Marcie laughed lightly. "Sarah, I wouldn't worry about it, at least not just yet. And I know what has you bugged. Even if Clara can squelch the confession as a Miranda violation, you had your ducks in a row before Elsea spilled his guts."

Sarah grinned sheepishly. "Am I that transparent?"

Marcie reached to pat Sarah's forearm. "Not usually, but ... yeah, this time you are. What has you worried about it now? Some sudden realization? A bad dream?"

Sarah shrugged, partially relieved by Marcie's answer and appreciative of the sincere concern. "I had not given it much thought until the Mayor made a comment."

"The Mayor. Humph. That explains a lot. She's not big on law enforcement, is she? Except, of course, the environmental laws that she creates." Marcie worked for the County. She had a broader vision of the city's politics than most people. She did not answer to the Mayor and was glad of it.

"No," Sarah sighed and smirked. "And it's budget time. I watched Chief Keck fight that battle year after year, but I never truly understood the stress. Now, I suppose it's my turn."

"Well, worry about your budget, not the case. There's plenty of legal precedent to support the admissibility of Elsea's confession if that helps settle your mind. You weren't interrogating him. You simply asked "why did you do it" without vocalized threat of arrest. He spilled his guts."

"That helps me feel better. I just wish I had thought about it before I arrested him."

"Miranda Rights are triggered once the suspect is taken into custody. According to your statement, his confession came during a conversation prior to arrest. You're good. And besides, like I said, there's plenty of evidence and at least one unimpeachable witness. It's a solid case. He got his rights before booking. Now, back to the Mayor ..." Marcie cocked her head toward Sarah to prompt her to respond.

Sarah shook her head and smiled bemusedly. "I have to wonder if every police chief in the country has to deal with a mayor like Jordon Kamen."

Marcie blew at her errant strand and smiled greeting to a passer-by. "I imagine some are worse. Stand up to her."

"I have to remember the power of the man ... or woman ... with the power. The Mayor can fire me on a whim. The only way Chief Keck has a chance to be reinstated is if I am still in position."

"First of all, Chief Keck will not be reinstated. Give up on that. From what I hear, he's happy as a retiree, living it up on the golf course and playing with his grandkids."

Sarah scowled. "I didn't want this job. I only took it because it would help Chief Keck and Devaney PD."

"And you being Chief does both of those things."

"How does it help the Chief?"

Marcie chuckled. "He can enjoy his retirement stress-free with the knowledge the department is in good hands, and the city is safe."

The Sheriff's office was in the Courthouse. Sarah went there next in hopes of catching Sheriff Herriman.

"Hello Sarah." The grayed Sheriff smiled greeting and rose from his creaking, wood-backed office chair. The central spring that supported the seat was sagged to one side. Years of use by a large man who leaned to one side caused it. He pushed against the arms to get to his feet before extending his hand across his cluttered desk. "What brings you out slumming?"

Sarah smiled, relieved that the Sheriff was willing to see her without an appointment. "I wanted to continue our discussion of the new annex. Get a feel for what resources you expended on that area."

The Sheriff's face twisted with uncertainty as he waved his hand toward a guest chair. "Have a seat. I'm not sure how much more I can give you, but I'll try." He lowered himself into his chair while Sarah made a slight adjustment to the offered chair before she sat in it. "What in particular has you bugged?"

"Nothing in particular. It's budget time in the city," Sarah raised her eyebrows and rolled her eyes to express her exasperation, "and I need to justify additional funding for the additional patrols. How many unit hours did you log for that area?"

The Sheriff pondered the question before he responded, "I'm not sure I can give you anything that specific." He pulled a pair of readers from his shirt pocket and rummaged through papers on the top of his desk. "Ah! There it is." He studied the paper a moment. "We don't ride predictable routes in the county. Too much scattered too far for that to make sense. Plus, all the little burgs break the flow of our coverage areas. The annex was an island for us. Surrounded by Devaney on three sides and Medfield on the other. To be honest, we didn't do much more than respond to calls …" he quickly added, "as a rule."

Sarah hid her disappointment as well as she could. "On the whole, how did you budget for miles patrolled per population?"

The Sheriff leaned back with practiced precision, sending the creaking chair to a point near loss of stability. He removed his readers and tucked them back into his pocket. He pursed his lips in thought. "I suppose my bosses just never asked for that kind of detail. I just show what we spent last year and adjust for inflation, replacements and raises."

Sarah nodded. It sounded too simple … and not necessarily good. "Mayor Kamen is demanding Zero Based Budgets."

The Sheriff shook his head. "I'm not even sure I know what that means."

"Basically, we have to justify every penny. We can't base it on what we spent in previous years."

"But those previous years are real numbers. That's what it costs." Sheriff Herriman shook his head harder and twisted his face at what he saw as idiocy. "Law enforcement requires money … resources. Resources that increase with population. Without the resources, crime goes up and people's lives are in jeopardy. You spend what you spend, not what some accountant thinks you should spend." He sighed. "I'm glad I don't work for that woman." He spat the last word.

Sarah ignored his derogatory emphasis on gender. "I don't mind justifying costs. I do mind dealing with someone who refuses to face the facts, refuses to accept justifications if they don't support her preconceived notions. You and I both know we can't shortchange law enforcement without serious repercussions. If you have anything that shows how much you spent on the annex, it will help me make my case." She was pleading.

The Sheriff leaned forward. "I'm sorry. I don't break it down that way. But if it will help, I'll join you when you meet with the Mayor. Maybe she'll listen to experience."

Sarah winced at the message in the older man's words. She knew he was not directing it toward her as much as he was directing it toward the Mayor. Still, she felt it. "I appreciate that, though I don't know if that would be well received."

Sheriff Herriman nodded. "Probably not. How else can I help?"

Sarah looked the man in the eyes. "Is your budget being reduced because of the annexation?"

"I can't say as I know that. Like I said, here at County we do things different. In my twenty years, I've not seen a time when I didn't have enough money to do what needed doing. But - there are more and more youngsters coming into office with different ideas, so that could change I suppose."

"Change is inevitable."

"That's what they say," the Sheriff mused. "I've not been much help so far. Is there something more I can do?"

Sarah thought before she replied, "I'm just concerned about how to patrol the annexed area. Without additional resources, we will be spreading ourselves too thin. Leaving too many gaps."

"That presents a problem, but …" the Sheriff paused as he tested his chair's continued viability by leaning back, "as chief law enforcement officer of the county, my department will always be there as backup."

Sarah studied the Sheriff's body posture. He was confident, maybe more than the statement merited. She knew some of his confidence came from the fact that his was an elected Constitutional position. By law, the Sheriff's office had to be funded. By law, the Sheriff was the superior law enforcement officer within the County. When push came to shove, the Sheriff had more authority than any police chief. More power. "Will you be available to assist if I need you?" She hated to ask the question, but she had to have a plan in case the Mayor won the budget battle.

"My county will not go unprotected," the Sheriff replied with a self-assured smile. "Even though there may be some jurisdictional disputes from time to time, I am the person ultimately responsible for the safety of the county's citizens – regardless of their address. I will do whatever is necessary to make that a reality."

Sarah nodded acceptance as she rose to her feet. "Don't be surprised if I hold you to that."

Sheriff Herriman stood and walked around his desk. He placed a reassuring hand on Sarah's shoulder and smiled as he walked with her toward the door, "I'll be here. Just call."

# CHAPTER 4

## Tuesday 1:27 A.M.

Sarah was invited to a dinner meeting. The role of Police Chief came with social obligations, generally unrelated to police work. Sharon Castleman, VP of Devaney's largest employer, a tire manufacturing company, invited her as guest speaker for the Chamber of Commerce Large Industry Council's monthly meeting. As its President, Sharon Castleman was a power broker within the business community of Devaney as well as within the national sphere of her company's influence.

The dinner was a buffet at a local eatery with an easily segregated dining area. The food was passable, standard fare, and the group was professionally polite, accepting Sarah's words without challenge. The topic of the evening was "Women in Business." From the dais, Sarah saw the uncomfortable detachment of the males and the eager attention of the few females in attendance. Regardless of ethnicity, the line was there separating the sexes, both sides sure the other was creating the divide. Sarah wanted to comment on what she saw from the dais, but she kept her focus on her message, nothing more. Words would not quickly change deeply held notions. Change was happening at an evolutionary pace; too fast for some; too slow for others. She was doing her part to expedite changes, but that was not something she aspired to do. She only accepted the mantel of leadership in the movement because it came with her success – as had Sharon Castleman's.

Sarah admired Sharon Castleman. The black woman achieved remarkable successes without pushing her racial or gender differences. Very few Devaney residents voiced Sharon's race or gender as a descriptor. Sharon never used either to advance her career. She was skilled enough to advance on merit. That was what Sarah wanted said about her. Even so, she used her success to support other women in the same way Sharon did; words of encouragement and proof that her successes were because of personal accomplishments, nothing more, nothing less. And yet, Sarah knew her gender set her apart and raised doubts in the minds of some about her ability. In the back of her mind, she knew eliciting support in the budget battle from the Councilmen sympathetic to Bill Keck would be affected by her gender. Devaney was still a "good ol' boy" town. The only thing she had going for her was that the Mayor was also female, so at least *that* battle line could not be drawn.

"Chief James, thank you for your participation this evening. There is no doubt that you provided confidence to some of the young women who doubt themselves. Better, you raised awareness that gender is not a criterion for success."

Sarah smiled at Sharon Castleman as they shook hands. "I hope so."

Sarah drove toward her apartment, her car's headlights and the city's streetlights guiding her way. Her mind quickly left the social aspects of the Large Industry Council meeting and returned to the Mayor and the budget. It was too late to call on Bill Keck. She wanted to tap his years of budget battle experience. She decided to call on him - maybe meet him for lunch - the next day.

A pothole jarred Sarah. It shook her hard enough to blur her vision momentarily. After mentally scolding herself for inattention, she thought about the Street Department. They needed money too. More money to repair winter damage as well as normal wear and tear. She thought about the female Street Department engineer, Emerson, who answered her questions about road construction during her investigation of Mayor Clairmont's accident. The Street Department would also be seeking an increased budget to cover the recent annexation. The annexation came with a lot of miles of road, most of them not up to city code. The Mayor would need to ask for money for that as well as for her pet projects. In the current national political climate, it would be easy for the Mayor to convince the public - and the Council, to reduce police funding. The thought angered Sarah as she dodged another pothole, not as bad as the one that jarred her.

A warm shower helped Sarah relax. Rather than crawl into bed immediately, she sipped a half glass of Merlot while she went over her budget figures on her laptop. She was anal about being correct when she made her next appeal to the Mayor, not that she had not checked and rechecked the figures for accuracy. The arguments, the justifications, were more critical than the numbers themselves. *"Figures don't lie"* rang through her mind, *"but liars figure."* A worn phrase, but a true one. The justifications, no matter how concise and precise, were subject to twisted semantics by detractors. The Mayor was a detractor of both Sarah and the police department. The democratic process was Sarah's only hope. Councilmembers represented the voice of the people. If she had their ears, she could influence the police department budget decision. Mayor Kamen was not the end-all. The scheduled Council budget meeting was in four weeks.

Sleep, when it came, did not come easily, nor did it last long. Sarah was not sure how many times her PD cell phone rattled on her nightstand before it dragged her from blank darkness. "Hello," she mumbled, her heart racing, her mind foggy and her mouth thick with sleep. Her eyes blearily read the time on her blue LED clock; *"1:27."* A deathly serious voice spoke urgently and yanked her into the moment.

"Chief, we've had a shooting. Officer Wyatt is down. I have a unit on the way to escort you to the scene."

Sarah sat bolt upright. Her mind raced to gather the names in her head. Officer Wyatt was five-year veteran. Five years as a Patrol Officer. His shift should have ended at midnight if her memory was right. *One twenty-seven.* He would have barely had time to finish his paperwork and go home. "Sergeant, how bad?"

The answer came too slowly to be good. "He's dead, Ma'am."

Sarah's heart stopped. She caught the gulp in Sergeant Blanchard's voice. The Shift Commander was struggling to maintain his professional composure. "What happened?"

After Sergeant Blanchard cleared his throat and inhaled deeply, he said, "We're not sure, Chief. Boston is already at the scene. Lieutenant McCuskey is enroute. I'm heading that way. One of Officer Wyatt's neighbors called it in. John ... Officer Wyatt lives on a cul-de-sac. He was found in another neighbor's driveway. His car was in his own driveway, a few houses away. We don't know much yet."

Fully awake, Sarah flipped on the overhead light as she stepped into the bathroom. "Thank you, Sergeant. I will see you at the scene ... and thank you for the escort."

The last time Sarah raced through the night streets of Devaney with an escort was when Detective Boston Mankowitz was stabbed. As she hurriedly dressed, selecting her Tuesday wardrobe of white blouse and slate gray pantsuit, she thought about Boston. His recovery and return to full duty was nothing short of miraculous. She still worried about him. He was worse than her when it came to pushing himself too far – physically and mentally. She thought about Lieutenant Taylor McCuskey. Taylor was shattered when Officer Micha Michalski-Jensen was shot. Micha survived. Sarah worried about her Lieutenant's state of mind with an officer lost. Random thoughts about how the community would deal with the death of a police officer swarmed her mind. The impact would be felt by everyone in some way.

As promised, a patrol car was at the apartment parking lot entrance with strobes flashing. All the driver needed was for Sarah to start her car's blue-colored grill and dash strobe lights to signal him into action. Both vehicles' sirens screamed across town toward Officer Wyatt's neighborhood.

Sarah parked her car out of the way on the street outside the cul-de-sac. She did not want to be an interference to the ambulance or the Coroner's wagon. She would not be in charge of the scene. That duty – and right - would fall to Boston, the investigating Detective.

The Coroner's wagon, an ambulance, two squad cars and an unmarked car were parked in front of a house with a two-car garage and an appropriately wide driveway that sloped toward the street. Sarah noticed that the garage was set back about six feet from the frontline of the house. The roofline of the house was a few feet higher than that of the garage, an indication of a second story or a useful attic. Sergeant Blanchard met her as she approached. He and his officers were herding a gathering group of curious onlookers. "Sergeant, have we learned anything more?"

"Not much. The homeowner is out of town. It appears John … Officer Wyatt walked from his house to here. Maybe he saw something suspicious. Boston will have to update you, Chief. I've been keeping the scene clear for him and the Coroner."

The word "coroner" caught in the Sergeant's throat. Sarah felt the same way. "Thank you, Pete. How is your team?" Sarah knew the effect an injured officer had on the members of the police department. She was unsure how the death of an officer would affect them. She did not know how it would affect her. A line-of-duty death was a dramatic change in her experience.

"Shook. Lieutenant McCuskey and several of them are with Celia." The Sergeant turned his head to indicate a house two doors around the cul-de-sac. "Family is on the way." An approaching siren caught his attention. "That may be some of them now." He immediately stepped into the street to clear a man and woman who arrived after Sarah.

Coroner Henry Mason saw Sarah crouch to pass under the police tape. Officer Wyatt's body was still sprawled on the concrete driveway, covered by a sheet. It was splotched with blood, especially near the head. His initial survey was completed. He was waiting for Detective Mankowitz to complete the scene investigation before he took the body. The scowling Detective was focused, apparently oblivious to anything other than the task at hand. "Hello, Chief."

"Coroner," Sarah responded an unemotional greeting. She nodded grimly at two paramedics who stood nearby. They were absently toying with their Nitrile glove encased fingers and watching anxiously as they waited to assist the Coroner if needed. She glanced toward Boston, who was searching the driveway and nearby grass with a Stinger, high-lumen LED flashlight. She knew the routine. A killer usually leaves something behind. The investigator simply has to find it. "Henry, what can you tell me?" She did not want to interrupt Boston until he was ready.

"Appears to be GSW to the back of the head. Several. It was an execution. Gruesome."

Sarah's gut wrenched and bile rose into her throat. She swallowed hard. "Execution? Why?"

Henry Mason's eyebrows lifted. "Chief, that will come from you guys. I can tell you the cause, but not the why. It would appear someone wanted him dead."

Sarah bit her lower lip until she had some semblance of control over her emotions. The Coroner's detached demeanor at a death scene was to maintain his own sanity. He was a Mortician by trade. He was used to death. She knew to ignore his detachment. As a trained detective, she needed to help the investigation to protect her own sanity. "I'd like to look at the body." She did not wait for permission, only a moment of hesitation until Boston looked her way. He surmised what she wanted and nodded his approval, still stoically searching the area with his light, placing evidence markers, and taking pictures if he found something.

Sarah pulled back the sheet. Officer Wyatt's head was a bloody mess. Exit damage to his face that she could see from her angle was horrendous. Gruesome was the Coroner's word. It fit. Sarah hoped Celia did not rush to the scene and see something that would haunt her memory of her husband. She knew the image would forever be in her own mind, just like every other grisly scene she had investigated during her career as a law enforcement officer. To help maintain emotional control, she asked the Coroner, "Has Officer Wyatt been moved?"

Boston answered. "I turned him to access his ID. Couldn't tell much from the face. I took photos first. He's close to the way I found him."

"Okay." Sarah grimly smiled at Boston. The former undercover cop was savvy. She knew he would dig out every possible detail and uncover every potential clue. She could only hope he would find the *best clue*, the one that would lead to the killer. Still squatted next to Officer Wyatt, she relied upon the shadow-casting streetlights to scan the immediate area. Boston had placed several numbered, tent-shaped evidence markers around the concrete slab. Spent brass. Blood spatter. A lit flashlight. A wadded fast-food wrapper.

Sarah stood and carefully backed away from the body. While Boston tended to the fine-detail search, she tried to envision the events that led to the final position of Officer Wyatt's body. A thought struck her. She squatted beside Officer Wyatt's body and lifted the sheet from around his waist.

"It's gone; if you're looking for his service weapon," Boston said from his position searching the area. Sarah's actions were not unnoticed. The experienced detective did not want his scene contaminated.

"Overpowered?"

"So it would seem."

Sarah replaced the sheet. She clinched her teeth. John Wyatt was only twenty-six. His dream job was police officer. A wife and two children. She saw Lieutenant McCuskey approaching in the streetlights' glow. She walked to meet her. Boston would speak up if he needed assistance. Taylor probably needed her more at that moment.

"Taylor," Sarah asked softly, "how is Celia doing?" She knew she needed to keep the seasoned officer's mind away from self-pity.

Lieutenant McCuskey grimaced. Normally fully armored with make-up, Taylor was unadorned. Hardly noticeable because her eight-point uniform cap cast a shadow down her face. The soft blue of the streetlights did not reveal stress lines like natural lighting. The lack of make-up meant no ruined mascara. Tears glistened on her cheeks. The older woman reached for Sarah, seeking the comfort of an embrace with another human. "She's in shock. The Chaplain should be here in a few minutes. We contacted her doctor. He grumbled, but he's on his way out here. She needs some meds." She broke into a sob. "Sarah, how can this happen?"

Sarah steeled herself. She knew she had no time for emotions at that moment. "How? I wish I knew for sure. Political rhetoric has made the badge a target. Don't worry. We'll find the shooter. We'll find out why."

Taylor's dyed blonde hair quivered against Sarah's neck. "Not soon enough." The Lieutenant pulled away. Even in the obscure lighting, her eyes sparked with angry determination as she composed herself. "What can I do to help?"

"We can start by interviewing every neighbor. Someone might have heard something, seen something. Boston is gathering the physical evidence. The Coroner will tend to the … to John. He will send him to the State ME."

"Delaney has never lost an officer on duty," Lieutenant McCuskey stated questioningly.

"Not in modern times," Sarah replied. Taylor needed tasks to stop her mind from chasing thoughts that served no purpose at that moment. "Taylor, gather a team and canvas the cul-de-sac. Get statements. Locate anyone with security cameras in the area and get the videos. Not many businesses nearby, so that won't be much of an option, but check all gas stations and quick stops that are open at night. Look all the way to the interstate."

"Yeah." Taylor nodded her head vigorously, her eyes wide. "Great idea! He's got to be running scared. Probably needed gas. I'll put out a statewide BOLO."

"Slow down, Taylor. We don't know what to look for yet. Gather information first. Let's make sure we get this right the first time. We *will* be watched." The final comment was made to caution herself as much as it was for Lieutenant McCuskey. The public would want to know everything about the murder – and the people investigating it.

"Of course. Make sure we're right," Taylor's voice was calmer, an indication she was returning to her normal, detailed self.

Sarah watched Taylor quickly walk toward Sergeant Blanchard. If anyone could organize a canvasing operation, the Lieutenant was that person. She told Boston that she would be back and walked toward Officer Wyatt's house. The thing she dreaded most had to be done, both for the sake of John Wyatt's family and for herself. John was her employee, her charge, her family, her responsibility in many ways. His family was part of the Devaney Police Department family. Celia was her family as much as was John. Sarah felt responsible for Celia too.

The Wyatt family members were anxiously gracious. Red eyed. Drawn faces. Eager to do something to help, to be supportive. At a loss. There was nothing more they could do. Celia was generally unresponsive, absently accepting a hug from Sarah and continual embraces from everyone there to console her. Her two children, two and four, too young to understand, overcame the initial excitement and fell asleep, the four-year-old in the arms of a red-eyed police officer, John's patrol partner, after repeatedly bragging, "My Daddy is a policeman." It broke Sarah's heart to see their peaceful faces, unaware of how their lives were forever changed. She swallowed the lump in her throat.

Burdened with the pain of the Wyatt family, Sarah returned to the crime scene after retrieving a flashlight and an evidence kit from her car. There was not much she could do without interfering with Boston's evidence gathering ... but holding the light and being prepared made her feel less useless.

Sarah shined the light on the brick veneer exterior of the garage and the house. She was searching for something or nothing, any clue yet unfound that might exist. She quickly noticed that the privacy fence gate was ajar. "Boston, were there signs of forced entry? Maybe John heard or saw something that drew him over here." Why the young officer would be shot dead in his neighbor's driveway was one of the questions that required an answer.

Boston paused and flexed his torso. Even though he was released back to full duty, his damaged abdominal muscles were not back to full strength after the knife attack that he survived. "The responding unit didn't say anything about it. I immediately focused on documenting the scene here before there was any more trampling."

"Do you mind if I swing around back?"

"Not a bit." For the first time that night, Boston grinned. "You do remember how to investigate without disturbing evidence, don't you, Boss?"

Sarah grinned back. "I'll make sure I do it right. You can critique me afterward." She donned gloves, picked up her evidence kit and walked to the gate.

Before she scooted the gate further open, Sarah dusted the handle for fingerprints. The thumb clasp yielded a smudged print. Probably unreadable. Like most privacy fences, the gate was installed before the grass was fully established. The bottom dragged on the lush sod that now controlled everything. It was difficult to open it wide enough to walk through without rubbing the wood gate posts. Mindful of everything and anything on the lawn, Sarah shined her light in every direction, lingering on the reflective spider eyes that shone from deep within the turf. Grass blades were bent from footsteps, not uncommon for a lawn. From the gate and in the short expanse between the garage and the side fence, regular foot traffic had created a shallow path in the grass. The path was mostly defined by the shadows created by the taller grass that bordered it when she moved her flashlight's beam. It was all grass. No chance of capturing a footprint. She slowly moved to the backyard and let the light lead her as she crossed behind the garage toward a concrete patio with sliding glass doors to the house. She dusted and then tested a pedestrian door that led into the garage. It was locked. The only scuffing on it or the door frame was in the bottom twelve inches, probably scraped by lawn care equipment stored inside the garage.

Before stepping onto the patio, she took pictures with the camera from her kit. Sounds of voices, officers talking with neighbors, neighbors' muffled voices gossiping, and dogs barking filtered through the night air. The only distraction that clouded her mind at the moment was the fact that she, the Chief of Police, should not be focused on minutiae. As Police Chief, she should have already appointed another detective, so the burden did not all fall on Boston. When push came to shove, while Boston was analyzing the evidence back at the station in the Situation Room, the Police Chief would be otherwise occupied. All the seemingly insignificant details that did not fall into the category of formal evidence, things a detective sees during the investigation, the clues that become the glue that holds the case together that might be observed by Sarah, could be lost during the analysis if she was not available. Sarah knew she had to do the right thing. She dialed Sheriff Herriman's number. He had detectives.

Rather than stop her search pending the arrival of the Sheriff's detectives, Sarah searched for footprints or scuffs as she walked toward the patio door. Her flashlight reflected off the glass. Cleaner than most patio doors. No smudged handprints one would normally see. The curtains were drawn. Before testing the door, she dusted the aluminum handle for prints. She got nothing but a smeared set of prints from an index, middle and ring finger, the fingers that would be used to pull the door open or closed. She was unsure whether they would provide anything of substance. She prepared to move toward windows along the back of the house.

"Chief?" Sergeant Blanchard's voice was loud and clear.

"Yes, Sergeant. Around back."

"The Press is here."

Sarah was crestfallen. She had a job to do - and it was not detective work. PR was among her primary functions as Chief. "Tell them I will be there in a moment."

# CHAPTER 5

Tuesday 2:30 A.M.

Sarah sucked in a deep breath. She had hoped the "Press" would be a gathering of few reporters with recorders and note pads. It was more than that. At that moment, she surmised Kyren Bailey and her camera crew must live together and sleep in their clothes. She knew the media monitored emergency scanners. Them knowing about the shooting was not a surprise to her. Their ability to be on the scene and ready to film so quickly was a surprise. They were efficiently mobile. The camera and lights were already set up on the street outside the cul-de-sac. Sergeant Blanchard had wisely directed them to that spot. After placing her evidence kit in the trunk of her car, Sarah straightened her jacket and stepped into the bright lights.

"Before I answer any questions, allow me to make a brief statement. This is an ongoing investigation in its early stages. I have very little information beyond what I am going to say. Sadly, an off-duty Devaney Police Officer has been slain. This is a shock to all our law enforcement team. We are trying to process the loss. I ask for your understanding as we process through this dark moment. The scene is locked down while we conduct our investigation."

Kyren, remarkably well-groomed considering the rush required to be at the scene, commanded attention above the few other reporters present. "Chief, what is the name of the slain officer?"

"Kyren, I can't give you that pending notification of next of kin." Sarah was uncomfortable with starting the gossip. She knew from experience that people tend to fill in the blanks when they did not know all the facts.

"We hear that he lived in this neighborhood," Kyren shot back.

"Kyren, I will release the name when it is appropriate. We are in the early stages of this investigation." Sarah's comment was harsh and to the point.

"Was it a home invasion?" asked a young, male reporter with a recorder and a small microphone jutted toward Sarah.

"Again, the investigation has just begun. I have asked Sheriff Herriman for assistance."

"Because you don't have enough detectives?" Kyren asked purposely.

Sarah thought about using the moment to publicize the need for additional staffing but thought better of it. Now was not the time or place. "Because this is personal to every member of the Devaney Police Department. We have lost a brother, a member of our family. Sheriff Herriman understands our pain and has agreed to assist."

"Do you have a lead on the killer, or killers?" shouted another reporter.

Sarah exhaled to calm herself. Answering reporters' asinine questions was not what she wanted to be doing in the middle of the night. Not this night. She was emotionally unprepared for the press. "We are in the early stages of the investigation. We are gathering evidence at this moment. Until that is done, there is nothing more I can offer. Please, allow our officers time to gather evidence so we can understand what has occurred. More importantly, allow our officers time to grieve. This is a tragedy that hits home to all of us. I will issue a statement later today as more information becomes available. Thank you and good night." Sarah turned away from the crowd and walked toward the crime scene.

Sarah's phone rang. Her personal phone. She looked at the ID. Zoey Kopechne. She let it ring a couple more times before she answered. "Hello Zoey."

The Mayor's representative spoke in a sleepy, cautious voice. "Chief, Mayor Kamen needs to you to call her."

"Okay. As soon as I can," Sarah responded and ended the call. Jordon Kamen wrapped the mantle of Mayor around her like a shield. Because of her "important position" and its "time demands," she seldom placed a call herself. She went through her Assistants, usually Zoey. The Mayor did not like to be in the position of waiting for someone to answer her call. In her mind, her time was too important to waste waiting. Sarah dialed the Mayor's cell number. It was answered after the first ring.

"What's happened? Why wasn't I called? Who did it?" The Mayor was angry.

Sarah held her tongue. She did not expect much from Jordon Kamen either as a person or as Mayor. Even so, she thought the Mayor of Devaney would feign concern for Officer Wyatt and his family first and foremost. Her tolerance for Jordon Kamen was low. Her disdain was something she knew she had to control if she wanted to survive as Police Chief. That was a fact. The Mayor was her boss. "Mayor, an off-duty Devaney Police Officer has been shot and killed. It occurred about an hour ago. We are on the scene now gathering evidence and trying to understand what has happened."

"That's all well and good, but why wasn't I called?"

Sarah took a couple of deep breaths. As unprepared as she was for the Press that early in the case, she was even less prepared for a turf war with the Mayor. "Mayor, other than waking you to tell you what has happened, what advantage is there to you knowing about it before we know something definitive?"

"I will be asked questions. I'm the Mayor. I need to know everything that goes on in Devaney so I can inform the citizens. I need to know if that officer was out of line and did something that turned the situation deadly. The citizens have the right to know. I expect you to tell me everything that is happening. Lieutenant Glasgow will be there shortly, as will Sergeant Locke. Read them in." The phone went dead.

Sarah pulled the phone away from her ear and scowled at it before she tucked it in her pocket.

"The Mayor?" Sergeant Blanchard asked.

Sarah blinked to regain her focus and composure. She shook her head side-to-side in disgust. "Yes. Afraid she'll miss the smell of someone's flatulence."

Sergeant Blanchard chuckled as they walked toward the crime scene. "That's a novel way to put it.

Sheriff Herriman and a plainclothes Deputy, Detective Faraday, arrived before Kyren and her crew left the scene. She detained the Sheriff with questions, and as a politician, he deftly fielded questions with non-informative answers for a few minutes. Sheriff's Detective Ben Faraday caught up with Sarah and Boston in the driveway.

"What's the situation?" Faraday asked, his eyes blinking away the sleep that tried to stay with him.

Boston answered, "When I heard someone was joining me, I held the body so you could see the entire scene." He glanced toward Coroner Mason whose impatience was obvious. "I've been over the scene with a fine-tooth comb. Lots of pictures. Very little substance. Off-hand, I'd say Officer Wyatt was caught off guard."

"Does he live here?" Deputy Faraday glanced around the neighborhood.

Boston pointed. "There where all the cars are. The people who live in this house aren't home. Out of town according to a neighbor who has a key."

"Have you been inside?"

"Not yet. Processing the outside first."

"Really?" Faraday looked toward the house and asked incredulously. After a pause, he continued. "So, why was the officer here this time of the night?"

"My guess is that he saw something. His shift ended at midnight. He left the station half-hour or so after midnight on his way home. Everyone on the cul-de-sac watches out for each other. They all know if someone is gone for a few days. Pick up the paper. Check the mail. Even mow the grass if necessary."

Faraday nodded. "That's good. So, if he was checking on something, how could he be caught off guard? Surely he would have been on alert."

"Good question. Maybe it was someone he recognized. Maybe it happened too fast." Boston pointed his flashlight toward a still lit flashlight several feet from the body. "He had his flashlight, so he was checking something. Other than that, I'm not sure. Not much here to go on. I don't want to speculate." The Detective deflected defensively.

Faraday inhaled, turned on his flashlight and walked toward the sheet covered body. He played the light around the immediate area. The bloody concrete at the edge of the sheet glistened, not yet dried. "Did he bleed out?"

Henry Mason grunted and interjected, "Not the cause of death, if that's what you're asking."

All three peace officers glanced at him before Faraday leaned over and pulled back the sheet. He jerked back. "My God! How many shots?"

"Don't know yet," grunted the Coroner.

Boston spoke as he pointed his light toward three of his yellow evidence markers, "I found three nine mil casings, likely from Wyatt's service weapon."

"You think the shooter was standing below him?"

"Brass could have ejected and rolled downhill. Not much telling at this point."

Faraday nodded understanding. He shined his light toward Officer Wyatt's waist and lingered on the empty holster. "Damn!" he muttered. After studying the body for a few minutes, he turned to the Coroner. "Coroner, do you mind if I move the body?"

"Whatever you need to do. I'm ready to take him to the morgue as soon as Boston releases the scene."

"Thank you," Faraday grunted. With his hands gloved, he carefully grasped Wyatt's shoulder and pulled the body onto its back. He jerked back with a gasp. "Good Lord! Are you sure there were only three shots?"

"Not sure of anything," Boston replied. "I only found three casings."

Even though Sarah had turned John's body enough to know the exit wounds were horrific, she cringed at the fully revealed damage. Almost no face left. Lots of pieces of flesh and bone scattered from what once was the top of the head onto the concrete. Extreme exit damage. In the bright beams of both Faraday's and Boston's flashlights, she saw something exposed that had been covered by the mangled face and the blood. Inside the coagulating blood were three gouges in the concrete. "What are those?"

Faraday and Boston both leaned closer, blocking Sarah's view. In unison, they redirected their lights toward the front of the house, carefully searching for something.

"Higher," said Sarah, regretting not having her flashlight.

"What?" Both detectives asked simultaneously.

"Move your lights higher. The bullets may have ricocheted higher."

"Depends on the entry angle," responded Faraday. "Unless it was a high angle of entry, the bullet would lose some velocity and exit angle because of drag on the concrete."

"True, but the driveway slopes upward. Assuming the shooter was standing below John, the angle would be lower on entry. Of course, the slugs could have missed the house all together on exit."

The two detectives walked to the right side of the garage doors. The blood covered gouges indicated the bullets might have traveled in that general direction.

Sarah followed with only her phone flashlight for added illumination. Not much. While the two men looked higher on the bricks, Sarah squatted and looked at the concrete near the edge of the building. "Here," she said while she held her light steady over what she had found.

"You find one of them?" Boston asked.

"No, but I'm sure at least one of them hit the bricks above me. I've got red powder and shards. Looks like pulverized brick."

The brighter lights of the detectives' Stinger flashlights more clearly revealed what Sarah had found. Both light beams went up to survey the bricks above the brick powder.

"There," exclaimed Faraday, his light fixed on a gray spot on a brick. "I think its lead. Do you have something to stand on? It's a little high for me to reach."

"I'll find something. I'm sure someone in the neighborhood has a ladder," replied Boston. He played his light around the area near the piece of lead. "I don't see the others. Maybe they caught the roof. Chief, do you reckon one of the officers can locate us a ladder."

"I'm sure they can. I'll talk to Sergeant Blanchard."

The Sergeant wasted no time finding a ladder. The next-door neighbor also provided the house key. "Chief, do you want me to send a team into the house?"

Sarah looked toward Boston. "It's Boston's scene. Boston, do you want a team to check inside?"

Faraday cautiously injected, "It would be good to know if someone is still here."

Boston glanced at Faraday, then took the ladder and nodded. "Just don't contaminate. Did you finish the perimeter?"

"No. I was called away."

"Have someone do that too while we check the roof. Oh, don't forget the attic if they have one."

Lieutenant McCuskey returned to the driveway, pointedly avoiding looking at the body which the Coroner and the two EMTs were carefully loading into a body bag. "Sarah, so far, we're not finding anyone nearby who saw anything. The next-door neighbor thought he heard gunshots, but he said he wasn't sure what it was. It was loud enough to awaken him. He said he laid in bed a moment wondering what he heard, and then thought he heard a vehicle leaving the area in a hurry. He's not sure of that either. By the time he put on clothes and came outside, everything was quiet. He said he was going to ignore it and go back to bed, but something made him walk over here. He said it was just a feeling. That's when he saw the body. In the streetlights, he didn't know who it was, but the amount of blood convinced him the person was in serious trouble. He didn't want to go any closer. That's when he called 9-1-1."

Sarah nodded. "Understandable. I didn't expect much. I was hoping some of the other neighbors were shift workers or night owls. Do you still have teams checking gas stops?"

"Yes. We'll keep digging. Is Boston finding anything here? Is there anything I can do to help here?"

"Blanchard has assigned teams to clear the house."

"I think I'll go check on Celia and the kids." Taylor's head turned toward the Wyatt's house. Even in the poor lighting of the streetlights, the pain was visible in her eyes.

"Good idea. I saw a car come in. Maybe it was her doctor."

Sergeant Blanchard came from inside the house shortly after Lieutenant McCuskey left Sarah. "Chief, we found a jimmied window in one of the back bedrooms. It was still locked from the inside though. No one broke in tonight. We're dusting just in case. Could have been the homeowner accidentally locked himself out sometime in the past."

"Probably. Is anything missing?"

"Nothing that we can tell. No ransacking."

"Odd," Sarah mused. "Do any neighbors have dogs?" She paused and answered her own question. "Never mind. They've been going crazy ever since we arrived. Talk to those people. See if any of them reacted to their dogs."

"Chief," a familiar voice called from the sidewalk.

Sarah turned and saw Lieutenant Glasgow. "Melvin. You're out early." She wanted to force him to tell her why he was there.

Glasgow stammered in response. "Uh … yeah … uh, the Mayor wanted me to get an update on the situation."

Sarah felt Sergeant Blanchard swell in resistance. "We're investigating. That's the update." She turned back to Blanchard, "Carry on, Sergeant. I know your people are busy." He needed to hear that she had it covered with Glasgow.

"Yes Ma'am." Even in the shadowy light of the streetlights, Sergeant Blanchard's scowl was clear and directed toward Lieutenant Glasgow. "If you need me …"

Lieutenant Glasgow cleared his throat, decidedly uncomfortable. "I understand that it might be Officer John Wyatt who was shot."

"I hope you also understand that *your understanding* is not public knowledge … and if I hear it announced before I make a public statement to that affect, I will end your career." Sarah's jaw clinched defiantly. If Glasgow knew, the Mayor knew – or would soon know – and the Mayor would rush it to the media to prove her value.

Lieutenant Glasgow immediately backtracked. "Of course. I understand. I was just trying to get a grasp …"

"No, Melvin," Sarah kept it personal, "you are trying to spy for the Mayor." She saw Keith Locke approaching along the sidewalk. She was sure both men were unhappy that Sergeant Blanchard's traffic control officers refused them vehicular entry into the cul-de-sac. She parked outside the cul-de-sac. The Mayor's lackies could do the same. "If you and Keith are interested in gathering information, why don't you gather information to help us find the perp? Coordinate with McCuskey. She's in charge of the off-site investigation. There she comes now."

Taylor McCuskey heard her name and saw the two Public Outreach Department officers. It took her only an instant to surmise Sarah's intent. "Guys, I'm glad the Mayor offered your services. This is a tough one. We are canvasing every all-night gas station and quick stop between here and the interstate. Here is my list of places we haven't covered yet. Two-man teams, just in case you stumble on the perp. Be on alert. He has killed a cop. He will kill again. He knows what he's facing."

The two men waggled in place for several seconds before they took the offered list.

Sarah and Taylor both suppressed the desire to laugh at the two dejected men as they walked back the way they came. When they were out of hearing, Taylor whispered, "You're going to catch Hell for this, you know."

"I'm growing accustomed to it," Sarah replied. She watched until the two men drove away in Lieutenant Glasgow's car. It grated on her nerves that he had a department vehicle at his disposal, as did Sergeant Locke. Both were among the newest vehicles in the PD fleet because *"it's better for public relations."* In her mind, she could hear the Mayor's nasally voice say the words.

As she observed the investigation proceedings, both of Sarah's cell phones rang several times. She checked the ID and either declined or ignored all of them. Zoey. The calls were not unexpected but answering them would do nothing to solve Officer Wyatt's murder. By six o'clock, the skies were lighter, causing some of the streetlights to flicker off. Boston released the scene to a Hazmat crew. Sarah watched as kitty litter sopped up Officer John Wyatt's congealed blood so it could be vacuumed. The stains that were not easily cleaned were then pressure washed into a liquid vacuum system. She felt obligated to remain until all trace of him was removed. She knew her presence kept the cleanup crew from making gallows humor remarks while they worked. It was the least she could do for her fallen officer. When completed, the only evidence that something had occurred were the three gouges in the concrete, a shattered bit of brick on the garage veneer and freshly trampled grass on a path from the gate to the back of the house. The second and third rounds were not found near the scene.

Sarah reckoned the Coroner was busy prepping John's body for transport to the State Forensics Lab. She also knew Henry Mason's curiosity would drive him to perform a mini autopsy. Even though it was obvious, she asked him for a preliminary ruling on cause-of-death, which would give authority to his curiosity. She would need to hurry to get to the Coroner's place of business before Henry physically released the body. No matter the hurry, she still had two stops to make before going to Mason's Mortuary and Funeral Home.

Thanks to the Doctor's help, Celia was asleep. Some family members, whose reason for being there was to console her, were also asleep. Those not dozing were drinking coffee. When Sarah arrived, they offered coffee and genuinely appreciated her presence and concern. They asked questions. She answered those that she could. "We will leave a squad car in the neighborhood for a few days," she told them as she prepared to leave.

Immediately, ideas formed, and the question was asked, "Are you afraid the murderer will return?"

Sarah cringed. She did it wrong. She should have prefaced the statement with an explanation. "No. Not at all. Once I make the public announcement, the press and the curious will swarm the neighborhood. We will keep them out of here until the novelty subsides."

Sarah spoke briefly with Lieutenant McCuskey regarding the neighborhood patrol before she left for her next stop. "Have you gotten any security camera possibilities?"

"Nothing yet," Taylor replied. "We'll keep hunting. The one thing we're reasonably sure of is that the perp *was* in a vehicle. I hoped we would find squeal marks from rapid acceleration, you know, get some tire prints, but after the Coroner and the ambulance left, there was nothing where they were parked. It's almost like we're looking for a ghost."

"It's early. The shooter left something. We'll keep looking. We'll find it." Sarah exhaled heavily, her hopes not as solid as her words.

"Are you going to the station now?" Taylor asked.

"I'm going to go see Micha, see if she's heard about John. Then I will go see the Coroner."

Taylor's eyes widened. "I didn't think about Micha. This could kill her. Should I go see her?"

"I'll do it. You still have work here."

Taylor nodded. "She'll appreciate that." She started to turn then paused. "By the way, I've been getting a lot of calls looking for you."

Sarah grimaced. "Imagine that. Zoey? Did you call the Mayor?"

Taylor averted her eyes. "I figured it would help you if I did."

Sarah smiled to ease Taylor's tension. "What did you tell her?"

"That we need Melvin and Keith because there is a lot of evidence to gather," Taylor replied, "and that you were busy with the investigation and the Press."

With a small chuckle, Sarah said, "Sounds better than I would have done. Maybe I'll call her back."

# CHAPTER 6

## Tuesday 7:00 A.M.

Micha was wide-eyed when she answered the door. The petite brunette with frosted highlights looked at Sarah hesitantly, anxiously. "Hello, Chief. What's going on?"

Sarah saw the anxiety in the young officer's eyes. She smiled to help allay the woman's fears. She should have called ahead. She should not have surprised her – especially early in the morning. Micha's husband worked nightshift at the tire company. That was the main reason the patrol officer preferred to work nights, even though her seniority qualified her for different hours. Without realizing it, Sarah's early morning arrival could easily be interpreted as a delivery of bad news. It was, but not to the extent Micha's mind was dreading. "I wanted to see how you are doing," Sarah replied, then with a cheery smile, she asked, "Do you have coffee ready yet?"

Micha, still suspicious, smiled momentary relief and opened the door wider. That allowed the smell of freshly brewed coffee to waft through to Sarah. "I do. Come in. Charlie will be home in an hour or so." The young woman was still hesitant; her eyes pleading for release from her fears.

Sarah accepted the offer she hoped would be made. "Thank you. Darn. I'll probably miss him. I really can't stay long. I was on my way to the station and thought I'd check on you two. How's Charlie doing? When does he finally get to go on days?" She knew all the reasons Micha worked night shift. The main reason was to have more time with her husband.

Micha laughed. Relief replaced the anxious concern on her face. "Probably never. He's doing well. He just got promoted to Line Lead. None of those spots will be available on days anytime soon. I suppose I'll retire from nightshift."

"Let's hope not." Sarah grinned. She did not hear the sound of a TV. "Have you been watching the news this morning?"

Micha handed a cup of coffee to Sarah and motioned for her to sit at the kitchen bar. Almost automatically, she reached for a remote control on the kitchen bar and turned on a TV in their line of sight. Her face showed interest, and concern. "No. Has something happened?"

"Yes." Sarah had to say the words right. "We had an officer shooting. John Wyatt was shot last night." The TV came on. Neither of them were focused on it at that moment.

Micha's eyes widened with shock. "Oh My God! Is he okay? How's Celia and the kids?"

Sarah solemnly replied, "He didn't survive. Celia is in shock. The kids don't understand."

Micha's eyes filled with tears. "I need to go see her. Those poor babies. What happened?"

"We're not sure. He was off duty. From the looks of it, he may have seen something at a neighbor's house. The neighbor is out of town. He was found in their driveway. We don't have much to go on yet."

"Did you say he was off duty?" That fact seemed to horrify Micha as much as the core fact that Officer Wyatt was dead. "That's not right. It makes no sense."

The possibility of death in the line-of-duty is always on the minds of law enforcement officers. It is part of the life they choose, the risk they choose to take to fulfill their desire to be police officers. Being killed while off duty, while on their own time … their family time … is not in their thought processes. Even so, every police officer knows punching the clock to go home does not mean the risk ends. Even in street clothes, they are duty bound to protect and serve. Sarah placed her hand on Micha's, hopefully to calm the shake. "No, it doesn't. It doesn't make sense regardless of duty status." She waited for Micha to process the news.

Micha's eyes fired with anger. "What can I do to catch the son-of-a-bitch?"

Sarah replied, "Boston has it under control for now. The Sheriff has loaned us a detective, Ben Faraday. He's helping Boston. The State Police will send help as we need it."

A "news alert" sounded on the TV. Both women looked toward it. Sarah was expecting to see Kyren Bailey emoting an update of the shooting. She feared the eager reporter would speculate on John's identity. Instead, the morning anchorman sadly stated, *"Local real estate developer and entrepreneur Terrance Overton, Senior has passed away. According to a family spokesman, he died suddenly last night. Repeat, long time citizen of Devaney and founder of Overton Enterprises, Terrance Overton, Senior has passed away. We will have a recap of Terrance Overton, Senior's career and his impact on the Devaney landscape this evening."*

As soon as the alert was replaced by normal morning TV programming, Micha continued as if nothing had interrupted the conversation. "But what can I do? I want to help."

Sarah thought about Micha's reaction to John Wyatt's death. Her concern, her reason for personally visiting with Micha, was how it would impact Micha emotionally. Micha survived an on-duty shooting that could have ... probably should have ... killed her. A nighttime traffic stop that escalated to an assault on a police officer by a deranged drug dealer. Micha physically recovered with chest scars that would forever remind her of that night. Emotionally, she recovered enough to be released by a psychiatrist. There were unseen scars. The psychiatrist cautioned Sarah that the emotional trauma could not be overlooked, especially if a violent assault on another police officer occurred. Any such incident could be the prelude to an emotional breakdown, could cause Micha to relive the trauma, trigger PTSD. "Micha, if you would like to reassign from patrol for a while, we can do that."

Micha scowled. "Never! I love patrol. I just want to help find the bastard." Her blue eyes were dark and intense.

Sarah was unsure whether the woman's reaction was healthy or a cover for pain. She *was* sure that by helping, by staying active, Micha could keep her mind focused on positive results rather than roiled with doubts and fear. "That's what I wanted to hear. Lieutenant McCuskey can probably use some boots on the ground the next couple of days, if you want some OT." It was Micha's scheduled days off.

"I'll do it without pay if I have to," Micha responded adamantly. "I know how the Mayor wants to cut funding."

Sarah smiled. "That won't be necessary. If we spend it, the city *will* pay it."

Boston called Sarah while she was driving from Micha's to Mason's Mortuary to follow-up with the Coroner. He sounded tired and frustrated. "Boss, this thing is going nowhere fast. Alicia has everything we gathered, but I'm not confident we have anything. No obvious DNA. No clear fingerprints. No tire marks. No footprints. The only thing we have is the fast-food wrapper."

Sarah knew Boston as a gruff, upbeat detective, ready to crack the toughest case and patient enough to wait for the break. He was a hunter, unafraid to wade into the darkness to stalk his quarry. She knew his emotional recovery from the stabbing was still ongoing. The wary … and situationally aware … detective was caught completely off-guard the night he was stabbed. That hurt his ego and confidence more than he would admit to his psychiatrist – or to himself. His release to duty was conditional, conditioned on his ability to perform. Sarah knew the measure of success was not as much about cases solved as it was about overall focus on duties. If self-doubts got in the way of his performance, she would send him back to the psychiatrist for further help. Physically, he was not yet one hundred percent either. "Boston, the break will come. All we need to do is keep our eyes open, stay focused and do the right things. If detective work was easy, anyone could do it."

"It may be harder than I can handle," Boston replied dejectedly.

"Boston!" Sarah exclaimed sharply to get his attention. "You and I both know better than that."

"I'm not so sure. No clues and the Press is all over me, plus the Mayor keeps sending her lap dogs over here."

Even over the phone, Boston's despair for the case and disdain for the two officers were clear. "Politics. Boston, just send them to me. I'll be there before eight. Let Alicia work her magic. In the meantime, you need to get some rest. I know you didn't get much sleep last night."

"You didn't either."

"I wasn't working as hard as you were. Go home. Take a shower. Crash for a few hours. You'll feel better after some rest. Things will be clearer. You're still recovering. Don't push yourself too hard."

"We have a cop killer on the loose," Boston said bluntly.

"You're right. But - you can't solve the case if you're too exhausted to see the clue that brings everything together. We need to get this right the first time. Go home. That's an order."

After a lengthy pause, Boston replied with some semblance of his normal demeanor, "Okay Boss. If you insist. I'll leave my phone on."

"Okay. I'm going to drop by the Coroner before I come in. If he tells me anything, I'll leave a message on your office phone."

"Or call my cell."

"Fair enough," Sarah conceded after a brief pause. Boston was the lead detective on the case. He deserved to know everything as soon as possible.

Early morning traffic moved slowly along the route Sarah chose to take to the mortuary. Officer Wyatt's murder was in the front of her mind. Close behind that was the impact the murder could have on her department. Everyone on the force would be angry, vengeful, ready to "*get justice for John.*" It was her duty as Police Chief to make sure everything was done right. Justice done right. Justice done wrong was not justice. There could be no mistakes caused by misguided, emotional responses. Devaney PD had its share of hotheads. She did not need one of them to provide the Mayor with ammunition. She hoped Henry Mason would have evidence, or even some clues that would help find the killer quickly. Somewhere in the back of her mind was the death of Terrance Overton, Senior.

Sarah's interactions with the Overton family were memorable, but not in a good way. Mr. Overton had two grandsons. The firstborn, Terrance Overton III, called Terry, murdered his brother, Bentley, in a bizarre, fake kidnapping case that required weeks to solve. The Overtons and Mayor Clairmont, their bought Mayor at the time, demanded a quick answer to the kidnapping of their elder son, the heir-apparent to the Overton empire. Sarah would not rush. She could not rush. The mistakes from a rushed case in her past forced her to make sure she was right. Patience was more than a virtue when working a criminal case; it was the difference between being right and being wrong. The Overton family did not like the answer eventually Sarah provided. Even though the evidence was there, even though Terry admitted he killed Bentley, the Overton's held animus toward Sarah for her role in bringing Terry to justice. Nonetheless, she felt sorrow for the family's loss of its patriarch.

The front door of the mortuary was locked, not yet open for business. Sarah did not expect it would be, but she tried anyway. She walked around the building to a backdoor marked *"Employees Only"*. She knocked heavily and then pressed a buzzer button. If he heard both, Henry Mason used that as his code for an official visit after hours.

Sarah stayed in front of a peephole so Henry could see her. She heard the panic bar's metallic clatter before the door opened. "Good morning again, Coroner." When fulfilling his obligation as County Coroner, Funeral Director and Mortician Henry Mason preferred that salutation.

Henry offered a dismissive grunt before he spoke. "It's been morning most of the night. But you know that. Come on in before the Press sees you."

"Have they been hounding you?"

"Don't you know it. They followed my van from the scene. If that blonde processes through my mortuary, I'm going to present her with a microphone shoved …" Henry did not complete the sentence. He just made a disgusted sound and led Sarah to his prep room. He looked toward one of his stainless-steel tables as he asked, "Do you want me to show you what I found?"

Sarah glanced toward the table that held the body bag with Officer Wyatt's body. It was partially unzipped, the upper portion of the officer's body exposed, still fully clothed. Clothes would be removed by the Medical Examiner at the state lab in case they contained trace evidence. The uniform did not draw her attention. The mostly missing face did. She closed her eyes and turned her head away from the grisly sight. She did not need to see it again. "Give me the executive summary."

Eyes still on the cadaver, Henry nodded knowingly. "I don't blame you. The boys at State may find more, but they won't find anything different on the COD. As we suspected, high caliber rounds to the back of the skull, left side. He was not exactly face down. But there was more damage than that. All that facial damage was not done by simple exit wounds. The victim was on the ground when he was shot."

Sarah gasped. That fact was generally determined by the ricochet evidence at the scene, but the Coroner's words made it real and final. "He was forced to lay down and then shot?" She could not imagine an officer willingly submitting – unless required to do so to save someone else. That finding added mystery to the case. Who was Officer Wyatt trying to rescue, and where was that person?

"Not necessarily. Let me finish. The facial damage was the result of exit wounds plus ricochet. That's what caused the damage to the top of his head. From what I can deduce, the right side of his face was against the concrete, not quite sideways. The bullets entered near the base of his skull, below the left ear. The bullets reentered after hitting the concrete." He held up a sealed evidence bag with bullet fragments. "Two of them decelerated enough to remain inside."

Sarah closed her eyes and gulped. "So, the three rounds are the COD?"

"Probably not. This fell out as I was studying the wounds." Henry held another sealed evidence bag containing a piece of lead. "There was a lot of damage from the three rounds. Not much intact bone to hold everything in place. It's a wonder it didn't fall out when we bagged him."

Sarah blanched at the image invoked by the Coroner's description. She kept her eyes averted from the table. "Part of one of the three bullets?" Sarah took the bag to get a closer look.

"No. As you can see, this bullet is smashed but relatively intact. It's probably a .22 caliber. It entered and stayed. It's not from his service weapon."

"Gang execution?" Sarah's stomach turned.

"That's for your people to determine." Henry glanced toward the body. "I know you don't want to see it, but there is a small entry wound through his right eye. It was almost unnoticeable because of the damage. I found GSR at the entry."

"So ... he was shot with a .22 first?"

"I'd stake my reputation on it. Point blank. Hard to prove, but I'd bet the barrel was within an inch of his face. The bullet did what .22s are famous for; it bounced around inside his skull. That was the Cause-of-Death. Killed him instantly would be my educated guess. Hard to confirm with the additional nine-millimeter damage."

"How did that happen?" Sarah asked automatically.

Henry shook his head. "You're the detective, Chief. You tell me."

Sarah's eyes strayed to John's mutilated face. She could not resist. She had to see the effects of the bullets whether she wanted to or not. It was difficult to do with someone she knew. She felt her anger growing greater than her revulsion of the sight. Time and evidence would prove whether her thoughts at that moment were right. The shooter must have been someone he knew. She handed the bagged slugs back to the Coroner.

"Don't you want to give these to Alicia?"

Sarah nodded. "Sure. Do you have the Chain-of-Custody paperwork?"

"Right here. Also," the Coroner pointed to a camera on a nearby table, "I have more pictures of the damage. I can send those to you."

"Send them to Boston." Sarah signed for the evidence bags and tucked them into her jacket pocket. "Thank you for everything. Thank you." She let herself out in time to answer a call from Zoey. "Yes Zoey?" she opened tiredly.

"Mayor Kamen needs you to call her." Zoey was no longer sleepy, but she was still cautiously apologetic.

"Thank you, Zoey." Sarah dialed the Mayor's cell number.

An angry "Why have you been avoiding me?" started the call.

"I haven't been avoiding you, Mayor. I've been focused on the investigation."

"Bull! Why did you send Glasgow and Locke away from the scene? I sent them there for a reason."

"I know you did, Mayor. You sent them there to gather information. That's what they are doing. Gathering information."

Jordon Kamen sputtered incoherently for a moment. "That is not what I meant for them to do, and you know it," she finally uttered.

"At two o'clock in the morning at a murder scene, I don't need political games, Mayor. I was dealing with an emotional event for my department plus dealing with the Press."

"What did you tell them?"

"Pretty much nothing other than a police officer was shot. I will make a formal statement in about an hour. Do you want to be there?"

"Make it two hours. I have an important meeting at eight."

Sarah shook her head as she opened her car door. "Okay. That will give me time to contact the Press." She disconnected the call.

Sarah called Boston's cell phone as she continued toward the police station.

Boston sounded tired. "Hello."

"Sorry to call, but the Coroner found something unexpected." Sarah tried to be concise, to let Boston get some rest. "John was shot in the face at close range with a .22. The Coroner thinks that was COD, not the service weapon."

A long pause preceded Boston's reply. "I wonder if there was more than one assailant."

Sara thought a moment before she asked, "What makes you say that? Did you see something?"

"Just a gut feel," Boston replied. "If it was an interrupted burglary, it was likely more than one person. Just a thought. I don't have anything else."

"Without proof, I don't want to go public with that. I can alert Taylor though. A manhunt changes if it's more than one person."

"Yeah. I'm not ready to commit to it," Boston relented. "Just a gut." He paused, then added, "A tired gut."

"I can understand that." As an addition, Sarah said, "I'm holding a presser about ten."

"Good. Get it done while I'm napping."

Sarah knew he would say something like that. The seasoned detective did not like speaking to the Press. His years as an undercover cop appealed to the introvert in him. She could not blame him, but he deserved the respect of being allowed to decline. "Okay. I'll take care of it. Not much to tell yet anyway." To become Senior Detective, he would have to overcome his disdain for speaking to the public.

# CHAPTER 7

## Tuesday 8:00 A.M.

The mood at the station was somber. Sarah went straight to the squad room. Her primary focus at the moment was on the patrol officers, the men and women who interacted with the public on the streets. Theirs was the toughest job. Theirs was the real job. They were required to rise above their emotions and fears. They were required to pretend their feelings did not matter.

Sergeant Blanchard was updating his relief, Sergeant Cron, and the oncoming dayshift officers in the meeting room. Many of them reported for duty early, either called-in to assist or made aware of the events of the night via the grapevine. They all paused when Sarah walked into the room, expectantly hoping she brought good news about the investigation. "Chief, have you heard anything new?" Blanchard asked hopefully. He knew he was in the information loop, but like a child's *"are we there yet?"* he was compelled to ask.

Sarah nodded greeting to the entire assemblage and walked to the front of the room so everyone could see her. In her short time in the Chief role, she became comfortable addressing her charges en masse. The faces looked to her for leadership without suspicions. "I wish I had something more, a break in the case. I will share what I know to be true, though it may be what you already know. John apparently went to his absent neighbor's house to investigate something and encountered an unknown assailant. An unofficial look at his wounds seems to indicate he was shot point blank and killed by the assailant. Afterward, the assailant took John's service weapon and turned it on him." Hands shot up.

"Was he overpowered?" challenged a veteran officer, one of Sarah's potential hotheads.

"It appears that he was surprised rather than overpowered. I cannot say that with certainty, though. The State ME might provide answers to that. Offhand, suffice it to say that either someone stepped out of the shadows and shot him, or it was someone he knew."

"A neighbor?" asked the officer as he looked to the faces around him for emphasis.

Sarah did not like the turn of the question. She sensed vigilante style suspicions. "I'm not going to get ahead of the evidence. I am asking you to follow suit."

"Maybe we need to shake down the neighbors," replied the officer.

Sarah grimaced. "I know how you feel. It's okay to shake the tree to see what falls out. But we need to put our emotions and feelings aside. Look for evidence and clues. Let's make sure we're right in everything we do. I know most of you have confidential informants and people who hear things. Get with your CIs. Listen to what they have to say. Some of those people may know something they don't realize will help us."

"We'll make that our focus," the veteran officer said. "Does the Mayor expect us to fill out contact cards?" he smirked.

Sarah bemusedly responded. "I expect every contact you make to be cordial. We won't get to the truth if we are too heavy handed."

"It would seem that they are the ones being heavy handed," the officer snarled.

"*One. One* of them. Not all. First and foremost, don't create an environment where the citizens of Devaney sympathize with the shooter. Our actions will dictate public opinion. And the public makes up the jury. In the end, we need the support of the public. We can be firm without being hostile. We want that *one* person."

"What about OT?" another officer asked. "I know some of the off-duty guys are interested in helping in the manhunt."

"I will leave that call to Detective Mankowitz, Lieutenant McCuskey and the Sergeants. They know my position on this case."

"Will the Mayor's cops help?" asked the veteran officer with a sneer.

Sarah forced a smile. "Yes. The Mayor was kind enough to send both of them to help shortly before three o'clock this morning." She saw Sergeant Blanchard's disguised grin.

"Good. I want to see all cops on this one. I have a family that wants me home every night." With that off his chest, the older officer allowed the more inquisitive officers to engage with Sarah, the ones who wanted to know rather than wanting a soapbox.

Sarah stayed with the officers until they were ready to disengage. She knew they needed to vent and to organize their thoughts. They were all going through the grief process. She was pleased with the dedicated focus they carried from the room to their squad cars, even the few angry ones.

Liz met Sarah at the top of the stairs. She held Sarah's motto inscribed coffee cup filled with coffee. Her face showed her concern and compassion. "Good morning, Chief. I am so sorry. John was a good police officer. Everyone liked him and respected him." She offered the cup of coffee. "I heard you were visiting with the troops. I was heading downstairs with this."

Sarah was slightly embarrassed by the attention. That part of the job, of the status position, was not yet within her comfort zone. "Thank you, Liz. Yes, he was."

"How are the field officers?"

"Angry. Resolved. Hurt."

"How are you?" Liz asked as the two of them walked side by side toward Sarah's office.

"Angry. Resolved. Hurt." Sarah paused before she sat at her desk. "But, more resolved than anything. The others are emotions. Resolved is a state of mind. Can you arrange a Press conference for ten o'clock? Notify the Mayor when you confirm." She rolled her eyes. "She wants to be in the loop."

Former Chief Keck knocked on Sarah's door while she was on the phone with the State Medical Examiner's office. She knew the death of a police officer would prioritize the autopsy for the State ME but adding her voice to the process made her feel more confident that it would happen quickly. She also knew it would be several hours before John's body arrived in Topeka. Sarah stood and extended her hand. "Come in, Chief." Old habits were hard to break.

Bill's face expressed his awareness and concern. "Morning, Sarah. How are you doing?" He grasped her hand with both of his.

"Worried about Celia. Worried about the officers. Worried about not enough clues."

"The clues will come. I have faith in you, Sarah. Not trying to be cold or seem unfeeling, but Celia *will* survive. So will the men and women of the force. Is there anything I can do to help?"

"Tell me who did it," Sarah replied. Her desk phone rang. The ID declared it was Alicia Kettering. She held up a finger. "Just a moment, Chief. It's Alicia. Maybe …"

"Chief, I'm sorry about John."

"Thank you, Alicia. We'll get through this together."

"I hope so. Boston called me in early to check some evidence he found. I heard you sent him home to rest. He needs it. But I've gone through the evidence he gave me and I'm nowhere near finding a clue."

Sarah felt her shoulders sag. "Have you found anything? DNA on the wrapper?"

"I swabbed it inside and out. I hope there is some transfer, but I'm not hopeful. It didn't have any fingerprints that I could find."

"What about the fingerprints I took from the gate and the patio door?"

"Smeared too badly. Smudges more than anything else. Nothing recognizable by AFIS. I'm sorry, Chief. I don't think I'm going to be any help."

"Oh!" Sarah exclaimed as she remembered the two evidence bags in her pocket, especially the one holding the .22 slug. "I have a slug I need you to run. If it came from a registered gun, maybe it can tell us something."

"Okay. I'll be up to get it."

Sarah gave the evidence bags and accompanying paperwork, folded to fit in her jacket pocket, to Liz. She knew Alicia would hurry. She also wanted to shut the door for her conversation with Bill. "Okay," she said when she returned and closed the door. "Where were we?" She motioned for him to sit.

"I'm just concerned for your wellbeing. I've had officers injured on duty, but it was always my good fortune that none died."

Sarah nodded and said bemusedly, "Good fortune. I suppose that is the line between tragic and catastrophic."

"Luck. They say there's no such thing, but you couldn't prove it by me. We were lucky to not lose Micha or Boston."

Sarah reflected before she answered. "True. I think the difference emotionally is that with Micha and Boston we had hope. Hope that they would survive. Hope that they would get back to normal. With John, there is no hope, other than hope we don't become bitter."

Bill nodded agreement. "I worry about you. I don't want to see you become bitter. I don't want to see you turn your back on police work."

Sarah studied Bill's eyes. The older man's eyes showed wisdom gained through experience, not age. "I'll be okay. But – in all of this, I still have a job to do. Budget. Do you have time to talk about budgeting?"

Bill's face reflected momentary surprise, then settled on acceptance. "Anything you want to talk about. What do you need to know? If it's how to deal with a novice Mayor with an agenda, I doubt I can help much."

"Don't say that. You're my last hope," Sarah said.

Bill chuckled. "Funny, but not funny. What is the sticking point, or points?"

"You're aware of the annexation?"

"Yes. What about it?"

"It comes with more than thirty miles of roads and streets plus over three thousand people. More area and people, more patrol resources required. The annexation came as a surprise. No time to plan or prepare. It came from out of the blue, and now I have to deal with it. The Mayor has dug in on reducing police spending, not increasing it. She says the Sheriff has been handling that area, so, he can keep handling it."

"What does Cecil have to say about it?"

"He'll support citizen safety, but that's not something he wants to do long term – or commit to officially. The County will lose tax base. The City gains everything the County loses, not to mention the higher property taxes that go with being inside the city limits."

Bill shook his head. "State law says a city must provide services to any area within its boundaries, even newly annexed areas. But I know what you'll be dealing with until the State steps in. Data. Put the numbers to it. There are national ratios of police headcount to population. Look for comparably sized cities for comparison. Present data and she will be hard pressed to ignore it."

"I have. She did."

"She rejected it?"

"Adamantly. So, how do I win the budget battle with someone who refuses to acknowledge facts?"

Bill thought a moment. "You know the budget is voted on by the Council, right? The battle doesn't end with the Mayor."

"I do. Who are the sympathetic Councilmembers? If any."

Bill grinned. "Ready for politics, are you?"

"No. But what *must* be *will* be."

"Talk to Jim Sloan. He's always been a strong police advocate. And he's savvy to how the system works in Devaney."

Sarah intwined her fingers and stared at them for a moment. "One thing I forgot to ask. Are any of the Councilmen upset about Elsea's arrest?"

Bill shook his head. "They aren't going to have a grudge against you for it if that's what you mean. Jim will take your data and use it. According to Joseph, Jim was absolutely against giving the mayorship to Kamen. He thinks she's unfit."

"That's a positive. Will he be enough?"

"Probably not, but Chase Mendelson will support you. He's a numbers guy. CPA by trade. Give him supporting data and he'll convince the Councilmembers who have good sense."

Sarah relaxed. "I guess I should feel better, but I'm still afraid the politicians will stick together. Good sense may not prevail. Reelection seems to be the coin of the realm."

"Politically, Kamen is standing on a thin ledge. Always has been. Joseph used his influence to put her there because he thought it was a good, long-term political move. Most of the Council didn't like her as a Councilwoman, so – to Joseph - it made sense to stick her in as an unelectable Mayor. She would be off the Council and, at the end of the term, out as Mayor. Out of their hair. A good way to get rid of her without making a martyr of her."

"Seems convoluted. Almost makes me sympathetic for her."

"Politics. Joseph was a schmoozer. He convinced the Council to go along with him. Talk to Jim and Chase. The two of them can sway enough of the rest to override Kamen."

"Sounds easy enough."

"Well …" Bill started slowly, "it won't be a slam dunk. This is still a "good ol' boy" town. You need facts and …" he paused to make sure Sarah was looking him in the eye, "the right attitude."

"Businesslike?"

"Not just that. Servile."

"Servile? What does that mean?"

"It just means that Kamen is your best weapon against Kamen. She's not servile to the men in power."

"Are you telling me I have to whimper just because I'm a woman?" Sarah's topaz eyes darkened.

"Just contain yourself. Don't be pushy."

"Just because I'm a woman?" Sarah's voice strengthened with incredulity.

"Sarah, you underestimate your power."

"You make it sound like I don't have any."

"That's not the way I mean it to sound. You have more influence than any Police Chief in Devaney history. Politically, the Mayor can't touch you. Women politicians are a dime a dozen. Female Police Chief's … not so much. And the fact that you didn't hesitate to arrest a crooked politician – that gives you political clout like you can't even imagine."

Sarah replied angrily, "I'm not looking for political clout. I'm a law enforcement officer."

Bill leaned forward and placed both hands on the desk. "It doesn't matter what you are looking for. You have it. Use it to your advantage. Just don't let it show. If you offend the Councilmen's egos … and don't ever forget that politicians are as much ego as they are BS … they won't rock the boat to support you. And you are asking them to rock the boat to the point of tipping it. Let them think they are in charge and you can lead them."

Sarah stared at Bill incredulously. Finally, she exhaled, "So, I have to play their game? Make them feel like big boys?"

Bill grinned and patted her right hand. "Now you get it. It's politics. There's a time to exert force and a time to divert counterforce. You have good political sense. Use it."

# CHAPTER 8

## Tuesday 10:00 A.M.

Kyren Bailey's crew was efficient. The camera and supporting lights were set and ready in the police station lobby before Sarah and the Mayor walked down the stairs. Sarah maintained her composure. The previous ten minutes had been filled with confrontation between her and the Mayor. The Mayor wanted to open the news conference. Sarah knew better than to allow it. Their upcoming battle required "spear in the sand" posturing on her part. She could not give the Mayor the upper hand. She needed the support of the people and of the City Council. She could not allow herself to appear weak. The investigation of John Wyatt's murder was not the only thing on her agenda.

Sarah cleared her throat before she stepped to a cluster of microphones fastened to the podium normally used in the squad room. Most of the microphones were put there by reporters. One was affixed with a quick disconnect for use with the squad room speaker system. It was not connected to anything at that moment. In truth, it was seldom used, but someone in the past thought it would be a good idea, and so it was attached. The reporters waited expectantly, impatiently. Mayor Kamen stood on her left, well within the field of attention. Zoey Kopechne stood two arm lengths away from the Mayor's left with Missy at her side. "At approximately 1:00 A.M. this morning, a yet unknown assailant ambushed and killed Officer John Wyatt. Currently, Devaney Police Department and the Sheriff's Office are investigating the incident. Detective Boston Mankowitz is leading the investigation with cooperation from Sheriff's Detective Benjamin Faraday.

"Our PD family is heartbroken by this loss. We ask for your prayers for Officer Wyatt's family. We also ask that you allow the family privacy as they try to cope with their tragic loss. Officer Wyatt is survived by a wife and two small children. They need our support and understanding.

"Officer John Wyatt was 26 years-old. He was a five-year veteran of Devaney Police Department Patrol Division. Being a police officer and protecting people was his dream as a young man. All indications are that he died while trying to protect a neighbor's property. Officer John Wyatt will be missed and mourned." Sarah turned toward the Mayor and invited her to make a statement.

Mayor Kamen adjusted the fixed microphone, so it was closer to her mouth, unaware that it was not attached to a speaker. She spoke softly which negated some of the whininess of her voice, "Times like this are unexpected. Shocking is a better word. The charged emotions between the community and the police department cannot continue. The loss of a young man, a husband, a father, demonstrates the need for a truce. Shooting anyone is not okay. It is not the way to resolve differences." Jordon glanced toward Sarah before her voice returned to normal, nasally and accusatory. "As we heard earlier on the national news, two Kansas City police officers were also shot during a traffic stop overnight. The animus between police and citizens must stop. In particular, I will not allow this to be the way of life in Devaney. I will be moving forward in the days ahead to further implement my initiatives so clashes of this nature do not reoccur in Devaney. We are better than that. Let's honor Officer John Wyatt, the first officer slain in the line of duty in Devaney's history, by embracing *Citizen Friendly* behaviors. It is time for a new Devaney. A citizen friendly Devaney."

Sarah felt her face flush. She knew her topaz eyes were dark and glowering. She could not help herself. She had seen Bill Keck's face during similar situations. She grasped her hands tightly to keep from throttling the Mayor. Most of the reporters were stunned by the Mayor's words, the politicization of the death of an officer. The Devaney PD employees and officers on hand were visibly enraged. She stepped forward to retake the podium before the Mayor could say anything further. The Mayor resisted momentarily by grasping the microphone but stepped aside when she saw Sarah's face. Sarah inhaled deeply and said, "I don't have a lot of answers at this point, but I will try to respond to questions."

Kyren asked, "Chief, Kansas City is not that far away. Are these shootings related? Is this part of a concerted assault on police?"

"We don't have any evidence that the incidents are related. I don't pretend to know a lot about it, but my understanding is that the Kansas City shooting developed spontaneously during a traffic stop. Officer Wyatt was off duty, apparently checking on a neighbor's home while the neighbor was out of town." Sarah hid her anger with the Mayor for using the Kansas City event to deflect focus on the Devaney event.

Kyren quickly asked a follow-up question. "Chief, if the two events are unrelated, was the shooting of Officer Wyatt a result of the feud between Devaney PD and the citizens of Devaney?"

Sarah's eyes narrowed. She could not stop her automatic facial response. She did not want to openly react, but it happened. "Kyren, despite recent political rhetoric to the contrary, there is no feud between Devaney police and citizens." She could not resist the urge to glare in Mayor Kamen's direction, "Last night's assault was the result of a criminal caught in a felonious act by an off-duty police officer. Criminals have always had a feud with law enforcement."

"Is the assailant a danger to the citizens of Devaney? Should we be worried?" asked an older, local newspaper reporter, Bernie Stone.

Sarah felt relieved. The right question at the right time. "I'm worried," she replied emphatically. "As I think we should all be. The killer has proven his disregard for human life by murdering a police officer. What is to say he would not kill anyone who gets in his way? I'm not suggesting people lock themselves in their homes, but I am suggesting that everyone should exercise caution. Report anything suspicious in your neighborhood."

Kyren pushed her question. "Will you be making changes in the department to support the Mayor's initiatives?"

Sarah composed herself before she responded, "Devaney PD will continue to protect and serve the citizens of Devaney. That is and has always been our objective. Officer Wyatt died protecting and serving, even while off duty."

Bernie Stone asked, "Do you believe the person who shot Officer Wyatt is still in Devaney, possibly hiding in plain sight?"

Sarah had a thought. In actuality, it was Boston's thought. There was nothing to confirm the number of suspects, but she had faith in Boston's gut. A good detective sometimes must rely on gut feelings, called hunches, intuition. Because of her "Maxie Moment" during her first solo case, Sarah avoided acting on feelings other than as an incentive to dig deeper. But, at that moment, standing before the microphones and cameras, Boston's feelings made sense. She was sure he was right. "I believe some, if not all, of the suspects are at large in Devaney. We believe we are closer to apprehending some of them than we were this morning." The statement was not wrong as far as she knew, and it would generate a reaction. Every criminal knows the act of killing a police officer is not taken lightly. Whoever killed Officer Wyatt was a marked man, even among his peers in the criminal world. They would not want to be associated with him when the end came.

The reporters responded to her words with shouted questions. Sarah held up her hands to quieten them, then pointed toward Bernie.

"Chief, you said you didn't have any new information earlier. Now you are saying you are close to an arrest. What are you withholding?"

Sarah answered quickly, "That statement was made about two thirty this morning. Evidence indicates that more than one person was responsible for the death of Officer Wyatt. Evidence is helping us tighten the net around the murderers. All of those involved will be charged with capital murder when apprehended."

Kyren shouted to be heard, "Chief, will the police act responsibly when making the arrests?"

Sarah suppressed a smile. The question is the one she wanted to hear. That question and her response would be played and replayed on the airwaves, out there so the killer and any accomplices would eventually hear it. It provided her the opportunity to set the stage, to instill doubt and fear in the minds of the killers. "We will proceed with caution, fully aware that these murderers are armed and dangerous. We will not allow another law enforcement or civilian life to be put in jeopardy when we apprehend vicious people known to be willing to kill to avoid arrest. Whatever it takes to protect the public." She saw astonishment on the faces of some of the reporters. The word would spread quickly, probably enhanced in typical media fashion. "That is all I have at this time. I will call another news conference when there are further developments."

Sarah saw Mayor Kamen's glowering face when she turned to walk toward the stairs. She heard the sharp click of the Mayor's heels on the tile rapidly approaching. She wheeled to face Jordon at the base of the stairs, timed to force the Mayor to stop suddenly.

"You didn't mention that you were about to make an arrest," Mayor Kamen whined accusatively.

"As I recall, we didn't discuss the case at all. You were more interested in the publicity role of the press conference than you were in the loss of John Wyatt. You tried to turn this into a war between the police and the citizens." Sarah turned and walked up the stairs. She did not have to look back to know the Mayor and her entourage left by the side door. She also noticed that the reporters, especially Kyren Bailey, were silently observing the interaction. The newshounds were sniffing.

"You haven't eaten today, have you?" Liz cared.

Sarah swiveled her neck to loosen the tension. She was tired. More tired than she was hungry. But Liz was right. She overlooked breakfast. Too many things too early. A steady stream of phone calls and follow-ups on the investigation kept her from everything personal. "I haven't even thought about it," she replied, a hint of shame in her tone.

"Go eat. You're going to make yourself sick."

"I think I already am. Heart sick." Sarah inhaled deeply to renew her resolve. "I'll go get a bite to eat." An idea formed. "I think I'll go to that little place near the street department compound. Call me if anything comes up."

Sarah drove to the café near the Devaney Street Department compound. She did not notice the name of the place when she ate there almost a year earlier. "Pearl's Café." As huge as the portions were, she expected it to bear a man's name. Burl's, or Butch's. The lot was nearly full, mostly with Street Department vehicles. She walked inside and glanced around the diner while she waited to be seated.

Sarah recognized Emerson, the Engineer who willingly shared information about the science of road surfaces. A smile crossed her face when she saw that Emerson was seated at a table with only one other person, a man she immediately recognized as Jackson "Jake" Farmer, the Street Department Supervisor. At least one thing was working in her favor.

"One?" asked a Server.

Sarah nodded toward the tables, "If they will allow it, I'd like to sit with Jake and Emmy."

"Sure Sweetie. Do you need a menu, or do you know what you want?"

"I'll probably just have the special and an iced tea," Sarah replied, knowing full well that she could not eat the entire meal.

"Hey, Kids," the Server said to Jake and Emmy, "do you mind if she shares the table with you?"

Jake looked up, momentarily puzzled until he recognized Sarah. "Of course. Sit down, Chief. We were just trying to make sense of what happened last night."

The Server reacted to Jake's words. "I'm sorry, Chief. I wasn't paying attention. I've been praying for Officer Wyatt's family. Terrible thing to happen in Devaney. I'll get your order in."

"Thanks for letting me join you," Sarah said as she adjusted the chair before she sat in it.

"How are your people holding up?" Jake asked sincerely.

"It's a struggle. It's hard to deal with the loss of someone in your family. Finding the shooter is keeping everyone focused for the moment."

"I am so sorry for your loss," Emmy said softly. "Is there anything I can do?"

"Pray for Celia and the babies. They need our support." The three sat silently solemn for a moment. Chatter from the other tables was uncomfortably noticeable. Sarah broke the silence. "I didn't ask to join you to disrupt your meal."

"Not at all. You're not a disruption," Jake replied quickly. "We're glad you joined us. But if there is anything we can do, any help you need ..." His words faded.

"There is one thing I can use your help with, Jake." Sarah was tentative.

"Of course. What is it?"

"Budget."

"Budget?" Jake and Emmy both looked puzzled.

"Budget. In particular, your budget for the annex. How are you justifying an increase?"

Emmy rolled her eyes and scowled.

Jake scowled and shook his head. "I'm justifying it by the added miles plus the data that shows most of those roads are not up to city code. Not that it's doing me any good. Kamen isn't accepting any increased spending on streets."

Sarah mirrored the scowls on the two faces. "Really? I would think your budget would automatically increase."

"You'd think, but apparently the Mayor has other uses for the money. She says the taxpayers don't want their money wasted on asphalt and concrete. Says road construction is harmful to the environment. Pretty much kicked me out of her office as soon as she said it." Jake's face reddened and his voice grew harder as he spoke. "I'm sure that if she had a trapdoor, I would have felt the floor open under my feet."

"Wow! I got the same treatment, for different reasons, but still the same. How are you going to move forward? Streets have to be maintained."

"I'll have to plead my case before the Council when the budget is on the agenda," Jake replied with a note of resignation. "I just hope we can survive another two years of her. So, I assume she nixed any increases you requested?"

"And insisted on budget cuts from current spending," Sarah replied. She sipped from the glass of tea the Server brought. "This nationwide "defund the police" mantra is her cup of tea." She held the glass up to accent her pun.

Emmy chuckled, "That's funny. I can't imagine, in light of what just happened, that she would still consider defunding police activities. That's insane."

"I think she is insane," Jake said. "We're facing a lot of repair work because of last winter. I get more pothole complaints than you can imagine."

Sarah nodded. "I can agree with the complainers. And … the Mayor seems to miss the concept that rough streets increase the wear and tear on police vehicles, increasing my costs to maintain the vehicles."

"It's a vicious cycle," Emmy inserted.

"What are you going to do on your budget?" Jake asked.

"I'm taking my case to the Council too," Sarah hesitated, then added, "but I'm going to start ahead of the budget meeting. I want to make sure I have someone on my side when it comes to a vote."

"Interesting," Jake said. "Very interesting. Do you think it will work?"

"It has to," Sarah answered and began eating from the overfilled plate the Server brought. The aroma was too inviting to ignore. Her stomach appreciated her attention.

"Do you mind if I tag along?"

"It might help. A united front, so to speak." Sarah's phone rang. Embarrassedly, she checked the ID. "Sorry, but I do need to take this." After receiving nods of understanding, she answered, "Hi, Alicia. Do you have something for me?"

"Hi, Chief. Not much. The smashed slug from the brick appears to be from a nine-millimeter, but it was too damaged to confirm whether it came from John's service weapon. The same with the mess in the one evidence bag you gave me. The .22 slug was readable, but it was not in the system. The only thing I can say with confidence is that it is from an unregistered gun. I have enough to match it if we find the weapon though. Sorry. Not much to go on, but it's all I have. I've been in touch with the State Lab. John's not there yet, but they assured me they will make him a priority."

"Okay. Thank you, Alicia. We'll keep looking."

Jake and Emmy watched attentively during the conversation. As soon as Sarah disconnected, Jake asked, "Any developments?"

"Not really. I know we don't have a lot of camera equipment on our streets, but do you have any out in the Glendale Avenue area?"

"Sorry," Jake shook his head, "we don't. Just the cameras for the user-actuated traffic lights. They just read. They don't record."

"Too bad. We're trying to find any video or security footage of traffic in that area from midnight until about two. It would be nice if we had a vehicle to hunt."

"No clues?" Emmy asked.

Sarah thought before she responded. "We have one potential. I hope it provides something of value." Even among those who supported her and the police, she did not want to reveal that the investigation was yielding nothing.

Sarah walked in the front door rather than through the back entrance of the police station. She wanted the Shift Commander to see that she was in the building and accessible in case there were any new developments. Upstairs, inside the bullpen, she noticed the Situation Room light was on. A lone figure sat in a chair and stared at the whiteboard. On the table in front of him, his index finger was hooked through the handle of a coffee cup. Boston looked disheveled, as normal but more so. Horizontally across the center of the whiteboard was a black line made with a dry-erase marker. The beginnings of a fishbone chart were there, starting with a dark line marked *"John shot"* slanted upward from the horizontal line. The next slanted line was marked *"9-1-1 call."* Nothing more to show for all the manhours of investigation since the shooting occurred. Sarah recognized the desperation in Boston's posture. She had been in that situation more than once. Not enough evidence and no clues. "Hi Boston. Did you get any sleep?"

Boston turned, took a sip of coffee and replied, "Not really. But I did get a needed break. I heard the slugs tell us mostly nothing." He nodded toward a diagram of bullet ricochet tacked to a corkboard with several scene photographs.

"Yeah."

"Anything on the radar? Faraday is down for the day."

"He is? I expected as much, especially with no breaks. Taylor's people haven't turned up anything. No cameras. No witnesses. Nothing. But we have a chance to get a break."

"What's that?" Boston scowled, suspecting Sarah was holding back information.

"A hunch based on your gut."

"My gut?"

"I told the press that there were multiple perps, that we are closing in, and that we would do everything possible to contain them without violence when we find them."

"Are we?"

"We will be if your gut is right and my words fall on the right ears."

"Chief," Liz said softly from the Situation Room doorway. "I'm glad your back. I hope you got something to eat."

"Thank you, Liz. Yes, I did. I feel much better. Did you need something?"

Liz whispered, "Terrance Overton is here to see you. Terrance Junior."

"To see me? Did he say what about?" Sarah's face twisted with bewilderment.

"No. He said he needs to talk to you. No one else. I told him you were busy with a case. Do you want me to tell him to make an appointment?"

Sarah looked at Boston. "Do you need me at the moment?"

"Not unless you have a clue about who did this and where he is … where they are," Boston shrugged. "I'm going to go back to the scene and dig around the neighborhood. Maybe one of those barking dogs knows something."

"Okay. I'll go see what Overton wants."

Terrance Overton, Junior aged more than he should have during the few years following the death of his younger son, Bentley. The frame around his bald head was completely gray. He appeared haggard. The death of the family patriarch probably added to the stress that made him appear drawn and gaunt. The good life turned bad when his happy home and his world fell apart. Sarah knew from general gossip that his wife, Christina, had not recovered from the emotional trauma after the murder of her younger son at the hands of her older son, Terry. Terry was in an institution, probably never to be released, unable to cope with the demons that drove him to do what he had done. Sarah met him at the door when Liz led him to her office.

"Good afternoon, Mr. Overton. I am sorry for your loss. Your father was a good man who made an indelible mark on Devaney. How may I be of service?"

Terrance, informally called Junior, did not waste time. "I want you to investigate the murder of my father. They're saying heart attack, but I know better. I want to know who killed him."

Sarah pondered his statement. "Please be seated." That gave her a few more seconds to formulate a response. "Other than the announcement of your father's passing, I have heard nothing. Who ruled the cause of death heart attack?" She only knew of two people in Devaney who could list

COD on a death certificate: the attending physician or the Coroner. She doubted Henry Mason was involved, considering the events of the night.

"The ER Doctor. But it's a lie." Junior stated adamantly.

"Was an autopsy performed?" Sarah doubted one was. That would have required transport to the State Medical Examiner. It was too soon for the body to be delivered. Definitely too soon for results.

"No. That's why I need your help." Junior was not asking for Sarah's help. He was demanding it.

During a past investigation, Henry Mason explained to Sarah the protocol for autopsies. Unattended death. Suspicious death. Police request to satisfy an investigation. "Did you ask the Coroner to authorize an autopsy?"

"He wasn't willing to authorize one. He said there was no reason to doubt the attending physician's determination." Junior clinched his jaws angrily.

Sarah studied the man for a moment. He still projected the power of a person accustomed to getting his way. His eyes were colder than she remembered. Less compassion. "What makes you believe your father was murdered?" she asked with as much concern as the day's events allowed for the new development.

"He was the picture of health. Never had a heart problem before this. I tried to get his regular doctor, Dr. Mertz, to look into it. He's out of town. My father was murdered. I have no doubts."

Sarah kept her focus, even though she wanted to ignore the man and his plea. As far as she was concerned, Junior was grasping at straws, firmly in the grasp of denial. He was in the initial stages of grief, a phase where she was not allowed to linger. "Where is your father's body now?"

"At Mason's Mortuary. I told that …" Junior paused and composed himself, "I told Mason to not touch the body until I gave the okay."

Sarah knew Henry Mason had limited storage space for bodies. He was not in the habit of keeping bodies in his cooler more than a day without starting the embalming process. "Mr. Overton, I can't promise anything, but I can delay the process until we sort through this. As you can imagine, the department is going through a struggle right now."

Junior scowled, "Your problems are not my problem."

Sarah pulled her shoulders back and glared at the demanding man, completely forgetting his grief. "Mr. Overton, the murder of a police officer should be everyone's problem," she seethed.

Junior's head jerked back, and his eyes widened, "What? What murder? When did this happen?"

Sarah maintained her posture, "One of our police officers was shot last night. That has the focus of this department and the Sheriff's Office."

"I'm sorry. I didn't know. I've been dealing with … that's probably why the Mason was so curt."

"Could be, Mr. Overton. Could be. Henry Mason is also the Coroner, in case you don't remember, and he has been up all night." Sarah rose. "Again, I am sorry for your loss. I will talk with the Coroner and do what I can as soon as I can."

Sarah watched Junior walk toward the stairs. His posture was subdued. She reckoned some shame was now mixed with his angry grief. Helping the owner of Overton Enterprises would probably be a good thing. It certainly would not hurt anything … if she could muster the resources.

# CHAPTER 9

## Tuesday 2:00 P.M.

Sarah eased into her chair. She was exhausted. It was barely two o'clock, but her day had started early. If she were still a detective, the Chief would have told her to go home and get some rest – like she did with Boston. As Chief, there was no one to tell her to get some rest. She was committed to a dinner meeting with a group of Devaney business leaders. She probably could beg-off under the circumstance, but it might upset some of the influential people in town. She could delay it until another evening, but she might be just as busy or just as tired then. Police work was too unpredictable. Besides, this was an opportunity to plant a few seeds that might grow into supportive relationships, relationships that could help Devaney PD in the long run, maybe even help in her battles with the Mayor. She refocused on her immediate tasks, a full inbox with several documents that required her signature.

By the time Sarah completed the critical items in her inbox, along with a quick update on the Wyatt case from Boston, it was almost four o'clock. She barely had time to visit with Henry Mason before she freshened herself for the dinner meeting. "Liz, are you aware of anything more I need to do before I leave? I need to go see the Coroner."

"You have the dinner meeting with the business group. Unless you want me to cancel it. They should understand if you do cancel."

"I know, but the contacts might be beneficial. Have you been monitoring the news?" Chief Keck installed a TV in Liz's office so he could be aware of any important news stories. The practice was especially helpful in dealing with a Mayor who played the Press to further her agenda.

"Just repeats of your statement this morning," Liz replied. "I suppose your plan was for Kyren to keep repeating your comment about being close to apprehending the suspects."

Sarah nodded. "The word needs to be out there. Anything else before I venture among the movers and shakers?"

"Other than that, everything else can wait until tomorrow. You need to get some rest."

Sarah went to the front entrance of the funeral home rather than the back entrance. A somber-faced woman with an empathetic smile and sad eyes greeted Sarah when she entered the carpeted lobby of Mason's Funeral Home. The room was decorated with fake lilies, lighted sconces, and over-stuffed furniture with easy-to-clean upholstery. Live flowers would replace the fakes during viewings. Tissue boxes were available on several small tables scattered around the perimeter of the room. The effect was a respectfully somber aura throughout the lobby, designed to give grieving families comfort.

As soon as Ellen Mason recognized Sarah, her somber expression changed to one of welcome. In a respectful tone, Henry Mason's wife and business manager extended her hand. "Hello Chief. I am so sorry for your loss."

Sarah replied, "Thank you," as she took the offered hand. She could not shake the eerie feeling of the hand she shook. Cold. At that moment, she realized she preferred the atmosphere of the morgue and the prep room. She expected those rooms to be physically cold. The coolness of the lobby and the chapel was not about room temperature; it was about the nature of the business. After exchanging obligatory greetings, she asked, "Is the Coroner available to answer a few questions?"

"He should be. He was going to prepare the remains of a client, but as I understand it, he is awaiting further instructions from the family. These things are not easy, you know."

While Sarah waited in the lobby, Ellen disappeared through a doorway that led down a hallway flanked on one side by offices. The older woman's footsteps were silent on the maroon carpet with golden-yellow swirls. A short time later, Henry Mason appeared dressed in his dark Funeral Director suit. For a man who also spent his night at a crime scene, he looked remarkably well rested. She reckoned he took a nap in his office at some point during the day.

"Hello Chief. How may I help you?"

"I have a few questions for you."

"I'm not sure I have any more answers than I had this morning. I did expedite Officer Wyatt's body to the State ME. I received confirmation of receipt if that is your question."

"Admittedly, that was one, but I'm here on a different subject."

"Oh?"

"Mr. Overton. I have been asked by the family to request an autopsy. Is there any information to support doing that?"

Henry Mason shook his head. "Junior was in here earlier, demanding that I perform an autopsy. Interfered with my nap. He couldn't understand that I don't do autopsies. I'm a Coroner; not a Medical Examiner."

"He is adamant that his father's death was not from natural causes. Anything to indicate that?"

"Nothing that I could see, Chief. What are you thinking?"

Sarah mulled the question. "Is there anything that can be done to get answers?"

"Well, I did draw some blood and take precursory tissue samples just in case. Maybe Alicia can find something if you want to do that."

"I assume you maintained Chain of Custody?"

"Of course. You know I always maintain COC." Henry appeared offended by the question. "Let's go get them, or do you want me to call Alicia?"

"I can take them. I want to keep this low key for now. What about an autopsy?"

"You're the Chief of Police. I have no reason to request one. If you do, just say the word …" the Coroner paused before adding, "but don't expect the Coroner's Office to cover the cost on a fishing expedition."

Sarah was forced to consider the options. She had no money in her budget for autopsies. She could charge it to Miscellaneous, but she doubted there was enough money to cover it, let alone hide it. "I don't have funds for autopsies," she finally said.

Henry cocked his head, "Since the family is wanting it, they can pay for it."

"Is that done?"

"I've only had one case as Coroner. The family pays for the autopsy with the provision that if foul play is discovered, the Coroner's Office reimburses the cost."

"Interesting."

Henry watched Sarah for a few moments before he asked, "So what do you want to do? I have the body in the cooler. I can send it out in the morning."

"Let me talk to Junior. See if he's willing to pay." Sarah left the funeral home with the evidence from Terrance Overton, Senior's body, and apprehension about the call she needed to make to Terrance Overton, Junior.

"Mr. Overton, this is Chief James. I'm following up on your request for an autopsy on your father."

"Are you going to get it done?" Junior harshly asked. His phone voice was strong.

Sarah inhaled deeply, "Mr. Overton, we have blood and tissue samples in the lab. We are unsure what they will tell us. To determine if your father did succumb to a heart attack will require a full autopsy."

"Then do it!"

"It's not that simple, Mr. Overton. Neither the Coroner nor I are authorized to pay for autopsies that are not indicated by circumstance. The fact that the attending physician, the doctor who treated your father at the time of death, is confident that heart failure is the COD means we aren't in a position to authorize spending public funds on an autopsy." Sarah phrased her statement as diplomatically as she could, knowing full well diplomacy would not temper the message.

"Then I'll pay for it!" Junior was angry.

"Are you sure you want to do that?" Sarah got the response she expected, but the whole affair was in unfamiliar territory to her.

"Yes. And I'm upset that the Police Department won't do its job and pay for a murder autopsy."

"Mr. Overton, let me be clear. The Police Department can't authorize an autopsy if there is no indication of foul play. The attending physician has certified COD. At this point, it is up to the family to cover the costs. On the other hand, if an autopsy reveals something other than natural causes, you will be reimbursed."

"You seem to think I care about the money. I don't. I want to find out what killed my father … and who."

Sarah collected her thoughts. "Mr. Overton, where are you right now?"

"I'm in my office. Why?"

"I will stop by there in a few minutes so you can sign an autopsy request form. It's a required document. The Coroner will send your father to the State Medical Examiner tomorrow morning." The request form also indicated the paying party, normally the Coroner's Office.

Sarah had to hurry. After she left Overton Enterprise offices and delivered the autopsy request to the Henry Mason, she had less than an hour before the business group dinner. Rather than go to her apartment, she freshened up in the Station locker room. She kept spare clothes in her locker. A fresh gray toned pantsuit and a paisley blouse. She also kept a few make-up items in case of emergencies. After a night with less than three hours sleep and a busy day, a dab of emergency make-up was in order. She longed for a warm shower or a lingering soak in the tub.

The business leaders jockeyed for Sarah's attention, as well as the attention of the Sheriff and the DA. Businesspeople know a good working relationship with law enforcement makes their lives better. Assets need protection. An extra patrol here. An extra patrol there. Every available eye to watch over valuable properties. Her official phone buzzed incessantly. On silent, she felt the vibrations against her left breast. She kept it in an inside jacket pocket so she could feel it. She could not stay out of touch, especially not under the current circumstances. Every call showed the Mayor's ID, either her official phone or her personal phone. Unusual to say the least. Sarah kept her personal phone in another pocket. She could not feel vibrations from it, but she was sure it rang as well.

The dinner, which included pre-dinner and after-dinner mingling, required more than two hours of Sarah's time. She put her phones back on sound when she got into her car. Six voicemails awaited, five on her official phone and one on her personal phone. Surprisingly, all of them from the Mayor, not Zoey. Each was a repeat of the first, with variations of words to express the Mayor's growing indignation that Sarah did not answer immediately. The Mayor was upset about a public statement from Terrance Overton, Junior regarding an autopsy.

"Mayor, I see that you called and left voicemails about Mr. Overton's requested autopsy."

"Why did you not answer your phone?" the Mayor demanded.

"I was indisposed. I don't sit around and wait for your calls. Now, what do you want?" Sarah was tired and in no mood to be civil.

"Don't take that tone with me. I can fire you in a heartbeat."

"Mayor, don't go down that road. You called me for a reason. Tell me the reason or I'll hang up. I've been working since two o'clock this morning. I'm tired."

The Mayor mumbled unintelligibly for a moment. "Sarah, have you even watched the news? Have you seen what Terrance Overton is saying about you?"

Sarah blanched as she drove and processed the Mayor's words. "I told you, I was indisposed. I was at a meeting with the Sheriff and the DA." That was as close to the truth as Sarah wanted to be with the overbearing Mayor. "What did Overton say?" She really did not want to hear the Mayor's version, but she could not hear the real version until the ten o'clock news – if it was replayed … and if she was still awake.

"He said his father was murdered and the Devaney Chief of Police refused to pay for an autopsy to find out what killed him, yet the city is paying for an autopsy on a police officer whose cause of death is apparent."

"Mr. Overton discussed his concerns about his father with me. At that time, he wasn't aware of John's murder. I respect his concerns and have started an investigation. It has only been a few hours since we met. Samples are in the lab."

"So, why is he going to the Press about you not paying for the autopsy?"

"Mayor, you know autopsies are funded by the Coroner's office, not the police department."

"He said you told him you would not pay for an autopsy."

"I can't. The Police Department does not pay for autopsies." Sarah was exasperated and could not keep it from her tone as she annunciated each word slowly. "Mayor, let me repeat – I told him neither the Coroner nor I could authorize an autopsy under the circumstance. The attending physician declared the COD was natural causes. The body shows no signs to indicate otherwise. Until we find something to contradict the doctor, we can't request an autopsy in good conscience."

"So, *good conscience* is a policy maker?"

Sarah shook her head. "Autopsies cost money. You should understand that. If there is no reason to spend that money, it should not be spent. I told Mr. Overton that if he wanted to pay for an autopsy, the Coroner would send the body to the State ME. In the meantime, we are testing tissue samples. If those samples show just cause for an autopsy, the Coroner will reimburse him. Overton signed-off on that."

"Then why is he on TV delivering his scathing message?"

"I haven't heard him, so I'm not going to speculate on his motive. He's upset about his father's death, apparently unexpected by the family. The Overton family is important. The Overtons are always newsworthy."

"Maybe we need to take him seriously."

"Mayor, I am. There is only so much I can do. The body will be sent to the State ME tomorrow. Alicia will have some results on the tissue samples within a day or two. We can't go any faster."

"Who's assigned to the case? I don't like it when a citizen goes on TV and disparages my administration."

Sarah was surprised by the Mayor's words, though not her tone. Without the tone, her words almost sounded like she was defending Sarah in a back-handed sort of way. "I don't take anything personally."

"It wasn't you he was attacking," Mayor Kamen snapped. "Get this straightened out. You're devoting too much time to a police death and not enough to the death of a prominent Devaney citizen."

Sarah was instantly hot. Rather than respond, she hit the end button. Angry tears blurred her vision, and she bit her lower lip so hard it hurt. A driver following her honked to express his irritation when she slowed to turn into her apartment parking lot. She turned on the left turn signal and slid into the center turn lane, later than she should have already done the maneuver.

# CHAPTER 10

## Wednesday 6:00 A.M.

At six A.M., Sarah was at the gym. She needed it as much as she needed her night's sleep. Running was her focus of the session. Not a hard run. A sweat generating, heart pumping, circulation inducing run. Only fifteen minutes, but she felt better when she stepped into the gym shower.

Short, not quit shoulder length brunette hair dries easily, quickly, and falls into place without much fuss. A touch of powder across her nose and an insignificant amount of colorless lip gloss gave her confidence. A tiny bit of perfume and a dab of underarm deodorant finished her preparation. Her suit bag held her daily selection. A slate gray pantsuit and a Forest Green blouse. It was Wednesday. It seemed like it should be later in the week. Tuesday was interminably long.

Sarah carried a paper sack containing an orange juice and a cup of cut fruit into the station, the finest a fast-food place had to offer. Sergeant Blanchard was at the Shift Commander desk. After a brief update of the night's patrol activities, and disappointment that there were no new developments in Officer Wyatt's case, she walked upstairs to her office. She knew there was nothing new, otherwise she would have received a phone call. It was still disappointing. She almost always arrived earlier than anyone else who worked upstairs. That morning was no different. She opened her office and set the sack on her desk. She then went to the bullpen coffee pot and started the first pot of the day.

Sarah checked her office phone voicemails while the coffee brewed. Three from the Mayor. All the same messages. Angry over Terrance Overton, Junior's statement to the press. When Sarah arrived at her apartment, she was too exhausted to stay awake for the news. She still did not know exactly what Junior said. She turned on the TV in Liz's office, hoping his statement would still be news.

It was.

Terrance Overton Junior appeared as agitated on camera as he was in Sarah's office, maybe even more so because he still did not have an answer an hour after they last spoke. Impatience in the extreme. The camera lighting was bright. Probably hot. Junior's brow and upper lip were damp with sweat. The lights and perspiration accentuated his anger. His words were crafted for impact.

*"It is an outrage,"* were the first words that blurted from the screen. Probably not the beginning of Junior's original comments. *"My father was in good health despite his age. He* **did not** *die of natural causes. He* **did not** *have a heart attack. Someone murdered him. Overton Enterprises has been under an orchestrated attack by city officials for more than a year. It is no secret that the politics of the day is to limit development within the city and within areas identified by the city for future annexations. My father made himself a target when he came out of retirement to personally confront those attacks.*

*"The current climate in Devaney will strangle development and developers. Preservationists hold a narrow view of the world. Their misguided environmental policies will ultimately lead to the destruction of this city's economic environment. That is the environment that needs protection.*

*"Because of this administration's funding policies, the Chief of Police is unable to pay for an autopsy on my father, an autopsy that will indisputably prove my father's death was murder, not natural causes. BUT – the city seems to have adequate funding to perform an autopsy on a murdered police officer, a case that is indisputable as to cause. Meanwhile, my father's murder will go unresolved because no tax money is available, tax money paid by me and every other Devaney citizen.*

*"I will pay for the autopsy myself because my father deserves justice."*

The screen reverted to the morning news anchors gathered around a semi-circular desk affixed with the station logo and a digital display of local time and temperature. Their giddy banter muted with the push of a button on the remote.

Sarah walked to the coffee pot with her coffee cup in hand. The pink letters emblazoned on the gray cup grounded her, *"Make sure you're right then go ahead."* She was glad she did not fully accept the Mayor's version of Junior's message. He was not attacking her. He was attacking the Mayor. His only references to her were to further attack the Mayor. Jordon Kamen tried to draw Sarah into the dispute on her side by twisting Junior's words. She reckoned the Mayor would also try to publicly spin Junior's words into a slap against the Police Department, against Sarah, before it was finished.

As she poured her first cup of coffee, Sarah heard the bullpen door open. She turned and saw the top of Lieutenant McCluskey's hair bob along the perimeter of the partition walls. "Good morning, Taylor. How are you?"

"Good morning Sarah. Maybe the better question is, how are you?"

"Still tired. I haven't done my rounds this morning. Anything new?"

"Not that I've heard – and I would have heard. Have you heard anything from Boston?"

"Not yet. Coffee's fresh."

Taylor dropped her personal belongings at her desk and circled toward the table that held the coffee pot. "Good. Care if I go with you on your rounds?"

"Let's go." Sarah paused long enough to turn on the Situation Room light. The whiteboard showed no more than it did when she left Tuesday afternoon.

The mood in the department was one of frustration. And anger. No clues to indicate the killer. No evidence to show progress. Though barely over twenty-four hours into the investigation, the urgency to capture John Wyatt's murderer was strong. Every Devaney police officer wanted him found. Someone had to pay. Vengeance drove them. Sarah felt the same, but it was her duty to keep the Department professional. Otherwise, they were no better than a vigilante mob. She talked. She empathized. She soothed. She felt the same pain, with one possible exception – they felt the pain of fear. Fear for their safety. Fear of that one unpredictable moment. Fear that the cop killer was still lusting blood. Something had to give soon.

Lieutenant McCuskey stayed with her Sergeants for shift change. Sarah returned to her upstairs office alone, empty cup in hand. She realized that she was in the defining moment of her career. How she handled herself, how she handled the investigation, how she resolved the case would determine what she and the Devaney Police Department would become, would determine if she *could* be a Chief of Police. That cup told her everything she needed to know.

Boston pulled himself upright when he saw Sarah walking around the edges of the bullpen. Sarah recognized the posture of a man who was trying to hide physical pain. Detective Mankowitz's abdominal injuries were not fully healed. His belly muscles might never get back to their former condition. "Good morning Boston," Sarah greeted him as she approached the coffee pot. "Have you learned anything new?"

Boston shook his head and winced. "Nothing. I've never had a case this dead. I questioned every neighbor out there. They are either good liars or sound sleepers. Even the ones with dogs."

"The dogs didn't wake them?"

"According to them, no. Boss, I've never been this frustrated by a case." Boston's eyes showed defeat as he blew across the top of his cup.

"This one is personal. Don't give up. It will come." Sarah said the only things she knew to say at the moment. She remembered the frustrations she felt when she doggedly hunted the man who stabbed Boston.

"Yeah. It is personal. I've lost friends on the force before … back in Baltimore. At least we had evidence. Clues to follow." Boston shook his head as he sipped his coffee. "I have nothing to write on the whiteboard."

Sarah heard the frustration in Boston's voice. If the lead detective sounded lost, the whole department would hang on that tone. "Something will break. It always does. This was not a hit." They both understood the statement. A professional hitman knew how to cover his tracks. Routine killers did not. Boston just needed to stay focused until the killer made a misstep. "What *did* you learn from the neighbors?" She knew his previous statement was born of frustration.

The two of them sat in the Situation Room to talk … and stared at the almost blank whiteboard. Some of the photos from the crime scene were tacked to a corkboard. John Wyatt's sheet covered body primarily displayed. Nothing on display prompted an epiphany.

"The next-door neighbor who found John was the only one to react to the gunshots. The neighbor on the other side didn't even wake up until the sirens. No one knows if the dogs started barking because of the shots or because of the sirens."

"Have you talked to the homeowner?"

"By phone."

"Did you learn anything from him?"

"Not a lot. He was surprised to hear about the jimmied window. Didn't know anything about it. That's his daughter's bedroom."

"Whoa! That's frightening. How old is his daughter?"

"Fifteen."

"Oh. Sneaking out at night and accidently got locked out?" Sarah asked.

"Or something. He did say that he has SimpliSafe installed on all perimeter doors, with a camera on the front door."

"Don't those notify you when someone comes into view?"

"Yes. He said his phone alarmed him when I first arrived, but he slept through it. It woke him when the house was entered later."

"It doesn't alarm on the other doors?"

"Not over the Internet. Just an audible ding indoors. If his daughter is sneaking out, she has to crawl out the window to avoid detection. She can't use a door without that ding. Maybe the window jammed a few times when she closed it behind her, so she had to jimmie it open."

"Do you think the dad or mom knows?"

"From his reaction, I doubt it. But they do now. We'll probably hear more on that." Boston raised his eyebrows and smiled knowingly.

"When are they coming home?"

"They're due back tomorrow. He said they could stay away a few more days if necessary. I think he wants to see that window. I told them to come home today if he wants. There's no evidence to disturb."

Sarah thought about the clean-up crew. Boston was right. Other than the bullet scars on the concrete and the brick veneer, there was nothing. She looked at the picture of John's sheet covered body. "The perp's car was on the left side of the driveway," she said confidently.

Boston looked at the photos on the corkboard. "What makes you say that?"

"It's a two-car garage, right?"

"Yeah. Why?"

"John's body was located to one side of the driveway, away from the shadowy side where the gate is. The left. The initial shot killed him almost instantly. He didn't run. He dropped where he was standing."

Boston got up and walked to the corkboard. He stood sipping his coffee, thinking. Sarah let him think. She knew she was right, but she did not want to get ahead of the evidence. Boston would either agree or disagree. "You may be right. We're sure the shooter had a vehicle, there for a burglary. Had to have transportation." He sipped and stared.

Boston shifted his cup to his left hand as he walked to the whiteboard. He grasped a marker with his right hand and traced a slanted line - a fishbone - up from the center line, immediately left of the bone noting time of death. He wrote on the new line in a neater hand than an observer might think possible *"Passenger shot John."* He put the marker back in the board tray and stepped back.

Sarah nodded when he looked toward her. "Your gut was right. He had a partner. At least one ... the driver."

"I'm glad you put the body position into perspective. I should have seen it."

"It was dark. The shadows were heavy." Sarah offered an excuse, knowing full well Boston did not want to hear one. She should have noticed it sooner herself.

"I should have noticed it because the food wrapper was near John's body. There was not enough wind to move it from where it was thrown."

"We both should have noticed the clues." Knowing there was more than one person involved did not move them any closer to solving the case, but Sarah still felt relief from knowing. She had not misled the Press or the public. She noticed that the local news was still putting the message out that the police were close to arresting "some" of the people responsible for killing Officer John Wyatt. And ... they were not hesitant to mention the potential for a violent end for those people. Exactly as Sarah wanted it.

"Good morning, Chief," Liz Sweeney stood in the doorway, apologetically waiting for Sarah's attention.

Sarah turned and responded, "Good morning, Liz. You're early today."

"I knew it would be busy for you. Sergeant Locke called your office. I answered. He's on his way over from City Hall."

"That's early. What does he want?" Boston snarled vehemently.

Sarah cringed. The physical separation of Glasgow and Locke from the routine activities of the Police Department created divisiveness and harmful animosities, especially under the circumstances of their separation. She did not know if those animosities would – or could - ever be resolved. In a conciliatory tone, she said, "I'm sure the Mayor sent him. Liz, let me know when he gets here. I think I may have a job for him. Probably not what Jordon wants, but …"

"Spies. I don't like it," Boston said, "but I don't have to deal with it. Unless you were planning on assigning him to me …" Boston raised his eyebrows questioningly as he made the last statement.

"No. But Keith was learning to be a fairly decent detective. I do have a case for him."

"Good. So, about this close arrest … what are you thinking?"

"Call it a hunch … or a hope."

Keith smiled sheepishly when he knocked on Sarah's open door. She knew it was an attempt to ingratiate himself. "Come in, Sergeant. What can I do for you?"

"Well, I thought I would come see if I could help. You told the Press that you were about to make an arrest. If you need help …"

"I have that covered. I do have something else I need." Sarah selected a folder from a wire file holder on her desk. She opened it and withdrew two pieces of paper with handwritten notes. "You probably heard that Junior Overton is convinced his father was murdered. I don't have anyone to assign to it, but with your experience, I'm counting on you to find out if he has a case."

Keith was shocked. "But … but …" And speechless.

"Are you here to assist or snoop?"

"Well … uh …"

"Good. Snoop it is. Snoop around on the Overton case. He sounds like he's got it in for the Mayor. You can get him off her case by taking on his case. If someone from Public Outreach is working on it, that should calm his attitude toward the Mayor. Do you think you can handle it?"

Sarah did not allow Keith time for rebuttal as she handed him the folder. "This is all I have to go on. Check with the attending physician and the Coroner to get up to speed. Find out what they know that we don't. Push the doctor. The body will go to the ME sometime today, but it won't be a priority. Alicia has some blood and tissue samples that might give you a clue." She stopped; satisfied Keith was sufficiently overwhelmed to prevent argument over the assignment.

Keith studied the notes and nodded. "Okay, but you may have to cover me with the Mayor."

"Just tell her that you are part of the solution. I will deal with her. We have some killers to apprehend. Thanks for your help." Sarah's words dismissed Keith better than a shove out the door. It was too early to call Henry Mason. She asked Liz to remind her to place the call after eight o'clock. A simple task, but she knew Liz would not let her forget it. She did not want to send Keith in unannounced. She also knew she would hear from the Mayor sooner rather than later.

# CHAPTER 11

Wednesday 9:00 A.M.

Dr. Chakrabarti did not appreciate Keith's presence at his door at nine o'clock on a Wednesday morning. His ER shift did not end until seven. The first few hours after shift-end were his unwind time before he crawled into bed. The appearance of a uniformed police officer at his door pushed his mind into overdrive. "What do you want?" he demanded. He wanted to be kind, but ingrained fears prevented it. He was a naturalized US citizen, but his brown skin and accent did not go unnoticed by some of his patients, and their reactions did not go unnoticed by him.

Sergeant Locke stood stoically on the front portico. The two-story house was in the Prairie View development, an upscale area of town with large lots. Upscale homes gave the area a safe appearance. The former patrol officer knew there were no safe places when it came to criminal activity. The inhabitants of Prairie View would feel safe until the first high profile crime occurred in their development. He almost felt sorry for their blissful ignorance. "I'm trying to gather information regarding the death of Terrance Overton, Senior. Records indicate you were the attending physician at the time of his death."

Dr. Chakrabarti shook his head in disbelief. "You disturb me at home for this? He died of heart complications. I even tried to revive him with a defibrillator. He was old. All that is in his file – if you have the right to see it."

"I understand that you valiantly tried to save Mr. Overton. This has nothing to do with your efforts. I spoke with his personal doctor, Dr. Mertz, before I came to see you." For emphasis, Keith produced a folded piece of paper. "I have a court order to access his medical records as necessary to conduct an investigation into Mr. Overton's death."

Dr. Chakrabarti was stunned. He still held the edge of the door, essentially blocking further intrusion. "Investigation? Why?"

"His family has expressed concerns that his death was not from natural causes."

"He had a heart attack. That's a natural cause, unless they want to blame red meat and his eating habits for suicide by diet."

"They believe the heart attack may have been induced," Keith said, still maintaining his steady composure. "I just have a few questions."

"They believe I did something to cause his heart attack?" the Doctor asked incredulously.

"No. But did you?"

"Of course not! Why would you ask such a thing? He arrived by ambulance. He was in distress. Clammy, gray face. Struggling to breath when the paramedics arrived at his house. Complained of chest pains. They sent telemetry of his EKG. He showed all the signs of arrythmia, myocardial ischemia. The patient was in severe distress when he arrived. His heart stopped. I defibrillated. Twice. Three times. Nothing brought him back."

"Was it two or three times?" Keith asked pointedly.

"What?"

"You said you defibrillated twice, then changed it to three times."

"No. No. That's not what I was saying. I defibrillated twice. Nothing. Then a third time. Nothing. I continued for several minutes. My notes in his file will tell you. Several times, but his heart was stopped. It did not respond. He was dead and to do more was cruel."

Keith made notes in a notepad. "Did you check his body for puncture wounds or any other physical marks?"

Dr. Chakrabarti blinked confusedly. "Marks? No. I was treating his heart. He did not suffer trauma. He had an IV when he arrived. The paramedics gave the patient an aspirin tablet, but he had difficulty swallowing it. To help with pain, they administered sublingual nitroglycerin. He was on oxygen when he arrived."

"Did Mr. Overton complain of anything."

"He was barely responsive when he arrived. I'm not sure he ever understood what was happening."

"Is that normal?"

"For myocardial infarction, yes. Too often. If people wait too long to react, to call for help, yes. Too often, men ignore their symptoms until it is too late. False bravado. Women's symptoms are ignored because they suffer differently and don't realize what is happening. We can only help if we get to them in time."

"Did you draw blood?"

"Always. His blood tests told us what we knew. Elevated BNP and Troponin-T."

"What do those tell you?"

"That his heart was damaged – severely damaged."

"How did you respond to the tests?"

"There was no time for response. He was pronounced before the tests were completed."

"If you …

"Had the test results sooner? Is that what you are wondering? He would still be just as dead."

"Then why do the tests?"

"If he was not as severely damaged, the tests could have guided treatment regimes."

"Did you find anything else in his blood?"

"Like what? Cholesterol? Lipids?" Dr. Chakrabarti was no less irritated after several minutes of Keith's questions.

"Toxins. Poisons. Something that could cause a heart attack."

Dr. Chakrabarti shook his head. "Of course not."

"The tests did not show anything that could cause a heart attack?"

"Other than cholesterol, no."

"Was his cholesterol high? His doctor said he wasn't being treated for any heart disease."

"Cholesterol was normal as I recall, but cholesterol is not the only measure of heart risk."

"What are some other measures?"

The Doctor was exasperated by the questions, "Age. Stress. Alcohol consumption. Heredity. Gender. Blood pressure. Inactivity."

"What toxins could cause heart attack?"

"Do you honestly believe the patient was poisoned?"

"I'm just investigating the case. I have to look at all possibilities."

"Look in his pantry. Maybe the answer is there. I don't know anything other than what I have told you."

"His pantry? Some foods could cause heart attack?"

Dr. Chakrabarti shook his head. "Officer, poor diet is a primary cause of many ailments. Red meat. Low fiber. High fat. Refined sugar. Our pantries hold many poisons. Investigate his diet and maybe you will find your answer."

Keith walked away with no progress made. Terrance Overton, Senior's personal physician was sure Terrance was in good health for his age, at low risk for heart failure. The ER Doctor was sure Terrance died of a massive, unsurvivable heart attack. He decided to talk with the paramedics, to find out anything they may have noticed during the call. He drove to the fire station that housed the responding unit.

Paramedics Tamara Jones and Carly Blakemore were still on duty. Barely.

"Sergeant, can we make this quick?" asked Tamara. "We've been here for seventy-two hours. It's time to go home.

Keith smiled understanding. He knew the Devaney firefighters and EMT personnel worked three-on, three-off, seventy-two hours straight. "I'll be quick," he assured the two paramedics. "I just have a couple of questions about one of your calls. A heart attack victim late Monday evening. Terrance Overton, Senior."

"I remember him," Carly said. "Nice place. His wife was really upset. The responding firefighters had to calm her while we worked."

"Did you notice anything unusual?"

"Unusual for what? He waited too long before telling his wife - if that's what you mean. He died in the ER before we completed our paperwork."

"Is that unusual?"

"I wish I could say it was. Happens too often. People just don't listen to their bodies. If it doesn't feel right, see a doctor."

"Yeah," Tamara added. "People are ashamed it will be a false alarm. Better to be ashamed than be dead, I say."

"Did Mr. Overton say anything out of the ordinary? Anything that made you think something was amiss?"

"By the time we got there, he was barely able to respond to our questions. He was confused. That's a sign that he was in distress. Blood flow was severely restricted by his arrythmia. We followed standard protocol and transported him as soon as we could."

"What protocol?"

Carly answered. "Tried to get him to swallow an aspirin. Set a saline IV. He was hurting. Clutching at his chest. Struggling to breathe. Sublingual nitro tablet. Oxygen. Strap him in place and run hot. Established an EKG to transmit enroute. Made the link. Dr. Chakrabarti met us at the door. He was trying to code before they got him off our gurney onto the table."

"Did you assist once he was in ER?"

"Stayed out of their way. Those people have way more skills. We removed our equipment as they cleared it, then waited for someone to sign off. He died before anyone could get clear to sign for us. Tough one."

Tamara nodded affirmation of Carly's statement. "His wife and a man who I think was their son showed up around the time we were rolling our equipment out. That was not a meeting I wanted to be part of."

"Did the wife say anything while you were in their house?"

"She was in panic mode. Like we said, the firefighters tried to calm her and keep her out of our way. In retrospect, maybe it would have been better for both of them if she could have held his hand while he died."

"Did you notice any signs of trauma? One of you inserted the IV needle. Were there other signs of puncture? Abrasions on his body."

"I won't say there were no marks on his body, but there was nothing obvious on his arms, chest or head. That's about all we see with a heart attack. He was fully clothed at the time, except shoes. He wasn't wearing shoes. Just socks."

The paramedics provided no unusual information, no clues. Keith's next stop was the Coroner. Coroner Mason was expecting him, somewhat perturbed that he did not arrive earlier. It was almost eleven o'clock. The two men sat in Henry Mason's office.

"The Chief says you're investigating Terrance Overton's death. What did the doctor tell you?" Henry got to the point.

"Not much. Neither did the paramedics. It's up to you, I suppose." Keith smiled devilishly.

"It's not up to me," the Coroner said dismissively. "I've done all I can do. I took blood and tissue samples. They are at your lab. Your people will have to tell you about the results. My part was to pick up the remains from the hospital morgue and then package for transport to the ME."

"Did you do anything with the body ... the remains?"

"Other than draw some blood and take a few tissue samples, no. It appeared that the morgue did some precursory cleaning around the face and neck. Probably to allow the family to say goodbye before the remains were sent to the morgue. I'm sure he vomited at some point during the procedures to save his life."

"Did you get stomach contents for the lab?"

"No. If there were any left inside his stomach, I left that to the ME They are better equipped. I didn't want to disturb the remains any more than I had to for the blood and tissue draw. Autopsies are precise, especially when it's an Easter egg hunt."

"You think heart attack was the right COD?"

"I generally trust the attending physician. He has a better view."

"Could it be murder?"

"Anything is possible. I would not make that call based on what little I know, though."

"Why do you think his son thinks it is murder?"

"Denial. I deal with grief on a daily basis. Denial is the first stage."

Keith studied the Coroner's cold glare. "So, it's a wild goose chase?"

"It's his goose. He's paying for it. I'll let the ME tell us the story. It's out of my hands. I'm just the mortician in this saga. I was called to pick up remains based upon family choice."

"I thought you were the Coroner." Keith was confused.

"I am if a Coroner is required. Until Junior Overton came to request an autopsy, I was the mortician chosen to prepare the remains for burial. Still am unless the ME says different."

"Did you start that?"

"No. Fortunately for him ... for Junior, I did not. Other than the light cleaning done by the ER staff and my blood and tissue draws, the remains are untouched. All that is noted in a file I sent to the ME. Mr. Overton is still in the clothes he was wearing when he was loaded into the ambulance."

"When do you expect results from the ME?"

"At best, a week. Depends on their case load."

"Can that be shortened?"

Henry Mason smirked, "I'm sure Junior is pulling as many strings as he can. It's not often that a citizen pays for an autopsy."

"What happens if the ME finds something to indicate foul play?"

"If that happens, the Coroner's Office will bear the burden of cost. We'll see how that plays out."

"I mean, what do you do if the ME finds something."

"It's not me who has something to do. That will be you ... the police department will have to investigate to find who did it."

Keith thought about what the Coroner said. He rose from his chair and handed the Coroner a business card. "If you think of anything else, please call me."

Henry rose, accepted the card, and walked around his desk toward the door. "You know I will."

# CHAPTER 12

## Wednesday 11:00 A.M.

"Chief James, this is Zoey Kopechne."

Sarah resisted the urge to laugh into her phone. The Mayor's Assistant answered the phone in a rapid, apologetic voice as if she had placed the call to Sarah rather than the other way around. Nerves. Sarah imagined the terror that welled in the Mayor's sycophant. The sense of fear carried through the phone. The young woman was learning quickly that her imagined ideals were not of much value in the real world. The recent college graduate was still being fitted for big-girl panties. "Hello, Zoey, how may I help you?" There was no need to be rude.

"The Mayor is in meetings, so she asked me to check on the status of the arrest, you know, of the people who killed the officer." Zoey relaxed in response to Sarah's conciliatory tone - but she remained warily hesitant. She was only doing what the Mayor insisted be done. She was doing her job. She knew the Mayor and the Police Chief were at odds, in perpetual clash mode. As much as she admired Jordon Kamen, she did not want to be stuck between two powerful women.

Sarah regretted making her public assurance of arrests. Not because she thought it was the wrong thing to say, but because the Mayor would pursue the subject like a baying hound. She needed to be careful to not overplay her hand. A wrong statement by the Mayor could unravel her plan, expose the bluff. "Tell her I expect something very soon. I appreciate her concern and I will keep her up to date." She hoped her derision did not transmit to Zoey's ears.

Sarah shook her head after the call ended. She knew the Mayor would still call her, demanding an answer. She did not know when that call would come. Her official cell phone chimed. She grimaced.

The ID on Sarah's phone indicated Devaney PD. A call from inside the building. She answered. Puzzled.

"Chief, this is Sergeant Jarrett in Booking. I'm not sure what's going on, but there seem to be some reporters gathering outside the jail entrance. Are you aware of it?"

Sarah responded, "I'm aware of nothing. Is Boston or Detective Faraday there?"

"Not that I can see. I put a couple of officers inside the door. Makes me nervous when people congregate outside the jail."

"I'll be right there." Sarah disconnected the call. She was not worried that someone would breach the door. The back entrance was not a public entrance. The door required a pass card, issued to all officers along with their badges. Once inside, entrants had two options, go through a second security door into Booking or ascend the stairs to the office area. She left her office and stopped at Liz's doorway. "Liz, is there anything on the news?"

Liz looked up from her desk and glanced at the TV. "No ... wait." She reached for the remote control and increased the volume. "Something is crawling across the screen right now." She read what they both could see. "*Breaking news at Devaney PD. Suspects in murder of Officer John Wyatt to be booked into jail.* Did Boston arrest someone?" Liz looked puzzled.

"I've heard nothing. BOSTON?" Sarah called loud enough to be heard in the bullpen.

Boston responded, "Yeah, Boss?"

Sarah walked around the corner to see Boston coming toward her from the Situation Room. "Have you identified someone in John's murder?"

"Not yet. Still cold. Why?"

"Channel 6 is prepping to go live outside Booking. They say suspects are about to be booked. Have you heard from Faraday?"

"Booking? Are they outside?"

"Sergeant Jarrett says they are. I'm going down. What about Faraday?"

Boston hurried to catch up with Sarah as she walked quickly toward the back stairs that led to Booking and the jail. "I talked to him a few minutes ago. He's been on the phone with the homeowner. The family will be back later this afternoon. The dad is incensed about the window, claims his daughter denies jimmying it. He's worried that someone might have found his wife's jewelry box."

"What's the girl's name?"

"Kendra, I think. Why?"

"Somehow, I think that might be important. She might be important."

Sergeant Jarrett's dour face greeted Sarah when she reached the bottom of the stairs. "They're not attempting to come in. They're looking toward the parking lot as if they are expecting someone. Do you want us to disperse them?"

Sarah glanced through the small glass pane in the door and shook her head. "Want? Probably. But I think I will go see why they are here. What they want."

"Backup?" The Sergeant asked.

Sarah smiled grimly. "Always."

"Parker. Jenson. Accompany the Chief." Sergeant Jarrett's order was heeded by the two officers at the doorway.

Kyren turned to look at Sarah when the door opened. Her eyes lit with anticipation and she motioned for her camera man to follow. The other reporters followed suit. "Chief! Chief! What can you tell us about the suspects? Will they be kept in city lock-up or will they be transferred to County?"

Behind Kyren's back, unnoticed by any of the reporters who were focused on Sarah, a gray sedan parked away from the small crowd outside the police station. Almost immediately, Clara Taylor climbed from the driver's seat. She scowled toward the building. Something upset her. She hesitated momentarily then opened the back door. A teenaged boy stepped from the car. The passenger-side back door opened. Another teenaged boy waited to exit until Clara and the other boy came around to his side of the car. Both boys fussed with their clothes, straightening any wrinkles that might show while Clara watched and directed their movements. Clara strode purposefully toward the Booking entrance with the two boys at her heels.

"Chief, do you have anything to tell us? We were told someone with knowledge of Officer Wyatt's murder would to be brought to the Booking entrance at noon today. What can you tell us?" Kyren impatiently, persistently pushed her microphone into Sarah's face. She failed to notice Sarah's momentary distraction.

Realization struck Sarah. Her plan worked. The accomplices' fear of harm overcame fear of arrest. She knew who Clara had with her. Her topaz eyes darkened. "Kyren, in all fairness to the suspects, I will allow their attorney to speak first." She motioned toward Clara and the two teenagers.

Kyren almost knocked her cameraman over when she wheeled in place. A newspaper reporter reached Clara first.

"Are these the murder suspects?"

One of the officers who accompanied Sarah, nudged her elbow to get her attention and whispered, "Just a heads-up, Boston says the DA is inside."

Sarah nodded understanding but kept her eyes on Clara and the two teens.

Clara was not happy that the event did not unfold exactly as she planned. She glared her disapproval toward Sarah before she responded. "My clients are *not* murder suspects. Let's make that very clear. They had nothing to do with Officer Wyatt's murder. They are witnesses to the murder."

Sarah watched with interest and allowed Clara to speak. Anything Sarah did or said at that moment could be turned against Devaney PD.

"Witnesses? We were told suspects would be arrested," chimed Kyren. She sounded disappointed and glanced toward Sarah.

"Rumors," Clara replied angrily. Her tip to the Press was misinterpreted. "They are not suspects … but that is how they would be treated by Devaney police if I were not present. My clients know who the murderer is. These two young citizens witnessed the murder. These two young men are here of their own volition to bear witness to that murder, to do their civic duty, to help bring the murderer to justice. If you will excuse us, we have business with the Devaney Police Department."

"So, they will be arrested?"

Clara pointedly glared toward Sarah. "I'm sure the police will try to book them. That is the only way Devaney PD functions. Accuse and arrest. Use duress and contrived evidence against good citizens. But they will not be arrested."

"What can you tell us about your clients?" Kyren hungrily asked. "What are their names? Where are they from?"

"I can tell you that my clients can identify the murderer. I can tell you that they tried to intervene, to stop the murderer. I can tell you that they are Devaney citizens, high school students with no history of criminal activity – no record of run-in with the law. I can tell you that they were frightened by the public, threatening tone of the Devaney Police Chief's message toward anyone who witnessed the murder. Honest, decent young men who I am here to prevent from coming to harm at the hands of overzealous Devaney police officers set on revenge. To keep them from being railroaded by vigilante justice at the hands of the police."

"Are you suggesting they will be harmed by Devaney police?" asked Kyren.

Clara glared toward Sarah. "That is a possibility. That is their fear. That is why I am escorting them into Booking. That is why I called the Press. I want a visual record of their physical condition at the time they present themselves to tell what they know. I want everyone to see that they have come here voluntarily. Yes, I fear for their safety in this jail, the treatment they might receive, and I will be asking Judge Varadkar to move them to County if the overzealous Police Department decides to make a false arrest. I will also ask the State Police to intervene and guarantee their safety if they are taken into custody and, even more so, after they are released on bail."

"Why didn't you take them to County in the first place?" a veteran newspaper reporter asked pointedly.

Clara glared and ignored his question.

The older reporter persisted. "If they are only witnesses, why would they be arrested?"

Clara hesitated. Kyren's camera was trained on her. All the reporters in attendance waited for her response. The rush of questions she wanted, the chatter she needed to cover questions she did not want to answer did not happen. Finally, she responded, "My clients were unwittingly involved with an evil person. Their role was unwitting, but they accept the fact some people … especially the police … may try to connect them with the killer. They are aware they may have to face the Judge to be exonerated. And, make no mistake, my clients will be exonerated." The wily lawyer saw that the mood of the Press was not as supportive as she hoped. "Now, if you will excuse me, my clients need to be booked so they can officially plead their innocence and get on with their lives."

Sarah watched. The shift in mood among the reporters was all she needed to see. Clara's stunt did not play as well as planned, but the lawyer had successfully planted seeds of doubt in the public mind about the safety of the two teenagers. Those seeds would grow and provide fodder for the Mayor's reduced police funding agenda. If Jordon could feed a steady stream of doubts and "what ifs" to the public, she could get support for lowering the police budget. With enough public support, even the Council would be politically inclined to support the Mayor's budget plans.

The reporters parted to allow Clara and the two boys entry. Sarah and the two officers stood between them and the doorway. Clara stopped and glared. "Are you going to stand in our way," she snapped curtly.

Sarah held the lawyer's glare a moment then turned sideways while motioning toward the door with her right hand, "Of course not. Gentlemen," she said to the two officers, "please escort Miss Taylor and her clients to the Booking Sergeant. And notify Detective Mankowitz of their arrival. I'm sure he has some questions." She knew Boston was inside the door watching, but she wanted to put Clara on notice publicly that the show did not end with booking. The attorney knew her clients would be arrested despite her posturing.

The reporters wanted to follow Clara and the two teenagers. Sarah knew they would. Booking was not off limits to the public, but it required the door to be unlocked by an officer. She had no desire for the event to become a dog and pony show for Clara. She turned to the converging reporters, "While they are attending to business inside, I will entertain any questions you still have." She met the veteran reporter's eyes, all but inviting him to ask.

Bernie responded, "Miss Taylor seems concerned about the treatment that might be afforded her clients while in Devaney PD custody. How will you address her concerns?"

"I'm glad you asked that, Bernie. As you can imagine, I take offense to her assertion – but I accept her histrionics as part of her legal strategy.

As an experienced criminal defense attorney, Miss Taylor knows it is in her clients' best interest to create as much doubt about fairness as possible to sway public opinion. Aside from that, the District Attorney's Office is inside for the booking to oversee the process. They will make sure everything is done legally." She assumed Clara had called for the DA to be present. By mentioning it to the Press first, she negated Clara's messaging. "Even as deeply hurt as we are at the loss of one of our own, we are professionals, sworn to protect and serve. We do not choose who we protect. We protect everyone equally, even the accused. Her clients will answer questions – or not - as Miss Taylor advises. No threats. No duress. No torture ... as some people unfamiliar with modern, professional interrogation might suggest. We will know the truth so we can charge the appropriate person ... or persons ... for the murder of Officer Wyatt. Accomplices to murder will also be charged for their role in the crime. That is a point Miss Taylor avoided to mention. But in the long run, the DA will decide who is charged and with what charges. That is not for the police department to decide."

"What will you do if Clara demands her clients be taken to the County jail?" Kyren asked hurriedly to prevent someone else being heard.

"That will have to be addressed by a judge, probably Judge Varadkar. I will abide by the Judge's ruling. If Judge Varadkar sees merit in her request, it's not my place to deny her clients that change."

The veteran reporter barged in with another question, "Yesterday you announced that this would happen, that an arrest would happen soon. Yet, you seemed surprised when Miss Taylor appeared with her clients."

Sarah's mind scrambled. She did not want to reveal that she was only playing a hunch, a hunch that the fear of a violent arrest would force a bit player in the murder to come forward and beg for mercy. "Surprised? Not really. Pleased. Yes. I am *happily* surprised they chose to turn themselves in rather than try to evade capture. We achieved a positive outcome without confrontation."

"What will they be charged with?"

"Specific charges will come from the DA's office. We have authority to arrest murder suspects. I will suggest that attempted burglary charges are also possible. But ... let's not speculate further. This is a serious matter. We must all make sure we're right every step of the way." Sarah looked toward Kyren to see if she had more questions. She knew one of the officers would come tell her when the booking process was completed. The booking would be delayed by Clara's legal maneuvers as she tried to convince the DA her clients were not involved. The booking would happen despite Clara's legal wrangling. She also knew Boston would have the two teenagers and Clara inside the Interrogation Room immediately after that.

"Chief, how does it feel to finally have someone in custody for Officer Wyatt's murder?"

"Kyren, as a citizen of Devaney, how do *you* feel?"

Kyren stumbled over words before she responded, "I suppose I feel better knowing the murderers are locked up."

"But, according to Miss Taylor, her clients are not murderers. They are witnesses to the murder. The actual murderer is still at large - according to her clients."

"Are you saying that the citizens of Devaney are still in danger?"

"I'm saying that we still have work to do. If a murderer is still in our midst, no one is safe until he is behind bars."

Questions continued, questions that danced around the subject and delved into a string of what-ifs that Sarah hated to dignify with a response, but she needed to bide time. Finally, Officer Jenson stepped out and leaned to whisper to Sarah. Sarah nodded understanding and said to the reporters, "Ladies and gentlemen, I wish I could continue but I am needed inside. I will try to have a statement early tomorrow. Maybe sooner if we learn the name of the murderer and feel it is essential to public safety to release the name. Thank you for your time."

Officer Jenson held the door open for Sarah. The reporters were pressing forward, but he allowed the door to close after him.

Sarah heard her cell phone. She guided toward the Interrogation Room before she lifted the phone from her jacket pocket. The ID indicated it was Zoey. She shoved it back in her pocket. Jordon must have been watching the news bulletin. As to be expected, the Mayor had Zoey call on her behalf as soon as Sarah was free. Sarah had better things to do than listen to the angry woman. Off hand, she could not think of anything that would *not* be better than listening to one of Jordon's rants.

# CHAPTER 13

## Wednesday 1:00 P.M.

Sarah greeted Marcie Ignack when she stepped inside the observation room. "I thought you would be in with Boston."

The perpetually overwhelmed Assistant DA grinned. "I didn't want to give Clara the satisfaction. You should have seen her performance at Booking." She laughed aloud, then clasped her hand over her mouth. "Oops! Too loud."

Sarah shook her head. "I doubt they can hear you. This room is pretty much sound tight. It's about time to get this started." Her cell phone rang. She shook her head and scowled. Zoey. She declined and put the phone on silence. She did the same with her personal cell. Zoey would keep trying. The Mayor would demand it. She sent a text to Liz. *"Interrogation. Do Not Disturb. !!!"* Liz would understand the exclamation points.

From behind the one-way mirrored glass, both women observed the Interrogation Room occupants. Clara Taylor was seated between her two clients on one side of a utilitarian table. The threesome was facing the mirrored wall. Boston was sitting with his back to the mirror, studying the contents of a folder. The folder held hand-written notes, evidence reports and photos of the crime scene. She knew he was waiting for her to signal that she was ready. Red lights shined from cameras that recorded activity in the room. Two cameras captured everything. One near the ceiling on the wall behind Boston. The other on the wall behind the two teenagers and Clara. Neither suspect was cuffed, the result of an agreement between Boston, Marcie, and Clara for the interview. Everyone understood they would be cuffed for the trip to a cell. Sarah flipped a switch on a small control panel. The lights turned off and on, an indication to Boston that she was in position.

Boston looked up and surveyed each boy in turn. "Please state your names and ages for the record." Command voice. Coldly unemotional. Boston at his best.

The teens looked toward Clara expectantly. She nodded. "Just your names and ages. Nothing more."

After a couple of false starts as the two boys determined who would speak first, the thinner boy began speaking. "Buzz, ah … Clarence Houston Paltrow. Seventeen." The blonde shock of hair on the nervous boy's head quivered as he spoke.

"Buzz? How did you get that name?" Boston's vocal tone postured his authority.

The boy's eyes widened. He looked at Clara.

"Why are you asking that question?" Clara challenged.

"Because I can. He can answer or not, but his refusal will be noted as uncooperative." Boston glared at the lawyer.

Clara nodded to the boy.

"When I was little, my grandpa said I was as busy as a bee, buzzing around. He called me Buzz. You know, like a bee." Buzz expectantly waited for Boston's approval.

Boston scribbled on a piece of paper and ignored Buzz's eagerness for validation. "And you, state your name and age."

Sarah watched the second boy. Stockier. Accustomed to the advantages his size gave him. His attitude was different than Buzz's. Less frightened. Less concerned. Barely concealed cockiness. His hair was dark, almost black. His brown eyes challenged the Detective defiantly. He had a mustache. Red rash on his cheeks and chin indicated that he recently had a beard. Sarah was sure Clara enforced a grooming code the boy reluctantly accepted.

"Bear Switzer. Eighteen. I suppose you want to know why I'm called Bear?"

Boston's eyes narrowed. "Makes no difference to me. I want your full name. Not a childish nickname."

Bear swelled angrily. Clara cleared her throat to get his attention and put her hand on his forearm. He yanked his arm away from her touch before he settled. "Brandon Dean Switzer."

"Now - that wasn't so hard, was it?" Boston said. "Your lawyer claims you boys didn't have anything to do with the murder of Officer John Wyatt." He pushed a graphic picture of John's body toward Buzz. "Tell me what you *don't* know about this." His statement was heavy with sarcasm. Throughout his career, he heard more suspects claim they *did not* know anything than claimed to know something.

Buzz paled. So did Clara. Bear glanced toward the picture but did not register that he saw it. Buzz's vocal cords were tight. He could barely squeak out a response. "I don't know anything."

"I thought you saw who put four slugs in Officer Wyatt's head while he was lying helpless on the concrete." Boston glared at Clara who seemed ready to speak. He jabbed a finger at the picture for emphasis. "This was an execution!" he bellowed. The Detective glared at Buzz and then Bear. Bear was startled by the outburst. Boston snarled, "I guarantee your lawyer can't save you if you don't tell me everything you know right now."

"Are you threatening my clients?" Clara snapped.

"No, Ma'am. I'm telling them like it is. You said they were here to tell what they know. What they need to know is what they are facing if they don't talk. They were party to an execution. Someone stood over Officer Wyatt while he was helpless on the ground, took his service weapon and shot him mercilessly. Now, Buzz, tell me why you were in that driveway with a killer."

Buzz slumped, cowed. "We were there because Bear's girlfriend's family was out of town."

"Stop!" demanded Clara. "I need to caution my clients that what they say can be used against them."

Boston leaned back. "You want me to read them their Miranda's again? They said they understood them when Sergeant Jarrett recited them. Are they mentally impaired?"

Clara glared at Boston then turned her eyes toward the mirrored wall. She knew from experience that Sarah and Marcie were in the Observation Room. "The police in this town seem to ignore Miranda Rights."

"Well, Counselor, at this point, we can prove your clients were at the scene of the execution of a police officer. They've freely admitted that fact, Miranda or no Miranda. That makes them guilty of being accomplices to murder. Even though the State frowns on lethal injection for killers under twenty-one, it is more than happy to lock them away for life. Sixty or so years in an eight-by-eight cell with a smelly cellmate. Not much of a life. But that's no secret to you, is it, Miss Taylor? You say they are here to cut a deal by turning state's evidence. By ratting-out someone they *claim* they tried to stop from executing a cop. What can I say? No talk. No deal." Boston closed his folder and leaned back in his chair for emphasis.

Clara twisted her thin lips, agitated by Boston's words. "Clarence, you can continue cautiously. Tell him why you were there. Nothing more."

"We were there to steal some jewelry and stuff." Buzz could not avoid drifting his eyes toward Bear who was scowling at him.

Sarah saw the displeasure in Clara's eyes. Buzz had said more than she had coached him to say. It was too late.

"Burglary? Whose idea was it to steal the jewelry and stuff?"

Buzz's eyes cut toward Clara.

Clara touched his forearm. "Tell him what you two told me – but no name yet."

"Uh … the guy who shot the policeman. It was his idea." Buzz gulped. "We just went along. Dumb like, you know."

Boston scribbled before he asked, "No. I don't know. Are you saying it was his idea to kill a policeman? That you went along with that plan to execute a police officer too?"

"NO! That's not what I'm saying. We didn't know he was going to kill anyone. It was his idea to steal the jewelry."

"Oh, I see." Boston liked the reaction he got. "Was the plan to break down the doors and hold the family at gunpoint while you robbed them?"

"No! I said they weren't home. We knew that. We knew they had security doors with cameras."

Marcie whispered to Sarah, "Gutless little twerp."

Sarah nodded, not wanting to miss anything, even though she knew the recording could be reviewed later.

"Bear," Boston abruptly switched his attention, "your girlfriend lives in that house?"

"I don't have to answer that."

Boston smiled. "No, but your girlfriend has told us a lot, about how you sneak into her house through the back window. How you showed her how to jimmy window locks."

"Stop!" Clara demanded. "My client doesn't have to answer any of those questions."

Boston scoffed, "I only asked one question, and your client refused to answer it. Another notation under the uncooperative heading. No talk. No deal. But no matter. Kendra has told us plenty. Enough that we knew Mr. Brandon Dean Switzer was involved and we have been watching him since first light the morning after the shooting. We knew he would lead us to the rest of the gang. He's not very good at this."

Sarah grinned as she watched Clara and the two boys squirm. Boston was good. She made a mental note to never play poker with him. He could bluff better than she could. He could also play egos very well.

"Now, Bear, do you want to answer my question, or do I let you two take your chances with an angry jury? Remember, without a name, you go down for accomplice to murder. Who knows? Maybe we can pin it all on you. After all, it was *your* girlfriend's house. The murderer found out about it from you."

"It wasn't me. We told Cutter not to do it. Yeah, Kendra lives in that house. But it wasn't my idea to rob the place."

Boston made a note. Cutter was a street name, or a nickname. Bear was coming under his control. Fear was a powerful tool. "How often did you and Kendra date?"

Bear squirmed, "We didn't actually date. Her dad is pretty strict. She hooks up with me and we go places every now and then."

"Sex?"

Bear's heavy brows met in the middle. "What?"

"Was the sex with Kendra consensual?"

Clara opened her mouth to speak but was not quick enough. "I didn't force myself on her," Bear replied disgustedly. "I'd never do that."

"Interesting," Boston mused as he scribbled some more. "Now, tell me how you were planning to get inside the house and locate the jewelry."

Bear looked at Clara, who was glaring at Boston. "Go ahead," she said, "but be cautious." She knew there was no going back. It was better for her clients to reveal the truth.

"The plan was simple. Go around back to Kendra's bedroom window. Jimmy it open. It's easy on those kinds of windows. There's a gap between that rubber stuff."

"The seal?" Boston asked without looking up from his notes.

"Yeah. The seal. It's easy to slide a screwdriver tip up there and unlock the window."

"Where was the jewelry?"

"We didn't get it."

"I understand that. But where is the jewelry in the house. Surely you weren't just going to ransack your girlfriend's house to find it. That would be pretty dumb."

"Of course not! They hide the jewelry when they go out of town. Stuck between the mattresses on her parent's bed. With the pillows and stuff, it's not even noticeable if you don't know it's there."

"You've seen it there."

"No. Kendra told me about it."

"Sounds like a good plan there, Buzz. What were you supposed to do? It wouldn't take all three of you to climb in a window to get a jewelry box if you knew where it was hidden."

Buzz was shocked by the sudden shift of attention to him. He stammered. Clara did not offer any extra cautions. "Uh ... I was the driver. It was my car."

"You're only seventeen," Boston noted casually, "and you have your own car? Impressive. Parents must be well-off."

Buzz relaxed and smiled proudly. "I work as a cart pusher at Walmart. I'm paying for it with my own money."

"That's good. I bet your parents are proud of you."

"My mom. Dad's dead. Died when I was five."

"I'm sorry. You know, Officer Wyatt's children are two and four. Younger than you were. Now their dad is dead. How do you think they are going to survive?"

Buzz gulped. Clara put her hand on his forearm to silence him. "What is that? Ask him about the murder. That question has nothing to do with what they know about Officer Wyatt's killer."

Boston shrugged. "Just curious. If anyone in this room can offer insight into what Officer Wyatt's children can expect in life, Buzz is that person. I thought maybe he could help us help them. But you're right. It has nothing to do with the case. But - if Buzz can help those babies …" His voice trailed. "So, you were the getaway driver?"

"The driver. Yes. That's all I did."

"What happened after you got to the Whitmore's house? That was their name, you know. Good to know your victim's name."

"Uh … yeah. I know their name. Kendra is younger than me, but I see her around school. And Bear …" Clara's hand stopped him.

Clara cautioned, "Just answer the Detective's questions. Ignore his sidebar. He asked what happened after you arrived at the scene."

"Scene. That's good. Impersonal. Helps erase the image of a bleeding, dying father begging for his life so he can go home to his children," Boston said as he pointed toward the photo in front of Buzz. He saw the boy's eyes struggle to avoid seeing the picture. "Buzz, what happened after you parked in the Whitmore driveway? On the left side of the concrete."

"We waited. Cutter said we needed to make sure no lights came on in the close houses. If someone noticed us, we were going to leave."

"Sounds like a good plan. Then what?"

"A car came into the neighborhood. Drove past us."

"What were all of you doing?"

"Just sitting there. Waiting."

"Where was everyone inside your car?"

"Bear was in the back seat."

"Which side?"

"What?"

"Which side of the back seat? Passenger side? Driver's side?"

"He was behind me. The idea was for him to get out on the dark side and go through the gate."

Boston looked toward Bear. "Alone?"

Bear responded with a snarl. "I thought I already told you that."

"Not specifically. But it's good to know. If Bear was in the back, was the murderer in the front passenger seat?"

Buzz began twisting his hands together.

"Was the murderer in the front passenger seat?"

"Yes. Cutter was in the front seat." Buzz's memory of the night began to take control of him. His hands twisted harder and he bit his lower lip.

"What was Cutter doing?"

"Eating a burger. We got something to eat earlier."

"What did you eat?"

"What difference does that make?" Clara interjected.

Boston bluffed, "It will tell me if he's lying."

Clara nodded and Buzz answered. "I didn't. I was too nervous."

"First time, huh?"

"Yeah. I shouldn't have agreed to it. But once Cutter heard Bear mention the jewelry, well it kind of got out of control."

"What was Cutter's job?"

Buzz looked toward Bear, confused. "I'm not sure. Guard. Lookout. I think?"

"Okay, a car drove into the cul-de-sac ..."

"The what?"

"Cul-de-sac. That's what that kind of dead-end street is called. What happened after the car drove past on the cul-de-sac?"

Buzz looked down at his hands and his eyes teared. In a barely discernible whisper, he said, "Cutter told us to get down while he watched." Buzz's voice broke. "He said it was a cop. He said the cop was coming our way. I told him we needed to go. So did Bear." Buzz's head leaned lower. A tear dropped on the table near his hands.

"My client needs a moment to compose himself," Clara said as she patted Buzz's shoulder.

"Fine. Bear, you can answer. What happened after Buzz said you should leave?"

Bear finally looked uncomfortable. "Cutter laughed. Not too loud, but he laughed and said, 'I've always wanted to pop a cop.' Then he pulled a pistol out of his pants." Bear's eyes widened, "I swear we didn't know he had a gun. It was just a robbery. Supposed to be a robbery. Take the jewelry and leave."

"Repeat what Cutter said," Boston demanded.

"He said he always wanted to pop a cop. Those were his exact words." Bear dropped his gaze to the top of the table.

Sarah saw the change in demeanor. Both boys were aware of the circumstance. Both boys were regretful, if not remorseful. They were telling the truth, or at least their version of it. She was anxious to hear the name of the shooter, and eager to go after him.

Boston made notes and stared at the folder. Carefully, slowly, he pulled several pictures, different angles of Officer Wyatt's bloodied head from the folder. He pushed them directly in front of the two subdued teenagers. "Tell me what happened next."

Bear talked in a suddenly timid voice. "The cop ... the policeman ... walked to the car. He had a flashlight in one hand. His other hand was at his waist. On his pistol."

"He drew his weapon?"

"Not exactly. He had his hand on the handle, from what I could see."

"So, you didn't get down like Cutter told you to do?"

"Not really. After he talked about killing a cop, I froze." Bear hated to admit his fear.

"Did Officer Wyatt say anything?"

"I think he asked why we were there. It happened too fast. Cutter's window was down but mine was up. He smoked and Buzz told him to open the window when we were driving."

"Cutter's window was down. Got it. The policeman walked to the window with a flashlight in one hand and his other hand on the grip of his weapon. What next?"

"It happened so fast. Cutter suddenly tossed his burger wrapper out the window. The policeman's head turned to watch the paper. It distracted him. Cutter pointed his pistol right into the cop's face. I heard a pop." Bear paused to bite his lower lip. He inhaled deeply. "He shot the cop. The cop fell. It must have killed him right away. From where I was sitting, he just dropped out of sight. Before either of us could say anything, me and Buzz, Cutter slung the door open and jumped out. I couldn't see anything real clear. Buzz did. He says."

Boston turned to Buzz. "Buzz?" The boy was struggling to stay in control. "Buzz. I need you to tell me what you saw." He waited but Buzz still stared at his twisting, entangled fingers. "Buzz, look at me," Boston commanded. "Did you see what happened after Cutter jumped out of the car?"

"Yes," Buzz squeaked. "He leaned over and grabbed the cop's gun and shot him in the head. Then he jumped in the car, slammed the door and said "Go. Go. Go.""

"What did you do then?"

"I froze … for a minute." Buzz turned his head to show his right temple. "Then he punched me and said "GO! GO! GO! I popped me a cop." He was mad and happy at the same time." He paused, then added, "He was crazy."

"Where did you go from there?"

"Uh … we drove to where he left his Beamer then I took Bear home. I went home."

"Where was his Beamer?"

Buzz paused to blink away more tears. "At the mall. A long way from the house."

Boston scribbled. "That's almost a mile away. Why so far?"

"I don't know. That's where he wanted to leave it."

"Probably so his vehicle wouldn't be associated with a robbery on the opposite side of town," Boston said derisively. "He was ready to let you two take the fall for the burglary if something went wrong." He paused and stared at both boys for a moment. "And something went wrong big time. Without your testimony, you will take the fall for the murder of Officer Wyatt. You get that … don't you?" He looked from one boy to the other.

Both teens nodded. Clara stared at Boston with her jaws set.

"What made you decide to come forward, to tell us about Cutter?"

Buzz answered. "Cutter said no one would know who did it. No witnesses. But when the Police Chief told the news she knew who helped. Said she was going to arrest them and hoped it didn't become violent. Me and Bear worried that we might get shot, so we went to see Miss Taylor so we could tell the truth. We didn't shoot the cop. We didn't even know Cutter had a gun."

Boston nodded. "I believe you. But there's one thing you're missing."

Clara bowed up and asked, "What's that?"

"Not a word about what was done to stop Cutter from killing a police officer. It sounds like you two are accomplices to murdering a police officer."

Bear exclaimed, "We told him not to. We didn't have time to stop him. It happened too fast."

"Then you did nothing to save Officer Wyatt's life. Who is Cutter?" Boston was sure undercover Detective Blake House could get the name from his street contacts, but it would take longer.

Clara placed a hand on each boy's forearm and leaned forward, "Before they reveal the name, do we have a deal?"

"I will do what I can to convince the Chief and the DA you were not a party to the murder. Just unwitting dupes. But Miss Taylor, you know how this works better than I do."

Clare glared at the mirror. "I know the Assistant DA and the Chief are behind that mirror. If they can't come in here and assure me of that, ..."

"Miss Taylor, you also know that withholding the name of a murderer is a criminal offense unless it's self-incriminating. Last I heard, giving the name of a murderer is not self-incrimination – unless they actually did it. The way I see it, they know who killed Officer John Wyatt and if I don't have the name in fifteen seconds ..." Boston out-glared Clara as he let his comment end.

Clara continued to glare at the mirror for a few more seconds. She exhaled heavily and reached into her briefcase. "This is the name Clarence and Brandon gave me." She pushed a piece of paper across the table to Boston. "I want your assurance that my clients will have a deal that will keep them out of prison."

Boston tugged the paper from Clara grasp. "Miss Taylor, if this name is the murderer, I will do what I can do. I can't speak for the DA." He studied the paper then turned to nod at the mirror with his eyebrows raised. He looked back at the boys, "How did you meet Cutter? Drugs?"

Buzz quickly answered, "We don't do drugs. Some of our friends do. We met him at a party. He's older and I think he sells them drugs."

"So, you just told him about the jewelry? You didn't know him, but you told him about jewelry at your girlfriend's house?" Boston stared at Bear.

"Kendra was with me. Somehow, she said something about it and that her family was going out of town. I don't remember. Cutter asked me later."

"Bear," Boston leaned forward, "I don't believe you. I think you're hiding something, like a habit of stealing."

Clara Taylor's face flared with anger, "You are out of line, Detective!"

Boston smiled derisively. "Am I, Miss Taylor? It might have been Cutter's idea, but I doubt Bear needed any encouragement. We're through here." He gathered the pictures and placed them in the evidence folder.

"Well, I guess it's time to get a warrant," Sarah said to Marcie. "What are the boys going to be charged with?"

"We booked them for accessory to murder. Clara wasn't happy. I think she hoped we wouldn't do that. Even accessory comes with a long sentence, but it's better than murder one. We can't overlook the crime, but the Judge can approve a reduced sentence if we recommend it."

"Off hand, I'd say Buzz was a patsy. Bear is a rebel without a clue."

Marcie nodded. "Based on the interrogation, Bear will also be facing statutory rape charges. That girl is underage."

"And the burglary?"

"Conspiracy to commit. Not much considering they all are facing capital murder anyway. But a jury will react to it. Murder during the commission of a felony comes with enhancements. If necessary, we will use it to get the jury's attention."

"Let's go see that name," Sarah said as soon as the two boys were led out of the Interrogation Room in cuffs, followed by the attorney. She felt the all too familiar vibration of one of the cell phones. She glanced at the offending phone. It was a text from Liz.

*"Mayor fuming, pacing the halls."*

Sarah responded, *"Tell her in five."* She shook her head and led Marcie to the Interrogation Room. She saw Clara in an animated conversation with the Mayor. Fortunately, neither saw her. She ducked into the room.

Boston was waiting for them. "That went well enough," he said as soon as they entered the room. He handed the paper to Sarah.

"Spencer Sheffield," Sarah read the name aloud. "Any kin to Wynn Sheffield?"

"Wow!" Marcie said. "I think it's his son. His youngest. This will make headlines all the way to Topeka. The DA needs to know this right way. I'll get the warrant for you." With her trademark overworked persona, she added, "And I'm sure he'll call a presser for this. I'll let you know." Marcie walked from the room while dialing her phone.

"BOLO?" Boston asked.

"Check DMV to see if that Beamer is registered in his name. Add *armed and dangerous.* Include the reason for the BOLO. I want this to get everyone's attention."

# CHAPTER 14

## Wednesday 2:00 P.M.

The hunt was on. Sarah felt the edgy anticipation of a predator stalking prey. But first, she had to engage with another predator, the Mayor. The politics of the case were elevated to a stratospheric level. Jordon Kamen would play it for all it was worth. Truth be known, Sarah did not care about the Mayor's games. She just wanted the killer in cuffs.

"There *you* are!" exclaimed the Mayor when she saw Sarah exit the Interrogation Room. Her heels clicked on the hallway floor. "You **do not** keep me waiting!" Her face was red and twisted.

Sarah ignored the assault, and asked with feigned innocence. "Did you need to see me about something?" She looked over her shoulder to see if the angry woman was following as she turned toward her office. "If you come into my office, I have an update on our case."

Mayor Kamen stomped after Sarah. She did not miss the opportunity to glare at Liz as she passed the Assistant's office. The Mayor sniped, "I think I have enough update. Clara told me about the heavy-handed way your detective treated her clients."

Sarah saw Lieutenant McCuskey walk past. Taylor scowled at the Mayor's back, then shook her head in disgust. Sarah held the door as she motioned for the Mayor to sit in a chair. She closed the door as soon as the Mayor was fully inside the office. No one else needed to be subjected the tirade. As Police Chief that was her job. "The Assistant

DA was there to observe. She can tell you the truth about the interview process."

"Don't gloss it over. It was an interrogation. Not an interview."

Sarah ignored the Mayor's comment. "The two accomplices named the shooter. The DA's office is getting the warrant. Boston is issuing a BOLO. We are setting out a dragnet."

"Why was I not notified of the press conference?" The Mayor was single-minded.

"I wasn't aware of it until they showed up at the door. That's why. Clara Taylor pulled a publicity stunt, plain and simple. She knows her clients are facing life in prison without parole, if not the death penalty. If she can sway public opinion, taint the jury pool, maybe she can get a lesser sentence. She will use every weapon in her arsenal to create doubt about her clients' involvement and how they are handled by the legal system."

"You let a lawyer outsmart you?" Jordon asked derisively.

"It backfired on her. Just don't let her outsmart you. She will twist every nuance to create a loophole for her clients."

"Whatever," The Mayor waved her hand dismissively. "She was able to get to them before your *stellar* Detective Mankowitz. A sad commentary if you ask me."

"She didn't *get to* them. They went to her. They knew we were coming for them."

"They're kids. Why didn't you just go get them?"

Sarah kept her calm. "Mayor, despite your misgivings about how the police department operates, we do not rush headlong into anything. To protect people, we must operate in a methodical manner. Clara knows that, which is why she made a spectacle out of the booking."

"I'm not stupid. Neither is the public. I heard what she said. Your department is a threat to society. Those boys feared for their lives. Afraid they would be killed rather than brought to trial. Killed by your officers. The same fears held by most of the citizens of Devaney."

Sarah leaned forward slightly. "Mayor, name one instance of proven police brutality."

"Oh, don't think I don't know what you're doing. Don't think I don't know about the *methodical manner* of the Devaney Police Department." The Mayor's tone oozed sarcasm. "Chief Keck set the standard for Gestapo tactics, supported by – or should I say in support *of* – the criminal element, in support of Joseph Elsea, your benefactor. I think it's very *methodical* how you conveniently provided him a path to get away with murder. No Miranda Rights. Every rookie cop knows about Miranda Rights, but it never crossed your mind. Yes, I know how the Devaney Police Department operates."

Rather than rebut Jordon Kamen, which would only devolve into a tit-for-tat spat, Sarah looked the Mayor in the eyes and said, "I thought you wanted an update. If not, I have a murderer to catch. Do you want to know his name or not? The DA will be making an announcement in a press conference shortly. I intend to be there. I thought you might want to be there also." Sarah thought it odd that Clara talked to the Mayor but did not tell her the name of the alleged murder. There was no way the Mayor had that information and did not mention it.

"Why is the DA doing it? It was our police officer who was killed. It should be the City, not the County." Jordon was indignant.

"Because capital murders are State crimes. The DA will prosecute the case for the State."

"I know the law," the Mayor snapped. "Who is it?"

"Spencer Sheffield." Sarah was surprised to see color drain from Jordon Kamen's face. The Mayor recognized the name immediately.

Slowly, color returned to Mayor Kamen's face. A dark, angry color. Her eyes narrowed. She pushed herself to her feet and snarled, "Let me know when you locate him. I definitely want to be there to represent the city and assure the public that Devaney PD will behave professionally." She wheeled and fumbled with the doorknob before she yanked the door open.

Sarah watched the Mayor's hurried escape. The woman's reaction was nothing like she had expected. Confusing. Only after a few moments did she realize her fingernails were hurting the palms of her clenched fists. "Liz," she said loud enough to be heard.

Liz met Sarah at the door, "Yes, Chief?"

Sarah smiled tiredly. "The DA may try to contact me through you. He will be holding a press conference shortly. If he does, tell him to also invite the Mayor."

Liz looked down the hall in the direction the Mayor rushed toward the stairs. "Are you sure?"

"Politics. We still report to the Mayor." Sarah went to the bullpen to find Boston. Sheriff Herriman called before she found the detective.

"Chief, Sheriff here. Your detective and Faraday said they are setting up a dragnet for this Sheffield fellow. I'm giving Faraday his head on this one. Too many variables, considering the suspect's name. I guess it's confirmed he's Senator Sheffield's boy, at least the same name. Gonna be dicey to say the least."

"Hello Sheriff. I agree. I'll do the same with Boston. My gut feel is that I'm going to have more politicians than just my Mayor to deal with."

"You can bet on that, Chief. I'll be over to see you as soon as I get the assignments out. Oh, if you see Faraday – I think he's with Detective Mankowitz – tell him everything's good to go."

"Will do. Thanks, Sheriff."

Sarah continued her search for Boston. He was with Lieutenant McCuskey in the main conference room addressing a group of Sergeants and a handful of Patrol Officers. Officer Michalski-Jensen was there, intently listening to the Detective and the Lieutenant. Sarah was pleased to see Micha was involved. The Officer needed to be there for therapeutic reasons above all else.

Sarah tried to slip into the room without disturbing the meeting. An impossible task for anyone. Especially difficult for the Chief of Police. She motioned with her hand for Boston to continue as she nodded greeting to everyone and slid into a corner. Detective Faraday was leaning against the wall in another corner. All the chairs were taken.

Boston acknowledged Sarah and continued. "Lieutenant McCuskey will coordinate searches throughout the city. Detective Faraday," he motioned toward the Deputy Sheriff, "will coordinate searches throughout the County. Captain Kyle Anderson with the State Police will coordinate the statewide search. All intel and activity updates will be funneled through me," he motioned toward Sarah, "and Chief James."

Sarah spoke-up, "Through Boston. Single point. The Sheriff and I will stay out of the way and deal with the Press … and the politicians."

Boston grimaced. "Thanks, Chief. We'll find him … sooner rather than later." He turned back to the group. "Now, let's go find this scumbag and put him where he belongs."

Sarah winced at Boston's exhortation. She did not want to see a feeding frenzy. "Be professional. Be safe. Let's all go home to our families at the end of the day."

A murmur swept across the room. General acknowledgement of either Boston's or Sarah's words. Maybe both. Sarah shook hands or patted the shoulders of each man and woman as they exited the room. Micha's face was firm with resolve. The Chief lingered longer with Micha's hand, clinched tighter. Liz got her attention from the doorway.

"Chief, Marcie called. The presser is in half an hour."

"Good. Did she tell the Mayor?"

"I asked her to," Liz replied with a shrug.

"I'll make sure." Sarah dialed the Mayor's number. Missy answered. "Missy, can you notify the Mayor that the DA is holding a press conference in half an hour?" Missy agreed to do so. Sarah then called Sheriff Herriman; in case he did not know. He needed to be there.

Cameras were set in front of the Courthouse steps. Microphones were attached to a podium that was set up on the top landing. The reporters were jockeying for position even though only a couple of courthouse staff were checking the sound system at that time. Sarah was glad she chose to enter through the County Jail entrance at the back of the building. Out of sight. She found the Sheriff outside his office door, talking with a female Deputy who held a handful of papers. "Hello, Sheriff."

"Hi, Chief. You ready for this?"

"I am. A necessary step on the path we chose."

The Sheriff nodded. "Ain't that the truth?" He turned to the Deputy. "Which of these do I need to sign right now?"

Sarah watched as the Sheriff signed documents presented to him by the Deputy. She wondered if he knew what he was signing since he was not wearing his readers.

Finished, the Sheriff said, "Well, let's go find the DA. I don't want to go out first. It would upset the apple cart."

Marcie was standing in the lobby, waiting for the DA. She appeared less flustered, less overwhelmed than usual. No need for the persona.

The DA would be the center of attention. Hers was a supporting role. "Sarah. Cecil. The DA should be here shortly," she said. She looked around questioningly. "I though the Mayor would want to be here for this. I talked to one of her people."

"She does. I called her too, just to make sure she knew," Sarah replied.

DA Charles Dunn came from the hallway with a folder in his hand. "Sheriff. Chief. Marcie." His acknowledgements were his greetings. "If you are ready, I'm sure the Press is." He lifted his hand to show the folder. "This is going to create a stir."

Charles paused in front of the threesome. "Chief, Sheriff, I assume one of you has an update on the status of the manhunt?"

Sarah looked at Cecil. He nodded for her to answer. "I can address that subject. The two boys have identified a picture of Spencer Sheffield as the person in the car with them. We have issued a BOLO. City, County and State resources are dedicated to the capture of Mr. Sheffield."

"Good. A coordinated effort. I assume this includes all police departments within the county?"

"Yes, it does. Detective Mankowitz is the point man on this."

The DA nodded, straightened his tie. "Are we ready?" He did not wait for an answer. He walked through the Courthouse door and approached the podium. The reporters moved forward in unison, still jockeying for position. Before he could speak, everyone was distracted by a female voice.

From her stance behind and to one side of the DA, Sarah watched Mayor Kamen barging through the periphery of the group of reporters and curious onlookers. Lieutenant Glasgow was dutifully clearing the way for her. The Mayor was warning the reporters that she needed room to pass, even though she could have achieved the same result by walking a different path. Six feet to her right and the Mayor would have encountered no one. Her charge through the small crowd was her grand entrance. No one would have noticed her if she had merely avoided the reporters and walked up the steps unimpeded.

When she reached the top of the stairs, the Mayor smiled at the DA and took a position to his left, blocking view of Sarah. Lieutenant Glasgow stood at her side, blocking view of the Sheriff. "Thank you for waiting, Mr. Dunn. I was detained by important business."

The DA dipped his head slightly as acknowledgement. He leaned toward the microphones and began. "Ladies and Gentlemen, shortly after noon today, an arrest warrant was issued for the suspected murderer of Devaney Police Officer John Wyatt. The warrant is the culmination of intense investigative work by Devaney PD," he nodded toward Sarah, though the cameras only saw the Mayor and Lieutenant Glasgow, "and the Sheriff's Department. Chief James and Sheriff Herriman are coordinating with the State Highway Patrol to execute a manhunt. The suspect has been identified as Spencer Sheffield, no confirmed residence. The BOLO was issued a short time ago, so we have nothing new to report on the manhunt. Is that correct Chief James?"

Sarah answered as loud as she deemed appropriate, "That is correct."

All eyes turned in Sarah's general direction. All eyes except Mayor Kamen's. She looked straight ahead; her lips pressed firmly together.

The DA continued, "As information becomes available regarding the hunt for Spencer Sheffield, Chief James will update the public. I will open for questions at this time."

"Mister Dunn. Mister Dunn." Bernie was quickest. "Is the suspect considered armed and dangerous?"

Charles Dunn said, "I will allow Chief James to address that question." He stepped aside.

Sarah stepped to the podium. "Yes. Our BOLO lists Mr. Sheffield as armed and dangerous. He has already killed a police officer and stole the officer's service weapon. He is still in possession of the Officer's weapon. That warning is issued so all officers know to approach him with caution."

"Who will make the arrest?"

"That will be determined by who finds him first. If you are wondering if there are jurisdictional lines, there are none. He is wanted on suspicion of capital murder, a State crime. At this point, I hope he hears we are seeking his whereabouts and he will turn himself in, like his accomplices."

Kyren managed to get Sarah's attention. "Chief, is the suspect kin to State Senator Sheffield, or is the name coincidental?"

Sarah dreaded that question. She would have preferred it not be asked. But it was. "It is my understanding that Spencer Sheffield is the Senator's youngest son."

"Is the Senator aware of this?"

Sarah looked to the DA. The DA nodded for her to answer. "If he is not, he will be within a short time. The State Police either have contacted the Senator as part of the search for Spencer or will very soon."

Without warning, a red-faced Mayor Kamen pushed her way to the podium. "I can tell you that Spencer Sheffield has not been found guilty of murder. He is an *alleged* murderer, and it will be prudent for the Press and law enforcement to remember that. The DA knows the law well enough to not brazenly imply the suspect is guilty. I will not stand by and allow a man whose only known crime is based upon accusations made by teenaged boys have his reputation ruined. A murder that they may well have committed and needed a cover story to save themselves." She made a point of looking toward Sarah. "If ... or dare I say *when* ... Spencer Sheffield *is* killed during arrest, it will be their word only. Spencer will be branded guilty and the real killers will walk free because they cooperated with the police. I fear that is the entire purpose of the armed and dangerous BOLO." She paused to calm herself. "To protect the integrity of this investigation and to protect the life of an innocent citizen, I am placing Lieutenant Glasgow in charge of the manhunt." She glared at Sarah, "There will be no lynch-mob justice in Devaney - especially not by the police department."

The audience and the people on the Courthouse landing were stunned.

Kyren was the first to recover. She asked, "Mayor, are you replacing Chief James?"

Kamen's face reddened further. "Not specifically. I just want to make sure the apprehension of Spencer Sheffield does not result in his murder."

Kyren was on a storyline. "Mayor, are you insinuating that Spencer Sheffield, the son of a State Senator, will be killed by the police rather than brought to trial?"

The Mayor glowered into the camera. "I am declaring that Spencer Sheffield *will not* be murdered by the police. To ensure that, I will ... Lieutenant Glasgow will oversee the manhunt."

Sarah closed her eyes for a moment to gather her thoughts. She then spoke loud enough to be heard without use of a microphone by the small assemblage. "Detective Mankowitz, Sheriff's Detective Faraday and State Police Captain Anderson are in charge of the manhunt." Attention immediately shifted to Sarah. "The fact remains that all criminal investigation and police activities within Devaney city limits are within the purview of the Devaney Police Department. The Sheriff is responsible for all such activities within the County and the State Police are responsible for all activities within the State. This is not a political investigation. It is a homicide investigation and Spencer Sheffield is being sought because his alleged accomplices have named him as the shooter."

The Mayor's face twisted angrily. Flushed and frustrated, she finally spoke, "Everything involved with this manhunt will be approved by me, by the Mayor of Devaney. The Devaney Police Department will not be given a license to kill."

Bernie asked, "Mr. Dunn, what are the expectations of the District Attorney's office?"

Sarah was relieved to see the DA gently nudge Jordon away from the podium. "Our expectations are that Mr. Sheffield will be brought before the Court for trial."

"Do you have enough evidence to convict Mr. Sheffield?"

"I am not prepared to discuss any evidence we have with the Press. Mr. Sheffield is entitled to a fair hearing and all evidence will be presented to his attorney before it is aired publicly." Charles Dunn glanced toward the Mayor and Sarah. "But first, he must be found and brought before the Court to answer the charges. A manhunt does not imply his guilt. It implies that he is still at large."

A slurry of related and unrelated questions followed until the DA dismissed the press conference. Sarah did not relax. The Mayor stayed but was visibly enraged, more so because no questions were directed toward her. Sarah knew she would have Hell to pay. She also wondered why the Mayor would have been blatantly obvious about wanting to control the manhunt.

Sarah walked into the Courthouse with the Sheriff and Marcie. Inside, away from the cameras and reporters, a shrill voice caught her attention.

"Sarah! We need to talk!" Mayor Kamen's heels clicked angrily on the marble floor. Lieutenant Glasgow kept pace easily with his longer stride.

Sarah stopped and turned, as did Cecil and Herriman.

"Alone," Jordon snorted. With an angry glare, she dismissed the Sheriff and the Assistant DA.

Sarah did not cower. "What do you need, Jordon?"

"Mayor. I am Mayor," the Mayor barked.

"And I am Chief," Sarah replied succinctly.

"Only at my pleasure," the Mayor snarled. "It would be good for you to remember that."

"Certainly," Sarah responded with a smirk. "Be sure to shout that out again so the whole town hears it in case they missed it all the other times you've said it. Stop the BS. What are you trying to do? Help a murder suspect escape?"

Jordon Kamen's face contorted for several seconds. Finally, she gained control of her overactive emotions. "As your boss, I want to know what is happening during this manhunt. I will not allow that man to be *accidentally* killed during arrest. And you know what I mean. Since you are conveniently too busy to tell me what is happening, Lieutenant Glasgow will be my eyes and ears until Spencer is brought to jail safely, unharmed. Is that understood?"

Melvin Glasgow looked at the floor when Sarah turned her eyes toward him. She felt compassion for the man who jumped on a long-awaited promotion only to find it was to become a lackey for an agenda driven Mayor. She also felt concern for the damage he could do to Devaney PD moral simply by being present in the station under the current circumstances. Lieutenant Glasgow was in a no-win situation. "I have no issue with another resource. Lieutenant, are you coming with me or will you come over later?"

Glasgow's eyes jumped back and forth between the Mayor and Sarah. His mouth was open, but he did not respond.

"He will be there within the hour. Make sure you keep him up to date." Mayor Kamen wheeled and stomped toward the front doors. Lieutenant Glasgow hurried to open the door for her.

# CHAPTER 15

## Wednesday 3:15 P.M.

Sheriff Herriman waited for Sarah in the hallway that led from the lobby. "Girl, I don't envy your situation. Stand firm. You've got more going than she ever will. Why did they ever put that crazy woman in charge?"

Sarah ignored the older man's diminutive and shrugged. "So she could self-destruct, apparently. Believe it or not, I'm actually growing accustomed to it. I don't let it bother me … too much." She smiled dryly. "Besides, we've got a killer to catch plus a budget battle to fight. Unfortunately, both involve Jordon Kamen."

"All I can say is, if she pulled that crap with me, she'd have to be reminded that I'm always armed."

The minute Sarah entered the Police Station, police personnel approached her individually and in groups of two or three. To a person, they offered encouragement and expressed outrage over the Mayor's actions. There was no doubt no one in the Police Department would vote for Jordon Kamen as Mayor in the next election. She assured every one of them that the Mayor's rant was nothing more than a politician's scramble to be relevant. She also asked all of them to remain professional at all times to avoid providing ammunition to the Mayor.

Boston was not in the field. The Situation Room was his command center. Extra phone jacks that were available in the room were pressed into service for additional phones. The TV normally used for review of evidence videos was tuned to Channel 6 and muted. Even though most TV newsbreaks would only contain information released by law enforcement, if an arrest was imminent, they might do a live broadcast from the scene.

Sarah stood in the doorway. She watched and listened until Boston was not preoccupied. "Any progress?" It was early, but the question was as good an opening as any.

Boston glanced up. "Nothing yet. Just getting set up. Lots of moving parts on this one. We have to be able to sort the real from the ghosts and shadows."

Sarah reflected on the night Micha was shot. The suspect was spotted almost immediately and there was a hot pursuit. Plenty of moving parts, but no ghosts to chase. In the case of Boston's stabber, the man tried to hide in the shadows, but shadows talk. "Are any of the CIs talking yet?"

"A little. Apparently, Sheffield got his nickname because he dabbles in drugs."

"Don't tell me. He repackages drugs."

"Yeah. Low budget. Walking around money at best. There's no way he made a living at it. He's barely a blip on the radar. A nothing. I guess he decided to add burglary to his repertoire." Boston snorted. "What are we going to do about the Mayor ... and Glasgow?"

"I'll take care of Glasgow. I have a chore for him. The Mayor will take care of herself."

"Well. Well. Speaking of the Mayor, there's one of her lapdogs."

Sergeant Locke approached the Situation Room, "Chief, when you get a minute ..."

Sarah nodded. "I suppose we can talk in my office. What do you have?"

"I've got an update on the case."

"My case?" Boston asked gruffly.

"No," Keith replied. "I'm on a separate case so you can focus on the murderer. I'm honestly just helping." He tried to sound conciliatory.

Boston sneered and shook his head.

Sarah said, "Let's see what you've got." She led Keith away from the Situation Room to prevent further interaction between him and Boston. Rightfully so, Boston's animosity toward the Mayor was greater than anyone on the Force. He readily shared that animus with anyone associated with the Mayor.

Keith shut the door after he followed Sarah into the office. "I heard you've got a name and have a dragnet out for John's killer."

"Yes. His accomplices turned on him."

"Oh? I didn't hear that part; just radio chatter on the BOLO." Keith glanced toward the door. "Of course, I don't get much from anyone in PD. I feel like an outsider."

"I hate that for you, but most of it's your fault."

"Because of Zoey?"

"Not Zoey. Your reaction to her when the Mayor stationed her after Chief Keck was fired."

"Well, *we* weren't going anywhere," Keith lamented.

"Go with that." Sarah replied with a crooked smile. "You're in a hole that only you can climb out of. Mayor Kamen drew the battlelines. You were standing on the wrong side at the time. You stayed there. You can come back, or you can remain an outsider." She stared at him until he was uncomfortable.

"I'm a police officer, not a politician."

Sarah nodded toward a folder the Sergeant was holding. "*That* is your passport back into the department. Do police work. Avoid political entanglements. What have you discovered?"

"Not much. From all appearances, it looks like Overton died because of a heart attack. The Coroner pulled some samples from the body before he sent it to the State ME. I took them to Alicia. She's looking, but it will probably be tomorrow before we know anything."

Sarah nodded. "Alicia has been focused on Wyatt's murder. But she should be free for other cases now. Is she cooperating?" Because of the Mayor's recently televised harangue, the barrier between anyone from the Mayor's office and the Police Department just got higher and thicker.

"No problem. You don't think she would hold the fact I work in the Mayor's office against me, do you?"

"I hope not," Sarah shrugged, "but after the news conference a few minutes ago ..."

"What news conference?"

"To announce the name of the suspect. Spencer Sheffield. The Mayor decided to put Glasgow in charge of the manhunt."

"What?" Keith Locke was genuinely shocked. "He doesn't know anything about running a manhunt. Sarah ... Chief, why would she do something as stupid as that?"

Sarah smirked. "Politics, Keith. She's been anti-police ever since she was elected to the Council. Defunding police has become a national movement. She's riding that wave to bolster her agenda. If she can paint the Police Department as modern-day Gestapo, she can sway the public to support her reductions on the police budget. Properly played, she can distract the public from other parts of her agenda."

Keith nodded slowly. "You think she's just on the bandwagon for personal gain? Like you said, it's a national thing, but most people know it's not real."

"Maybe so, but political rhetoric forms opinions and perceptions. Perception becomes reality after opinions are formed. I have to wonder how she plans to use the money not used for police protection. Public safety is the primary reason for government."

"I understand that. Is there something I can do to help with the Mayor?"

"Other than keep her away from microphones and the Police Department, I doubt it."

"I know Zoey's not real happy over there." Keith stopped abruptly, as if he had said too much. His eyes danced anxiously.

"What has Zoey upset? I thought she was in her element with the Mayor. Being a change agent for public opinion." Sarah saw an opening.

"I think she's seeing some things she doesn't like. But I've said more than I should. It's Zoey's problem."

"You're probably right. We've all got our own problems." Sarah wanted to pursue the subject, look for a loose stone in the Mayor's castle wall. She pushed a little. "It would be nice to know what could upset someone as energetic as Zoey." She nodded thoughtfully, hoping Keith would continue.

The Sergeant, former tryst of the Chief, leaned forward secretively, "She says the Mayor wants to use any money saved from departmental budgets to fund green initiatives. A business venture group wants to build an alternative energy manufacturing company near Devaney, but they won't do it without tax incentives. On the downlow, the site has been selected. Zoey hasn't said, but I think its somewhere in the new annexation. If Devaney is the taxing authority, the Mayor can commit to those incentives. That's why she pushed the annexation so hard and fast."

"It's not uncommon for the Mayor of a city to know about new businesses, though I would think the Council would also be involved. She wouldn't be the first politician to offer tax incentives to a company. It would bring jobs and, theoretically, a bigger tax base."

"I know. That's what I told Zoey, but Zoey says there is more to it. She won't tell me." Keith stopped. The finality of his statement made it clear he had said all he intended to say on the matter.

Sarah gave him an out. "Back to the Overton case, what does your gut tell you? Is it natural causes or is there reason to suspect foul play?"

"I'm torn. The Doctor is adamant that it was just another heart attack statistic. The Paramedics said heart attack. The Coroner is non-committal. Alicia said that if there was anything out of the ordinary, either she or the ME would find it. I guess I wait."

"Have you spoken with Overton Junior?"

"Does he know something?"

Sarah shrugged. "Obviously, he suspects something. Our meeting was brief. Only as long as it needed to be. John's death was … and is … key in my mind, so I didn't push him. But it would probably be good for him to know someone is taking him seriously. Maybe he's calmer now."

"Okay. I'll go talk with him while I'm waiting for the Lab." Keith stood to leave. "Chief, is there anything I can do to help on the manhunt? I want to see John's killer captured as much as everyone else. After all, I *am* a Devaney Police Officer."

Sarah saw the pain in Keith's face. "Sergeant, I know you are. I know you care. As big as the spotlight is on Spencer Sheffield, we still have other cases to solve." She smiled with resignation. "In all of this, I still have budget and political battles to fight. The Overton case is in the political column. You are helping." She watched Keith leave the door open as he exited. She wanted to feel sorry for him.

# CHAPTER 16

## Wednesday 4:15 P.M.

Boston appeared in the doorway. He looked toward Sergeant Locke's retreating back with a sneer. He then turned to address Sarah, "We have a break."

Sarah quickly stood. Boston's face showed more emotion than normal. "What do we have?" Her heart rate increased.

"A unit just pulled over a car that matches the DMV description. Something is happening at the scene. Other units have been dispatched."

Sarah gulped. "Where is it? I'll dispatch to the scene. We can't have this thing escalate."

"I'll follow," Boston said as the two of them rushed across the bullpen and down the stairs.

As they raced to their vehicles, Lieutenant Glasgow hollered to get Sarah's attention. She paused to glance back at him, "What do you need?" She was curt.

"The Mayor sent me ..."

Sarah did not wait for him to complete his statement. "Get in the car. A unit thinks they've located Spencer." The Lieutenant did not ask questions. He buckled into the passenger seat of Sarah's car, his eyes wide with anticipation, his face flushed with excitement.

Both unmarked vehicles ran with lights and sirens toward the address given. No matter how many times Sarah heard sirens, ran with sirens, they always quickened her pulse rate. Whether it was the effects of the sound that caused her heart to beat faster or the knowledge that something potentially dangerous awaited, she did not know. Nor did she give it much thought. Her mind was focused on clearing slow-to-yield traffic while she drove as fast as she deemed safe to the public. Loud radios and cell phones in the hands of drivers created a whole world of hazards for emergency responders.

At the scene, the street was filled with flashing lights. Several Devaney squad cars were in a semi-circle, noses pointed toward a silver-toned BMW coupe. Two Deputy Sheriff vehicles were parked at the intersection through which Sarah and Boston had to navigate. The Deputies prevented traffic from moving through the stop site, motioning a detour to everyone other than official vehicles. Rubbernecking pedestrians were as yet uncontrolled. At the other end of the block, Sarah saw other flashing lights. More Deputies diverting traffic.

A flurry of activity was underway near the BMW. Sarah parked and quickly approached. From a distance, she had a difficult time distinguishing rubberneckers from police officers. Officers were on the ground, wrestling with the driver of the vehicle. Some onlookers held their cell phones up, obviously capturing video. From what Sarah could determine, the driver was not a large man, but apparently, he was extremely powerful. Two officers were standing over the melee with Tasers at the ready. Another was holding a baton, prepared to use it if additional force was required.

Micha was one of the officers wrestling with the suspect. She was the first to get a good grip on the man. From behind, she immediately put him in a chokehold. Slowly, the fight left him. An expert in martial arts, Micha released to allow him to breathe but maintained position in case he renewed his resistance. He did. Almost as soon as he regained awareness, he writhed and punched at the arresting officers. Another minute of squeezing and he slumped again. The other two officers in the melee managed to cuff the suspect while he was subdued. Micha did not release until the cuffs snapped shut. Even with his hands uncomfortably cuffed behind his back, the suspect began cursing as soon as his airway cleared. With his arms behind his back, his only recourse was to kick at the officers.

A baton whacked the man's knee. "Stop!" the officer wielding the weapon commanded. "Next time, I'll break it!"

"Anita!" Sarah barked. "He's cuffed." To the others, she ordered, "Roll him on his stomach and restrain him until he quits fighting."

Micha obliged, using her hold around the man's neck like a steer wrestler. A larger male officer knelt with a knee in the middle of the suspect's back to allow Micha to get clear of the suspect. It did not shut his mouth, but it limited his ability to writhe and kick with any force. Micha stood up and smiled triumphantly at Sarah. "We got the bastard," she said. "We got him!" The young officer could barely contain her excitement.

Sarah glanced at Lieutenant Glasgow. "Melvin, clear these people. Back them up at least thirty yards for their own safety." The cell phone wielding onlookers irritated her. The fact none of the officers took charge of the scene irritated her more. Everyone wanted to get a hand on the suspect. She made a mental note to address the need to control the scene in its entirety with Lieutenant McCuskey. She wondered why the Lieutenant was not already on scene.

Sarah and Boston moved close enough to ensure no officer made any threatening moves on the prone, cuffed suspect as they patted him down for weapons and ID. Concerned with the suspect's continued thrashing, she said, "Shackle his feet so we don't have to keep hands on him. Is he on something?" Sarah recognized the behaviors that accompanied chemical enhancement.

"Sure seems like it," Micha responded breathily, the result of her excitement, not the physical exertion. "He's a lot stronger than I would have guessed him to be."

"Read him his rights and get him in a squad," Sarah ordered when the pat-down finished empty-handed. She glanced at the man and at the officers. "He needs some medical for his injuries. Probably some of you need it too." The suspect was bleeding from his lips and from scratches on his arms. "Take him to the hospital for an evaluation before you transport him to the jail. Is he drunk?"

"Drugged up, I think," said one of the officers who was in the melee. "When we approached the car, he bailed and attacked. Crazy."

Sarah nodded to the senior officer of the original contact squad car. "Sean, do we know if he is Spencer Sheffield?"

"Can't say for sure, Chief. We've been sort of tied up - if you know what I mean. He fits the physical description and looks like the picture on the BOLO. But we didn't find an ID on him and his only language seems to be cuss words." The officer grinned, an obvious attempt to relieve his tension, created by the physical take-down.

"Find out before you leave. Make sure he didn't drop his driver's license during the arrest - or leave it in the car." Sarah watched as one of the officers checked the BMW's registration paperwork. All the officers were on adrenaline highs. She calmed herself so she could act as a calming force for her charges.

"No ID of any kind on him or in the car," Officer Sean Holmes said when they finished their search. "The registration is for Wynn Sheffield and Spencer Sheffield. It appears that it *is* his car."

"With daddy's money," Sarah said. The suspect began cursing and banging against the inside of the car. She shook her head derisively. "Have him drug tested. I'll call for a warrant to draw blood. Read him his rights, make sure he's secure, and go."

Three of the squad cars drove away toward the hospital, lights but no sirens. Sarah knew there would be plenty of eyes on the suspect. She also knew the onlookers could pose a problem for her and Devaney PD. Clara Taylor would not be Spencer's lawyer, but any savvy defense lawyer would know what to do. Private videos were not always accurate records of incidents or of the truth, but they were always easily manipulated tools for a defense. Even Micha's exuberance would be misinterpreted if it was captured – and Sarah was sure it was.

Lieutenant McCluskey arrived. She exited her unmarked vehicle and looked around the area. "Boston, is there anything you need from me here?" Her tone and demeanor indicated she was back to her usual self. Capturing a cop-killer can do that.

"I need someone to set up a tow. We'll process the car at impound. Other than that, not much left here. Rubberneckers with cells." Boston nodded his head toward a group of people held at bay by Lieutenant Glasgow. "The real excitement is headed to the ER and then to Booking." Despite the onlookers, he was more relaxed as well.

Taylor looked askance of Sarah, "Chief, do you care if I go to ER?"

Sarah nodded. "I insist on it. I want this on the up and up." Sarah glanced toward the onlookers. "Too many eyes, ears and mouths here. Is Sergeant Cron in the field?" Not only did she notice that Lieutenant

McCuskey was not on scene, but also, the Shift Commander was nowhere to be seen.

"Yes. Jim is commanding a TA fatality scene near the Interstate. I was there with him when the call came on this."

Sarah was reminded once again that normal police services are required regardless of circumstances. Catching Officer Wyatt's killer was just one piece of police work, no more important to the average citizen than any other piece. She shook her head. "Do you know the cause of the TA yet?"

"From witness accounts, speeding. Lost control." Taylor shook her head. "With all the emphasis on citizen friendly, I think we are offering too much leeway. You know how people push the limit."

"Give an inch. Take a mile," Sarah said. "The driver or an innocent?" As bad as it was for drivers to lose their lives in traffic accidents, it always seemed worse when it was someone other than the person behind the wheel.

"The driver this time." Fatal traffic accidents were too common, even in a city as small as Devaney. Taylor McCuskey was extremely detail oriented when it came to TA investigations. If her officers did a sloppy job, she caught it and made them redo it. Her final report would be something the insurance company and the lawyers could rely on for accuracy.

"No police involvement, I assume?" Sarah hated the fact that the political climate in Devaney, probably in the whole country, forced her to vocalize what should have not even been part of her thought processes. But – that was another thing changed in her life.

"Just the investigation," Taylor replied, her face showing puzzlement at Sarah's uncharacteristic lack of compassion for the life lost.

"Good. Let me know when you approach the station with Spencer. I want to be downstairs when he's booked." Sarah again glanced toward Glasgow and the onlookers. "I have a feeling it's going to be a circus." She shook her head and walked toward her car. She called out to Lieutenant Glasgow, "Melvin, I'm going to the station. Are you coming with me or hitching a ride?"

Lieutenant Glasgow hesitantly turned his back on the curious crowd then hurried to Sarah's car. "I'll go with you."

"Okay. First, I need to survey a TA fatality scene." Without speaking, Sarah drove across town to the accident scene.

The ambulance was still there, along with a fire rescue vehicle and a fire truck. Red and yellow strobes warned of the activity. Sarah turned on her blues as she approached and parked her car. She and Lieutenant Glasgow walked closer to the scene. Firemen and paramedics were in the final stages of removing the driver from the twisted and smashed vehicle. It was obvious that the car tossed and rolled several times before coming to rest against a power pole. Electricity was off in the immediate area. Yellow and white strobes on a power company lift truck and a wrecker added to the light show. Both were standing by, ready to go to work as soon as the Firemen gave them the okay.

Sergeant Jim Cron walked to meet Sarah. "Hello, Chief." He paused to look at Glasgow. "Lieutenant," he said tersely as acknowledgment. "Looks like he was going too fast to maintain control. Corporal Canton is leading the investigation to get the details."

"Good. Canton is thorough. Don't overlook the EDR." Sarah learned a lot about vehicle Event Data Recorders during the investigation of former Mayor Clairmont's fatal auto accident - the accident that set the stage for Councilwoman Jordon Kamen to be appointed Interim Mayor.

Sergeant Cron nodded understanding. "We'll follow up with the salvage yard – unless you want us to tow it to impound." His comment ended in a questioning tone.

"No, the towing company's impound will be fine. The EDR might pinpoint the cause in case Corporal Canton doesn't find evidence of it."

Sergeant Cron spoke hesitantly, eyeing Glasgow as he said, "Radio chatter says we caught John's killer. Is that true?"

Sarah nodded. "We have a man we believe is Spencer Sheffield in custody."

"Believe?"

"He's not very lucid and he wasn't carrying any ID, but he was driving Spencer's car. He kind of looks like the photo we have. Is there anything you need from me on this?" Sarah motioned around the scene.

"No. It's been slow because the driver was trapped inside the mess. Investigate and clear the scene so folks can have their street back. Wrong time of day for this to happen."

"Is there a good time?"

Sergeant Jim Cron shrugged, "Never a good time to die."

Sarah returned to the police station. She and Lieutenant Glasgow listened to the police radio while she drove, tracking the progress of Spencer Sheffield from ER to Booking. Her Bluetooth buzzed several times to indicate an incoming phone call. She declined immediately each time, before the ID had time to flash on the dash screen. She knew who it was. The calls from Zoey started while she was at the accident scene. As soon as she turned into the parking lot, Lieutenant Glasgow's phone rang. He answered, hung up, and immediately placed another call. Sarah listened to the one side of the conversation she could hear.

Glasgow was nervous. His responses were short. Mostly "Yes Ma'am" and "No Ma'am." Finally, he said with forced confidence, "We have just arrived at the station. The suspect … yes, Ma'am … the alleged suspect … is not here yet." He paused to listen, his face contorting as he listened. "We're tracking their arrival on the radio. Yes, that's the noise. Yes. Well … as we understand it, superficial bruises when he resisted." The Lieutenant never once looked toward Sarah. "No. It wasn't that way. Yes. Yes Ma'am. I'll look into it."

Sarah parked and exited the car before Glasgow's call ended. When he caught up with her as she walked toward the police station, she said derisively, "I guess she couldn't wait until it was safe for me to talk on the phone." She glanced sideways and waited briefly for a response that did not come. "Did you answer all her questions, or do I need to call her? Oh, by the way, he is not an alleged suspect, he is a suspect – period. Alleged murderer." Glasgow needed to be a police officer or an overpaid go-fer. It was his choice to make.

"Uh … well … I'm sure … she'll probably call you … or you can call her. She just wants to make sure everything's done right."

Sarah ignored his scrambled excuse. "Apparently, you made a point of calling her from the scene?" She did not hide her displeasure as the two of them walked toward Booking entrance.

"She'd be upset if I didn't. But" Lieutenant Glasgow paused, "social media is lighting up with videos. She's concerned about the image they project. They aren't complimentary of the arrest, of Devaney PD. I tried to tell her it wasn't the way the media is presenting it."

"I'm sure she listened to you," Sarah said with a sarcastic snurl.

"She wants to make sure the city is not presented in a bad light. That's all."

"Of course." Sarah led the way into Booking. She was glad to see Boston already there. "Anything new?" she asked him.

"Nothing. We'll go through the car when it gets here. But … interrogation first." Boston gave Glasgow a sideways glance. "How was the TA scene?"

"Brutal. What's that?" Sarah reacted to a noise from the stairwell. She noticed Glasgow step toward the bottom landing and stiffly wait.

Jordon Kamen's heels clicked on the soft rubber stairs treads. Lieutenant Glasgow extended a hand to help the Mayor make the final step. Her face was flushed. "Chief, why is it that every time Devaney police make an arrest, someone has to go to the hospital?" Her voice was loud and shrill.

Before Sarah could respond, Sergeant Jarrett said, "Chief, the Press is outside."

"Post a couple of uniforms outside the door. No comment. I'll be with them shortly." The car with the suspect would enter a fenced compound and drive into a garage with its own doorway to the jail. Sarah knew the cameras would capture any activities they could for use as backdrop during news reports. TV required moving pictures even if they were only vaguely related to the story.

"A show of force?" the Mayor snarled.

"Protocol, Mayor. Protocol. We are obligated to protect the suspect."

"Is that why he was beaten into submission?"

Glasgow stiffened at the Mayor's question, an action that did not go unnoticed by Sarah. Sarah replied, "Mayor, when will you quit getting your news from social media?"

The comment angered the Mayor further, unsurprisingly to Sarah. "Chief, videos don't lie, no matter where they are viewed."

"Don't they? I haven't seen the videos you are using for information, but I can assume they came from one of several cell phones that I saw at the scene. Most of those cell users arrived after I did, and I was late to the scene. They don't show the entire episode. Why don't you wait for the official footage from body cameras before you pass judgement?"

"I don't need your contrived footage. I find it amazing that every video you have is complimentary to the police and makes the citizen appear as a criminal."

Sarah shook her head. "Mayor, that is generally the case. We arrest criminals, not innocent citizens."

"This police abuse must stop. Your actions on this arrest will be your undoing."

"Chief," interrupted Sergeant Jarrett without consideration of the Mayor's tirade, "the unit with the prisoner has entered the compound."

"Mayor, excuse me," Sarah said in a syrupy tone, "I am needed elsewhere." She immediately used her police ID card to open the security door to the protected area of Booking. The public area was seldom used, generally only for surrender suspects. She did not hold the door open for Glasgow or the Mayor. She smiled to herself when she heard Glasgow's pass card unlock the door. She would have preferred to keep the Lieutenant out, but she knew he would enter and bring the Mayor.

A disturbance at the compound entry commanded the Chief's attention. Sarah knew the Mayor was still yammering about something, but her focus was on the disturbance noise. The commotion included swearing, mostly from the prisoner, grunts and the sounds of bodies contacting the wall. The prisoner was still resisting. She knew treatment at the ER was cut short because of the man's belligerence. A blood sample and a couple of swabs with sterile solution on the most obvious abrasions was all the ER staff was able to do. A sedative was not something she, or the ER Doctor, was willing to authorize, considering the undetermined drugs already in his system.

Sergeant Jarrett commanded the man to calm, to no avail. Finally, frustrated, the Sergeant said, "Take him to the drunk tank. He needs to come down from whatever he's on before we can book him. He's raging too much to understand what's happening." Four officers prodded, pushed, and pulled the writhing man along a narrow hallway toward the drunk tank. "Be careful," the Sergeant admonished to the escorting officers. "He's banging himself up on the walls. Don't let him bang you too."

"I want to see the man you've arrested," the Mayor demanded over the din.

Sarah turned to face Kamen, "Mayor, no one is going to see him until he sleeps this off. You just saw a small sample of how he has been. Before he was shackled, he was hurting himself and everyone within reach." Micha and her partner approached, smiling victoriously. Sarah nodded toward the petite Officer. "If it wasn't for Micha's martial arts skills, it would have been worse." Her eyes challenged the Mayor to say more.

Mayor Kamen looked at Micha and said maliciously, "Yes, I saw the video of the Officer's glee. Like a giddy schoolgirl. If someone that small was able to subdue him, …"

Sarah did not allow the sentence to be completed. She shut the Mayor off by turning to Micha. "Micha, how are you?"

Micha glared at the Mayor. She rolled her arms to show her elbows. "Road rash from wrestling." She lifted the end of a cord that was once attached to her body cam. "Broke my cam. Some of the others took some hard hits. Cal has a broken finger, and he's going to have a shiner. A few cuts and bruises, but all in all, we got John's killer. I'd say it was a good day at the office." She sardonically grinned at Mayor and left.

The Mayor huffily addressed Glasgow, "Lieutenant, let's talk to the Press. They need an official statement. Those videos are stoking a feeding frenzy."

"*I* will talk to the Press. I am Chief of Police," Sarah stood between the Mayor and the exit. "There is only one message. A suspect we believe to be Spencer Sheffield has been taken into custody. We will not address anything else at this time."

"You can't suppress the truth."

"I don't intend to suppress anything other than speculative gossip. I suggest you do the same." Sarah's withering glare caused the Mayor to flinch.

Sarah walked through the door and nodded to the two officers Sergeant Jarrett had posted. "Thank you." She faced the clamoring group of reporters. She wanted to begin before the Mayor recovered from their conversation. "Ladies and Gentlemen, thank you for being here this late in the day. Earlier this afternoon, a suspect driving a vehicle registered to Spencer Sheffield was apprehended. At present, he is in a holding cell awaiting booking." She knew the right words. "As of this moment, we can only assume the person we are holding is the alleged murderer of Officer John Wyatt. Until such time as identity is confirmed, he will be held pending further action."

Kyren was front and center. Her camera gave her an advantage over the other reporters. "Chief. Are you saying the person you have in custody may not be Spencer Sheffield?"

Sarah responded slowly, "I am saying we do not have a positive I.D. on the suspect in custody. Until we do, we will not book him on murder charges."

"If you don't know who he is, why is he in custody? Why was he beaten during his arrest?"

"I will address the second question first. The suspect *was not* beaten. He was under the influence of an unknown substance and extremely combative. Devaney Police Officers followed protocol to subdue the suspect. He and the arresting officers were taken to the ER for treatment of minor injuries. He continued to be combative in the ER. His treatment was cut short because of his continued violent behaviors. His actions were putting ER staff, the officers, and himself in danger. He is still not lucid enough to be questioned – or to even tell us who he is. He had no ID on him. To your first question, he is in custody because he was operating a motor vehicle while under the influence."

"Social media is full of videos that prove he was taken to the ground and beaten with a baton. Some witnesses say he was also Tased."

"I was at the scene. People with cell phones seldom capture the complexities of an event. The force used to subdue the combative suspect was within department protocol and necessary to prevent the subject from harming himself or others." Sarah was aware the Mayor and Glasgow were now standing near her. "No one was Tased. Because of the combative nature of the suspect, the arresting officers were in close physical contact with him at all times. Tasing the suspect would have transferred to our officers. At one point, an officer did use a baton on the suspect's leg to stop him from kicking the arresting officers."

Bernie stepped in front of Kyren. "From the videos, it would appear that a large number of officers were required to make the arrest. Was that necessary?"

Before Sarah could respond, Mayor Kamen interjected. "Absolutely not! This kind of brute force is unnecessary. Our officers behaved irrationally, driven by revenge. That is why I was demanding that Lieutenant Glasgow be in charge of the manhunt. He has a level head and is not swayed by emotions of the moment." She glared at Sarah, "Of course, the DA and other law enforcement officers stood in my way."

Sarah closed her eyes to center herself, then stated, "The suspect is in the drunk tank until he becomes lucid. If those officers had not done their job as they did, the suspect would have driven away in his vehicle, still under the influence." She cast a sideways glance toward the Mayor. "If our officers were driven by emotions or revenge, it would have been easier to use lethal force than to risk personal injury subduing the suspect. There is more to this case than the social media videos show." Sarah paused and looked directly into the Mayor's angry eyes, "Unknown to the Mayor, at the same time the suspect was being taken into custody, a fatal traffic accident occurred on the other side of the city. I think we can all surmise his presence behind the wheel of an automobile in his condition could very easily have resulted in at least one more fatality. Was it necessary to use the amount of force the officers used? Yes. The suspect's behaviors demanded it. If he were capable of rational thought, if he were lucid enough to comply, no force would have been required. As it was, the only way to protect the public was to physically subdue him. As one of my officers said after the suspect was secured in the cell, "It's a good day at the office." Everyone will be able to go home to their families."

The Mayor lost credence for the moment and Sarah was the focus of the reporters' questions. The social media aspect was still in the forefront of Sarah's mind. The first message the public received was from those videos. For too many members of the public, it would be the only source of news they would see. The burden of proof fell on the police department. The police were guilty until proven innocent. It was Sarah's duty to share the truth. Sarah knew she had a nearly impossible job in front of her. Even so, she returned to her office tired but satisfied because John Wyatt's killer was in a cell. At least, that thought gave her comfort.

# CHAPTER 17

## Wednesday 6:30 P.M.

"Congratulations."

Sheriff Herriman's soft drawl was a welcome relief to Sarah's ears. The Mayor's nagging, whiney voice grated on her nerves. She had her phone on speaker so she could double-task with a stack of papers Liz left in her Inbox. The bullpen was generally empty. Afterall, it was after normal office hours. As far as she knew, Boston and Taylor were the only two people upstairs, completing obligatory paperwork. "Thank you, Sheriff. I just hope we have the right man."

"Is there doubt?"

"Some. No one here is familiar with Spencer Sheffield. The suspect is in the tank until he sobers enough to get prints, take mugshots and answer a few questions. He fits the general description, but I won't be satisfied until we've completed the process."

"Combative?" The Sheriff did not wait for a response. "I saw some of the videos. I hate those damn cell phones." After a brief pause, he added, "And the idiots who use them."

Sarah sighed. "Me too."

"The reason I called; my people pulled together some information for me. The kind of stuff you can use to convince that Mayor of yours to give you a decent budget."

Sarah perked-up. With the killer … hopefully … in custody, she could focus more on the budget and the Mayor's efforts to reduce funding for the police department. "Does it clearly justify my request for additional funds?"

"If that *woman* is smart enough to read, it does," the Sheriff replied derisively. "But after hearing her comments to the Press over the last couple of days, I'd say the jury is still out on that one." He snorted to accent his comment.

Sarah shuddered lightly at the Sheriff's words. She knew his sexism was part of his character, unmistakably clear to anyone who paid attention to his words. She also knew that he probably did not even know it. It was second nature, never challenged and never changing. "I don't think it's because she's a woman. It's because of her agenda and her misguided politics."

Cecil Herriman chuckled dismissively, "Yeah. I know her being a woman has nothing to do with it, but I still doubt she has the smarts to understand anything other than her own brand of politics. Just saying, she doesn't have a lick of sense. I can run the stuff over if you need it right away. From the looks of it, even Mayor Kamen should understand it."

Sarah thought a moment before she responded. "I need to go see Celia Wyatt. I've been so tied-up that I haven't been to see her today. I don't want the family to lose sight of the fact that Devaney PD is here for them. I can drop by your office on my way in tomorrow if that's okay."

"Sure. I know you get around early. Our public entrance isn't open until eight, but you can use the after-hours entrance at the jail. I'll have the stuff in a big envelope for you. Just ask the night Deputy. How is Missus Wyatt?"

"Struggling, of course. Her family is staying close, especially her mother and father. There's a hole in her heart that can never be filled." A gentle knock on the doorframe got Sarah's attention.

Lab Technician Alicia Kettering was standing in the doorway, her head turned as if watching something in the hallway. She had a puzzled, perturbed look on her face.

"Sheriff, I'll probably talk more tomorrow." Sarah ended the call. "Alicia, come in. You're here late. On your way home, I hope."

"What was he doing out here?" Alicia asked, still looking down the hallway and ignoring Sarah's question.

"Who?"

"Lieutenant Glasgow. He was standing in the hall, like he was listening. At first, I thought you were talking to him, then I realized he wasn't with you. I think it startled him when I came up behind him. He grunted "Hello" and walked away." Alicia moved inside Sarah's office.

"Really?" Sarah quickly recapped her conversation with the Sheriff. Phone speakers were not always a good thing. She did not immediately recall anything that the Mayor did not need to hear, at least, nothing that came from her mouth. "I thought he followed the Mayor back to City Hall." She shook her head and then smiled at Alicia. "What brings you by so late in the day?"

"I wasn't sure if I needed to call Keith ... Sergeant Locke ... first or run it by you. I think I found something on Mr. Overton."

Sarah's eyes widened with curiosity. "What did you find?"

"Aconite poisoning. It causes arrythmia in extreme cases."

"I've never heard of it."

Alicia beamed proudly. "I know. It's an oddity, not a crime drug, and the test for it is not something anyone would think of. I decided that if Mr. Overton was murdered, a smart killer would use something an ME wouldn't normally consider. Something that could easily go undetected."

"Are you sure?"

"Sure enough to call ME Assistant Stacy Kemper to ask her to hurry a confirmation test. I also sent my blood sample to her; in case she can't get good samples from the body. She's excited about this."

"What made you think of aconite?"

Alicia grinned, "A hunch. Sometimes, even a scientist has to play a hunch."

"Is aconite readily available? Again, I've never heard of it."

"It's used a lot in Asian countries. It's from a plant, the aconite plant. You may have heard of it as wolf's-bane. People use it as a homeopathic analgesic. It can also be used to lower blood pressure or to slow rapid heartbeat. Spooky stuff."

Sarah felt a sense of dread. Killers who use poisons are wily and diabolical. Finding Terrance Overton's killer would not be an easy task.

Keith might not be up to that level of investigating. She would need to assign the case to Boston's leadership. Oil and water. "How is aconite administered?"

"Most commonly, it is applied as a salve or lotion, like CBD oil. The external applications are usually as an analgesic for joint pain, an anti-inflammatory ointment. It can also be used in an oral dose. Not very common, though. My guess is he was given something orally. More potent and quicker."

"Can the ME find it in his stomach?"

"If he didn't vomit all evidence of it. It *can* cause intense vomiting at some point."

Sarah remembered Keith's update on his interview with the Coroner. Overton vomited at the hospital. The ER staff cleaned his face before allowing the family to see him. They had no reason to save the vomit. "Am I to assume this is non-prescriptive?"

"Yes. It can be bought at most homeopathic shops. It can even be bought on-line."

"And we know Mr. Overton wasn't using it for an undisclosed heart issue? You know how some people put a lot of faith in homeopathic medicines – and very little in doctors. They believe that because the medicines are natural, they are safe."

"I don't know that, Chief. I suppose Sergeant Locke will need to ask that question."

Sarah nodded. "Give Locke a call. Let him know what you've learned. Be sure to tell him it's preliminary, not something for open discussion. We don't want him to overreact, but he will need to determine if Mr. Overton was using aconite homeopathically."

"Okay. Will do." Alicia paused. "The hospital finally sent the blood sample taken in the ER - you know – from the murderer. I should know if he is on drugs or anything before morning."

Sarah smiled warmly, "Outstanding, Alicia. As always, you are doing an amazing job."

"Thank you, Chief." Alicia left with a noticeable spring in her step.

Sarah shuddered with dread. Killers who use poison as their weapon are difficult to find. They are confident that they can and will elude detection. She wondered if Keith, with his limited investigative experience, was up to the task. If John Wyatt's killer was in the cell downstairs, it would be in the best interest of justice for her to assign Boston as the lead on the Overton case. The move would not go over well with either man. But she was Police Chief. If it was a murder, it had to be solved as quickly as possible. She would have to make that decision.

Sarah's phone rang. The caller ID indicated Zoey. She started to press the "Speaker" button but thought better of it. Glasgow might still be in the station. "Hello, Zoey. You're calling late."

Zoey sounded frustrated. "Chief, the Mayor wants you to call her."

Sarah dialed the Mayor's number and responded as soon as the phone was answered. "Mayor?" Short and simple.

Mayor Kamen did not waste time on formalities. "Why is the Sheriff involved in city budgeting? Are you incapable of doing your job?"

Sarah instantly reached a boil. Not toward the Mayor. Toward Lieutenant Glasgow. There was no other way Jordon Kamen could know about her conversation with the Sheriff. Not that it was any of the Mayor's business anyway. "Mayor, I am gathering information regarding the Sheriff's budget allocated to the new annexation. To get that information, I have to talk to the Sheriff."

"And telling the Sheriff that I'm not smart enough to understand the numbers is part of that?"

Sarah shook her head and seethed before she replied. "Before you call to accuse me of something like that, you need to get a better spy. If Glasgow told you I said that then he is lying."

"I trust Lieutenant Glasgow's word over yours, *Chief.*" Mayor Kamen accented the word "Chief" with a contemptuous tone. "It may be time for me to have a Police Chief I can trust. Someone who cares about the entire city and not just her little kingdom."

"Mayor, have a good evening. I have business that requires my attention." Sarah ended the call and stared at the phone for several seconds, waiting for Jordon to call back for the last word. The phone did not ring. She could only hope the Mayor gave thought to her comment about Glasgow's veracity. Probably not. In truth, knowing the Mayor's habit of playing loose with facts, Glasgow probably told the truth and the Mayor twisted it to throw Sarah off balance.

# CHAPTER 18

## Thursday 5:45 A.M.

Celia Wyatt was still in shock, worried about John's funeral and the fact that she was unable to see his body. Sarah fought her own emotions as she compassionately reassured the distraught wife and mother that John would be ready soon. Celia was simply trying to hold herself together, wanting closure, tending to the things her mind told her were important at that moment. Sarah avoided words like "Medical Examiner" and "autopsy" as she held Celia's hand and embraced her. The red eyes of attending family members expressed grief that would not quickly subside, even after closure. Sarah also knew something Celia and the family did not yet know. By necessity, it would be a closed casket funeral. She was emotionally exhausted by the time she crawled into the comfort of her bed.

Harsh dreams of ongoing battles and unresolved conflicts made her sleep uneasy. Sarah frequently awoke, Wyatt's funeral, the Mayor's budget, and a killer washed through her mind as she slowly returned to restless sleep. The sudden rattle of a cell phone on the nightstand was a disturbingly welcome relief from the turmoil in Sarah's mind. She fumbled through two more rings and checked the blue LED display of her clock before she answered. It was her normal wake-up time anyway.

"Good morning, Boss." Boston's tone was almost teasing. "Did I catch you before you started your workout?"

Sarah recognized his tone, intentionally used to put her mind at ease. "Good morning, Boston. What has you out early?"

Boston responded apologetically, "You sound sleepy. Sorry. I thought you would already be at the gym. Our boy is awake and ready for a lawyer. I thought you might want to be here."

Sarah sat up on the edge of the bed and ran her fingers through her hair. She pushed the night's thoughts from her brain and focused her mind. "Yeah. I do. Is the lawyer there already?" she asked skeptically. She looked at the clock again, proving to herself that she was not late.

"No, but he said he would be here shortly. Not sure what that means in lawyer speak."

Sarah yawned to clear her lungs and widened her eyes to get the sleep out of them. "That means I have time to shower and buy breakfast."

"I've got fresh donuts," the Detective said with a chuckle. He knew Sarah preferred a healthier option.

"Any other time, I might take you up on donuts, but not today. I'll be there in an hour or less."

Sarah navigated the familiar gauntlet of potholes as she drove from her favorite breakfast drive-thru to the police station. When she stepped from the car in the parking lot of the station, she adjusted her charcoal gray jacket and checked her rose-colored blouse using the reflection in her car's side window. It was only Thursday, but the preceding two days felt like a week. A random thought flashed through her mind. She wondered if Liz had set a meeting with Councilmen Sloan and Mendelson. It was essential to resolve the budget issues, even though Officer Wyatt's killer was her primary concern at that moment. She wondered why Chief Keck stayed in the job as long as he did … *how* he stayed in the job as long as he did.

"Good morning, Boston. What do we have?" Sarah poured coffee into her cup as she waited for his response. She watched the spoonful of sugar in the bottom of the cup swirl and disappear into the coffee. She did not stir. The last few sips would be sweeter than the first. That was the way she liked her coffee – start bitter then fade into comforting sweetness.

Boston's face twisted as he put words together for his response. "The suspect claims his name is Winston Baines – not Spencer Sheffield. After booking, we returned him to his cell. Waiting on his lawyer."

Sarah stared at her gray coffee cup. The pink words stared back at her. *Make sure you're right then go ahead.* Apparently, they were not right. She exhaled heavily. "It would seem we are back to square one."

"Not really," Boston replied. "Once we get Winston - or whoever he is - into Interrogation, we'll find out where Spencer is."

"We can only hope it's that easy." Sarah's fitful night was wearing on her positivity.

"Oh, he'll talk. Otherwise, I'm pushing for accessory to murder." Boston smiled wryly. "I'll explain the consequences of that. He's not ten-feet tall now that he's off the Angel Dust. It will be that easy."

Sarah nodded approval. She liked Boston. Only a few years older than her, but far more seasoned because of his years with Baltimore PD as a detective and undercover cop. Of all the law enforcement officers Sarah had ever known, Detective Mankowitz was the least concerned about honorifics. His years undercover conditioned him to wince when he was called "Detective", though he was getting used to it. He liked the down to earth style of an undercover cop, the task for which he was originally hired by Chief Keck and Lieutenant Kendall. He was good at it. He learned a lot about pulling information from suspects using his wits as the means. "I'm glad to hear you say that. We know it was PCP?"

"Just my guess. All the signs say it was."

"Understood." Boston's guess was almost as accurate as a lab test when it came to illicit drugs. "I need to do my rounds. Call me as soon as the lawyer arrives."

Sergeant Blanchard updated Sarah on the night's events. It was his week for four nights. He would be on shift one more night. The night had been generally quiet. Citizen calls regarding noises in the night. Routine traffic stops and no drunks. She should hear nothing from Zoey regarding calls. Contact cards from the previous weekend should be available if the mail was on time. If the sleepy driver who placed the hot-line call sent in his contact card, she would have to relive that episode. The Mayor would not automatically connect the two. In fact, Sarah had no doubts that the Mayor would play it as a separate incident for effect. Her cell rattled in her pocket. Boston's ID. She finished her rounds with the officers and PD employees before she returned to the bullpen. Boston would hold the Interrogation rather than start without her.

No one was in Interrogation when Sarah arrived. She remembered she needed to go to the Sheriff's Office for the data Sheriff Herriman promised. An oversight on her part. She found Boston, drinking coffee and staring at the whiteboard in the Situation Room. "Is he with the lawyer?"

Boston looked annoyed. "Yeah. The lawyer wanted to spend some time with him before interrogation. He wants to understand what is going on."

"How long do you suppose it will be? I need to run by the Sheriff's Office to get some documents."

Boston shook his head. "You should have time if you hurry. I'll delay until you signal me."

Traffic was heavier, bogged at some intersections. It always amazed Sarah how slowly most drivers react when a light changed from red to green. It irritated her more than normal. The fact that the person she had in jail was probably not John's killer disturbed her more the longer she thought about it. Somewhere in her city or in the state, a murderer was in flight. A cop killer who apparently felt no remorse for his deed. Everyone in the Department would again be on edge. A roller coaster of emotions.

The Sheriff's car was in the parking lot. Sarah entered the after-hours entrance. She was not surprised to see Sheriff Herriman talking with a group of Deputies on the other side of the plexiglass window that separated the public from the rest of the building. He waved when he saw her and opened the security door to allow her to enter.

"Good morning Sarah. Running late, I see." Cecil grinned big. "What's the news on our boy? Has he sobered up enough to talk?"

Sarah twisted her mouth before she responded. "He's sobered up. And he's talked. He claims he's not Spencer Sheffield. Says his name is Winston Baines. We're waiting for his lawyer to allow interrogation."

Sheriff Herriman's facial expression deflated. "Not Spencer? That puts a whole new light on things. Does Faraday know?"

"To be honest, I don't know. But, knowing Boston, I'm sure they've talked."

"I'll call him and ask, to make sure." The Sheriff blew hard as if releasing pressure from his brain. "And I thought today was going to be a good day."

"It will be. We'll find out where Spencer is hiding." Sarah went with Boston's positivity. "I need to hurry back to the station for the interrogation, but there is another item to discuss. Are you on board with the escort for John's funeral?"

"Escort Hell! I intend to give the man a hero's parade. I'll have as many of my units as possible involved. When is it planned?"

Sarah cautioned, "The ME hasn't released the body, but as soon as he does, Celia needs the closure. No delays."

"When do you expect it?"

"I should hear something from the ME today. I'll call them if I don't hear something by noon."

Sheriff Herriman was pensive for a moment. "Whenever. Just let me know. We're ready to respond. I imagine every PD in the county will be there. Probably the State as well."

Sarah felt a lump in her throat. The law enforcement community was always supportive, especially when one of their own fell in the line of duty. An attack on one was an attack on all. Along with everything else, she had received calls from numerous Police Chiefs from across the state … and beyond. "I will contact the Highway Patrol to make sure of it. Tony Kendall called late yesterday. He wants to know when the funeral is so he can be here." She gathered the information she came for and hurried back to the station.

Steven Cantrell was relatively young, early thirties at most. Dark brown hair and blue eyes. An eager lawyer with only a few years of experience. Devaney did not have any big law firms. Devaney *did have* several lawyers in private practice or grouped under one roof. Steven Cantrell spent his early years learning the trade working at a law firm in Wichita. In Devaney, he was on his own and hungry for clients. A frantic call from a high-profile suspect at five o'clock in the morning could provide the jumpstart he needed for his career.

Sarah stared bemusedly at the young lawyer. Winston Baines was still in a jail cell, returned there as soon as the attorney-client meeting ended. The prisoner was not new to jails. His prints were in the system. He was who he claimed to be. That was a let-down, even though she expected nothing different. Boston called while she was enroute from the Sheriff's Office to tell her the lawyer was demanding his client's release. The attorney wanted to see her personally. She found the young lawyer held at bay by Liz near her office and listened politely to his practiced diatribe.

"Chief, my client has made it abundantly clear that he is not your suspect. He was driving the BMW with the owner's permission. I am advising him to not answer any questions at this time."

"Mr. Cantrell, your client may not be our murder suspect, but he apparently was in contact with the suspect recently. He knows where Spencer Sheffield is hiding, which makes him a suspected accomplice to murder. He was also driving under the influence of a controlled substance and resisted arrest – violently. He has to face those charges. He's not walking until a judge says so."

Steven Cantrell smiled knowingly, "And he was subjected to police over-reaction. We will pursue that with the Judge as well. False arrest. Police brutality. I believe he may have a case against the city and the police department."

Sarah smiled in return. "And I can show you the videos from the police cameras. As a matter of fact, I would appreciate they go on public display with as much exposure as the little cell phone clips people are so eager to display. Everyone can then see just how violent your client really is, the kind of violence that explains why he would kill a police officer without a second thought."

The lawyer stepped back. "You can only charge him with DWI or DUI. Not murder."

"Actually, Mr. Cantrell, I can charge him with accessory to murder. Now – for your benefit and his - he needs to start talking before his attitude gets him in more trouble than he can handle." Sarah turned and walked away before the lawyer could respond.

"Wait. Wait." Steven Cantrell called after Sarah. "He will talk, but off the record."

Sarah stopped and turned. "We don't do off-the-record."

"Very well. Bring my client and we will answer your questions." Steve Cantrell tried to maintain the façade of being in control.

Sarah nodded to Sergeant Jarrett who was observing the conversation in the booking area. "He'll answer Detective Mankowitz's questions in Interrogation. I'll escort you up there. Sergeant, please see to Mr. Baines. Shackles. He's done nothing to convince me he won't be a violent flight risk." She watched Steven Cantrell's face contort before he relented and followed her up the stairs.

Sarah watched through the one-way glass. She ached to be in the action, demanding answers to questions. She had to allow Boston his space, just as she had been allowed her space when she was a detective. Boston was not yet in the Interrogation Room. He was allowing the suspect and his lawyer to stew. When he did walk into the room, he ignored the two men as he carefully placed a stack of folders on the table before he sat across from them.

Steven spoke first, indignantly. "You are intentionally dragging this out. Do your interrogation so my client can be released."

Sarah did not notice from her vantage point, but Boston's smirk was caught on one of the cameras. He stared at the lawyer for more than a minute, waiting for the young attorney to react.

"I'm not sure what your game is ..." Steven started.

Boston interrupted gruffly, "To catch a murderer. That's what my *game* is, if you and your client think this is a game."

Steven tried to cover his shock by leaning toward Boston, but his eyes revealed he was somewhat intimidated by the gruff detective. "Of course not. But my client deserves some respect and has rights. The police can't ..."

Boston was ready. As the attorney spoke, he pulled a stapled document from one of the folders. "The police are not Mr. Baines' problem. He is his own problem. Wichita PD has a warrant for his arrest. Something to do with multiple failures-to-appear. Looks like he likes to mix chemicals and gasoline. I suppose that's why he didn't have a driver's license when he was pulled over. Maybe that's why he resisted arrest. He knew his time was up and he was going down."

The lawyer reached for the warrant.

"That's not yours. You can get your own," Boston said bluntly, still clinging to the papers.

"I understand. I just want to see it." Steven's eyes were pleading.

Boston allowed the lawyer to hold the warrant and waited for him to return it.

Steven's mouth twisted as he read the document, and his eyes cut toward Winston when he finished. He handed the warrant back to Boston.

"We will address his Wichita warrant separately. We can satisfy these with a rehab program, but you know that."

"Rehab won't satisfy accomplice to murder." Boston glared at Winston as he responded.

Winston moved his arms far enough to reach the end of the restraints that held him to the table. He angrily said, "I don't know anything about a murder."

"Tell it to the Judge. Until you tell me the whereabouts of Spencer Sheffield, you are part of the murder. You own it as if you pulled the trigger yourself." Boston's eyes were steely.

"Don't threaten my client," demanded Steven.

Boston deliberately replied, "No threat. A promise." Fluidly, the Detective turned his full attention to Winston, "Where is Spencer Sheffield?"

"Your police beat me," Winston blurted, still belligerent.

Boston glared at Winston for a moment, slowly began to smile and said, "Do you want to see the videos, the real ones? As high as you were, you don't remember anything from the arrest. PCP turns a man into a superman without a hint of a brain. Where is Spencer Sheffield?"

Before Winston could blurt anything else, Steven commanded, "Winston, I recommend you answer the Detective's question. Everything else can come later."

The two men held eye contact for several seconds before Winston relaxed. "I don't know where he is."

"Abetting," Boston said plainly as he made a note on a page inside one of the folders.

"What?" Winston asked.

"I'm adding abetting to the charges. You're helping a murderer avoid apprehension by not telling me where he is. That's abetting. Maybe aiding. That adds up to more charges that the murderer will face – and he gets the death penalty." Boston smiled. "But that's your call, Boy."

"I'm not a boy!"

"Then act like a man. Own up to your mistakes. Tell me where Spencer Sheffield is."

"I'm not a rat either."

"Good. There's a cell in the pen with a big, lonely lifer as a roomie."

"Stop," Steven said. "You're intimidating my client."

"Not as much as Bubba will. Lansing has a couple of vacancies over there in Leavenworth County. A young man like Winston here is probably worth at least a half-a-pack of cigarettes. As you can see, I don't care about your client's feelings. I want to know where I can find Spencer Sheffield."

"I don't know." Winston appeared deflated. He was not a large man. Thin and average height. He looked smaller at that moment. Boston's words had an impact. "I don't know where he is."

Boston nodded. "You *did* know where he was when you got his BMW. How long have you known Spencer?"

"What? Oh, I don't know. Since high school. Cutter and I knew each other in Wichita. He ran with a different crowd, the rich crowd."

"When did you see him last?"

"A couple days ago. He was supposed to help me with … give me a ride. He said he couldn't take me, but he could loan me his Beamer. He gave me a couple of hits of Angel Dust and I left."

"He gave you Angel Dust then loaned you his fifty-thousand dollar car? Knowing your DUI history? That makes no sense to me."

"Right?" Winston made a quizzical face. "I thought he was being awfully generous, but I didn't argue. I needed wheels."

"And Angel Dust," Boston added. "Where were you when he loaned you his car?"

"Over at his pad."

"His pad? Here in Devaney?"

"Yeah."

Boston glanced toward the mirrored wall. "Where in Devaney? Do you have an address?"

"It's in that ritzy area on the south side. I'm not sure what street. Those streets aren't straight like in the rest of town."

"Western Plains?" Boston pressed.

Winston pondered the question. "I don't think that was the name of the street. Sounds familiar, but I don't think so."

"That's the name of a development area. Big houses. Big lots. Is that where Spencer's house is?"

"Sounds about right. I could drive you to it if you want me to," Winston offered with a smirk.

"Not necessary. How did you get there? You don't have wheels, as you put it."

"Another friend dropped me off there. Like I said, Cutter was going to give me a ride. He was high when I got there."

"Marijuana?"

"No, high. Like really happy. Stupid happy."

Boston's neck stiffened and his face turned red. "Did he say why he was happy?"

"No. He just said he couldn't take me," Winston paused to correct his sentence, "give me a ride like he promised. That's when he offered to loan me the Beamer. I left quick, before he changed his mind."

"Where did your other friend go?"

"Back to his pad I suppose."

"Does he go see Spencer often?"

"Can't say for sure. He knew the way okay."

"Does your friend have a name? What does he do?"

"I told you, I'm no rat." Winston leaned back in his chair.

"And I told you there are cells available in Lansing."

"He gave you a location," Steven protested.

"He gave me an area."

Winston leaned forward. "If he knows you're looking for him, he's probably not at his house anymore. What difference does it make?"

"It makes a lot of difference," Boston replied angrily. "Evidence. Clues to where he could be hiding. What's your friend's name?"

"Rewind. Tyrone Jamison. They call him Rewind."

Surprisingly, Boston recognized the street name. Tyrone was a parttime pusher with a low tolerance for applied pressure. He would give up anyone to save himself. Boston occasionally used Rewind for information during his undercover days. Rewind maintained a low profile, pushed a few bags to supplement his income as a retail clerk, and gave up information for a few dollars more. Boston wrote on a piece of paper while Winston and Steven fidgeted. He looked up and said, "That should do it. I'll have the officer escort you back to your cell." Without further interaction with the two men, he left the Interrogation Room.

Sarah waited until an officer took Winston from the room. She knew the attorney would ask for one more private meeting before he left. To be expected. The light in the Observation Room changed when the door opened. Liz entered apologetically.

"I waited until Boston came out of Interrogation. I heard that the suspect isn't the murderer after all."

Sarah shook her head. "Good morning, Liz. No. I'm afraid not, but Boston got a good lead to his whereabouts. I'm sure he's updating the BOLO. What do you have for me this morning?" She knew Liz would not have been there if it was not something relatively urgent.

"Zoey Kopechne called. She said the Mayor needs you to call her immediately."

"That's odd," Sarah said as she pulled her cell phone from her breast pocket to check for missed calls. It was on vibrate. She would have felt it if someone called. She would have ignored it, but she would have known. "I don't have any missed calls. Did she say what the Mayor wants?"

"No, just said to call her immediately."

"Okay. After I catch up with Boston. What else do we have today? Are the Councilmen scheduled?"

"Yes, Councilman Sloan is scheduled at ten o'clock. Councilman Mendelson is scheduled at eleven. Street Department Supervisor Farmer said he can attend both meetings but may have to cut the second one short. He has something at twelve-thirty."

Sarah was puzzled. "Could they not meet at the same time? That's two hours. I don't mind the amount of time, but that means I will be repeating myself."

"FOIA. They are concerned that two of them meeting to discuss official business would fall under the Freedom of Information Act. Public notice for an open meeting would be required."

Sarah shook her head. "I guess that makes sense ... but I can't see it. All the budget information will come out in the Council meetings."

"The public has the right to know what its officials are doing. Sorry."

"That's fine. Maybe by doing it separately, they will ask more questions. The more answers I have, or have to get, the better off we will be when I face the City Council. I certainly don't want the Mayor to know I'm politicking. She's aware that I've got the Sheriff working with me ... thanks to Glasgow."

"Speaking of Lieutenant Glasgow, he's roaming the station. Taylor said he was here when she arrived." Liz shook her head. "And to think, I used to like him."

Sarah wondered why the Lieutenant did not come looking for her. If he was worth his salt, he knew she was involved with Winston Baines' interrogation. She shook her head. Not seeing him was a good thing. Not knowing what he was up to was a bad thing. "And therein may answer the question of the Mayor's *immediate* phone call demand. Liz, please arrange a press conference in the lobby. Nine o'clock should be good."

"That's not much time for them to get organized," Liz responded.

Sarah chuckled. "I've seen how fast they can respond in the middle of the night. Daytime should be a cinch. They'll be fine." She walked to the bullpen in search of Boston.

Boston was in the Situation Room writing on the whiteboard. Sarah refilled her coffee cup before going into the room with him. She waited until he stepped back to review what he had written. New fishbones were added. Some older fishbones were updated. "What next?"

Boston replied, "We go get him – if he's still around. I checked county records. No record of a house owned by a Sheffield in Devaney. If that house is his, it's in someone else's name."

"Or an alias."

"There's no indication that he has aliases."

Sarah did not reply. She would let Boston process the idea.

"I called Blake. He's going after Rewind. See what he knows." Boston mulled something before he said anything else. "If Spencer is still in Devaney, he has to have an alias. Something that isn't associated with the Sheffield name. Even with pictures out there, in his secret identity, his associates would probably not make the connection."

Sarah nodded. Boston was opening the options.

"That house. We need to know the address. He may not be there, but it could lead us to his alias."

"He might have another vehicle also. More for the BOLO."

"Kind of stupid," Boston said off-handedly.

"What?" Sarah was shocked by the response.

"It's kind of stupid of him to allow low-lifes like Winston and Rewind know where he lives under his alias – if that's the case."

"Oh. Well, nothing he's done so far indicates he's very bright."

"True. His stupidity may be our big break. I reinstated the BOLO as soon as I got Winston's ID confirmed. I'll add more as we get it." Boston stopped and scowled. "What's he doing here?" He walked over and closed the Situation Room door in Lieutenant Glasgow's face. "Private conversation. Come back later."

# CHAPTER 19

## Thursday 9:00 A.M.

Sarah cringed. She did not need fuel added to the fire. "I'm sure he's looking for me. The Mayor wants me to call her."

"So, she sent her lapdog," Boston scoffed.

"Maybe. Is there anything you need from me right now?"

"I don't think so. The next step will begin when Rewind gives up the address. I have asked Taylor to pull back patrol of Western Plains, so we don't spook him if he *is* there."

Sarah greeted Lieutenant Glasgow with the friendliest tone she could muster. She disliked spies for the Mayor as much as she disliked the Mayor's behaviors. "Good Morning, Lieutenant. What brings you to the station so early?" Conversation starter.

Lieutenant Glasgow scowled toward the door of the Situation Room. "He knows the Mayor put me in charge of the manhunt."

Sarah smiled bemusedly as she led Glasgow toward her office. "He knows the Mayor *tried* to put you in charge of the manhunt. Detective Mankowitz is officially in charge. It would be good for you and the Mayor to keep that in mind. What do you need to know that you don't already?"

"Everything, especially since the person in custody is not Spencer Sheffield. The Mayor needs to stay informed, so she doesn't say the wrong thing to the public."

Sarah smiled bemusedly. "It is not her role to say anything to the public regarding police work."

"The Police Department *does* report to the Mayor's Office."

Sarah paused at her office door and turned to face Glasgow. "And the Mayor makes a point of telling me she's in charge every time we talk. I don't need someone who reports to me saying it. Now, what do you really want?" She walked into her office and sat at her desk. She unlocked the desk and removed a bundle of folders from a deep side drawer. "I have work to do if you are only here to visit."

"No. I need to know what is taking place in the manhunt. Boston could give me that – if he would bother to talk to me."

"We are still relying on the BOLO and informants. As you might suspect, we dropped the search when we thought we had Spencer in custody. The search is back on. Now, you are updated. By the way, I need to call *my* boss. *Your* boss is telling you to check with Lieutenant McCluskey to see if she has any leads that require your assistance. There's a lot to be done." Sarah knew it would grate on Glasgow to go face Taylor, who was his boss prior to his promotion. She dialed the Mayor's number while she watched Glasgow leave.

Zoey answered the Mayor's number. "Good morning, Chief. I will connect you to the Mayor."

"Good morning, Mayor." Sarah feigned good humor when the Mayor answered. "Liz said you wanted me to call you as soon as I finished what I was doing."

"I said no such thing," Jordon Kamen snapped. "I wanted you to call me immediately. You seem to think you can ignore me whenever you want to."

"Mayor, that is not true. I was involved in an interrogation of our suspect. Interrogations cannot be disrupted once they start."

"What harm would have come from interrupting the interrogation? It appears the Devaney Police Department has messed up again. The person arrested was not the same person you were trying to find. All I can say is that I still think we need someone capable of leading a simple manhunt."

"Mayor, you know the circumstances. The man was driving Spencer Sheffield's vehicle, under the influence of drugs with no ID. We have found that he doesn't have a driver's license. It was suspended in Wichita for multiple DUIs. But he has given us a very strong lead on Spencer Sheffield's whereabouts."

"Where is that?"

"A lead, Mayor. A lead. From what we have learned, Winston Baines was a dupe. Spencer Sheffield loaned Winston his car to distract us, to disrupt the search. We have now learned how to find Spencer. The dragnet is tightening."

The Mayor paused momentarily. "I suspect you will mess that up as well, but that is not the purpose of my call."

Sarah shook her head. She resisted the urge to remind the Mayor who dialed the phone to make the call.

The Mayor continued intensely, "Why do you have Sergeant Locke investigating Terrance Overton's death? He works for the Department of Public Outreach."

"Sergeant Locke works for the Devaney Police Department." Sarah struggled to keep calm. "Most of our resources are assigned to the capture of Officer Wyatt's killer. Sergeant Locke availed himself and I assigned the Overton case to him. As you told me, Mr. Overton is a prominent Devaney citizen. He deserves consideration. Sergeant Locke has detective experience. I gave him instructions to investigate the case, to determine whether Mr. Overton Senior's death is suspicious." She saw no reason to tell the Mayor more than that. It would be a test of Keith's allegiance. If the Mayor knew more than she just said, it could only come from Keith.

"Your instructions to Sergeant Locke were very poor, not that I'm surprised considering your demonstrated lack of leadership skills. Mr. Overton is extremely irate over the fact that Sergeant Locke interrogated his mother about the death. Does that sound like you gave the Sergeant good instructions? The woman is in shock."

"Mayor, it was not an *interrogation*. It was a few simple questions." Even though Sarah did not know what Keith asked, or what he learned, she was going to defend her officer. "Sergeant Locke was following a lead. Mrs. Overton is the only person who can provide answers to the questions that arose. That is very good detective work. Despite Mr. Overton's discomfort with it, he is the one who insisted we get answers."

"I didn't say he was uncomfortable, Chief. I said he was irate. *Yelling* in my ear irate. I won't have any more of that. Do you understand? Pull Sergeant Locke off the case."

Sarah gave herself a moment to control her emotions. Slowly and deliberately, she said, "Mayor, until you make good on your constant threat to fire me, I will operate this police department professionally in the way I deem appropriate. Our differences non-withstanding, Sergeant Locke is needed on this case. First, he is the only person with the right skill sets available and, second, he's too deeply involved to stop now."

"Well, keep Terrance Overton Junior away from me. Solve it fast. Understood?"

Sarah shook her head. The Mayor had wasted fifteen minutes of time she could not spare. "Understood. I'll talk with Junior as soon as I can. In the meantime," she changed subjects, "I have scheduled a press conference at nine o'clock in the station lobby to let the public know what has transpired with the manhunt. You're welcome to join and give your side of the facts." Sarah's closing comment was intentionally sarcastic.

"That's too soon. Change it to ten."

"I can't. My schedule is full all day. These things don't follow anyone's schedule. I need to prepare for the Press. I will see you if you can attend." Sarah ended the call. She imagined the Mayor was further incensed because the call ended abruptly.

As expected, Kyren Bailey's film crew was ready at nine o'clock when Sarah descended the stairs to the lobby. So were several other local reporters with their microphones, cell phones, I-Pads and even notepads. The Mayor followed Sarah down the stairs with her high heels clicking on the treads, unhappy that Sarah was in the lead. Lieutenant Glasgow was dutifully on the Mayor's heels.

Sarah opened with a statement. "As you are aware, a suspect in the murder of Officer John Wyatt was taken into custody last evening. The suspect was intoxicated, under the influence of PCP, commonly known as Angel Dust, and unable to communicate coherently. As a result, he was allowed to detox in our drunk tank overnight. A few hours ago, he sobered enough for us to formally process him, to run his fingerprints and mugshot. He is *not* Spencer Sheffield, even though he was driving

Mr. Sheffield's vehicle. His name is Winston Baines, formerly of Wichita and a long-time associate of Spencer Sheffield. Mr. Baines has been very forthcoming regarding the whereabouts of Mr. Sheffield. The new information has been released to all agencies involved in the manhunt. At present, there is nothing more I can share. If you have any questions, I will try to answer them."

Mayor Kamen moved forward. The press conference was prepped quickly, but Liz managed to procure the squad room podium. The Mayor wanted control of it at that moment. Sarah yielded without resistance. Predictably, the Mayor adjusted the inoperative microphone. Sarah knew the Mayor would have words. She did not expect the words she heard.

"The Chief has dismissed the suspect in custody as the murderer and seems bent on chasing after the son of a highly respected State Senator. I am deeply concerned that the Senator's son's reputation is being dragged through the mud as a self-serving aggrandizement of the Chief's resume. Even though the Chief's actions have not risen to the level of incompetence that requires me to replace her, I do believe the investigation into this man - Winston Baines - must continue." Mayor Kamen turned her head to indicate Lieutenant Glasgow. "I have asked Lieutenant Glasgow, head of our Department of Public Outreach, to do the necessary follow-up to ensure we don't keep chasing the wrong person. Evidence will prove Winston Baines is the murderer of Officer Wyatt." She looked at Sarah with a smug smile.

Sarah simply stepped back to take the podium. "Any questions?"

"Chief, is there any reason to believe Mr. Baines is actually the murderer?" Kyren asked louder than the rest.

"None. We have the testimony of two young men who were with Spencer Sheffield the night he shot Officer Wyatt."

Mayor Kamen hedged forward and quickly added, "Those two teenagers, easily influence young men, are basing their testimony on the word of a killer. The murderer told them that his name was Spencer Sheffield. He offered no proof of identity. After the brutal murder of Officer Wyatt, he had them drive him to his vehicle – the same vehicle driven by Winston Baines when he was arrested. Winston Baines *claims* that Spencer Sheffield loaned him a $50,000 BMW. Why do you think Winston Baines was so resistant to arrest that it required six officers to subdue him? I'll tell you why. It was because he didn't want to be captured for murdering a police officer. He lied to the two gullible teenagers. Now he's lying to the Chief and Detective Mankowitz. Winston Baines murdered a Devaney police officer in the guise of Spencer Sheffield. Lieutenant Glasgow will get to the bottom of this – hopefully before an innocent man, Spencer Sheffield, is brutally arrested."

"Chief! Chief!" Bernie asked hurriedly to beat Kyren. "Is there any reason to believe the suspect in custody has been lying about his identity?"

Sarah responded emotionlessly. The Mayor's words gave her an idea. Let Spencer Sheffield believe there was doubt. Let him believe focus on him might lessen. Let him make a mistake as great as the mistake of allowing Tyrone Jamison and Winston Baines know where he lived. Let his stupidity be his undoing. "Bernie, there is always a reason to doubt the veracity of any testimony given." She intentionally glanced toward the Mayor. "People say what suits them best. Our job is to read people. Our training and experience help us avoid following bad leads based upon testimony. I believe we are on the right course ... but the Mayor is within her authority to direct Lieutenant Glasgow to pursue her theory on behalf of the Mayor's Office."

The reporters asked questions until Sarah called the press conference to a halt at nine-thirty. She had a busy schedule.

# CHAPTER 20

## Thursday 10:00 A.M.

Boston waited for Sarah to finish the news conference, and for the Mayor to stomp out the door. "Chief, the ME called. They've finished the autopsy. John's body will be returned later today."

Sarah felt a sense of relief, as much for herself as for the family. "Thank you, Boston. Did they find anything?" They had eyewitnesses to the murder, but substantiating physical evidence would bolster the case. The Mayor's public speculation provided "reasonable doubt" for the eventual jury to ponder.

"Nothing we didn't already know or surmise. COD is just what the Coroner said it was. The .22 round through the eye socket was lethal. Everything else was hate."

"I don't suppose Alicia found anything more?" Sarah asked hopefully.

"No. We're relying on eyewitnesses. The food wrapper gave us nothing concrete. He's a neat eater. No saliva or epithelials to test. The .22 is not in the system."

"Any feedback from the field?"

"Other than keeping my ears tuned, I'm waiting for Blake to find Rewind. I had to wake him. He was on a case last night. It shouldn't take too much longer, though. Rewind is easy to locate."

Sarah heard a whispered male voice from the hallway. Liz's voice was not a whisper. Liz's words were prefaced by a laugh. "I saw her leave the building. I think I hear the Chief talking with Detective Mankowitz. I'll tell her you are here."

Sarah apologetically said to Boston. "I guess my ten o'clock is about to start. Interrupt me." She met Liz in the hallway, saw Jake Farmer leaning against Liz's doorframe, and smiled at both. "Thank you, Liz. Good morning, Jake. I'm glad you could make it. How is your day going so far?"

The Street Department Supervisor laughed and replied, "When I saw the Mayor's rig out front, I thought the jig was up. I came in the back way. I hope she doesn't see my truck."

Sarah grinned. "I always think that when I see her. We'll meet in the Conference Room. Do you want a cup of coffee?"

"Just as well," Jake replied to the offer.

Liz magically appeared with Sarah's coffee cup. "Chief, I have your files ready for the meeting. I'll lay them on the conference table for you. And I'll close the blinds." The conference room chosen was suitable for four or five people and had windows on the inside wall that abutted the bullpen, as well as the outside wall.

"Thank you, Liz." Sarah led Jake to the coffee pot. As they approached the conference room, a well-dressed man with graying hair came through the doorway at the top of the front stairs. He paused and looked around, he smiled and nodded when he saw Sarah. "Councilman Sloan, welcome to Devaney PD." She shook his hand and motioned toward Jake. "Have you met Street Supervisor Jackson Farmer?"

The Councilman shook Jake's hand. "Certainly. Jake and I have worked together before. How are you today, Jake? The Street Department probably gets more bad press than the Police Department," he said with a grin.

Jake laughed, "Everyone wants the streets fixed but they don't want construction to slow them down."

"It's a no-win," confirmed the Councilman. "I suppose we need to get to this." He lifted a briefcase slightly to indicate the task at hand.

Liz interjected, "Councilman, would you like a cup of coffee?"

"It's a little late in the day for me, but a bottle of water would be nice."

The three of them settled into the conference room and began discussing the needs of the Police Department and the Street Department. Sarah shared copies of her budget requirements along with the statistics she compiled and the ones the Sheriff gave her. Her budget requests included rational and supportive data derived from those statistic.

Councilman Sloan studied everything Sarah pushed before him. He finally said, "Chief, nothing in this is unreasonable. As a matter of fact, you probably need to go in high, so you have something to bargain with." He grinned. "Budgets in government are steeped in politics."

Sarah glanced at Jake and then back to Jim Sloan. "I'm just trying to be honest about it."

"Honesty looks good on camera, but it doesn't play well in the meeting room. You have to have a bargaining chip. For instance, why are you only asking for five officers and two new cars when your data shows you need at least seventeen more uniformed officers plus another three cadre personnel? That's twenty and you're only asking for a quarter of that. You also need to consider replacement of some of your older vehicles. Every budget cycle since I've been on the Council included replacement vehicles." Jim nodded toward Jake. "I assure you Jake has a few replacements in his."

Jake replied with a vigorous nod. "I sure do, though the Mayor has already indicated she won't stand for it."

Jim smiled. "And that may be her thinking at the moment. She's new at this Mayor thing. We have to help her understand the *cost* of reduced budgets in police and street work. Delayed spending invites safety problems. Chief, I recommend you up the ante. Put in the numbers you need for best case. Be prepared to settle for something less, but not much less. Despite the national cry for less police funding, I assure you the Devaney City Council is not on that bandwagon. Not yet anyway. I see the Sheriff included his budget in the documents he shared with you. Without cutting to the core, I assure you his staffing is greater than one officer per four-hundred fifty population like the National Statistics support. He got that because he asked, not because the Commissioners simply handed it to him."

Sarah's mind flushed with the prospect of additional officers. And better equipment. "I see your point. Especially on replacements. My maintenance budget could be reduced by having better equipment."

"Exactly. Don't short yourself in the budgeting process. You may not get everything you ask for, but you will get more than you are asking for right now."

Sarah cautiously said, "Will my new numbers be considered by the Council, since the Mayor has already denied any increases?"

Jim nodded. "Of course. Like I said, the Mayor is new at this. Every Mayor tries to imprint his ... or her ... ideas on the budget. As strange as it may sound, budgets become the legacies of executives. If you can convince Chase with these numbers, your numbers will be very highly considered by the rest of the Council. Can I promise you everything? No. That's why I'm saying - budget high and be ready to bargain." He turned to Jake. "What have you got for the Street Department, Jake? Good stuff I presume."

"I've got everything I need in it, but ... like with the PD ... the Mayor has nixed a huge chunk of it, especially the increases associated with the annexation."

The Councilman studied the documents the Street Department Supervisor handed him. After a few minutes, he said, "These numbers are in line with every annual budget I've seen while in office. Your arguments seem to be based on the premise that good infrastructure will attract investors, companies with jobs. I'm not sure that is the best approach with Mayor Kamen. What is the impact of bad roads on the citizens? If you can break it down to that level, she should listen. I know the Council will."

After another half hour of review of the two Department's proposals, Sarah felt more comfortable. It was pure serendipity that she met with Councilman Sloan first. Councilman Mendelson's CPA acuity might have been less supportive if she had met with him first.

Chase Mendelson arrived a few minutes early and was waiting in Liz's office, absently watching the muted TV. Sarah escorted Councilman Sloan to the lobby and Jake escorted Councilman Mendelson to the Conference Room. Liz met Sarah as soon as she entered the bullpen.

"Chief, Channel 6 keeps repeating the Mayor's comments from this morning. Apparently, she said more after she left the building. It's now being tagged as *possible identity theft*."

Sarah rolled her eyes and shook her head. "Jordon is playing right into a good lawyer's hands. Reasonable doubt. If I didn't know better, I would say she is doing it intentionally."

"She seems to hate the police department," Liz commented softly, "always interfering."

"She has something on her mind. Some agenda. I don't understand it yet. Anything else?"

"Yes. Lieutenant McCuskey is visiting with Celia Wyatt. The Coroner called to confirm he will receive John's remains later today. Taylor is there to accompany the family to the funeral home so they can make arrangements. We will know something later today."

"Good. If I'm unavailable when she returns, contact the Sheriff and the State. The Highway Patrol and KBI want to be involved." Sarah walked to the Situation Room to see if Boston was there. He was. He was adding a fishbone to the whiteboard. "I see Blake found something."

Boston turned and nodded. "Not much, but it's a start. Rewind rolled like a ball bearing. The house where they met Spencer is at 4376 Meadow Lane. A short street on the fringe of Western Plains."

"A dead-end street?"

"A loop. We're getting prepped to roll that way. The Sheriff is lending his SWAT. The State has a couple of units enroute as well." Boston pointed to a city map tacked on a corkboard. "We're going in from this street first to block foot escape." His fingers traced an imaginary line that formed a semi-circle around the backside of the looped street. "Blake is sitting in his unmarked car at a house that has a view of both ends of Meadow Lane. When we're ready, we'll block those entrances and SWAT will move in."

"Are you going with them? I'd like to be there."

"Yes, and not necessary. You have a job here," Boston nodded in the general direction of the Conference Room. "Looks like you're planning an assault too. I'll take care of this." Boston adjusted his shoulder holster to reassure himself his weapon was in place. "I've got this one, Boss."

"Be careful … and don't give the Press anything."

"You know I don't talk to the Press."

"You know what I mean," Sarah chided tactfully. She knew the reticent Detective would avoid talking to anyone outside of the Police Department. He might not be as concerned about how the arrest looked on the news. She went to meet with Councilman Chase Mendelson.

"Chief, there is a lot of detail here. You have done your homework," Chase said after he reviewed Sarah's budget proposals. "I'm impressed. What do you need from me?"

Sarah did not expect that question. "Uh … support. The Mayor has already told me I cannot increase my budget, even with the annexation. In fact, she's telling me I have to reduce my budget. There's no way I can do that and run an efficient police department to ensure public safety."

Chase nodded in thought as he studied the numbers further. "I see you penciled through the number five and changed it to seventeen. You have also inserted three cadre. What do you mean by cadre, exactly?"

"Lieutenants. Lieutenant Kendall left for another job. I moved up to replace Chief Keck. Lieutenant Glasgow and Sergeant Locke are counted in the current staff, but they report directly to the Mayor and not to the Department."

"That is four."

Sarah leaned back. "I didn't want to appear greedy." She smiled sheepishly; an action ignored by the accountant Councilman.

"I see. I see. I can support your personnel requests. This city is growing, and if Mayor Kamen is successful, that growth will become exponential. For sure, the Police Department needs to be prepared." Chase glanced toward Jake. "The same can be said for the Street Department. Public safety and infrastructure are critical for growth. Most cities react to growth, always behind the curve. Devaney is no different." He studied the data for a moment. "Chief, I see you made another change. You delineated new vehicles from replacement vehicles. You were asking for two new vehicles. You changed that to four new and three replacements."

"Yes. The need for seventeen new officers will require at least four additional vehicles for patrol. Also, if you look at the maintenance line item, that number has grown over the last few years because our fleet has aged faster than we have replaced vehicles. If we don't systematically replace units, we will find ourselves grounded."

With lips pursed, Councilman Mendelson studied the scribbled notes on the budget pages of both Sarah and Jake. Finally, he looked up and said, "I find no fault with your budget requests. That does not mean others will not." Almost as an afterthought, he asked, "Have either of you considered hybrid vehicles?"

Jake scoffed, "I certainly haven't. I don't think they make electric dump trucks."

Chase looked Jake in the eyes. "No. Probably not proven reliable yet. But I see a lot of pickups and one-ton trucks with Street Department logos on the door. Have you considered hybrids for those applications?"

"Electric doesn't run very long on a charge, not like a gasoline or diesel engine," Jake protested.

"True. But hybrids are different than totally electric. How far do your service vehicles normally drive in a day?"

"Oh ... uh ... it's not how far. It's how long. They are driving all over town every day."

"Constantly moving or going from work site to work site?"

Jake's face twisted angrily, "What are you asking me? Do we just drive around, or do we use the trucks to go to work sites? Both. Most of them are hauling tools and supplies. Some are used to transport employees. Some are used to inspect streets."

"Some. That is an important word." Chase looked at Sarah. "I am unsure about police work, but if even some of your fossil fuel vehicles can be replaced with hybrid vehicles, that argument will go a long way with Mayor Kamen. She is concerned about the environment."

Sarah thought Jake had a response, but he scowled and stared at his budget data. "I have done some precursory research on hybrid police vehicles. There are some with pursuit capabilities on the market. They are not cheap, compared to internal combustion vehicles."

"As your data indicate, a fully outfitted police unit is not cheap."

"True, but the hybrids are much more expensive. Life expectancy and maintenance costs are inconclusive."

"I am not the City Financial Officer, but I know the numbers. The city is not destitute. Why do you think Mayor Kamen is adamantly against your budget?"

Sarah shifted in her chair. The question made her uncomfortable. She did not want to give a petty response. "I think the Mayor is caught up in the national outcry against police overreaction. Defunding or reducing police budgets is thought to be the solution."

"That may be part of her position. I can tell you –," Chase paused and smile wryly, "and if you say I told you I will say you lied – Mayor Kamen wants more money spent on green initiatives. Hybrid city vehicles will get her attention. Maybe her approval."

Sarah saw the brilliance of the Councilman's suggestion. "I can do that. I'm not aware of any major issues with hybrids – not yet."

"Supervisor Farmer, what do you think?"

Jake relaxed, "I don't know much about hybrids, but I reckon if it will help get what we need, I can put some in the fleet."

Sarah appreciated the input from both Councilmen. She also saw the value of Bill Keck's words. Both men walked out of the Police Station feeling large and in charge, but they also recognized Sarah's strengths. She handed her copy of the budget with notations to Liz so it could be revised for eventual presentation. She felt more relaxed … about the budgeting process. She was not ready to truly relax just yet.

"Jake, if you have a few minutes, let's do some research. Councilman Sloan's comment about bad roads costing citizens has me curious." Sarah waited for Jake to reply.

Jake said, "I do have time, if you have data."

"The internet and government statistics are easy to access." Sarah led Jake to her office and starting keying on her computer. "There! This thing is loaded with statistic … and lawyers looking for clients. Over three-billion dollars a year! That's the cost of auto repairs caused by potholes. Extrapolate that." She pushed a calculator toward Jake.

"Three-billion?" Jake asked. He began calculating once Sarah confirmed the number. His eye widened when finished punching buttons. "WOW! If I break it down to Devaney's population, that's over half-a-million dollars a year that our citizens have to pay for repairs. And a lot of that is tire replacements."

"Use that for sure. Here's something else. Approximately a third of all traffic fatalities are linked to bad roads. That's over ten thousand per year." Sarah paused a moment. "As a matter of fact, I might find a few examples in Devaney MVARs that you can use. Mayor Clairmont's accident was road related." She saw Jake squirm when she mentioned Mayor Clairmont's accident.

Jake recovered quickly, "What's an MVAR?"

"Motor Vehicle Accident Report. Lieutenant McCluskey is extremely thorough. They'll offer something of value, I'm sure."

# CHAPTER 21

## Thursday 12:00 Noon

After Sarah escorted Jake Farmer down the back stairs, she went to see Liz. She wanted to call Boston, to check on the status of the raid at Meadow Lane, but she knew he could be in the middle of a tense situation.

Liz was eating her lunch at her desk and watching the noon news. The volume was loud enough to hear for a change. Sarah walked in and gave a thumbs-up. "Thank you for your help, Liz. There may be hope after all." She glanced at the TV. Kyren was standing with a backdrop of a residential area, one with large houses and large lots. Her blood froze in her veins. She recognized the area as Western Plains. A single police car blocked the street. The only other vehicles in view were residents' cars parked in nearby driveways.

Kyren was completing her commentary of the scene and introducing another part of her story, *"I spoke with Mayor Kamen on the phone earlier about the manhunt that continues for Officer Wyatt's killer. She still maintains Officer Wyatt's murderer stole Spencer Sheffield's identity."*

The screen faded from Kyren and filled with a stock photo of Jordon Kamen. Subtitles appeared across the Mayor's picture, keeping pace with her voice. *"I am concerned that the situation will turn deadly if we don't handle this rationally. While I understand the urgency in the minds of our police, the urgency to capture a murderer, I maintain that emotions can lead to mistakes, potentially fatal mistakes. Rather than knock on the door,* over-emotional police might resort to a SWAT team to batter down doors and go in guns blazing. All for naught considering the murderer is already in custody. Those are the reasons I have assigned Lieutenant Glasgow to this case, to protect Spencer Sheffield's right to life. Lieutenant Glasgow will prove the killer is already in custody. Winston Baines, the man who used Spencer Sheffield's identity to murder a police officer."

The screen switched to Kyren in the act of reading from her cell phone. "As you heard, earlier this morning, the Mayor expressed her position that Winston Baines is the actual murderer, and the manhunt is over. It has grown into an ongoing battle between Devaney Mayor and Devaney PD." She turned and looked down the street. The camera followed her move. "The house where the police believe Mr. Spencer is hiding is located on Meadow Lane, further inside the development. We are prevented from going any closer. Western Plains is an upscale neighborhood, inhabited by business and professional leaders. It is not the type of neighborhood where one would expect to find a wanton killer. The raid has been underway for almost half-an-hour with no indications of gunfire or tear gas. We will remain on the scene and will break in if there are further developments. This is Kyren Bailey reporting from the scene for Channel 6 News at Noon."

Sarah controlled her rage. "How did …?" She stopped, aware that Liz did not need to see or hear anything she had to say at that moment. No one did, except maybe the Mayor. "Liz, I'm going to Western Plains. Call me if you need me." While on the phone with Liz, her other cell phone rattled in her pocket. Zoey. She called Zoey to get the message to call the Mayor.

The Mayor was irate, as usual. "Why didn't you tell me you located Spencer Sheffield? And why wasn't Lieutenant Glasgow told?"

"Insofar as telling Glasgow …"

"That's Lieutenant Glasgow!"

"Insofar as telling Melvin, you specifically ordered him to prove Winston Baines is the murderer. You made that clear in two press statements. I didn't want to upset you by interfering with your orders." Sarah smiled as she listened to Jordon Kamen fume in response to her petulant tone.

"And you didn't tell me because I stepped on your toes? That's rather petty, unbecoming a Police Chief."

"No, I didn't tell you because I saw no reason to bother you until the suspect was in custody. If I called you for everything we do, you would not be able to do your job."

Mayor Kamen fumed a while longer. "Don't worry about me doing my job. It would be nice to know about these things before they make the news. What is happening out there?"

"Mayor, I can't tell you."

"Why!??!"

"Because I'm not there. Detective Mankowitz is in charge of the manhunt. The Sheriff is there. I trust both men to do the job. Boston will contact me as soon as something happens. I will call you as soon as he updates me. Is that good enough?"

"How did the media know about this raid before I did?"

Sarah thought a minute. Her initial thoughts about a leak when she saw the broadcast apparently were incorrect. She did not like being wrong, even about something as simple as that. "Mayor, my first thought was that Lieutenant Glasgow told you and you told the media. This operation was being planned this morning during our presser. I approved it before I went into scheduled meetings. Detective Mankowitz is highly experienced. He didn't need my participation."

"That's debatable," Mayor Kamen snorted.

Sarah ignored the comment. "Part of the plan was to surround the house on foot from the backside. There is a possibility an amateur newshound alerted the media. Our radio comms are encrypted, but there are some high-tech snoops in the media with scanners. Either or, the Press found out. So, I'm a bit incensed that Kyren was there too."

"Well, let me know. I'm sending Glasgow over."

"Over where?"

"To the scene."

A beep indicated Sarah was receiving another call. She glanced at her phone. "Mayor, Boston is calling. I'll see if he has an update and call you back." She knew a call back would be expected. "Yes, Boston."

"Nothing here." The Detective sounded exasperated.

"Nothing?"

"Well, no one. We're combing the house for evidence and clues. Just before we started the raid, I got a call from County Records. The house is owned by Samuel and Joyce Reed. I'll follow up on those names when I get back."

"It's a lead. I can have Liz do it for you," Sarah offered.

"Okay, Boss. The sooner the better. Gotta go."

Sarah did not intend to burden Liz with the task. It would not be that difficult. The digital age made property searches and people searches relatively easy, especially for someone with law enforcement level access. She called the Mayor and gave her the update. Surprisingly, the Mayor did not rant.

Sarah's search yielded a location for the owners. They bought a house in Texas, near San Antonio, less than a year earlier. They were in their mid-sixties. Records indicated cell phones for each. She called the phone attached to Samuel.

"Mr. Reed, this is Police Chief Sarah James with Devaney Police Department. Do you have a moment to answer a couple of questions about your property on Meadow Lane?"

"Police Chief? I thought Bill Keck was Chief."

Sarah cleared her throat. "Chief Keck recently retired. I was selected to replace him. Is this a good time to answer a few questions?"

"Retired? Good for him. I waited too long … I think. Finally took the leap a year ago. Moved to a warmer climate. Playing golf and fishing. Should have started sooner. What about the property? Has there been a break-in? Or a fire?" Samuel was concerned but he had his priorities. The house in Devaney came after retirement.

"No. I am wondering if anyone is house sitting for you."

"No need. We leased the house to a man. Said he didn't have any children. We didn't want young kids in the house, in case we decide to sell. They can do a lot of incidental damage. Not that kids are bad. They just like to play and don't understand. You know what I mean?"

"I do. What is the man's name?"

"Sends a check the first of every month. Has for the last seven months." Samuel paused to address someone on his end. "No. It's not the kids. It's the Devaney Police Chief asking about the house. Yeah. I know. We probably should sell it. Sorry, Chief. My wife snooping. Thought it was one of the kids. His name is Arthur Stevens. His background check was good. Didn't show any legal issues. Seemed stable. Has he done something?"

Sarah knew Samuel or Joyce would immediately call a former neighbor. She did not want to send out any signals. "We were just responding to a reported incident in the neighborhood. We saw that you lived in San Antonio but thought you might be in town ... in your house on Meadow Lane."

"No. Not there. Getting ready for some golf with Joyce and some friends. Maybe Mr. Stevens can tell you something."

"Do you have his phone number or where he works?"

"It might have been in the background check, but I'm not sure where we put that. As long as the monthly check shows up, we don't worry about it."

"Understood. Enjoy your golf."

Sarah performed a search for Arthur Stevens. She found eight in the State. Most were older than Spencer Sheffield could pretend to be. Only one had a Devaney address. 4376 Meadow Lane. Her heart rate quickened. Computer searches could be as exciting as physical searches. Discovery was always exciting, regardless of method. She pursued the name. She found DMV records for most of them. No driver's license for the one in Devaney, but there was a vehicle registration. A late model, Silver Sky Metallic Toyota Tundra. She called Dispatch to update the BOLO with the alias. She then called Boston to give him the information. The dragnet was tightening. She could feel it. This was not predator versus prey; this was predator versus predator.

Corporal Canton knocked on Sarah's office door. "Excuse me, Chief. Lieutenant McCluskey told me to bring this to you." He held a folder in his hand.

"Come in, Brandon." Sarah recognized the folder as one normally used for MVARs. "Is Lieutenant McCluskey back from the funeral home?"

"No. She's still there." The Corporal added apologetically, "I forgot she was there and called her. It's my preliminary report on the Tuesday morning fatality."

"The Lieutenant hasn't signed-off on it yet?"

"She said she would double-check me later, but she said you might want to see it since the Press is always hunting for something. It's pretty cut and dried. The EDR verified the physical findings, starting with the severe loss of control when the right front tire dropped into a pothole and lost air pressure. That indicates a blowout at a high speed. He was driving fifteen over. It's forty-five through there."

Sarah studied the report. She needed to look at past MVARs. When she was a Detective, she only had reason to investigate Mayor Clairmont's accident because Chief Keck suspected foul play. There was none, but she learned a lot about TA investigations, stuff that was routine to Lieutenant McCuskey and Corporal Brandon Canton. "Corporal, can you provide a list of TAs caused by hazardous road conditions, other than weather?"

"Cause or contributing?"

Sarah pondered the Corporal's question a moment. "Both. Anything that can prove unkept streets cause accidents."

"Of course they do. Is someone doubting it?"

"Not really, but Street Department Supervisor Farmer needs all that data we can provide. How much effort will it be to put that list together?"

Corporal Canton grinned. "Easy. It's all in the Department's data base. Maybe half an hour. Do you want me to bring it to you?"

"If you can have it hand delivered to Jake Farmer, that's what I really want. And, Brandon, only Taylor needs to know."

"Understood." Brandon grinned wider. "Maybe we can get some of these potholes filled."

Sarah paused as she handed the folder with the MVAR to the Corporal. "Also, could you give him a few photos like this one?" She pointed to a picture of the wrecked vehicle with the driver still in it.

"You bet. High impact statement. Gotcha, Chief."

Sarah called Jake to let him know what was coming to him. They both had to win the battle. Dead people could be an asset in the budget battle, especially for the Street Department.

"Thanks, Chief." Jake was excited. "I'm going to hit her hard with the damaged tires too. Those things are a hazard to the environment when they're scrapped."

"Good point."

Taylor McCluskey returned from the funeral home with schedule for Officer John Wyatt's service. "The family will be at the funeral home for visitation 1:00 to 4:00 Saturday afternoon. The funeral will be at the

United Methodist Church starting at 10:00 Monday morning. Burial will be in the Oak Grove Cemetery in Bourbon County."

"That's a long drive. Is that where John was from?"

"His grandparents are buried there. Apparently, the family owns a large lot there."

Sarah nodded understanding. "I'll set up escorts and coordinate with Henry Mason. Thank you. How is Celia holding up?"

"She's not. Did you know she was pregnant?"

"What?" Sarah felt her jaw drop. "No. How far along?"

"Eight weeks. They found out Monday."

"Did John mention it to anyone?"

"Not that I've heard. I'm sure his partner would have already said something if he knew."

"Lord have mercy! She's carrying a heavy load." Sarah felt a lump growing in her chest and throat. If crying would help, she would let loose. "I know the people in the Department will do everything to help her through this ... if someone can ever get through the loss of a husband and the father of her children."

Sarah was heartbroken but she called Tony Kendall. She still had a job to do. She had no time for heartache. "Hello, Tony. This is Sarah. How is your new job shaping up?"

"Hello, Sarah. Not as tough as yours, I'm sure. The Department is struggling to recover from a long-running conflict between the former Chief and the Mayor. Actually, two Chiefs. How are things going in Devaney?"

"Sounds like a contagion among small city PDs. Budget battles and meddling Mayor. I have the information on John's funeral."

"How's Celia and the kids? I've called the house, but I don't get much from her father."

"She's struggling. The whole family is struggling. They found out she was pregnant on Monday."

"My God!" Chief Kendall was stunned into silence for several seconds. "Is there anything I can do?"

"I'm not sure what anyone can do to help Celia, but I thought I would give you the memorial information. Visitation is planned for 1:00

to 4:00 Saturday at Mason's Funeral Home. Funeral service will be at the United Methodist Church here in Devaney at 10:00 Monday. Interment will be at Oak Grove Cemetery near Fort Scott, timing dependent on transit time."

Tony was silent as he wrote and digested the information. "Wow! That's a long drive for a funeral procession." He paused for a moment, then continued. "If you want, I can loan some units to cover Devaney so your people can attend the funeral and escort John to Fort Scott."

"I was hoping you would say that. Let me know how many you can bring. Other towns have put their name in to help." Sarah exhaled heavily. "I appreciate your help Tony."

"Anytime Sarah. I assume intersection control will not be an issue."

"It shouldn't be. We'll have enough units with lights to control traffic as we roll."

"I bet. Have you caught the killer yet?"

"Not yet. We know who. We just don't know where. But the net is tightening. I'd like to have him locked up before the funeral. We all need the closure."

"We've been on the look-out over here. No telling where someone like that will run."

"That's true. We're not sure he has run far. Hiding under an alias … and a rock. He's a State Senator's son."

"Really? A Senator's son? What does the Senator have to say on the matter? Defending his son publicly?"

Sarah thought about the question. "Oddly enough, I've not heard any public comments from him on the subject."

"You'd think he'd be using his political clout to create doubt at the very least."

Sarah's brow wrinkled at the comment. She simply replied, "You'd think."

Boston returned to the Station before three o'clock. He checked in with Sarah as soon as he came into the office area. "Boss, I handed some prints and items that may have DNA to Alicia. She said she can process them quicker than sending them to the State Lab where they would go into the queue."

"I have faith in Alicia. It would be nice if we could get some of those portable fingerprint scanners." Sarah mused aloud. She made a note on a Post-It pad. "I think I'll put one or two in the budget. If we had one of those, we could have checked Winston easier."

"Yeah. We had a few in Baltimore. I didn't have one – undercover. The crime scene guys used them on DBs to get a quick ID, if they were in the system."

Sarah nodded. "I don't think they are that expensive. They could save money by getting answers quicker. Less legwork and hours spent. What did you find? Any drugs?"

"Scout hit on something, but we couldn't find anything. We swabbed the area."

"You did follow protocol, didn't you?" Sarah asked, ashamed that she did not ask that question first.

"Of course. I'm not going into a potential drug scene without PPE. These stupid wannabe pharmacists don't have a clue about the dangers. Corporal Reeves said Scout was reacting to trace. Nothing big."

"He didn't keep drugs there?"

"I doubt it. Just enough for friends or personal use. We didn't find paraphernalia. It wasn't his drug house. We didn't find enough trace to check against the Angel Dust we found on Winston."

"I guess we keep digging. Make sure we're right. This could blow up in our face if we don't. A Senator's son is a hot commodity."

"Are you having doubts?" Boston asked sincerely.

"No. Not at all. I just want to make sure we're right. I don't want to leave any wiggle room for a shady lawyer. And I want to make sure we do the arrest right. Oh. I have something I want investigated, but it has to be kept quiet."

"You know I will keep it quiet, but …"

"But I don't want it to interfere with the manhunt. If Taylor can provide assistance personally or provide someone who we can trust to keep it quiet …"

"Now I'm curious. What do you need investigated?"

Sarah handed Boston a Post-It note with a sentence on it. "Read it. Burn it the next time you smoke a cigarette. Destroy it and any evidence of it. I don't even trust a shredder."

"Wow! I quit smoking, but you don't know how much pleasure this gives me. Is it for real?"

"Only a hunch. If I thought I could do it quietly, I wouldn't have dumped it on you."

"No problem, Boss. My pleasure." Boston left for the Situation Room and the all-important white board.

# CHAPTER 22

## Thursday 8:00 P.M.

Sarah's exhaustion was intensifying. She would not be able to rest until Spencer Sheffield was behind bars. And she wanted him behind bars, nothing more. She worried for the safety of her officers and her city while Spencer Sheffield was on the loose. A man who would brazenly kill a cop was either a sociopath or a psychopath. Regardless of what the professional evaluation might be, he was a danger to society. She also worried about Spencer's safety. She was not worried that he would get treatment he did not deserve; she was worried that he would get treatment he *did* deserve. She saw the lust for payback in the faces of every law enforcement officer she encountered prior to Winston Baines' arrest. That lust was back. She felt it in herself.

Sarah had seen the satisfaction, the overwhelming sense of relief on those same faces when Winston was captured. Now that it was clear that Winston was not the killer - the Mayor's suggestions aside - she saw overwhelmingly angry resolve in the faces of Devaney police officers, stronger than before the arrest. They wanted closure. They wanted vengeance. She was not sure she could contain them. She was sure Bill Keck would have no doubts about how to handle the situation.

Sarah wanted to flop across her bed and crash into a deep sleep. She accepted the fact that simply lying supine with her eyes shut would be better than nothing. She was skipping meals and skipping her exercise routine because of work, but she was not intentionally skipping sleep. Her mind was working too hard for her to sleep. Simply relaxing to decompress was not even an option. She poured a partial glass of Merlot, the last of the bottle she opened days earlier. She prepared the last of her garlic and herb cheese. It was not much for a meal, but she was more tired than hungry.

The day was not a total loss. Boston had a good lead on John's killer. She had a better understanding of the budget process. She had support on the City Council. Keith was making progress understanding Terrance Overton, Senior's death. But she still had Jordon Kamen. The day was not steeped in victory either.

Sarah pushed up from the dining chair and removed her jacket so she could remove her shoulder holster and service weapon. She seldom wore her waist holster and the larger pistol it carried. She did not need it in her role as Chief. She unlaced and kicked off her shoes after she placed her weapon inside her bedroom gun safe. She removed her shirt and pants. She placed them and her jacket inside her dry-cleaning bag. She then removed her socks and bra. She tossed those into a laundry hamper. She donned her PJs and returned to the living room. She had time to sit and calm before bedtime. Calm meant finishing her glass of wine and cheese snack while she mentally recapped the day's events. It did not mean relax. Her mind was too busy to allow her body to relax.

As good as Sarah felt about the budget presentation, she could not allow herself to bask in the warm glow that confidence brings. Jim Sloan's and Chase Mendelson's suggestions and words of encouragement elated her at the time they offered them, but additional time allowed doubts to grow. She still had to convince at least four more Councilmembers to support her budget requests to offset the Mayor's influence, and she was not sure she could do that. Bill Keck would not have those doubts.

Sarah considered the Mayor's assertions that Winston Baines was the murderer of John Wyatt. In her mind, her commonsense screamed the Mayor was wrong. She was positively sure the Mayor's reason for the assertions were nothing more than to garner public support for removing her as Chief of Police. The Mayor was a political person with an agenda. Jordon Kamen would allow nothing to stand between her and her goals. Not a bad characteristic, but the Mayor was vicious rather than tenacious. Winston was not a killer. Of that Sarah was sure. Glasgow could not prove otherwise.

Sarah worried about Celia and her plight. A pregnant widow with two tiny children. Finances would not be her problem. Emotional support would be. Even with the support of Devaney PD personnel, nothing could – or would – replace the love and support of her husband. Sarah wished there was something she could do or say that would make it better. Nothing came to mind.

Terrance Overton's death plagued her mind. It should not be a bother, but it was. Keith found evidence that supported Junior's assertion his father did not die of a natural heart attack. But that same evidence supported the possibility Terrance Senior was using homeopathic treatments for arthritis that came with inherent risks. That case promised to prove to be a red herring during her time of crisis. She did not need the distraction. She needed to pull her mind away from Terrance Overton's heart attack and focus on Spencer Sheffield's capture.

Spencer Sheffield in custody would settle her mind, allow her mind to rest. Sarah brushed her teeth and crawled into bed to continue thinking and to hope for sleep.

*A man with a smudged face grimaced as he swung a long rifle like a baseball bat. Blood was splattered on his leather jacket. Sweat poured from beneath an animal fur cap. Something swished side to side with every blow he delivered, with every spray of blood from each head he struck with his rifle's butt. He stopped and stared at Sarah. "Make sure you're right then go ahead." A loud noise ended him.*

Sarah sat upright in the bed. Her eyes were wide open. Her bedroom was bathed in a blue aura. For a moment, her staggered mind grasped for something real. Her cell phone rattled on the nightstand. The glowing blue numerals on her clock said 2:02. Her shaking hand reached for the phone. The ID indicated Devaney PD, the hardline. "Hello? This is Sarah."

"Good morning, Chief. Sorry to wake you." Sergeant Blanchard's voice cut through whatever fog remained in Sarah's mind. "Arthur Stevens' truck has been located."

Sarah's heart raced. "Where? Have they found Sheffield ... Stevens?" She corrected herself, even though she was sure the two were the same.

"It's in the Northwind Place Apartments parking lot. I've notified Lieutenant McCluskey and Detective Mankowitz. They said they want to establish a perimeter before they go door-to-door."

Sarah was already out of her PJs and in the process of dressing. Her Charcoal pantsuit and Royal Blue button blouse were already laid out for wear. She knew she would not be coming back to her apartment. Her day was planned by the wake-up call from Sergeant Blanchard. "Have you contacted the Sheriff's Office for back-up?"

"Yes, Ma'am. And the Highway Patrol. Units are enroute," the Sergeant paused, then added, "running dark and silent. We don't want to give him a chance to escape before we establish the perimeter."

"Good. I'll be on my way to Northwind in a few minutes." Sarah felt a rush of excitement. She suppressed it as well as she could. It was not over until Spencer Sheffield, or whatever he called himself, was in shackles. The words returned, *"Make sure you're right ..."* They helped center her thoughts as she locked her apartment door behind her.

Boston and Sergeant Blanchard were setting up the Mobile Command Center a block from the apartment complex when Sarah arrived. The complex consisted of four two-story buildings in a long row. Each building contained twenty apartments. The parking lot wrapped the entire complex with an inner row and an outer row of parking spots. According to the discovering police officers, Arthur Stevens' Tundra was parked on the inner row, almost dead center of the four buildings. Not hidden, but easily disguised by the number of vehicles parked closest to the apartments. The perimeter was larger than ideal. "What's the situation?" Sarah asked.

Boston nodded toward Sergeant Blanchard. "Blanchard did a good job assigning positions as soon as he got the word. Fortunately, it's Thursday night. Not a busy night for traffic. Easy to contain and watch."

"How soon do you expect to begin the sweep?"

"Taylor is calling in as many off-duty uniforms as she can muster. Faraday is arranging for SWAT and Deputies. The Highway patrol has both local units on hand. Six more coming."

"Are we waiting for them?"

"Not really, but they should be here within an hour. It'll take us that long to get everything else set." Boston forced a grin. "We want to make sure we get this right."

Visibility of the complex was poor from the MCC. The site was chosen intentionally to avoid detection from the apartments and to avoid putting Command in the line of fire. Sarah assisted establishing communications with everyone around the perimeter and doling out assignments as new officers arrived. She could not ... would not ... simply watch.

Zoey called. Sarah's blood immediately rose to a boil. Before she answered, she asked Boston, "Is Glasgow aware?"

Boston scowled at the mention of the Lieutenant's name. "I didn't tell him. Why?"

"The Mayor may know about this."

"Well, she didn't get it from me."

Sarah answered her phone, "Yes, Zoey."

Zoey's sleeping voice muttered, "The Mayor wants you to call her."

Sarah dialed the Mayor's cell number. The Mayor was ready for her.

"What do you think you are doing?"

"I was sleeping. Why?" Sarah was not going to give the Mayor the satisfaction of a simple answer.

"That's not what I hear."

"What do you hear, Mayor? And from whom?"

"It doesn't matter who tells me what I hear. Why are you arresting Spencer Sheffield without notifying me first?"

"Mayor, I think we've had this conversation before. There are a lot of things I do without notifying you first."

"Apparently too many things. Lieutenant Glasgow should be there shortly. Bring him up to date as soon as he does."

"I'm sure Boston will tell the Lieutenant all he needs to know. Mayor, I have a job to do." Sarah ended the call and shook her head as Boston and Sergeant Blanchard watched, both shaking their heads in disbelief.

"I'm not telling that rat anything," Boston said angrily. The Mayor was too loud to not be heard.

"Just the essentials. Found the truck. Searching apartments. End of discussion. Do we have a master key for apartments with no response?"

"Believe it or not, we do. Sergeant Blanchard's brother-in-law is the apartment manager."

Lieutenant Glasgow appeared from the darkness surrounding the subdued lighting of the MCC. He greeted Sarah and began following her but kept quiet and avoided Boston. Sarah acknowledged him and tossed out a brief overview of the situation. He disappeared for a few minutes. Sarah knew it was to call the Mayor with an update. She got a small amount of satisfaction knowing the Mayor's sleep was disrupted. She still did not know how the Mayor knew about the pending raid on the apartments.

Channel 6 news van arrived, led by a small car with Channel 6 logos on the sides, top, hood and truck. Kyren exited the car and immediately began barking orders to a crew that required no instructions. Kyren tried to approach the MCC but was turned away by a uniformed officer. She shouted for Sarah's attention and the officer cautioned her to keep her voice down. The MCC was close enough, and the night was quiet enough, for the sounds to be heard.

"How soon?" Sarah asked Boston.

"Maybe ten."

"Let me give Channel 6 a sound bite and a caution to not broadcast until the operation is over." Sarah walked to the eagerly awaiting Kyren Bailey. She wondered if the news reporter simply wore a pull over mask. The young blonde-haired woman always looked the same, except for the clothes. The clothes changed with the seasons. The camera lights hit Sarah in the face. She did not wear a lot of makeup. She randomly wondered if she looked as tired as she felt.

"Chief, are you arresting Spencer Sheffield at this time?"

"Kyren, before I answer any of your questions, I need you to understand that this is an ongoing operation. I request that you not broadcast any part of it before the operation is complete."

"The citizens of Devaney have the right to know what their police department is doing," Kyren retorted.

"Indeed, they do, but if the object of our operation is forewarned by your report, you will be charged with obstruction of justice."

Kyren looked amazed. "That's a reach, isn't it, Chief?"

"Not for a judge, if it results in the failure of the operation."

"I assure you this will not be broadcast until the 5:00 A.M. news. No one is awake for news bulletins anyway."

"Can we agree on that?" Sarah asked pointedly.

"Yes. Now, is the subject of this operation Spencer Sheffield? Are you about to make an arrest?"

"All I can say for sure is that we have located the vehicle registered to Arthur Stevens, a suspected alias of Spencer Sheffield. We won't know for sure until we have him custody. If he is in the area, we will find him."

"You only *think* it's Spencer Sheffield? Are you saying you don't know if Spencer Sheffield is in the area?"

"Our investigation indicates that Arthur Stevens *is* Spencer Sheffield. The proof will be when we take Arthur Stevens into custody." Sarah knew her explanation was weak to an outside observer. She could not communicate her gut feel as evidence.

"Where is he exactly?"

"In the area."

"We've heard he is in the Northwind Place Apartments. Is that true?"

"All we know for sure is that he may be in the area."

"So, you don't know if it is Spencer Sheffield or if he is actually here?" Kyren could not hide her suspicion and disappointment.

"I don't. That is why I'm asking you to hold the broadcast until we complete the operation. It could be nothing." Sarah hoped that would take the wind out of the reporter's sails. She noted that no other reporters were on the scene. Kyren had a source. She was sure of it. She walked away, looking to see if Glasgow was still shadowing her. He was.

As soon as she was out of sight of Kyren's crew, Sarah turned to Lieutenant Glasgow and pushed close to his face, "Lieutenant, I don't know what your game is, but if I find out that you tipped the Press, I will have your badge. If you think the Mayor can protect you, you are wrong. Do you understand me?"

Melvin Glasgow blanched, visible in the glow of the streetlights. He drew back and answered, "Yes Ma'am."

"Chief, we're a go. Any reason not to?" Boston asked as he glowered at Glasgow's retreating back.

"Give the order," Sarah replied.

Sarah and Boston listened to the action from within the MCC. Every radio call and comment was captured by the van's recorders. Some of the body cameras were live feed. Those that were showed orderly, polite, 3:30 A.M. interactions between the police and sleepy, frightened renters. A few were resistant to sweeps of their apartments, but in all, no one physically resisted. Within less than an hour, every apartment was searched. The maintenance rooms and equipment sheds revealed nothing out of the ordinary. Spencer Sheffield, AKA, Arthur Stevens, was nowhere to be found in the complex.

"How many houses within easy walking distance of the parking lot?" Sarah asked.

Boston glanced at a detailed map of the area. "Looks like ten or fifteen, depending on what you call easy. The area is mostly stand-alone shops and strip malls."

"Search the houses. Maybe he's being cagey."

"Wouldn't put it past him." Boston called Lieutenant McCluskey over the radio and instructed her to route searchers to nearby homes within the established perimeter. Then it was wait and see.

Shortly after 5:00, the searchers reported nothing found. The adrenaline rush associated with the possibility of success faded and the tiredness returned. Sarah was dejected. The manhunt was still in effect. Lieutenant McCuskey and Sergeant Blanchard returned to the MCC.

"Are we through here?" Blanchard asked Boston, his eyes including Sarah.

Boston glanced toward Sarah. Sarah took the hint and responded. "I think so. You can take the box back to the compound. Tell everyone to keep their chins up. We'll catch him. I'll see them back at the station later. Tow the truck to impound. If Arthur Stevens is legit, he'll report it stolen."

Detective Faraday arrived at the MCC as Sarah was talking. "Are we through for the day?"

Sarah replied, "We can stand down but don't go too far. I have a feeling this day is not over. We need to talk to the State Troopers. They may need to rotate out, especially the ones who aren't local."

Faraday nodded.

Boston said, "Before we release everyone, I'd like to search all the shops around here. He might have a connection. He could be hiding in one of them."

"Okay," Sarah approved. "Taylor, can you give him some support?"

"Absolutely. We'll keep the MCC operational while we do it," Taylor's words were directed toward Sergeant Blanchard.

One of the Highway Patrol officers approached the group. "Has anyone talked to the Press? They grabbed me as I walked by. I told them

I was not in charge. That blonde was upset. Said the station was waiting for her report."

Sarah's cell phone rattled in her pocket. She glanced at it. Zoey. "I'll go talk to them." She ignored three more calls until she finished her statement to the reporters.

"We have finished our search. Apparently, Mr. Stevens has left the area. We found no evidence of him in the apartments or the surrounding houses."

Kyren was visibly irritated. "You keep insisting that Spencer Sheffield is a suspect. The Mayor seems satisfied that Winston Baines is the murderer."

"I believe the Mayor wants that to be the case. She, like all of us, would like to see the murderer brought to justice. It would be nice to rest at ease on this. But the evidence does not support the easy answer. Whether she is correct or not will be determined when we interview Mr. Sheffield."

"Will Spencer Sheffield be interviewed, or will he meet his demise during his arrest?" Bernie asked the question without emotion.

"Despite the rhetoric, we only want to talk to Mr. Sheffield. If he will walk into the station and provide proof of his innocence, I will welcome that."

"Who is Arthur Stevens?" Kyren asked.

Sarah looked squarely into Kyren's camera, "I'm sure we covered that. Arthur Stevens is an alias connected to Spencer Sheffield. That is all I have at the moment. It has been a grueling night and I have other duties." She walked to the MCC.

Lieutenant Glasgow caught her attention. "What is it, Melvin?"

Glasgow cleared his throat, "The Mayor needs you to call her."

"Of course, she does. She has so much to offer in this time of crisis." Sarah did not mean to be flippant, but she could not help herself.

"Yes, Mayor. I'm avoiding you. It's been rather busy out here," Sarah said before Mayor Kamen could say anything.

"Busy doing nothing. I'm actually glad you waited. That gave me time to see the live report. Nothing. A total waste of time and resources. You have the killer in your jail, but you keep spending money as if the taxpayers don't care. I want a full report of the cost of this fiasco. On my desk before noon! And, by the way, you do not threaten Lieutenant Glasgow ever again. Is that understood?"

"Then keep him away from my operations. We are doing real police work here. And the costs associated with this operation will be in my usual monthly report."

"I think it is time for your performance review," the Mayor snapped.

Sarah ended the call.

# CHAPTER 23

## Friday 7:30 A.M.

The search of the shops and strip malls was slow going. Precursory searches for signs of break-in yielded nothing. Old signs of jimmied doors and windows were there, but they also showed indication of repairs or added security. Some shops were vacant. Some shops did not open until 10:00. The owners or managers of the individual storefronts were not easy to locate and contact. Those that were contacted promised to be there as soon as possible. And it started raining. Not hard at first. It began as a steady rain that quickly filled all the potholes in all the poorly constructed parking lots and weather damaged city streets. Then the skies opened. Rather than wait for the search, Sarah went to the station. She wanted to meet with the oncoming officers and Sergeant Casey Spader.

Casey was Sergeant Honeycutt's daytime counterpart on the Command Desk. She was a seasoned veteran with about the same time in grade as Sergeant Blanchard. She welcomed Sarah into the squad room as day officers gathered for their updates. The grapevine had them all talking about the ongoing search for Spencer Sheffield. Some heard Kyren's "Breaking News" report as they prepared for work. All were eager to get out in the field, especially the patrol units who could excusably go to the search area.

Sarah greeted the officers with as much of a smile as she could muster. She saw the expectations in their eyes. "As most of you have heard, and as I answered some of your questions before the meeting, we found a vehicle we believe to be Spencer Sheffield's pickup at Northwind Place Apartments. This is the vehicle registered under the alias Arthur Stevens. A thorough search of the apartments and surrounding houses revealed nothing. Currently, all the shops and strip malls within reasonable walking distance are being searched."

"Is there evidence that he is in any of those?" asked a corporal.

"To be honest, no. We are operating on the assumption that he parked the truck in a reasonably unnoticeable location and walked to wherever he intended to go. He likely tried to hide it in plain sight."

"That's a broad assumption, isn't it, Chief? What if he has an accomplice who gave him a ride from there?"

"It is a broad assumption – among several possible assumptions, to say the least. Our first assumption is that he is still in the area, and he may have become aware of our apartment search and slipped away unnoticed. But there is a chance we can still find him … or a clue. Of course, if he did have an accomplice, it will be wasted effort. I would rather search than assume he's gone and not search."

"That makes sense. How about CIs? Are they talking?"

"Nothing of value yet. I'm eager to hear from your CIs," Sarah challenged. "I know you want to get out there and help. If you have a CI, ask. If you think of anything, let Sergeant Spader know. If your beat allows it, assist in the search. But most of all, don't forget to guard the bank."

Boston updated Sarah on the search status. It was after 8:00 o'clock and only half the storefronts were searched. As strong as the desire to capture Spencer was, everyone in the search knew protecting the public was crucial to success. That meant no unnecessary damage to personal property. They would not break down doors unless there was an unimpeachable need. The rain made the search more difficult by obscuring outside visibility beyond a few yards. The loud thunder kept the searchers on edge as they listened for unusual sounds.

Sarah walked to the bullpen coffee pot for a refill. Only 8:45 and she was feeling the pressure to bring John's murderer to justice. The pressure was internal. The only pressure from her boss, the Mayor, was to cease the search for Spencer Sheffield and pursue charges against Winston Baines.

Glasgow was staying close. He was in the Situation Room staring at the whiteboard. One would almost think he was trying to solve the case. Under different circumstance, Sarah probably would have given him the benefit of the doubt, except she knew better. He was there because the Mayor wanted him to find an evidential link to place the murder weapon in Winston Baines' hand. Her cell phone rattled. Boston.

"Do you have something, Boston?" Sarah's anxiety strained her voice.

"We have someone cornered in a storeroom."

"Is it Spencer?"

"The Deputies who saw him says it could be him. Same height and build, but they only got a glimpse when the team started searching a clothing shop in one of the strip malls. I'm headed that way now."

"Don't do anything until I get there. Keep him contained." Sarah notified Liz that she was leaving the station.

Sarah wasted no time traveling to the location Boston gave her. The wet streets and heavy rain made driving hazardous. The rainwater hid the potholes. Every hole she hit jarred her spine. Standing water became a curtain of water on her windshield when she drove through it. Boston had moved the MCC closer to the search zone, a strip mall with a variety of eclectic clothing outlets. Boston was waiting for her, his clothes dampened by the rain.

Boston pointed toward a darkened storefront in the mall. "SWAT is in position. The search team has pulled back. We're waiting for your GO." He spoke louder than necessary. The falling rain filled the air with a wall of sound and muffled words. A clap of thunder caused them to flinch.

Sarah was better prepared for the weather. She had a raincoat with a hood. She offered Boston an umbrella from her car. He gratefully accepted.

"What is the situation? Are civilians clear?"

"Yes. All clear. We haven't allowed anyone inside the shops. When managers came to open, we borrowed their keys and searched their shops."

"Where are they now?"

"We told them to wait in the apartment parking lot for an *all clear*. The shop he's in is the last one to search. If it's not him, we're out of options."

Sarah evaluated what Boston told her for moment. "Okay. Let's move closer so we can see this. Everything on the up and up. I want him with the least damage possible."

"Of course," Boston replied. He then scowled and glared behind Sarah. "Did you call them?"

Sarah turned to see the Channel 6 News van and Kyren's company car come to a stop. The crew lept from the van and began retrieving equipment, carefully protecting it from the rain. The lightning flashed. The heavy cloud cover caused the streetlights to remain on even after sunup. The flash caused some of them to go off. "I thought they were still here."

"No. They left when the heavy rain started."

"Well, she got her early scoop. That sealed the story as hers. Did you call anyone else, someone who might tip off the Press?"

"Not me. You know better than that." Boston stopped and glared another direction. "Did you tell him?" Glasgow approached, generally unmindful of the conversation because he was focused on avoiding puddles of water on the asphalt.

"No," Sarah sighed, "but he was in the Sit Room when I went for coffee and you called. I told Liz where I was going."

"Snoop," Boston snorted.

Lieutenant McCuskey met the two of them, three if Glasgow lagging a few paces behind was counted, as they neared the storefront where four Sheriff's SWAT members stood at the ready. "Chief, we are just waiting for the GO."

"Is the back covered?"

"Yes. He's not going out the back without being seen. We've got eyes on the back door. The manager of the building says all of these shops have only two ways in and out. One front and one back."

"Okay. Do it." Sarah wanted to pounce, to rush along with the SWAT team. So did Boston and Taylor. They all knew protocol. Let the people with the skills and knowledge perfected by years of training do the job.

Shouts of "Clear!" came from inside the building, muted by the glass front and increased rainfall intensity. Silence replaced the shouts. Boston's radio barked. "No one here."

Boston looked confused and angry. "Are you sure?"

"Not a soul to be found anywhere in the store or in the storeroom."

"Back Team. Have you seen anything in the back?"

"No," came the reply.

Boston stood in stunned silence for a moment.

Sarah spoke into her radio. "Sergeant, is it clear for us to go inside out of the rain?" Her question was for the Deputy who led the SWAT.

"Clear. Come in."

Sarah, Boston, Taylor, and Detective Faraday entered the shop, careful to avoid the continually sweeping laser beams from the SWAT weapons. There was no intruder, but the Team was still vigilant. Every mannequin in the dress shop was inspected to make sure it was inanimate. Lieutenant Glasgow cautiously followed. "Where was he first sighted," Sarah asked of anyone who would answer.

"The initial search team said they saw him scamper from behind a rack in the back corner. The lights were off, like now, so they were using their search lights. They only got a glimpse." Taylor answered for the on-scene cadre.

Sarah looked around the semi-dark store, darker at the back away from the windows, which allowed intermittent lightning flashes to briefly illuminate the store with a strobe light effect. The lightning darkened streetlights under the heavy rain clouds meant there was only the dim light of a cloudy day to filter through the front window of the shop. "Does anyone have a flashlight I can borrow?" Taylor offered her flashlight to Sarah.

Even though Lieutenant McCuskey worked out of a cubicle in the bullpen, she wore a uniform. She was proud of it and wanted to be recognized as a police officer when she was on a scene. She wore her equipment belt every time she left the office area.

"Thank you, Taylor." Sarah slowly moved the light across the back of the store, paying particular attention to a rack near the storeroom entrance. She was looking for shadows. "Do you know where the Team was standing when they saw him?"

"No. I can call them in here. They are helping to watch the backside," Taylor replied. "The heavy rain and dead streetlights make it hard to cover the entire alley without additional officers."

"That makes sense. Call them in if there is enough coverage for the immediate area behind this store. It wasn't much darker then than it is now, right?" The question needed to be asked and answered.

"About the same," replied Taylor. She radioed for the team that first went inside the store.

The two Deputies involved responded quickly. "Can you show me where you were when he ran into the back room?" Sarah asked.

The Deputy who initially saw the suspect flee, stood in an aisle, and offered that as the spot. The second Deputy agreed that the position identified was within reason. Sarah stood in that area and played the flashlight across the back of the store as if she were searching. Shadows from the high-intensity light danced as the beam moved. She broke the silence that developed while she looked. "Could it have been a shadow from one of the mannequins?"

"No," the reporting Deputy replied indignantly. "I know what I saw. It was a moving person."

His partner quickly agreed. "It was a person. Not a shadow. Shadows don't have color. I can't swear it was our suspect, but I can swear it was a person."

"Good enough," Sarah said. She walked toward the storeroom. She looked at the SWAT Sergeant. "You're sure it's clear?"

The Sergeant growled, "I'd stake my life on it."

Sarah raised an eyebrow and replied, "It's *my* life you're staking on it." She stepped into the storeroom. It was dark. She slowly swept the area with Taylor's flashlight. The room appeared to be eight by ten with a single pedestrian door marked by a reflective EXIT sign. The room's ceiling was the same height as the store ceiling. No obvious secret hiding place above the drop ceiling. The walls were lined with shelving that contained boxes. The boxes were labeled as containing clothing items. The center of the room held a rack laden with factory garment bags filled with dresses and jackets.

After a careful search, Sarah turned off the flashlight, told the others to do the same, and asked, "Do you see what I'm seeing?"

"Light," exclaimed Taylor.

The SWAT Sergeant stepped toward shelving against the boundary wall that abutted the shop next door. "Looks like a doorway behind here." In the darkness, light filtered around a poorly aligned door reveal. The faint outline of light came from the shop next door, almost blocked by the boxes on the shelves. The bottom shelf was generally empty, especially in front of the doorway.

"I thought there were only two doors in and out," Sarah said sternly.

"That's what we were told," replied Boston.

"And I thought no one was in the other shops. Is there something you haven't told me?"

The SWAT Sergeant responded quickly, "There isn't. Some of the shops leave lights on in the storerooms. The owners with security systems usually enter through the back. It's closer to the keypads."

Sarah nodded. "Check it out, just in case."

"We've already ..." the Sergeant began.

"Humor me," Sarah cut him off. A moment of silence following her remark allowed the sound of heavy rain on the flat roof to fill the awkward tension. Deputies do not like taking orders from city police, even the Chief.

The Sergeant looked at Lieutenant Faraday who frowned a warning. "I'll need the key."

Boston handed the SWAT Leader a key. The team rattled out the front door.

Sarah opened the back door and peered out into the rain. Lightning flashed followed closely by a clap of thunder. The streetlights that provided poor lighting for the back alley flickered off again. It would be several minutes before their photocell switches reset if another lightning flash did not restart the process. Rain blew in her face. The storm seemed unending. The remaining officers assigned to watch the back of the strip mall were hunched against the wind.

"Careful," Taylor cautioned.

Briefly, a flash of light washed across the alley. Sarah's first instinct was to withdraw into the storeroom and close the door in reaction to lightning. Reality struck. She shined the flashlight toward a dark figure that had bolted from the mall and crossed the alley. The flashlight's bright beam was tempered by a flurry of raindrops that obscured visibility beyond a few feet in front of her. "There!" she shouted. "There!" She pointed her flashlight beam, vainly trying to focus it on what she was sure was a running person. "Do you see it?" she yelled in attempt to be heard by the officers watching the alley.

One of the officers looked her way then tried to follow the beam of light. He yelled, "Stop!" His hand pushed his rain gear aside to access his service weapon. A flash of lightning revealed the figure running toward a drainage ditch. The figure disappeared with a sharp report of thunder that followed the lightning.

Sarah ran outside, allowing the others to follow her into the alley. Lieutenant McCuskey grabbed her arm and commanded, "Stay! Let them get him."

Sarah scowled at Taylor but heeded her command. She was not wearing her vest. Not a wise move. She watched Boston and Detective Faraday rush the direction the two guarding officers ran. Sarah saw the SWAT emerge into the alley, again throwing the splash of light from the adjacent shop's back door into the rain, accompanied by the sound of the shop's activated alarm. The delay time passed without an input code. Their running feet splashed water with every step. The officer with weapon in hand reached the drainage ditch first.

And the rain stopped. Suddenly and unmistakable. The horizon showed a break in the clouds, too far away to offer light, but close enough to offer promise. The sound of beating raindrops was immediately replaced with the sound of water gushing from downspouts along the backside of the little shopping center. And the rush of water in the drainage ditch.

"Stop! Police!" shouted the first officer.

The sound of a gunshot was followed by angry voices as the SWAT and the cadre rushed into the now full ditch. Sarah watched the Team stumble against the rush of the water before they emerged on the other side. Ahead of them, a figure approached a 3-foot chain link fence that demarcated a home's backyard from a greenway between the strip mall and a row of houses. The runner placed his hands on the top rail and launched himself over the fence. His toe caught and he fell face first into a child's rain-filled wagon.

The SWAT closed the distance quickly. Before the runner could recover, two SWAT members were inside the fenced area with him. Sarah saw the man's hands moving, searching for something. She heard indistinct shouts from the Deputies as the entire SWAT crossed into the backyard, along with several other Deputies. The sounds of moving water drowned out their voices. A crowd of State Troopers and Devaney police officers converged on the fence but did not cross. A sharp command from the SWAT Sergeant was apparently ignored. Sarah was sure she saw a muzzle flash and heard the muffled sound of a gunshot. The suspect writhed on the wet ground and screamed in pain. The scream was clearer than the voices. The worst had happened. She dashed against the increasingly fast flow of water in the ditch and ran to the fence. A bullet from a SWAT assault weapon at close range would likely be lethal.

Sarah's heart pounded. Her mind raced faster than her water-filled shoes could carry her. She did not want a dead suspect. She was there, on the scene. Nothing, no words, could erase the fact that she was in charge, even if she were not the "scene commander." She was Chief of Police and Spencer Sheffield was the subject of her manhunt. "Stop!" she screamed in hopes of preventing a barrage of bullets.

Out of breath, Sarah pushed past the officers outside the fence, leaned across the top rail, and looked at the man on the ground. He was soaking wet. More than just the rain. He was muddy. Blood mixed with water and mud. His identity was obscured by the mixture. He was clutching his leg. "Who shot him?" Sarah demanded.

"I did," chuckled one of the SWAT members. "He was trying to pull this from his belt." He held up a pistol. "50 thousand volts changed his mind."

"He shot me!" screamed the runner. "He shot me!" His hands pressed against his thigh.

"Why does he think he's been shot?" Sarah asked, her voice shaking more than she wanted. "And where's the blood coming from?"

"He faceplanted on the wagon. Cut his face pretty bad. And, apparently, when his fingers twitched, he shot himself." The Deputy was still chuckling.

"It's not funny," screamed the runner. "I need an ambulance."

"How bad is it?" Sarah asked, finally regaining her composure.

"Looks like it grazed the inside of his thigh. He's lucky it didn't hit his femoral."

Another Deputy sneered, "Too bad it didn't hit his sack."

Sarah glared at the man for his insensitivity. She did not say anything to him. His eyes averted. He knew his adrenaline driven words were inappropriate.

A siren screamed toward the house. The Paramedics were on standby near the MCC. The easiest access was around the block to come in from the street. The ditch between the mall and the residential area was full.

"Bag the weapon," Sarah commanded. She said what was on her mind, even though the officers and deputies did not need to be told.

"Of course, Ma'am."

"What is it?"

"A street piece. .22," replied the SWAT Sergeant.

"Is it Sheffield … or a burglar?" Sarah needed confirmation.

"He has a credit card that says Arthur Stevens," replied the SWAT Sergeant. "Isn't that his alias?"

"Yes." Sarah watched as the Paramedics prepped Spencer Sheffield, aka Arthur Stevens, for transport. "Don't forget the shackles," she said before she turned to leave. Glasgow was standing at a distance, close enough to hear, watching with a cell phone to his ear.

Boston, who leaped the fence to be close to the suspect and collect evidence and personal effects, called to Sarah, "Chief, the Paramedic says the Press is set up on the sidewalk."

Sarah shook her head and turned toward the street. In the back of her mind, she thought that talking to the Press might allow enough time for the ditch to recede. The western sky was clearing. Maybe it would be a sunshiny day.

Kyren's camera crew was not yet ready. A first. As Sarah approached, she watched bemusedly while the eager reporter exhorted her crew to hurry. "Kyren," Sarah called to get the reporter's attention.

"Chief," Kyren said frantically, "can you wait until the camera is ready. They got wet, and …"

"Kyren," Sarah motioned with her hands to indicate her condition, "so did I. Can we meet at the station? I need to notify all outlets before I make an official statement."

Kyren was visibly upset. "We've been on this all night. We deserve the scoop."

Sarah relented. "Kyren, I'll give you a quick statement without footage so you can do a bulletin. Otherwise, you can wait like everyone else. We don't do these things to give you a scoop."

Kyren considered Sarah's words. "Okay. We can shoot some of the activity from here to go with your quote." She activated her phone recorder, "Okay. Give me your statement."

"As a result of a joint operation between local, county and state law enforcement, a suspect has been taken into custody. At this time, we believe the suspect is the object of our manhunt for Officer John Wyatt's murderer." Sarah turned and walked toward the strip mall, prepared to wade the ditch.

Zoey called. Sarah called Liz while she stood at the brink of the ditch and looked back toward the arrest scene. "Liz, it looks like we've caught our man. Set up a news conference in the lobby for 10:00. I'll be there after I get some dry clothes and shoes." She saw Glasgow observing the final activities as the Paramedics loaded Spencer into the back of the ambulance. The camera crew was taping everything they could see from the sidewalk.

Zoey called again. Sarah returned the call, then dialed the Mayor. Mayor Kamen was furious. Sarah expected it. "Hello Mayor. I've been busy, but I'm sure Melvin has kept you up to date."

"Sarah, you will stand accountable for shooting Senator Sheffield's son." The Mayor practically screamed into Sarah's ear.

"I'm not sure what your minion told you, Jordon, but we did not shoot anyone. He shot himself in the leg when he tried to pull his weapon." Sarah stared at the ditch. The water was receding rapidly, as rapidly as it had risen. Flash storms were not uncommon in that part of the country, especially early in the morning or late in the evening. If she waited a few minutes more, she would only have a simple wade in her still wet shoes. She heard Taylor and others sloshing across the green space toward her.

"I am Mayor Kamen to you!" the Mayor snapped angrily.

"And I am Chief James to you," Sarah replied. "Quit playing games. Why are you calling?"

"I have a witness to your brutal police tactics this time, Chief James. When I bring this before the Council, they will demand that I fire you."

"Mayor, I really don't care who you have as a witness. I have body camera footage that will refute any accusation you throw out. No shots were fired by law enforcement." Sarah recalled the sound of a gunshot early in the chase. She may have been mistaken. It could have been storm noise. Lieutenant McCuskey and Detective Faraday were on either side of her. "Mayor, if you care to hear the facts, I have a Press conference scheduled for ten in the station lobby. Until then, bye."

Sarah addressed the two cadre officers, "Lieutenant, Detective. I need a check of all service weapons. Who fired that shot when we first discovered the runner?"

Lieutenant Glasgow, lagging on a few paces back, overheard the question.

Sarah turned to check the water level before she stepped into the ditch. The roiled, muddy, opaque water from earlier was replaced by a slower, clearer, translucent stream. Something on the grassy bottom of the ditch caught her eye. She stepped into the ditch, bent, and reached for the object. With her fingertips, she lifted a 9-millimeter pistol by the barrel. She looked at Taylor and grinned. "I think I need an evidence bag. First, one of you glove up and clear the weapon. It's ready to fire."

# CHAPTER 24

## Friday, 10:00 A.M.

Sarah felt better. The warm water drained from her hair. The soft, cotton bath towel sopped the water droplets from her skin. The shower she missed earlier revived her now. That and the fact John Wyatt's murderer was in custody. She used her towel to remove as much water from her auburn hair as she could. The dryer would get the rest. She sat on the edge of her still unmade bed and rubbed body lotion onto her skin. For most people, the hours she had already logged would be considered a full day. But there were a lot more hours for her to log before she could call it a day.

Arthur Stevens was taken to the ER for treatment. The faceplant into the little red wagon left marks … and required a couple of stitches. His .22 caliber pistol left a mark. Sarah amusingly hoped the steel manacles did not leave *too* much of a mark. She knew the hospital would make his treatment a priority, but he still might not be booked into the jail by the time she cleaned and returned to the station.

Sarah's phone rattled. Zoey. A quick look at the call history indicated three missed calls from Zoey, one from Missy and one from Liz. She called Liz before she dried her hair. Liz told her the Mayor wanted her to call immediately. "If she calls again, tell her I'm in the shower."

The Channel 6 news van was parked in a visitor's spot in front of the police station. Kyren's little car was in the space next to it. From the number of vehicles in front of the station, Sarah was certain the Press was already prepared to hear her statement. She parked near the back entrance. No need to walk right into the lion's den. She was surprised that neither the Mayor's car nor Lieutenant Glasgow's car was in the parking lot. The Sheriff's car was there. Liz called while she was enroute to tell her the District Attorney was waiting to see her before the press conference.

Sergeant Reeves extended a cheerful greeting when Sarah walked through the door. She imagined spirits would be high. She was not disappointed.

"Is he here yet?" Sarah asked. She received a head shake and frown as an answer. "Don't worry. He will be, if not at County."

"Bars. That's all I care," replied Sergeant Reeves.

Sarah checked with Liz when she passed Liz's office. Liz handed her a folder attributed to Lieutenant McCuskey, who was home taking a shower. DA Dunn and Sheriff Herriman were milling around in the bullpen.

Cecil's cheerful face split wide with a grin when Sarah walked around the corner. "There's our hero. Congratulations, Chief." Cecil extended his hand.

Sarah blushed and shook his hand. "Don't congratulate me. Congratulate Boston, Faraday, McCuskey and all the field officers who did the work. I was just an observer."

The DA smiled professionally. "Never sell yourself short. You never know when you might want to run for office. Congratulation."

"Politics is not my forte. I trust you are here to lend credence to the case?" Sarah asked the DA.

"I *am* running for office," Charles Dunn replied with a grin.

"Me too," the Sheriff added with a laugh.

"I hope you are also ready to answer questions," Sarah said.

More seriously, the DA replied, "If necessary. I'm also here to represent the State and the County. We don't want this one to be lost by bad Press."

Sarah appreciated the DA's words, but she did not appreciate the insinuation. "I won't expose any weaknesses, if there are any."

Sarah led the two men down the stairs to the lobby. As always, Liz had the squad room podium ready. This time, she had it on a riser, so Sarah and the others were visible to everyone in the lobby. "Thank you for being here this morning. The men and women of several law enforcement agencies, the State Highway Patrol, County Sheriff, Devaney PD, and more nearby Police Departments than I can enumerate have been engaged in a manhunt led by Devaney Detective Mankowitz, Sheriff's Detective Faraday and State Police Captain Anderson. Their dogged efforts have resulted in the capture of the man suspected of murdering Devaney Police Officer John Wyatt.

"Shortly after 8:00 A.M. this morning, a man identified as Arthur Stevens, a known alias of Spencer Sheffield, was taken into custody with minimal resistance. As of this moment, the suspect has not been booked. He is receiving treatment for a self-inflicted gunshot wound to the leg. District Attorney Dunn has a statement." Sarah stepped aside for the DA.

Charles Dunn had the skills. The right facial expressions for every word, honed for maximum impact with his audience. "Ladies and Gentlemen of the Press, I appreciate that you are here to get the facts to report to the citizens of the City, the County and the State." He glanced toward Sarah and the Sheriff. "I want to extend my congratulations to Chief James and Sheriff Herriman for the safe culmination of an intense manhunt. Chief James' tenacity and persistence have made all our lives safer.

"The alleged murderer of Officer Wyatt will be booked into the city jail after he is released from the ER. As Chief James indicated, his injuries were self-inflicted as he struggled to resist arrest. Our law enforcement officers conducted themselves professionally to make this happen without serious consequences to the suspect or to themselves. I congratulate all officers involved for their dedication and professionalism.

"The suspect will be booked on suspicion of capital murder for the death of Officer John Wyatt. Unless legal objections are raised, I will prosecute the case. As the State's Prosecutor of the case, I prefer any legal questions be directed to or channeled through me. If the Chief or the Sheriff seem to be dodging your questions, it is because they have been instructed to leave matters of law to me. Chief." He nodded toward Sarah and smiled as he relinquished the podium.

Sarah stepped forward and nodded toward the DA. "What the District Attorney is saying is that law enforcement's job is essentially complete. The suspect's fate is in the hands of the Court from this point. Sheriff Herriman may have something to add."

Sheriff Herriman stepped forward. "I can't add much more at this time, but I want to congratulate Chief James for the job she has done on this case. Devaney should be proud of this woman." He beamed a smile in Sarah's direction. "She is doing the job as good as any man." He smiled at the camera as he stepped back.

Sarah hid her feelings about the Sheriff's cringeworthy comment. "Thank you, Sheriff. The support from your office, Detective Faraday, and the SWAT members, was instrumental in the success of this arrest. If you have questions, I will try to answer."

Kyren, as always, shouted first and loudest, "Do you have proof that this Arthur Stevens is really Spence Sheffield?"

Sarah nodded, "We have all the evidence necessary to prove the two names are for the same person."

"What evidence do you have?"

Sarah had no results from fingerprints yet, but she was sure she was right. "The suspect arrested was in possession of two weapons." The note Taylor left for her had two bits of information. "He possessed a .22 caliber pistol we believe was used in Officer Wyatt's murder, and he possessed Officer Wyatt's service weapon."

"You said you believe the pistol was used in the murder. Shouldn't you know that?"

"We are performing ballistics tests on the weapon now. That information will be available shortly."

"Are you saying the suspect had Officer Wyatt's service weapon on him when he was arrested?"

Sarah was suspicious of Kyren's question. The reporter was not in a position to see or know John's service weapon was found in the ditch. She slowly responded, "The suspect dropped the weapon when he fell into a flooded ditch during flight. The weapon was identified as Officer Wyatt's by the serial number."

"Are you sure he dropped it? I understand shots were fired during his flight, shots from a police weapon."

"Am I sure he dropped it? Absolutely. Regarding shots fired by police officers, that is totally false. No police weapons were discharged during the arrest or the flight leading up to the arrest." Sarah kept from glowering. The discovery of Officer Wyatt's service weapon was only witnessed by law enforcement personnel. Someone spoke out of turn. The defense would have that information to be used during the trial. It was not for public, pre-trial discussion.

"But my sources tell me that there was a shot fired and that it could have come from the weapon found, discarded by the officer who fired it."

"Were I you, I would get new sources. Next question." Sarah coldly dismissed Kyren.

"But ..."

"But ... let someone else ask a question. This is a press conference, not a Channel 6 symposium." Sarah was blunt. Other reporters chuckled gleefully. Their feelings toward the only local TV reporter were clear.

Bernie asked, "Mr. Dunn, are you satisfied the case against Mr. Stevens, or Sheffield, will result in conviction."

"Beyond a doubt. As Chief James has stated, we have irrefutable evidence to support conviction." The answer was partially a bluff. None of the evidence was fully vetted at that time. In his mind, the presser was premature for his office, though necessary for the police department.

Kyren pushed back to the front. "Are you satisfied that the arrest was executed in legal fashion? For example, the Chief's arrest of Councilman Elsea is tainted with the fact that he was not read his Miranda Rights when Chief James arrested him."

Sarah seethed. Someone fed the question to Kyren. She was reasonably sure that someone was not Clara Taylor, Joseph Elsea's attorney and counsel for the two teenaged witnesses against Spencer Sheffield. Someone else was trying to put doubt into the minds of potential jurors for Spencer Sheffield's trial.

The DA quickly answered. "I have no doubt the arrest was legal. Mr. Sheffield, aka Stevens, gave no statements to the police other than scream about the bullet wound he inflicted upon himself." He inhaled and leaned toward Kyren. "Insofar as the case of Councilman Elsea's arrest, I prefer to make no comments about a pending trial, but – to put this to rest in the public venue - I will note that all of Mr. Elsea's comments to the police were made prior to his arrest, a conversation between two acquaintances. The Supreme Court has ruled that confessions given without duress prior to arrest are admissible in court. Anything you have heard to the contrary is posturing by Counsel, and perfectly understandable for a defense attorney to do. The tactic does not lessen the charges or diminish the certainty of conviction."

"But my sources indicate the Defense Attorney can get the confession thrown out."

"As Chief James suggests, maybe you need new sources. Regardless of what is said pretrial, in the final analysis, the Judge will rule, and the Jury will decide – not the Defense Attorney or the Prosecutor."

Kyren was subdued during the remainder of the conference. When it was finished, the print and blog reporters left quickly to file their reports. Kyren lingered while her crew packed the cameras, lights, and microphones. Sarah excused herself from the DA and the Sheriff and walked to Kyren.

"Kyren, time for a question from me. Who is your source?"

"Confidential," Kyren responded dismissively.

"Confidential or compromised? I'm not sure who's playing you, but you are being played." Sarah turned to walk away from the blonde-haired woman.

"Chief. I'm on your side. I hope you know that," Kyren pleaded.

"You couldn't prove it by me. You are planting doubts to help the defense. You and I both know how the legal system works. If a good defense attorney can plant seeds of doubt, she can grow a garden of reasons for a confused jury to free her guilty client."

"My source isn't an attorney," Kyren offered.

Sarah nodded, "I know who it is, Kyren. Sometimes the game is not so much as to free the accused as it is to vilify the accuser."

# CHAPTER 25

Spencer Sheffield had no fingerprints on file. Arthur Stevens' fingerprints had no comparisons in the system. Regardless of the inability to identify Arthur Stevens as Spencer Sheffield, the prints on Officer Wyatt's service weapon and the physical possession of the .22 caliber pistol would prove the arrested suspect, Arthur Stevens, was the murderer. If Arthur Stevens was an alias, further investigations of his background would prove no such person exists. DNA, available from Arthur's ER visit, was ready to be compared to Sheffield familial DNA. Sarah signed the paperwork for a court order to gather DNA from a member of Senator Sheffield's family. Highway Patrol Captain Anderson was tracking down handwriting samples from both Arthur Stevens and Spencer Sheffield. Somewhere in the recordkeeping world was a sample of Spencer Sheffield's handwriting. It only had to be located for comparison. And there was always facial recognition software at the State Crime Lab. Those pictures were already faxed. A few extra steps, but in the end, the DA would go to trial with proof that Arthur Stevens and Spencer Sheffield were the same person.

Sarah's only worry was that the investigative process had to be unimpeachable. There was no doubt in her mind the murderer was inside her jail pending the arrival of an attorney. She oversaw the booking. She oversaw the incarceration. Yet - the physical similarities between Arthur Stevens and Winston Baines were disturbing. A quick glance, a meeting in the dark – one could be confused for the other by someone not well acquainted with either. Sarah also made sure no one asked any questions that could be misinterpreted as an interrogation. The only thing that did not make sense to her was the fact Arthur Stevens did not ask for a phone call. When offered an attorney appointed by the court, he simply stated, "My attorney will be here soon enough." Sarah had no doubt that was true.

Sarah's detective senses tingled when she saw, or suspected, inconsistencies. It made no sense that Spencer Sheffield openly identified himself to the teens and to Winston Baines. If he was going to commit a criminal act, it would make more sense to do so under an alias. Yet, Arthur Stevens appeared to be a model citizen, without access to or use of the Sheffield family name. The tangle was too tight to unravel. Her instinct told her to ignore it, but it nagged.

The booking process was rather quick. Glasgow arrived in Booking shortly after Boston and Detective Faraday arrived with the suspect. He tried to be anonymous, as much as the small area allowed. He said nothing. He nervously observed. Sarah saw Lieutenant Glasgow exit through the Booking entrance rather than follow her and Boston up the stairs. Whatever the reason for his presence, his mission was completed.

"Good job, Boston," Sarah said as they ascended the skid-proof, rubber tiled stairs. "You look like you could use some sleep."

Boston grinned. "Look who's talking. I've got some paperwork to do first. My boss is a taskmaster."

"Okay. Satisfy your boss' penchant for paper, then go get some rest."

"I will. What time does visitation start tomorrow?"

"It's from 1:00 to 4:00. That's a three-hour window."

Sarah slumped into her desk chair and looked at the pile of papers waiting in her Inbox. Another, smaller stack of manila folders were in the center of her desk. Liz considered those as critical. She decided to get a cup of coffee first. An aroma made her mouth water as she walked into the bullpen. She had not eaten anything since the partial glass of wine and the cheese before she crawled into bed, a bed she seemed to be ignoring of late. That and a single cup of coffee with a teaspoon of sugar after she showered.

Sarah said aloud in a teasing voice, "Okay. Who brought the tacos?"

Lieutenant McCuskey replied with her mouth full. "That would be me. Do you want one? I have plenty."

Sarah filled her coffee cup with coffee that was hot but not fresh before she walked to the Lieutenant' cubicle. "If you have plenty, I'll take one."

Taylor pushed a box with four soft tacos toward Sarah. "The six pack was on special. Same as the price of three. I thought I was that hungry, but after two, I think my eyes were bigger than my stomach." She laughed.

Sarah picked up one of the tacos and took a bite. She was not a fan of fast food, but her hunger did not require her to be a fan of anything. "Thank you, Taylor. I forgot I haven't eaten since I snacked last evening. Too much going on to think about food."

Taylor took another taco from the box and grinned. "Or sleep. But the excitement has my adrenaline pumping." She chewed a moment then said, "I can't tell you how good it felt to see that scum go down. Too bad it was a taser."

"By the book, Taylor. By the book. You know that better than anyone."

"Yeah, but sometimes ..." the Lieutenant took another bite. "But, according to the book, the Sergeants are finishing the officer debriefs and filing their reports. I guess it's not finished until the paperwork is done."

"True. Dot the I's and cross the T's. It's now in the Court's hands. We can't have anything coming back on us."

"Chief," Keith walked into the bullpen. "Do you have a minute?"

"Sure, Sergeant. What do you have?" Sarah hesitated to take another bite.

Taylor saw the hesitation. "Eat, Sarah. Whatever Keith has can wait until you eat something."

Keith nodded. "For sure. I'm in no hurry."

Taylor asked without offering the box, "Do you want one, Sergeant?"

"No, I ate before I came. Thank you, though. I'll wait in your office, Chief." The Department of Public Relations Sergeant felt Taylor's cold reception.

"I wonder what he has," Taylor asked, nosily suspicious.

Sarah replied between bites. "I gave him an assignment. It upset the Mayor, but he doesn't seem to worry about it."

"Be careful, Chief. You know not to trust that woman ... and he works for her."

"I know. Friends close. Enemies closer," Sarah said after she finished the taco. "Thank you, Taylor. That hit the spot. I'm good for another day or two." She chuckled.

"Another week like this one and you're going to have to get a new wardrobe." Taylor glanced at Sarah's hips with a mischievous grin and wink.

Sarah pulled her pants up and laughed. "The waist is a little bit looser."

Sarah stood in her doorway. "Senior?"

"Yes," Keith responded.

"Okay. I'll shut the door." Sarah sat in her chair and rolled it closer to the desk so she could lean on her elbows with her chin resting on the backs of her hands. "What do you have?"

"A lot, I think. When I upset Junior by talking to his mother, I did learn that Senior used an aconite salve on his shoulders and knees. Arthritis. I've learned a lot about aconite. It is used for several things in homeopathy, mostly arthritis pain. Sometimes it is used in a tincture for heart rate control and blood pressure control. It slows the heart."

"Do you think he overdosed on his salve?"

"Very unlikely unless he ate some of it. Even then, if it's prepared properly, he'd have to ingest a significant amount of salve to cause a heart attack."

"I think Alicia told me something along those lines."

"Did she tell you that consuming the leaves of the aconite plant is deadly?"

"She mentioned something about it and Wolf's Bane."

"She gave me a lot of information. Aconite goes by several names, but the name *aconite* doesn't have the baggage of some of the other names. People think of it as medicinal under the aconite name. Apparently, they only think it's poisonous under the other names." Keith opened a large, manila envelope he was clutching protectively and pulled a typed document from it. "Alicia got the results back from the State ME. The ME found chewed bits of aconite in his lungs."

"Lungs?"

"Aspiration. Not uncommon for heart attack patients who undergo resuscitation."

"I see." Sarah nodded. I remember you said the Coroner told you the hospital cleaned the vomit before they allowed the family to spend time with the body."

"There's no doubt he ingested some aconite. A small amount causes severely upset stomach and vomiting. A larger amount releases too much toxin for vomiting to clear it from the body. A heart attack can cause vomiting. No one noticed. Too much aconite toxin causes heart arrythmia. It's generally lethal. There's no specific antidote."

Sarah studied the lab results Keith handed her. "Did Mrs. Overton say how bad his arthritis was?"

"According to her, it was a nuisance. He complained a lot, but it didn't interfere with his life. He resorted to homeopathy because he didn't trust drugs."

Sarah twisted her mouth and shook her head. "I guess some people don't realize home remedies are drugs too."

"Natural. That seems to be the key in most people's minds. I didn't ask her if he had any aconite plants available. I did check a few homeopathic shops and on-line. Dried roots are available, along with a variety of tinctures, salves, and balms. You can buy aconite seeds to grow your own, but I didn't find any fresh plants that were readily available."

"What does aconite look like? Can it grow around here?"

"It can grow about anywhere temperate. You can find it on the Internet." Keith nodded toward Sarah's computer.

Sarah took the hint and did a quick search. She was surprised how much information filled her screen. "Wow! The blue ones are beautiful. I'd like a blouse that color," she said absently. "I suppose they would have to be in a large bed to really show their beauty, or used as undercover to fill open spots." She turned back to Keith. "Can you find out if the Overton's have big flowerbeds? Especially if they grow blue flowers. I'll clear it with Junior if you can go to the Overton house."

"Can do." Keith arose and started to leave. He turned back. "Thank you."

"For what?"

"For giving me a chance. I'm ready to do real police work."

Sarah smiled. "I'm glad to hear that. Tread carefully."

Keith nodded and left.

Sarah thought about what Keith had said. One more bit of information would determine whether there was a reason to assume homicide was the cause of death for Terrance Overton, Senior. Or if his death was the result of an accidental overdose of a sketchy homeopath. She hoped Keith could find the information without upsetting the Overtons. She did not want to hear anymore from the Mayor. She dialed Overton Junior's cell number. It rang several times before he answered.

"Hello, Chief James. I'm in the middle of my lunch. Is this important?"

"Hello, Mr. Overton. I wouldn't call if I didn't think it was important."

"What do you have?"

"We are finding some suspicious issues regarding your father's death. My detective needs to inspect the grounds of your parent's house. He will not interact with Mrs. Overton unless she initiates it."

Overton was silent for several seconds. "I'll call Mother and tell her to stay inside. If he rings the doorbell, ..."

"He won't, Mr. Overton. He's aware of your conditions. Thank you."

"Have you found out who murdered him?"

"We are still in the early stages."

Junior replied with sarcasm. "I know. I've heard all this before. You can't discuss an ongoing investigation."

"Something like that. I should have an answer within a day or two. Call me if you have questions."

"I will. Is that all you have?"

"Yes, for now. Thank you again, Mr. Overton." Sarah disconnected the call. As uncomfortable as that call was, she had another that needed to be made. She dialed the Mayor's number.

The Mayor did not answer immediately. She waited until it was one ring away from voicemail. "Chief, I am eating lunch."

"Must be nice. I grabbed a taco from Lieutenant McCuskey's taco pack. The first meal I've had in ... I can't remember when. I received several calls from Zoey. I assumed it was to call you. I've been extremely busy. I haven't had time to call until now."

"You had time to eat a taco," the Mayor retorted. "I called to tell you that your budget presentation needs to be ready for Tuesday's Council Meeting. We're going to get this behind us, so we can get to work on the city's business. The money tap will be shut off."

Sarah felt the taco roll in her stomach and push against the bottom of her throat. "Mayor, that is more than a month earlier than planned. Officer Wyatt's services will consume the weekend and Monday."

"Well, Chief, if you can't handle the job, maybe you should consider a different line of work."

Sarah allowed her good sense to control her tongue. She changed subjects. "Mayor, another thing. I have an update on Terrance Overton's death."

"The supposed murder? The Overtons demand too much of our city."

Sarah tried to make sense of the Mayor's reaction. Unable to do so, she continued. "Apparently, Mr. Overton's heart attack was caused by a toxin. Something he ate. I will know definitively within a day or two."

The Mayor's reaction was unexpected. "That's BS and you know it. You're dreaming this up to ingratiate yourself with the Overtons. Are you in their pocket? Never mind. I don't need you to answer. I am eating lunch. Bye!"

Sarah stared at her phone, totally shocked by the conversation.

# CHAPTER 26

Friday 6:00 P.M.

Liz protected Sarah the rest of the afternoon. No calls. No visitors. No interference while Sarah attended to the folders on her desk. One of those, the largest, was Liz's latest update on the PD budget proposal. Sarah gave it a lot of attention and made a few more changes for Liz to update.

Sarah did not go home early. After checking to see if Arthur Stevens' attorney called, she visited Celia Wyatt. She felt it was important for the Chief of Police to discuss the arrest with the family. Celia was still in shock. On the couch with her two children nestled against her while family members walked on eggshells. Celia's mother seemed to be the only one who could get through the bubble of grief that surrounded her daughter, and then only for minutes at a time. Because of her pregnancy, Celia's doctor was reluctant to prescribe strong medication to help her rest. The widow was in her own world.

Sarah ordered Chinese food delivered while enroute to her apartment. If she timed it exactly right, she would have time to change into shorts and a tee before the food arrived. She wanted to be barefoot.

A fresh bottle of Chardonnay breathed while she changed. The food arrived as planned. The evening promised to be good. Sarah set her glass of wine on the coffee table and turned-on the TV. She had nothing particular in mind. Drivel. Mind numbing drivel was all she sought. Something that required minimal thought while she ate her beef and broccoli with a side of lo mein noodles. The 6:00 P.M. news began almost as soon as she settled onto her couch.

The intro teaser was a brief recap of Arthur Steven's arrest and the assertion that the name was an alias used by Spencer Sheffield. Several pharmaceutical commercials interrupted by a local Ford dealership ad helped numb Sarah's mind while she ate and waited for the news broadcast to return. The wine tasted good even though a connoisseur would argue in favor of a red wine with the beef dish. She did not care about connoisseurs. She wanted what she wanted.

The Channel 6 news anchor read from his teleprompter, *"Senator Sheffield broke his silence today regarding Devaney Police Department's assertion that his son, Spencer, is the murderer of Devaney Police Officer John Wyatt."* The backdrop was a stock photo of Senator Sheffield. That evolved into a recorded "live" video of the Senator with captions. *"I am aware of the accusation against my son, but I can assure you he was at our family home in Wichita the night he was alleged to have murdered the police officer. As I understand it, the real murderer is in police custody, and has been for several days. I'm not sure if the Devaney Police Chief is engaged in a manhunt or a political witch hunt. Afterall, this is an election year."*

Sarah's appetite was gone. She stared at the TV as it droned on with more news. She did not hear, or see, any of it. In her mind, she recapped every detail of the murder, of the manhunt, of the Mayor's insistence that Winston Baines was the killer. The Mayor's insistence made no sense to Sarah, except to make Sarah appear incompetent as Police Chief. For the sake of the city, potential lawsuits non-withstanding, a competent police force is a necessity for attracting new people and businesses. Sarah was sure everything pointed to Spencer Sheffield, aka Arthur Stevens. The evidence was there – if the evidence was right. Before she left the office, Alicia assured Sarah the .22 pistol taken from Arthur Stevens was the same weapon that fired the slug into John Wyatt's head. The shot that killed him. The slug from Arthur Steven's thigh matched the slug from John's head. John's service weapon was dropped in the ditch by Arthur Stevens after he fired a shot toward the pursuing SWAT. He lost his grip on the pistol when he misjudged the depth and fell into the rush of the waterfilled ditch. His fingerprints were all over the 9-mil pistol. The only way Spencer Sheffield, aka Arthur Stevens, was not the killer was if Winston Baines was a criminal Houdini. Winston's sleight-of-hand would require him to convince two teenaged boys that he was Spencer Sheffield. In a stroke of genius, Winston would have to pass the murder weapons off to an unwitting Arthur Stevens. A doubt hit her mind. If she had doubts, so would a jury. What if Winston Baines traded the guns for drugs? Cutter had a reputation in the illicit drug world. Was there a remote possibility that the Mayor was right?

Sarah no longer cared for the taste of her Chardonnay. The weather woman was fast-talking her way through the forecast, including scientific data and analysis that only a meteorology aficionado could appreciate. Her cell phone rattled on the kitchen counter where she left it. It startled her. She set her cardboard fast-food box aside and retrieved the phone as it continued to rattle. The ID was Devaney PD. She answered, fearful of what would follow.

"Chief, this is Sergeant Fink in Booking. Some lawyer called. Said he represents Arthur Stevens. He wants to talk with the prisoner when he arrives."

Sarah sighed. "When is he supposed to arrive?"

"He said he was driving in from Wichita. Should be here in about half an hour."

"He can't talk to him until either Boston or I get there."

"Understood. Do you want me to call the Detective?"

Sarah thought a moment. Boston should be reasonably rested. Maybe even nourished. She no longer had an appetite, but she was exhausted. "I'll call him. I need to make sure he got some sleep this afternoon."

Boston was groggy but became fully alert when Sarah mentioned the situation. "I'll get over there. I've been tossing and turning. Thinking about the questions I want that scum to answer."

Boston's response was enough to convince Sarah that she needed to be there. If the Detective came on too strong, he might give the attorney something to use against the case, against Devaney PD. She called Lab Tech Kettering as soon as she ended the call with Boston. "Alicia, I hate to bother you at home on Friday evening, but I need something first thing Monday morning."

Alicia was gracious. If the call interrupted her, she did not express it in words or tone. "What do you need? If it's important enough, I can do it tomorrow morning." She was always eager to please.

"It's not critical. I just wanted to know if Arthur left any fingerprints on the bullets when he loaded the pistols."

Alicia chuckled. "I should have given you the written report. I checked the bullets in both weapons. The 9-mil has a capacity of eight rounds. It still had five rounds in the clip that were loaded by John … Officer Wyatt. There were only seven left in the clip, like it had recently been fired – which it had. The top two rounds were a different brand, from a different manufacturer. They had Arthur Stevens' fingerprints all over them. If you are wondering if he loaded the weapon, he did."

"You are way ahead of me. What about the .22?"

"Not as easy on 9 mil for prints. The bullets are so small. It was a revolver. I got partials on every piece of brass. Smudged and only partial, but they do seem to match Arthur's prints."

Sarah grinned into her phone. She wondered if Alicia could detect the fact she was pleased with the outcome of the conversation. "I suppose I don't need you to do anything first thing Monday after all. Enjoy your weekend, Alicia. Thank you."

"Oh. One other thing," Alicia added quickly, "the prints inside the pick-up match Arthur Stevens. Thought you might want to know."

"That is important to know. Thank you again."

Sarah dressed for work. It was Friday night. She was exhausted. She would have preferred a pair of jeans and a sweatshirt. It might be after hours, but she was Police Chief at all hours. She could easily refuse the lawyer until Saturday, but that would create a bond hearing issue. She needed to look the part of Police Chief. She wore the same gray pantsuit she donned after her shower that morning. She chose a paisley blouse rather than her usual Friday blue tone.

Attorney Grant Hesseman was in the Booking lobby when Sarah arrived, allowed to wait there by the night jail Sergeant. "Are you Chief James," he asked as soon as Sarah came through the door.

"I am. You must be Mr. Stevens' attorney." Sarah extended her hand. Cordiality was of value.

Grant Hesseman did not break his stony look as he accepted the handshake. "Grant Hesseman. I have requested to see my client, but there seems to be some delay. I expected him to be ready for my arrival."

"We don't sit around waiting for anyone's arrival. Your phone call was a nice head's up, but we don't begin prep of the prisoner until you are physically in the building. Security." Sarah saw Boston on the other side of the Booking security door. He was talking to one of the Jailers, a retired police officer from a small town in a nearby county. "They will let you in as soon as your client is in the meeting room."

"Our conversation will be privileged," Grant stated in a demanding tone.

"The room is secure. You will have complete privacy," Sarah assured him. She used her ID card to pass through the security door and left the attorney in the lobby. "Hello, Sergeant Fink. Hello, Detective. Is Mr. Stevens ready?" The question was for either man to answer.

"I just got here about five minutes before the lawyer," Boston replied. "Ellis is going for him now."

"Good. I'll go get Interrogation ready."

"Why did he bring in a Wichita lawyer?" Boston asked.

Sarah smiled, "That's Wynn Sheffield's hometown."

Boston snorted. "It will get interesting if Arthur denies his real identity is Spencer Sheffield."

"The court orders for DNA from the Sheffield family will end that. But I have a feeling there won't be any denial."

"Why so?"

Before Sarah could respond, loud voices echoed from within the jail area. More voices joined the original outburst. Sarah heard scuffling. Sergeant Fink bolted toward the security door that separated the booking desk from the jail cells. He checked through a small window in the door before he inserted his security card to unlock the door. Yells and the sounds of scuffling grew louder when the thick door opened.

"You're hurting me! Help! They're trying to kill me!"

Other voices added to the fracas. Shouts of "They're killing him! Stop the killing!"

Sergeant Fink's commanding voice took charge before the door closed and muted the sound. Sarah and Boston waited. She had to allow the jail staff to control the situation. If help was required, the call would go to the Command Desk. Finally, Sergeant Fink came out the door, his face red with an angry scowl.

"What happened?" Sarah asked.

"Stevens decided to launch himself as soon as Ellis opened the cell door. He began screaming ... well, you heard what he was screaming."

"I take it he's under control now?" Sarah asked.

"He is. Ellis said he slammed his own face into the cell bars a couple of times after Ellis got him in an armlock. The old man isn't to be trifled with."

Sarah looked at Boston and grimaced. "Stevens wanted marks. I'm sure this isn't going to end well for the PD."

"We've seen it before. We've handled it before." Boston reassured her. He turned to Sergeant Fink. "Can you get me a copy of the cell video?"

After Sergeant Fink nodded, Sarah replied, "But times were different before. Get your video and I'll go explain what has happened to Mr. Hesseman. He's either going to be angry or feign anger. Lawyers love this stuff." She walked through the primary security door into the Booking lobby.

Grant Hesseman was red faced and angry. "I've heard Devaney PD is run by thugs. I want to see my client immediately."

Sarah let the man rant. It was for show. She knew it. He knew it. He did not know Boston would have video if he raised the question during interrogation. "As soon as he is secured in the privacy room, I'll escort you there. You will be required to go through a metal detector. No weapons. No phones."

Grant Hesseman stewed until he was in the room with Arthur Stevens. He glared at Sarah, "Why is he shackled to the table? I demand you release him."

"He wouldn't be if he had not attacked the Jailer."

Arthur spat angrily, "The Jailer tried to kill me! Twisted my arm! Almost broke my shoulder. Shoved me into the bars. Look! Look at the bruises! Did he cut my face again? I'm gonna sue. I'll have your badge. I'll own this jail."

"Calm down, Mr. Stevens," said Grant while patting Arthur's shackled forearm. "We'll get you out of here first, then we can pursue justice for the mistreatment. If you're not going to unshackle my client, leave." The attorney glared at Sarah. "And the Judge will hear about this. What you're doing here is a violation of every basic right my client deserves."

Sarah left. She and Boston went upstairs to prepare a pot of coffee and plan the interrogation.

After a couple of hours, the lawyer was escorted to the lobby. With his cell phone back in his possession, he place two calls. He spoke softly so he would not be overheard by Sergeant Fink.

In the Interrogation Room, Grant Hesseman again requested that Arthur Stevens' shackles be removed. It was a request quickly denied by a dour Boston. Sarah stayed in the Observation Room.

Boston let the lawyer and his client stew while he studied a folder filled with several documents.

Grant finally erupted, "Are you going to ask my client questions, or are you playing some hick town game?"

Boston cut his eyes toward the lawyer and resumed studying the folder's contents. After several minutes of angry throat clearings by Grant and angry snorts by Arthur, the Detective looked at the suspect. "State your full name."

Arthur looked toward the lawyer before he replied with a scoff, "I don't have to answer your questions."

"Actually, you do, unless answering would self-incriminate." Boston looked at Grant. "Maybe you should get a better lawyer. One who knows the law."

Grant's face reddened. "Answer the question, Arthur."

"Arthur Stevens," the suspect said.

"Middle name," Boston said.

"What?"

"Middle name."

Arthur glared. "I don't have one."

"Really? Eighty percent of Americans have a middle name. Those who don't are usually older citizens. It's unusual to meet someone as young as you without one." Boston scribbled on a piece of paper inside his folder. He looked up and smiled commandingly, "Okay, now tell me your real name."

"What?"

"Tell me about your childhood. Where you went to school. Childhood friends. What kind of car your father drove. Where you played Little League baseball."

"What does that have to do with this case?" Grant demanded as he held Arthur quiet with a hand on the forearm.

"Everything. I want to make sure we are charging the right person."

"What? You arrested my client, and you don't even know if he's the right person?"

"Not exactly. We know we arrested the man who gunned down Officer John Wyatt in cold blood – in front of two witnesses. I just want to make sure we identify your murdering scumbag client by the right name."

"He has told you his name repeatedly," the attorney replied forcefully.

"He told us *a* name," Boston replied dryly. "Funny thing about names. They are not just associated with a person, with a human being. They are also associated with things humans do. Growing up with friends. Going to school. Having parents. Working. Your client's name doesn't indicate he has ever done any of those normal human things."

"That's ridiculous."

"Is it? Despite what you want to believe, we do things by the book here in this hick town. Simple things like using the correct name for murderers." Boston narrowed his eye and looked at Arthur, "State your name."

"I told you. My name is Arthur Stevens."

"Where were you last Monday night and early Tuesday morning?"

"Asleep in my bed."

"Can anyone corroborate that?"

"I was asleep. I live alone."

"Convenient. What did you do Tuesday?"

"I think I mowed the lawn," Arthur said with a smirk.

Boston made a note. "Okay. I can check with the neighbors. That will be easy enough to verify. If you lied …"

"I was being a smart aleck," Arthur quickly added.

Boston looked toward the lawyer. "I suggest you advise your client that being a smart aleck is a sure-fired way to win that lethal injection our state offers winners of the stupid game."

The two men played chicken with glares. Boston won. Grant told Arthur to answer correctly.

"I don't remember. I don't dwell on remembering things like that."

"Maybe I can help. You were meeting with these two gentlemen Tuesday before noon." Boston shoved pictures of Winston and Rewind in front of Arthur.

"I've never seen either of them."

Boston retrieved the photos. He slowly pushed a photo of Officer Wyatt's body, emphasis on the head, in front of Arthur. "And I know who you were with shortly after midnight Monday." He watched Arthur's reaction as the man studied the picture.

"I don't know why you're showing me that picture. I was home in bed."

"What is your father's name?"

"What does that have to do with this?" Arthur responded angrily. He lurched forward slightly. The move caused his wrists to reach their limit with the shackles. He glared at the chains and relaxed.

Boston saw Arthur's reaction and that of the lawyer. He made notes inside the folder after he withdrew the photo of John's body. "I think we're through for today. I'm not sure how long your appeal process will last before you are finally executed, but I hope it's not very long. I hate seeing taxpayer money wasted." Boston opened the door and told the Jailer to return Arthur to his cell.

Grant told Arthur, "I've talked to Judge Varadkar. Our bond hearing will be tomorrow afternoon."

Sarah cringed. She would have to be at the hearing to present the Police Department's objections to bail. She immediately dialed the DA. He could change the time. She knew Judge Varadkar would agree to the change request. She also knew the timing was not unintentional.

Boston met Sarah just as she was ending her call with the DA. "You heard that, didn't you?"

Sarah knew what he meant. "I just got off the phone with the DA. He said he would get that changed. Maybe tomorrow before noon." She walked toward the coffee pot with Boston at her side. "I noticed you left them hanging."

Boston grinned. "The scumbag is lying through his teeth. The lawyer knows I saw it. His name is not Arthur Stevens. DNA will bring that out. The lawyer knows that too. He hates his father."

"Is that why you stopped?"

"That combined with his reaction to the picture of John's body. A sociopath can't hide his satisfaction. There's no doubt he killed John and there's no doubt he's Spencer Sheffield. No need to keep talking to the scumbag and listening to his lies. Just looking at him makes me want to puke."

"Let's call it a night," Sarah said. She knew the DA would not have a drama-free trial, but she was positive he would get a conviction. The DA promised he would call her as soon as he received confirmation of the bond hearing time from the Judge. She walked down the back stairs while Boston filed his evidence files.

Sergeant Fink saw her coming and called her to the Booking desk. He spoke softly. "Chief. You might want to go out the front. That lawyer has some reporters out there."

Sarah peered through a small window. Kyren's camera crew was almost ready. Grant Hesseman was patiently waiting, confidently chatting with Kyren while he waited. "I'm going to go stand in the compound. I think I can see and hear from there without being seen."

A few minutes later, Sarah was hiding in the shadows close enough to see and hear when Grant Hesseman began his news conference.

"My name is Grant Hesseman. I am Mr. Arthur Stevens' attorney. As you may be aware, the Devaney Police Chief has arrested and falsely accused my client of the murder of Officer John Wyatt. Up front, I will state that my client was supposed to die during the arrest. We all know that. Police justice. Judge and executioner. But, fortunately, the presence of the media played a pivotal role in his safety. I thank the media on behalf of my client for their diligence. If not for the Press, we would all live in constant fear of over-zealous law enforcement.

"On that note, when I arrived to meet with my client earlier this evening, he was being assaulted by members of the Devaney Police Department under the watchful eye of Chief James. As you are all aware, the Mayor of Devaney, Mayor Kamen, is on a crusade to root out bad police officers from Devaney PD. The brownshirt tactics of Devaney PD is so inherent in the culture that the Mayor has established contact cards and an anonymous hot line so she can address citizen's concerns about brutal police tactics.

"While my client and I both are saddened by the death of a police officer, it is apparent from evidence that the officer was overly aggressive and instigated the violence that led to his own death. That same evidence makes it apparent that the two teenagers who claim to be able to identify a mystery murderer are in fact guilty of that murder. One of the boys, who imagine themselves as men, is facing charges of statutory rape. Not a very reliable witness when a man's life is at stake.

"As a result of attacks by the police on a helpless man inside a jail cell, my client will be filing a lawsuit for police brutality and bodily harm. Thank you and stay tuned." Grant did not answer questions. He hurriedly walked toward his vehicle while answering his phone.

Sarah watched Grant pause after opening his car door. He was far enough away that she could not hear him, but he was upset. After he ended the call, he glared toward the station before he entered the car. Her phone rang. She hurriedly answered it and moved away from the compound fence to avoid detection by Kyren and her camera crew. It was the DA. Judge Varadkar acted quickly. The bond hearing was at 9:00 A.M. She was ready.

# CHAPTER 27

## Saturday 7:00 A.M.

Sarah was able to sleep until 5:30. She was able to go to the gym for a short workout. Boston was right. There was no doubt that Arthur Stevens was the man who murdered John Wyatt. There was also no doubt Arthur Stevens was an alias used by Spencer Sheffield. The State Police would provide the proof within a matter of days, if not hours. Assistant DA Marcie Ignak planned to meet with her at the station to coordinate their presentation to the Judge for the bond hearing. She had time to go through the drive-thru for breakfast. She bought two egg white sandwiches and two cups of fresh fruit. Marcie would be hungry too.

"Hello, Sweetheart." Sergeant Honeycutt's cheery greeting welcomed Sarah as she entered the front door of the station. In a more subdued tone, Maria said conspiratorially, "*Have* I got something you're going to want to see." The Sergeant's equipment belt rattled as she walked to meet Sarah with a folder in her hand. She offered the folder and said, "Here. Let me hold your sack. I think you want to read this before you eat. It'll make your food taste better."

Sarah's curiosity was piqued. She opened the folder and perused the contents. Her eyes widened and became more focused. She could not help but smile as she read it. Detective Mankowitz chose the right person for the confidential task. There was no one on the force she trusted more to be quiet and supportive than Maria Honeycutt. "Where did you get this?"

"It's all out there, if you know where to look," Honeycutt said with a grin. "I've told you before, the Internet hides nothing – especially with official clearance."

Sarah read Sergeant Honeycutt's concise, bullet-point notes again to absorb every nuance.

---

- *Thomas Williams is father of Robert Williams.*
- *Robert Williams is father of Rosaline Williams.*
- *Rosaline Williams married Martin Kamen.*
- *Rosaline and Martin Kamen are parents of Jordon Kamen.*
- *Maude Williams is youngest sister of Thomas Williams.*
- *Maude Williams married Charles Sheffield.*
- *Maude and Charles are parents of Wynn Sheffield.*
- *Wynn Sheffield is father of Spencer Sheffield.*
- *Spencer Sheffield is first cousin of Jordon Kamen's parents.*

---

Sarah stared in awe at the piece of paper. She slowly raised her head and grinned at Maria. "Sergeant, I don't know how you do it. You are amazing."

Sergeant Honeycutt beamed with pride. "I knew you'd come around. BUT there's more." She pointed toward the folder.

Sarah put a second piece of paper on top of the first and read it. The information on the page confused her because it seemed to be a disconnect.

---

*NEO-Energy Sources, LLC*

*NEO-Energy Sources, LLC is an innovator in the field of sustainable energy, using revolutionary technology to increase the efficiency of wind driven turbines to generate 200% (two hundred percent) more energy than conventional turbine technology.*

*NEO-Energy Sources, LLC is a limited liability company principally owned by CEO Carter L. Laughlin, MSEE. Carter L. Laughlin assembled a team of like-minded*

---

> *engineers to develop the proprietary technology that will revolutionize the power generation industry, creating more electricity without compromising the environment.*
> *Additional information available upon request.*

Sarah re-read the blurb in search of its significance. "What is this?"

"The next page," Maria replied.

Sarah pulled up the third page.

> *For Immediate Release*
>
> *NEO-Energy Sources, LLC CEO Carter L. Laughlin announced that NEO-Energy Sources, LLC will break ground on a large-scale manufacturing facility within the next twelve months. The location of the site is pending environmental impact studies and zoning approvals.*
>
> *NEO-Energy Sources, LLC is an innovator in the field of sustainable energy, using revolutionary technology to increase the efficiency of wind driven turbines to generate 200% (two hundred percent) more energy than conventional turbine technology.*

"I'm not sure where this is going. Is the city wooing NEO-Energy?"

"I didn't find anything on that. I was just researching the Mayor's background. This popped up in one of my searches. Nothing is secret anymore. Read on." Sergeant Honeycutt motioned to encourage Sarah to look at the last piece of paper.

"This is a list of names," Sarah mused as she read. "Some of them seem familiar. Is there something special about this list?" It was simply a list of names.

The Sergeant leaned forward and answered conspiratorially, "I didn't print it in context. I found it in a scathing comment about NEO-Energy. It seems Carter Laughlin has made enemies along the way. The company is a rejuvenation of another company, NEO-Technologies, LLC. NEO-Technologies came after NEO-Enviro, LLC. Carter finds investors for his company to produce and sell his innovative inventions." Maria paused to make sure Sarah was attentive. "So far, his efforts have not resulted in success. Oh, he gets plenty of investors, lots of money, but the companies fail to produce anything. He reinvents his company under another name and uses the same spiel. Carter Laughlin is an innovator in the eyes of potential investors. To many of his former employees and vendors, he is seen more as a con-man."

Sarah looked up at Maria, who was still beaming proudly. "What does this tell me? Are these the people who were conned by Carter Laughlin?"

"This is a list of current investors. Read carefully. You may have missed it. Whoever put this on the Internet misspelled some names. Maybe I should have highlighted it."

The small print did not have wide spacing. The lack of sufficient white space made following the lines of print more difficult. Sarah read again, more slowly. The name was misspelled. *Winn Shefield.* "Wow! Is that our Wynn Sheffield?"

"My guess is yes," Sergeant Honeycutt leaned back and hooked her thumbs in her belt. "It fell out while I was doing a broad search for Wynn Sheffield using variations of spelling. Wynn Sheffield is part of the Mayor's family – with an interest in green stuff, and I'm not just talking about the environment."

"Can I keep these?" Sarah asked. Her excitement grew.

"I got it just for you. I can pull it again if I have to." Maria was pleased with herself.

Marcie interrupted the two. "Good morning, Chief. Are you ready to face the Judge?" She blew the errant blonde lock away from her eyes, only to have it return to its planned location.

"I think I can convince him to not offer bond." Sarah retrieved the food sack from Sergeant Honeycutt and held it up. "I bought breakfast. We can eat while we prep."

The two high-energy women reviewed their presentation. They settled on a list of reasons Arthur Stevens was a risk for flight and for further violence. The fact that his ID was suspect. A man with a hidden identity could not be trusted to remain available. The fact that his fingerprints were on the two weapons and ammunition used to kill a law enforcement officer proved he was capable of unprovoked murder. The fact that he exhibited violence, even when incarcerated – verified by the jailhouse video from his attack on the Jailer. Sarah and Marcie approached the Judge with confidence.

Grant Hesseman won two things for his client. Arthur could get a new bond hearing after his identity was confirmed. Arthur would be allowed to await his next hearing in the general population cell rather than in isolation as Sarah requested.

Bill Keck called Sarah while she was driving back to her apartment.

"Good morning, Sarah. Just checking in to see how you're doing. Everything flowing okay?"

Sarah replied, "Surprisingly well. We just convinced the Judge to not allow bail on Sheffield-Stevens, at least until the suspect's identity can be confirmed."

"That's good. I saw that slimeball lawyer's interview this morning and wondered how it affected you." Bill's voice expressed empathy.

"I was there last night when he called the presser. It was a standard attempt to sway the public and the bond hearing. He didn't help his cause with the theatrics. Judge Varadkar took him to task."

Bill chuckled. "Good. I love it when a lawyer overplays his hand like that. At least, you have John's killer in custody."

"He may get a second bond hearing after we confirm his ID. His lawyer got him that. The lawyer asked that he be transferred to the County Jail for his *protection*, which the Judge denied. That would suit me. Less to worry about."

"Good point. But he is in jail. That's the good thing. I suppose we can honor John and be there for Celia now. Get back to living."

Sarah thought of something. "Chief," Bill Keck would forever be Chief in her mind, "I have a dilemma. Maybe you can help."

"Oh? I'll try. What is it?"

"You're probably aware that the Mayor is very vocal and very public about her belief that Winston Baines is the killer. She's even got Lieutenant Glasgow investigating to prove Winston killed John, not Spencer Sheffield."

"I have heard her public statements. Is there a chance she has it right?"

Sarah inhaled deeply, fearful of indecision. "None. Arthur Stevens is an alias used by Spencer Sheffield. He left fingerprints all over the murder weapons and the ammunition, plus in his truck and the house. There is no doubt Winston Baines is a sap."

"I thought I heard that Senator Spencer has provided an alibi for his son, for Spencer."

"Yes, he has publicly stated that Spencer was at the family home on Monday night."

"And ... that's in Wichita. Right?"

"That's my understanding. Yes."

"Kind of hard to commit the murder from Wichita. Is there some other explanation?" Bill Keck leaned further forward inquisitively.

Sarah twisted her lips as she put words together in her mind. "I've never met a politician who wasn't loose with the truth. Spencer could have been in Wichita at the family home earlier in the day, say late afternoon, and had plenty of time to be in Devaney by midnight. Senator Spencer isn't stupid. He knows a murdering son would be a drag on a political career."

"Okay," Bill said musingly, "a father covering for his son. Half truth. Half lie. It's been done before. But - now it begs the question, why is Jordon so keen on shifting focus?"

"At first," Sarah began slowly, "I just assumed she was trying to discredit me. She wants to fire me but can't muster Council or public support any other way."

"At first?" Bill asked. "That says your assumption has changed."

"It has, and that's my dilemma. Mayor Kamen is Senator Sheffield's cousin."

Bill was silent for several seconds. "You're sure?"

"Positive. I have the proof locked in my desk."

"That is a dilemma. What do you plan to do with that information? Confront the Mayor? Go public?"

"Both make sense. They both sound risky. My primary concern is to bring the murderer of John Wyatt to justice. I don't want to get political."

"You may not have a choice. Have you talked to anyone on the Council?"

"I have not. The Mayor moved the Budget Review Meeting up to next Tuesday. It's no secret that we are locked in a budget battle. I don't want to make this look like a move to help my budget presentation."

"True. It must be done right. Why is she rushing the budget? Budgets are part of the publicly published schedule. It's not time for the final review at Council, is it?"

"I don't know why she's moved the review up. In a hurry to "get on with city business" is what she said."

"There has to be a reason. I sense it's not something good. You need to discuss this with someone. Are you familiar with Councilwoman Cary Beecher?"

"Not really. I'm too new in this game to know all the players. Other than that, I only generally know the names and faces of the Councilmembers."

"Cary is head of the Personnel Committee. She doesn't do city Human Resources per se, but the HR Supervisor has a dotted line to her. That way all personnel decisions are not exclusively at the whim of the Mayor's Office. The Mayor has to follow the law. Cary might have some advice."

"Thanks, Chief. I'll talk to her. I'll see you at visitation."

# CHAPTER 28

## Saturday 1:00 P.M.

Sarah stayed at Mason's Funeral Home during the visitation. Most of the time, she was outside, quietly visiting with out-of-town law enforcement officials paying their respects. The details of the escort from Devaney to Fort Scott required attention, completion of final preparations. It gave her the opportunity to put faces with voices that had carefully set the details in place. Sarah made notes on her phone for every finalized detail. Intersections. Traffic control on divided highways with two lanes in each direction. Traffic control for head-on two-lane roads. Traffic control through towns. Every aspect of the journey required specific instructions for the escorting vehicles. Most of the law enforcement officers would be paying their respects by keeping the convoy and the mourners safe as they traveled to and from the cemetery. A Highway Patrol vehicle would be in the lead both ways.

Surprisingly, Celia held herself together. Family attended to the children, entertaining them as necessary. Everyone, family and visitors, were pleased to know the man responsible for John's death was in custody. Sarah was embarrassed by repeated congratulations for a job well done. That was neither the time nor the place as far as she was concerned, but she could not stop it.

Most of the non-family civilians who came to pay their respects stayed no longer than half an hour. Some attended the visitation in lieu of the funeral. In nearly every case, Sarah was sought out as a contact that needed to be made. Her loss of an officer was seen for what it was, the loss of a family member.

Sergeant Locke and Zoey approached Sarah with appropriately long faces. "Chief, I know how this affects everyone, especially you, but we will make it through this together." Keith's words carried a different message than the words.

Sarah accepted his words without judgement. Zoey's comment was puzzling.

"Chief, I just want you to know that Keith and I support you one-hundred percent."

Reporters roamed the edges of the crowd. Like a lion pride anticipating a straggler, they lurked after paying their respects. The funeral of a police officer killed in the line of duty was not just a tragedy, it was news. Reporting the news was their livelihood. Sarah kept her reactions to what she viewed as disrespect in check and avoided the fringes.

Mayor Kamen did not. Her behavior was proper and fitting while she visited with Officer Wyatt's family members. Less so when she exited the funeral home. She scowled and hurried past Sarah without speaking. She spoke with Zoey briefly. Zoey's body language telegraphed discomfort.

Zoey called someone. The conversation was short. Her eyes cut toward Sarah while she talked, then averted guiltily.

Kyren Bailey suddenly focused on and called out to the Mayor. Her camera crew began recording. Far enough away from the funeral home doorway to not interfere with the proceedings, the two engaged in an animated interview, quickly attracting the other reporters.

Sarah's curiosity tugged. She wanted to get closer, to hear what the Mayor was saying. Her paranoia was strong. She imagined the Mayor's words involved an attack on Devaney PD in general, the Police Chief in particular. She knew Zoey's call was to Kyren. The Mayor wanted the media to come to her. Sarah saw Councilwoman Cary Beecher arriving to pay her respects. She casually drifted back inside so she could stay close to the Councilwoman. She would herd her aside at an appropriate time.

Cary Beecher's eyes were red when she completed her visit with the family. Sarah positioned herself in the Councilwoman's line of sight, offering herself as a beacon. Cary Beecher took the bait. "Chief James, I am deeply sorry for your loss. I can't imagine the pain." She hugged Sarah.

"Thank you, Councilwoman Beecher. My pain is for Celia and her babies."

"Absolutely. Absolutely. I wish I had the power to remove the grief. I am surprised the coffin is closed. Most of the time, the visitation is open, even if the funeral is closed."

Sarah grimaced. There was nothing to gain by telling everything. "That is how Celia wanted it. Councilwoman, do you have a moment so we can talk?"

Cary Beecher looked concerned. "Is this the appropriate time to discuss anything other than condolences for the loss of a loved one?"

"I – like you – don't get a day off for grieving, or anything else. I have information that must be revealed. It was suggested that you are the first person I should contact." Sarah watched Cary's eyes and face as the Councilwoman processed what she heard.

"Is it something we should discuss openly?" Cary looked around furtively.

"It is not subject to FOI, if that's what you mean."

"Not just that. Is it private?"

"It *is* personnel related. I've been told that you are the personnel contact on the Council." Sarah looked askance as she continued. "I have use of an office where we can talk privately."

Sarah led the Councilwoman to Henry Mason's private office and closed the door. "Councilwoman, I have come across information that indicates something of a conflict of interest between the Mayor and our suspected murderer."

"How so?"

"The Mayor is his cousin."

"How is this a conflict of interest? She is not conducting the investigation of Officer Wyatt's murder."

"In a sense, she is. The conflict is her public insistence that Spencer Sheffield is innocent, and Winston Baines is the killer. She has assigned Lieutenant Glasgow to investigate the case to supersede our PD investigation in an effort to prove Winston Baines is the murderer. Winston Baines' fingerprints are not on the murder weapons. Spencer Sheffield's, under his alias Arthur Stevens, are. The Mayor's constant beratement of the Devaney PD puts doubt into the minds of potential jurors when this comes to trial."

"What do you expect me to do?"

"I'm not sure what you can do. Or anyone else for that matter. I just felt it was important for someone other than me be aware of this. I have shared the information with the DA's office. I suspect they will find the proper use, if any, for that information."

Councilwoman Beecher nodded thoughtfully. "Chief James, I appreciate the confidence you have shown by sharing this with me. I'm not sure how I can temper the Mayor's posturing. We both know that is what is happening here. There is no secret there are unresolved issues between you and the Mayor."

Sarah ignored the personal attachment Cary made. "I understand your position. Are you familiar with a company called NEO-Energy Sources?"

"I don't think so. Who are they?"

"They are a green company. They apparently manufacture a high efficiency electricity generator for wind turbines."

"Really? How does that impact me, or Devaney?"

"To be honest, I'm not sure. Apparently, the Mayor's cousin, Senator Sheffield is an investor."

"I truly don't see the connection, Chief." Cary was showing irritation. "I'm sure many people in politics invest in companies – and are related to other politicians."

"I don't know what the connection is either, but I was hoping you might know something about the company."

"I don't," the Councilwoman stated.

Sarah shrugged. "Thank you for speaking with me." Cary Beecher did not offer much hope.

Bill Keck and his wife invited Sarah out to dinner. Sarah did not refuse the offer. A steak and good company were too inviting to ignore. They tried to not talk police business, or about the Mayor. They did not want to bore Margaret Keck. But Margie, as she was generally called, asked, "I suppose you saw the Mayor's press statement earlier today. It shocked me that she would use Officer Wyatt's visitation as a backdrop for her politics."

Sarah glanced questioningly toward Bill. He made a face to indicate he did not see it. "I wasn't aware of it, Margie. I almost hate to ask. What did she have to say?"

"Just the usual. The real killer is that Baines person. The police are bad. Blah. Blah. Blah. I question her sanity at times." Margie shrugged and took another bite.

# CHAPTER 29

## Sunday 1:00 A.M.

Sarah did not want to open her eyes. She was deep in sleep. The rattle on her nightstand persisted. She reached for the lighted face of her cell phone. Devaney PD ID. "Hello." The voice she used was weary and partially blocked by nighttime phlegm.

"Chief, there has been a fight inside the jail." Sergeant Honeycutt was not her usual, cheery self. "Arthur Stevens attacked Winston Baines."

"What? How? They weren't even in the same cell." Sarah was confused.

"After a fracas at dinner, Arthur was put into a different pod."

It was not an uncommon occurrence. Disorderly prisoners were moved away from potential personality conflicts. Testosterone fueled egos clashed frequently in jail. "How bad?"

"A shiner. A facial cut or two. Maybe a broken nose."

"Has a doctor been called?"

"Just the Paramedics. Nothing serious enough for a doctor."

"Do you need me ... just a minute. Someone else is calling." Sarah groaned when she saw the ID. Zoey. "I'll be there in a few minutes. Looks like the Mayor is calling."

Sarah called Zoey as she walked across the room to turn on the lights. She then dialed the Mayor's number.

The Mayor screamed. "What kind of jail do you run? The killer almost killed an innocent man!"

Sarah shook her head as she walked to the bathroom and squatted to pee. "Mayor, we don't have any innocent men in the jail. This sort of thing is routine in a jail house. Egos clash. Stevens, or Sheffield, was moved from his original pod to a new one because he got into a fight at dinner time. Apparently, he doesn't play well with others. We could shackle him to his bed. Maybe that will keep him from hitting people." She knew her words would incite the Mayor, but she did not care. Winston should have been turned over to Wichita PD on outstanding warrants, but Lieutenant Glasgow, prodded on by the Mayor, did not want the warrants executed until he found evidence that Winston was John's murderer.

"No. You put an innocent man in harm's way. A man that you have falsified evidence against for some inexplicable political reason. Chief, this is the last straw. I am sending Lieutenant Glasgow to the jail to take command of the situation." The call ended.

Sarah finished getting ready to go to the station. Blue jeans and an Oxford shirt. Her side holster rather than the shoulder holster that was normally concealed by her jacket.

Night Booking Sergeant Foster greeted Sarah when she came through the Booking entrance. "Sorry about this, Chief. Fink moved Stevens into Pod Two after he started a fight in his assigned pod."

"Protocol. Who's in Pod Two other than Winston Baines?"

"If you mean who's in there that might be connected to Stevens, no one. Just the usual."

Sarah nodded. Lieutenant Glasgow opened the outer door and lowered his eyes when he saw Sarah. He looked sleepy. "Melvin," Sarah greeted him tersely.

"Hello, Chief. The Mayor said there's been some trouble." Glasgow did not act like a man who intended to take command of anything.

"A scuffle. A clash of egos. Nothing more. How did the Mayor find out about a routine fight in the jailhouse?" Sarah's phone rattled in her shirt pocket. "Excuse me." She looked at the ID. Unknown Wichita. "This is Chief James. How may I help you?"

"Chief, this is Grant Hesseman. I'm getting my client out of there before you have him killed. I knew this was going to happen. Expect a call from the Judge very soon." The lawyer cut the connection.

Sarah shook her head and looked between Sergeant Fink and Lieutenant Glasgow. "How did Stevens' lawyer find out about this?"

Lieutenant Glasgow shook his head. "Chief, I swear I didn't. I was sound asleep when the Mayor called and told me to rush over here. Said something about a jail riot." He looked around. "Apparently, an exaggeration."

Sarah scowled. "Apparently," she said sarcastically. "Sergeant, I want that question answered ASAP. How did the Mayor know about this before I did? How did a lawyer in Wichita know before I did?"

"Yes, Ma'am." The Sergeant disappeared through the security door.

"Lieutenant, why are you here?" Sarah glared at Glasgow.

"Ma'am?"

"Don't Ma'am me. I'm Chief of Police and I want answers." Sarah's phone rattled. ID showed DA Dunn. "Melvin, are you a police officer or a politician's pawn?"

Melvin Glasgow's face paled. His eyes danced, seeking an avenue of escape.

Sarah's phone continued to rattle. "I need to take this. You stay here until you have an answer to that question for me." She walked through the security door into Booking so Glasgow could not hear her conversation. "Hello, Mr. Dunn. How may I help you?" She was puzzled by the call. The DA would not call after hours unless it was important.

"I just got a call from Judge Varadkar. He wants us on a conference call in five minutes. Something about an attempt on Arthur Stevens' life inside the jail."

"It was a fight between two inmates. He and Winston Baines clashed egos." Sarah gave the only answer she had.

"Are you at the jail?"

"Yes."

"Is he hurt?"

"I just arrived. From what I've gather so far, sore fists and maybe a broken nose on Winston, not Stevens. I'll know more shortly." The security door opened just as the call ended. Sarah looked to see Glasgow holding the door open for two paramedics.

"Sorry, Chief. They said they were called to check on the prisoners." Glasgow was subdued.

"Let them in. Stay in the lobby and consider your answer to my question," Sarah reminded the Lieutenant. "I have work to do in my office." She hurried up the stairs.

Sarah's connection to the hardline call required more than five minutes to complete. Judge Varadkar's grumpy voice indicated he was beyond angry.

"Is everyone here?" the Judge asked. After a flurry of yeses, the Judge said, "Court is in session. I want a rollcall. Go slow and speak distinctly. This call is being recorded and I am scribing as we go." He added sarcastically, "I don't have a Court Recorder in my bedroom."

Sarah was shocked when Mayor Kamen identified herself as one of the callers.

"Mayor, what is your part in this emergency bond hearing?" the Judge asked sharply.

"Your Honor, I am here to testify that Mr. Stevens' life is in danger, as was demonstrated tonight."

"Are you at the jail?"

"No, Your Honor. I was made aware of …"

"Mayor. The Court does not allow for hearsay, and apparently your part is hearsay."

"Your Honor, I protest. Winston Baines is the murderer of Officer Wyatt. Mr. Stevens was wantonly placed in the same cell as a murderer …"

The Judge cut the Mayor off. "Miss Kamen, let me be clear. I do not appreciate calls in the middle of the night about attempted murders in a jail. I appreciate even less any disregard for proper legal decorum and any opinionated histrionics by the participants in this call. If you are not Counsel for either party, the Chief of Police, or the District Attorney, you sit quietly as a public witness as if you were in my courtroom. Is that clear?"

The Mayor sputtered for a moment.

The Judge said, "Good. We have an understanding. Now, participants, identify yourself and your purpose for being on this call. By the way, I trust none of you are recording this call. It is an official hearing, and I will not allow unofficial recordings. If you chose to disregard that rule, then I suggest you hang up immediately or prepare to face the consequences. Understood?"

After identifying themselves and their roles, the Judge said, "Mr. Hesseman, you are the one who initiated this emergency bond hearing in the middle of a Saturday night. You asserted that a known murderer attempted to kill your client. Explain yourself."

"Yes, Your Honor. I received a call informing me that my client, Arthur Stevens', wrongly accused of murder, suffered grievous, life-threatening harm at the hands of another inmate, an inmate that evidence supports is the true murderer. It is only by the Grace of God that my client survived the attack."

"I thought you told me in your urgent request for this hearing that he killed a man in self-defense."

"Yes, Your Honor." Grant scrambled to respond. "That was my initial understanding. Later word was that he was attacked and beaten to within an inch of his life. He's currently receiving medical attention."

"Mr. District Attorney, what do you know of this situation?"

"I know two prisoners were engaged in a brawl. Paramedics were called to treat their injuries, none raising the level of life-threatening. That is the extent of my knowledge because no official investigation has been completed. This hearing happened rather suddenly."

A long pause followed the DA's statement. Judge Varadkar finally asked tiredly, "Are you prepared to change your stand regarding bail for Mr. Stevens?"

"Absolutely not, Your Honor. We have no facts to support a cause for change."

"If the man's life is in jeopardy while in the city jail, would it not be fitting that legal system save his life by freeing him on bond?"

"I believe we need to hear from Chief James regarding the occurrences at her jail tonight. As far as I know, she is the only one at this hearing who has firsthand knowledge."

"Who has been present at the city jail other than Chief James?"

After a brief pause, time for a quick text message, Grant Hesseman replied, "Your Honor, a member of the Mayor's staff has been present at the city jail. He can also add to what we are presenting."

"Is a member of the Mayor's staff there in the jail, Chief James?"

"No, Your Honor. Lieutenant Glasgow, who works for the Department of Public Outreach out of City Hall, arrived a few minutes before this phone call began. He has no knowledge of the events of this evening other than what he has been told by the Booking Sergeant, who is in charge of the jail." A knock at Sarah's office door distracted her.

"Then he has no firsthand knowledge of the alleged incident?" Judge Varadkar asked.

"No, Your Honor. He does not." The knock became more insistent.

"Chief James, I doubt you were in the jail cell at the time either. I have to assume, as a good police officer, you have done some investigation of the matter."

The knock was too persistent. It screamed urgency. Sarah hit the speaker button so she could listen and hurried to crack the door open. It was Lieutenant Glasgow. She scowled at him, held a finger to her lips and shrugged to indicate she was questioning his motive.

Lieutenant Glasgow whispered, "Chief, Sergeant Foster suggests you check the jail video he e-mailed to you. He said he has the phone. It might help with your bond hearing. Also," he paused and nervously added, "Stevens' lawyer called earlier and asked if Stevens was being manhandled for killing Baines. Odd, don't you think?"

"Chief James. Are you still with us?" Judge Varadkar's voice asked.

"Yes, Your Honor." Sarah nodded her appreciation to Lieutenant Glasgow, somewhat taken aback by his assistance. She also wondered, and answered herself, how he knew she was in a bond hearing in the middle of the night. "I believe I can provide something of value regarding the incident, if you will allow me a moment to review investigative evidence that was just delivered to my office." She quickly opened her e-mail and downloaded an attached file.

"Granted," the Judge replied.

The video was a wide-angle view of the sleeping quarters inside a cell. The lighting was subdued but not dark. Stark, metal framed bunk beds were in rows across the room. Camera coverage of the room allowed sight of every bunk, which meant there were multiple cameras at different angles. Sarah only received a small portion from a single camera. The grainy video showed Arthur Stevens in a jail uniform. He held something in one hand. He appeared to be dialing a cell phone. He held it to his ear and spoke for a moment. When he was through, he wiped the phone and tucked it under the mattress of another inmate. He then walked to a lower bunk and grabbed the sleeping occupant by the throat. Several seconds that seemed like an eternity that would surely end with the occupant's death passed before the sleeping person struggled and broke free. Arthur then punched the occupant in the face repeatedly until the occupant was able to get a leg free and kick Arthur away. Other prisoners began to move, most looking on curiously.

"Chief James, are you still there?"

"Yes, Your Honor. I have a copy of the jail cell video. I'm reviewing it now. If you will allow me a few more seconds."

"I object," Grant insisted. "The Chief is presenting evidence without review by Counsel."

Judge Varadkar snapped, "Mr. Hesseman, this is a bond hearing, not a trial."

"Judge Varadkar," Mayor Kamen's whiny voice cried out for attention, "the Chief is trying to create a smoke screen to cover her …"

"Miss Kamen," the Judge interrupted her, "I thought it was clear that you have no part in this hearing other than to be a witness. This may be a phone hearing, but it is still my courtroom and I will hold you in contempt if I hear another word out of you. Understood?" After a muffled okay from the Mayor, the Judge asked, "Chief James, have you had time to review the jail cell video?"

The interlude provided by the attorney and the Mayor allowed Sarah time to watch the video. When another prisoner became involved and kicked Arthur away from his target, Winston Baines' angry face became clear. He used the momentary lull to get out of his bunk and meet Arthur head on. Both men were of comparable size, equally matched for a street fight. Jailers appeared. Arthur took a swing at one of the Jailers and was hit with a baton for his effort. The video ended.

"I have, Your Honor. The video shows very clearly that Arthur Stevens was the aggressor. He attacked a sleeping cell mate using a stranglehold. The intervention of another prisoner prevented him from murdering the man."

"I see," said the Judge pensively. "Chief, what do you suggest at this point?"

"We have isolation cells. They are generally reserved for suicidal prisoners, but they are also used for prisoners who pose a threat to others.

I suggest Arthur Stevens be placed in one of those cells, as I requested in the original bond hearing."

"Remind me," the Judge said.

"I object," Grant exclaimed.

"To refreshing my memory?" the Judge asked. "Objection overruled."

"No. I object to my client being isolated. He is the one whose life is in danger. The danger is inside that jailhouse. I want him released on bond."

"Mr. Hesseman, at this point, it would appear the danger *from* him is greater than the danger *to* him."

"I want to see the video. How do ..."

Judge Varadkar interrupted. "Mr. Hesseman, you are trying my patience. You wake me in the middle of the night with a request for an emergency hearing because your client's life is in danger. Video from the cell indicates something entirely different. Chief, does the video have a time stamp?"

"It does, Your Honor." Sarah felt elation because of the Judge's question. "Arthur Stevens attack began at precisely 12:48 A.M. It was interrupted by the Jailers at approximately 12:49 and forty-five seconds." She waited.

"So, you're saying the fight was broken up at twelve fifty?"

"Forty-five seconds after 12:49. Yes, Your Honor."

"What time were you notified of the fight, Chief James?"

Sarah anticipated his question and opened her cell phone's recent call record. "A few seconds after 1:00 A.M."

"One o'clock," the Judge mused. "Is that unusually fast?"

"No. Not under the circumstance ... considering the parties involved. Not at all."

"So, you see nothing suspicious or unusual about your call?"

"Not about that call, no."

"There were other calls?"

Sarah grinned. The joy of discovery is a great feeling, even at 1:30 in the morning on a phone call with a judge. "There is one that stands out, Your Honor."

"And that would be?"

"A call from the Mayor's Assistant requesting that I call the Mayor immediately." Sarah heard a muffled sound that she was sure was the Mayor stifling a comment. That made her smile more.

"What time was that?"

"During the call from the station. 1:00 and fifty-two seconds according to my phone record."

"Was Lieutenant Glasgow at the station when you arrived?"

"No. He arrived a couple of minutes, two or three, after I arrived."

Complete silence for almost a minute. Judge Varadkar asked slowly and distinctly, "Chief James, do you have any idea how knowledge of an incident that occurred in your jail at 12:50 would be known to Counsel by 1:01, the time Mr. Hesseman woke me from a dead sleep?"

"Your Honor," Grant said, "Speculation!"

"Mr. Hesseman. I will allow you to answer that question. What time did you hear of the incident?"

Grant seemed confused. "Uh … I'm not entirely sure, Your Honor."

"Then I will allow Chief James to speculate. Chief, do you have any idea how Mr. Hesseman … or the Mayor, for that matter … could have become aware of the incident, apparently before you, the Chief of Police?"

"I have a suspicion." Sarah did not wait to be asked. "The time code on the video was about 12:47 when Arthur Stevens made a phone call using a contraband cell phone."

"Are you sure?"

Sarah replied, "Positive."

"So - if my notations are correct, the phone call was made *before* the attack."

"That is correct, Your Honor."

"Bond denied with no chance of rehearing in this Court. Remand Arthur Stevens to a solitary cell pending further review. I am hereby issuing a court order for the last two hours of cell phone and home phone records of Mr. Hesseman, Mayor Kamen, District Attorney Dunn, and Chief James along with those of the contraband phone. I am voluntarily submitting my records for the same time period for review by the District Attorney's office to construct a timeline of calls between all parties."

"Your Honor," Grant protested. "Attorney client privilege …"

"I'm only seeking numbers of incoming and outgoing calls. Do you deny you have spoken to your client tonight? Remember, you are under oath."

"I have other clients," Grant lamely continued his protest.

"If they are not among the numbers in the aforementioned group, they will be ignored. Mr. Dunn, can you see to the matter and submit the timeline to me?"

"I will, Your Honor."

"I expect there will be a reckoning for this hearing. Mr. Hesseman, Mayor Kamen, I will be demanding answers for your part in this. Adjudication complete. Court adjourned."

Sarah walked to Booking to give Sergeant Foster the Judge's orders. Lieutenant Glasgow was still in the booking lobby. He smiled nervously when she walked down the stairs. "Thank you, Melvin. That helped."

"Chief, I *am* a police officer." Glasgow sounded hurt.

"And a darn good one, Lieutenant. I think it's time to get some rest."

# CHAPTER 30

## Sunday 8:30 A.M.

Sarah did not sleep late even though it was Sunday and her return to the comfort of her bed was after three. She might have, but Keith called at 8:30.

"Chief, I know you were up last night, but I think I may have something more on the Overton case."

"Okay," Sarah said as she brushed her hair aside and sat on the edge of the bed. Even with the shades drawn, it was light in her bedroom. The blue glow of her LED clock had no impact on the light level. "What do you have?"

Keith hedged. "I think it would be better if we discussed it in person. We can come over to your place if that's okay."

"We?"

"Zoey and I."

Any residual drowsiness Sarah felt instantly evaporated. "Sure. Give me a few minutes to get dressed. Maybe put some coffee on." She stood and began shedding her PJ bottoms. Hearing Keith's voice while she undressed made her self-conscious.

"We'll bring some breakfast if that's okay. Good stuff. Not just donuts."

"Sure. See you in a bit." Sarah peed and took a shower. Her short hair would dry fast. She would have preferred a visit to the gym on what she thought might be a day off. Apparently, that was not to be.

Shortly after 9:00, Keith knocked. Sarah, still flushed from her hurry to get ready for the visit, opened the door for the couple. Zoey entered first, a hesitant smile on her face. "Good morning. Come in. Coffee is fresh and ready." The young woman's petite size was more apparent in a pair of shorts and a tee. Zoey almost looked like a schoolgirl. Sarah had to remind herself that the recent college graduate was not far removed from school age.

None of them discussed business or the purpose of the visit while they sat at the table and ate fast-food breakfast. Keith ate biscuits with gravy while the two women ate egg sandwiches with sausage. Sarah coaxed Zoey into talking about her family and her upbringing in Omaha. Sarah sensed an undertone of uncertainty, a lack of self-confidence. The young woman did not seem to be as aggressively in charge as she first appeared to be when the Mayor hired her to improve the Police Department's public image. Reality set in, a state that must be encountered to allow real growth.

Food gone with only coffee left, Sarah wiped her lips and asked, "Keith, what have you uncovered?" She was hesitant to mention Overton even though she assumed Zoey knew what he knew.

Keith looked at Zoey, "I think Zoey can tell you better, at least she can tell you what gave me a lead, maybe a clue. This Overton thing has a lot more to it than we thought. Zoey." He gently nudged the young woman.

Zoey hesitated slightly, then began, "Chief James, first – I want to apologize for the way I behaved when we first met ... and up until now. I realize ... I know you are an excellent police officer and a professional police chief. I may lose my job by saying anything, but ..." she paused and gathered her thoughts, "something is not right." She stopped, her lower lip quivered and her eyes teared.

Sarah waited patiently. She refrained from following her instincts to cradle Zoey's hand. Too personal with someone not personally accepted yet. She was glad to see Keith grasp Zoey's hand. Zoey needed support at that moment.

"I manage the Mayor's calender ... even for afterhours meetings." Zoey's lips twisted nervously. She wiped an overflowed tear. She glanced at Keith who nodded encouragement. "Last Sunday, I arranged a dinner for the Mayor and someone at Dave's Steak and Seafood." She stopped and stared at the hand Keith held.

Sarah knew Zoey expected affirmation of some kind. "I've never been there. I've heard good things."

"It is a good place to eat. The Mayor insisted that I go with them." Zoey's eyes begged for a question rather than just prattle.

"That sounds nice. You get to enjoy a good meal and meet the Mayor's acquaintances. That helps you plan events for her. Who was her guest?"

"Mr. Overton. Senior." Zoey paused before adding, "The one who died."

The Mayor dining with Terrance Overton, Senior was not alarming. He was a prominent citizen, her own words. Sarah wondered where Zoey was going and how that could be a lead for Keith's investigation. "Interesting. Did Mr. Overton seem well?"

"Upset with the Mayor, but he wasn't sick. Unless his blood pressure was up."

"Why was he upset with the Mayor?"

"He was upset with the Mayor for changing zoning and imposing a development moratorium on the new annexation. She wanted him to meet with someone who wants to put a factory in the new annex."

"A developer?"

"Not really. More like someone who wanted a factory built to his specifications. His company would lease it."

"Why would that upset Mr. Overton? He's a developer. Overton Enterprises recently built a factory on the old plastic factory site. They develop, sell and lease properties all the time. It's something they do."

"According to Mr. Overton, Overton Enterprises already has plans in place to develop that area. The Mayor's environmental moratorium that was applied to the new annex stopped his company's development. They can't develop it as planned. He was rather upset with the Mayor's proposal."

"It sounds like she offered him a path to recovery. Build the factory rather than houses."

"He said Overton Enterprises did not like to be told what kind of investments to make. Overton would have already been building the houses if the Mayor had not annexed when she did. The grade work was almost completed." Zoey paused, then almost whispered, "The Mayor rushed the annexation through. I scheduled a lot of meetings with area movers and shakers as well as the Councilmembers. It was a priority for her."

Sarah avoided politics as much as possible, though she was finding that to be more difficult in her role as Police Chief. She did recognize the sudden addition of the annexation, done with minimal advance notice. Sarah's budget battle was generally precipitated by the Mayor's reluctance to acknowledge the impact of the annexation on law enforcement resources. Streets, water, and sewer services were also an issue for budgeting, but those were other Departments' battles. "The annexation *was* a bit of a shock," Sarah noted.

"Reflecting back on it, it came as a shock to me. Suddenly, it was the Mayor's priority. She talked about saving the environment at the beginning. It seemed like a good thing, annex nearby areas to protect the environmental integrity of the city. The Mayor said she wanted Devaney to be a showpiece for proper environmental usage. I didn't connect the dots until recently. The environmental agenda morphed into private meetings with the man who wants the factory. It became an obsession. Initially, I was glad when the annexation was approved. I hoped that meant she would relax. Calm down." Zoey paused to sip her cup of coffee.

Sarah watched Zoey's reaction to the coffee. It was apparent that the young woman was more accustomed to lattes and cappuccinos. "I'm sure it's a lot of work, guiding an annexation."

"It didn't end there, not like I thought it would. Overton Enterprises was incensed. It cost them their project. Mr. Overton, Senior was relentless in his battle with the Mayor. I covered for her more than I care to admit. She said she didn't want to listen to his tirades. But I didn't blame him. The moratorium cost him a lot of money. Overton Enterprises already had money in site planning, architecture designs and engineering costs."

"Was the dinner a peace offering?"

"Not really. I think it was a last-ditch effort to sway Mr. Overton, to set up a meeting with the company that wanted the factory built. The company wants the factory in that area."

"Was the company representative at the dinner?"

"No. That was the reason for the dinner meeting. The Mayor wanted to convince Mr. Overton to have a meeting with the company."

"Did it work?"

"It did. Mr. Overton was to meet at Dave's on Monday, just him and the CEO."

"Do you know if he did?"

"I don't. In truth, the Mayor has been silent on the matter. Probably because of the murder of Officer Wyatt."

Sarah thought about the possible implications of the dinner meeting. She could not make a connection between the dinner on Sunday evening and Senior's death on Monday. She glanced toward Keith. "I suppose you could find the answer to that question. If I can get Junior to agree to a meeting with Mrs. Overton, you could ask her."

Keith nodded toward Zoey. "Zoey has more. Go on, Zoey."

Zoey cleared her throat. "The way the Mayor managed to get to Mr. Overton was odd." She formed her thoughts. "Only after Keith and I were talking last night," she glanced toward Keith who twitched at the revelation, "did I make a connection. Keith said something about aconite. Mr. Overton told the Mayor he used aconite for his arthritis. Again, I didn't think anything of it. Just the Mayor trying to schmooze someone."

"What prompted that conversation?"

Zoey answered carefully, "It was no secret to the Mayor, Mr. Overton's arthritis. The Mayor's grandmother suffered with arthritis, so it was a point of commonality. The Mayor does a lot of research on her opposition. She looks for every possible chink." Zoey looked at Sarah, "You upset her because she can't find your weakness, other than Maxie Smoltz."

Sarah shuddered to think of the brash, foul-mouthed teenager who was the knee-jerk suspect on her first case. That was Sarah's *Maxie Moment*, the time she learned to make sure she was right before she formed an opinion about guilt. "Thorough," she mused.

"She is. She doesn't like to engage with someone without information she can use. She knew Mr. Overton had problems with arthritis. She also knew he used aconite. She didn't tell me that specifically, but during the dinner, when she played with his mind, she guided him to discuss his pains and what he used. I didn't know what aconite was, not until Keith told me." Zoey paused, "But I suppose you want to hear the important part."

Sarah nodded, "Of course." She still did not see the connection between the Mayor and Mr. Overton's death.

"The Mayor made a point ... though I didn't notice it at the time ... of talking about Mr. Overton's arthritis when the Server, Kimmie, was at the table. Almost every time, she would bring it up as if that was the topic of conversation. I assumed it was to keep Kimmie from overhearing anything."

"That makes sense," Sarah said to encourage Zoey. "It's not as awkward as suddenly going silent. But you're right. That is an interesting coincidence. Odd that she would talk about aconite with Mr. Overton the day before he died of aconite poisoning." She glanced toward Keith who was watching her intently.

"It gets better," Keith said.

Zoey nodded. "That's not the oddest part. After Mr. Overton left, the Mayor asked Kimmie if she would be on duty Monday. Kimmie said she would be. When we were leaving, the Mayor told me to wait in the car. She said wanted to give Kimmie an extra tip for good service and discuss the menu for the meal on Monday."

Sarah stared blankly. Giving extra for good service was not all that uncommon.

"You don't understand. The Mayor never gives anyone credit for good service. And, if she wants something arranged, she always charges me with that task. That's my job."

Sarah considered what Zoey had said. She agreed with Keith's assessment of the information. Too much coincidence to ignore. Not enough factual data to be useful. "Keith, it might be worthwhile to talk with Kimmie. Find out what the Mayor said to her. See if it leads anywhere." She leaned back and sipped her coffee. It was cool. "I need a warm-up. Anyone else." As expected, both of her guests declined. "Zoey, is there anything else you would like to drink? I have some sports drinks."

"I'm good. Thank you, Chief."

"Call me Sarah when we're away from work." Sarah smiled at the young woman's reaction to the overture. "The Mayor loves all things green. I always wondered if she grew an organic garden or something. She seems the type who would."

Zoey laughed. "She's not that kind of green. She's a meat eater. Besides, she lives in an apartment, one of those nice ones on the northeast side. She doesn't have room for a garden." She gently pulled her hand free from

Keith's, no longer in need of the support. Almost as an afterthought, she added, "Once, she did show me a flower bed near the entrance to her apartment building. She was proud of it. It was very pretty. She said the groundskeeper lets her maintain it to suit herself. She said it's her escape, even if it's not technically hers."

"Everyone has to have an escape," Sarah said with a nod of understanding. "The gym is my escape ... when I get to go there." Sarah said.

Keith asked, "Do you think I should talk to Mrs. Overton? See if she knows anything else?"

Sarah thought for a moment. "The only thing she could offer is confirmation that he made the dinner engagement, but Kimmie can do that – if she worked Monday evening."

"Zoey, you wouldn't happen to know the name of the CEO Mr. Overton was to meet, would you?"

Zoey grimaced. "Bates. Carlton Bates. But I don't think that was his real name."

"What makes you say that?"

Zoey squirmed. "I learned in college that when a company is planning to locate, they keep their intentions and identities secret. Burner phones. Secret deals with Realtors. Sometimes the representatives use aliases until the deal is done."

Aliases seemed to be in vogue.


After Keith and Zoey left, Sarah made a list of things she needed to do for the rest of the day. Monday was booked with John's funeral and the procession, so everything needed to be done before Monday. She knew she could accomplish everything on her list. First would be a visit with the on-duty staff at the police station. No matter what, she could not ignore that need. Second would be a drive to the northeast side of town. She liked the scenery in that area, so much so that she had an implacable desire to pick some flowers.

# CHAPTER 31

## Monday 6:00 A.M.

The day would not be routine. Nothing about it could be. John Wyatt's funeral was at 10:00, followed by the long drive to the cemetery. But Sarah chose to begin her day with her normal routine. The fact that she had no overnight phone calls allowed her to do that.

Sweat pressed her hair against her head, that and her sweatband. Sarah sipped from her water bottle before she began a cool-down run around the gym's track. After a week without normal exercise, her body trembled after the weight machine and the stairs. Lack of proper nourishment added to the weakness she felt. Her workout pants, normally tight against her hips and thighs, hung loose at the waist. Lieutenant McCuskey's comment about her clothes rang true. Sarah was six pounds lighter than the previous Monday. She felt the weakness that comes with exhaustion caused weight loss. It did not stop her from finishing her run. It did slow her somewhat.

After Sarah showered in the gym locker room, she meticulously donned her uniform, the dark blue, crisply tailored pants and jacket that was adorned with gold epaulets and chest medals representing her accomplishments. The loss of six pounds kept the suit from fitting snuggly. She carried the accompanying eight-point cap under her arm. She would only wear it when appropriate.

Sergeant Honeycutt greeted Sarah when she descended the stairs from the office. Sarah smiled at the woman's cheerful, suggestive banter. The jovial Sergeant was the one solid thing in a world that had lost sight of normal. And things were not back to normal yet. They might never be. Too much had changed for normal, but things could regain some semblance of normal – a new normal. "Good morning, Sergeant. I trust the fact that I did *not* get an early wake-up call means the city is safe." Her comment bordered on being a question. Sarah knew to not count on it.

"Safe as can be in the lighted places. The shadowy places are always in doubt. You look refreshed this morning, Chief. Nighttime help?" Maria asked suggestively.

Sarah rolled her eyes expressively, "I was finally able to go to the gym."

"Whatever works for you," Maria chuckled. Her tone changed. "Are we still set for the funeral?"

"As far as I know. You and Taylor will ride with me. Liz isn't going to the cemetery, so she will be my connection to the station while we're gone."

"Too bad everyone can't go."

"Some duties can't be left unattended, even with outside assistance. The jail and dispatch aren't easily transferred. The Mayor finally signed off on my authorizations for external resources to cover the streets."

"Oh, is she still around?" Mayor Kamen had no support among Devaney's police officers.

"Yes. Jordon Kamen is still our Mayor. We need to learn to live with it," Sarah chided. She did not want her conflict to become a problem for the rank-and-file members of the Department. That would not be fair to them.

Sarah completed her morning rounds. She talked with each officer she met, in particular the Sergeants who would be handing off the Department's duties to police volunteers from nearby towns. Some of Devaney's officers would not make the long drive, for various personal reasons, so the city would not be entirely in the hands of strangers. The banks would be guarded. The mood was somber overall. Burying a friend, a family member, especially one as young as John Wyatt, was not an easy thing to do.

Sarah refilled her coffee cup when she returned to the bullpen. Boston was sitting in the Situation Room, sipping coffee and eating from a box of fresh donuts. The TV that was normally used to review evidence videos was still tuned to the local news. He watched intently as he ate his high calorie breakfast.

"Good morning, Detective," Sarah said.

"Morning, Boss," Boston replied after he swallowed his bite. "Want one?" He moved the box toward Sarah. Boston sported his official uniform, creased like it was brand new, which made sense because he only wore it for official occasions, and he avoided those if at all possible. Even his hair looked fresh.

Sarah started to decline, as usual. Instead, she took a napkin from a small stack near the box and selected a blueberry, cake donut. "I think I will." Her weight loss gave her permission to indulge. "It's going to be a long time until dinner."

Boston nodded and grinned, "Besides, it has fruit in it." He indicated the whiteboard with another nod. "I haven't heard anything on the DNA. Have you?"

"No. I'm not sure how soon that will come."

"Doesn't matter," Boston said as he shoved another bite in his mouth. He chewed, swallowed, and stated, "We know who he is. He hates his father, you know."

"You said that earlier. Why do you think that is?"

"Who knows, besides the son." Boston shrugged. "The rebellious son of a powerful man. The other kids turned out okay, if being like their dad is okay. This one is the black sheep. Every family has one. I was my family's."

Lieutenant McCuskey arrived, dressed in her formal uniform, her eight-point riding jauntily on top of her head. She wore the uniform well. She was comfortable in it. She joined the two in the Situation Room, commented on how good they looked, and readily accepted the offer of a donut. The discussion in the room was generally personal, focused primarily on the logistics of the funeral procession. Boston would drive with three uniformed officers as passengers. They were nightshift personnel who could nap during the drive. He was also the emergency response contact for the department. If something critical occurred that required a senior officer, he would break away from the procession and rush back to Devaney. Because of the distance the mourners would be traveling, Fort Scott PD had the foresight to provide a mobile bathroom facility at the cemetery, something better than port-a-potties.

Sarah was edgy for no reason. Despite the distractions, and with the assistance of a variety of law enforcement professionals, the day's events were set to flow like clockwork. Officer John Wyatt's death was a seminal event in her career, in her life. Nothing could change that fact.

Keith appeared, his expression torn between uncomfortable and eager. His uniform fit his body well. "Good morning, Chief. Lieutenant. Detective. Chief, I have an update, if you have time."

Boston scowled without speaking. Taylor smiled and said, "Good morning, Sergeant. You look dashing."

Sarah finished her donut, wadded the napkin, and dropped it in a trash can. She glanced at her watch. "We can go to my office. I need to make a phone call to the ME Lab first. Stacy should be there by now."

While Keith nervously waited with his notebook in hand, Sarah called Assistant ME Stacy Kemper. "Good morning, Stacy. This is Chief James, Devaney PD. I wanted to give you a head's-up. I overnighted a package to your attention. I need a DNA match, or genetic match, whatever you call it, run it against the Overton evidence you found. And … as you might imagine, it's a rush. Maybe even a super rush. Call me as soon as you know something. Leave a message if I don't answer." She ended the call and stared at the top of her desk. "Darn. I thought she would be there by now. I guess it is a little early, especially on a Monday. Voicemails always make you wonder if you explained everything clearly. Okay, what did you learn from the Server?" Sarah leaned forward. She always had good posture, but the stiffness of the uniform jacket forced her shoulders back.

"Kimmie's a flirt," Keith said.

"And you aren't?"

Keith grinned sheepishly. "Sometimes. But she talked a lot. And smiled a lot. The Mayor – she didn't know it was the Mayor. I didn't tell her. Didn't want her to gossip. She's relatively new in town. Doesn't keep up with politics. Kimmie's parents live in Enid, Oklahoma. Her dad was in the Air Force during Vietnam. She started college at Haskell Indian Nations University, but decided college wasn't her thing. She's Native

American. She moved to Devaney because she didn't want to go back to Enid."

Sarah listened carefully. "Keith, did you get her phone number?"

"What?"

Sarah grinned and shook her head dismissively. "Did you find out what the Mayor wanted?"

Keith blushed when he realized what Sarah implied. "I was just being thorough. Yes, the Mayor talked to her about the old man who was sitting at the table with her and Zoey. That would be Overton." He leaned an elbow on the edge of Sarah's desk.

"I assumed that."

Keith paused in reaction to Sarah's comment. He nodded and continued. "Anyway, she said the Mayor – she called her the *older woman*." Keith chuckled. "I thought that was funny. She said the older woman gave her a gift."

"A gift? You mean an extra tip?"

"No. A wrapped gift. She said the Mayor first asked her if she was working on Monday. Kimmie told her she was. The Mayor then told her the next day was the old man's birthday and that he would be there with some business associates. She wanted Kimmie to wait his table." He paused and waited for a response from Sarah.

Sarah said, "Go on."

"Kimmie said the Mayor told her to present the gift to the old man with a flair. She wanted a group-sing as soon as the salad was served. Said the Mayor told her to set the old man's salad to the side so the gift could be set directly in front of him. The Mayor requested for the whole group to sing. You know, where the staff gathers and sings to the birthday guy."

Sarah nodded expectantly, "I assume she did all that."

Keith chuckled. "Sure. The Mayor gave her a fifty-dollar tip so she could share with the other staff that joined."

"I assume Overton was there as planned," Sarah commented.

"Yes. She said Overton, "the old man", winked at her when he ordered his salad."

"Overton winked at her?"

"That's what she said."

"I've never thought of Overton as the flirty type." Sarah shrugged. "But that's me. Go on."

"Like I said, Kimmie's a flirt. She said she thought that meant he already knew about the surprise. But ... one thing she made a point of saying was she didn't think the three men were friends."

"Three men? There were three?"

"A man *about forty* - her words - and a younger man. The fortyish man smiled and laughed a lot, but the old man didn't."

"And the younger man?"

"Kimmie said he just listened with a foolish grin on his face. She said every time she heard him say anything, he seemed to be *"brownnosing"* the man in his forties."

"I wonder who he was," Sarah mused.

"An aide apparently. She said the two men came in together. She did say she thought the younger man switched salads with the old man while they were singing, but she wasn't too sure. She was focused on the gift and the song."

"How did Overton react to the gift?"

"She said he looked shocked and said thank you. She did say the old man seemed upset afterward, when the meal started, and conversations began. She said the conversations were serious, a little bit heated at times. Said he was upset. Said he was upset enough that it affected his appetite. He ate most of his salad but didn't finish his entrée."

"Back to the salad. You said she thought the younger man switched salads? Did she say anything else about that?"

"I didn't pursue it. She wasn't sure."

"I think you should follow that lead," Sarah said. "Did you ask her about the aconite and Overton's arthritis?"

"I did. But she said she didn't remember anything. She doesn't listen to specific conversations at the tables. Do you think it's important?"

"Probably just some attempt at auto-suggestion. Maybe to plant doubt if any questions arose." Sarah thought about it for a moment, then asked. "Did she overhear any names?"

"She said she always asks names. Likes to seem personal. But they laughed it off."

"Who paid?"

"What?"

"Who paid? Overton or the other man?"

"Overton. He used his card. She said both of the older men stood up, then the young one stood up, his eyes wide in shock. She was getting drinks from the bar for another table and couldn't hear what was said. The old man was upset, but he kept his voice low." Keith checked his notebook as he recited his information. He read what he had written, "*The other man seemed like he wanted to continue talking, but the old man waved his hand to cut him off.*" He paused to make sure Sarah was following him. "Then she said the fortyish man tried to reach out, but the old man put his hands on his hips. The other two men left the old man standing there. There was no doubt in her mind that the older man was accustomed to being in charge. At first, she thought all of them were going to leave, stiff her with the tab. But the old man sat down and held his head in his hands. She went to the table and asked if his friends had left. He muttered something like *They're no friends of mine.* She figured it was a business deal gone bad. She said a lot of business meetings happen in the restaurant."

"Did Overton appear ill? From what I've read, aconite reacts rather quickly if a lethal amount is ingested."

"If he was, she didn't notice it. Maybe he had his face in his hands because he was starting to feel it. She thought it was because he was upset over a deal gone wrong. Said he then settled the bill and left. Left her a decent tip."

Sarah mulled what Keith had told her. If her suspicions were right, Overton's death was a daring, well thought-out plan. Aconite poisoning was not something a forensics lab would look for. The symptoms of aconite poisoning were consistent with a heart attack. No reason for forensic analysis under normal circumstance. The perfect poison under ordinary circumstances. Even the most suspicious detective would not consider poisoning by aconite. Only because of Alicia's curiosity was it brought to light. Now it was up to the Assistant State ME. If Stacy could confirm a match between the aconite leaves found in Overton's lungs and the flowers Sarah harvested for analysis, Sarah could go to the DA. Everything was circumstantial, but it was worth pursuing. It was a hunch, a gut feeling. She had to make sure she was right before she acted. "Anything else?"

"Zoey's upset." Keith's tone changed to one of concern.

"Upset? About what?" Sarah sensed a shift in the young woman's attitude on Sunday. Maybe Keith could provide a reason for the change.

"The Mayor. Her job. Our relationship."

"Your relationship? You two seemed fine to me yesterday." Sarah felt queasy. Even though she and Keith mutually ended their relationship, she still felt a twinge of jealousy toward Zoey.

"Not Zoey and me. Me and you," Keith said, his eyes averted.

"We have no relationship," Sarah leaned back as she responded. The subject made her nervous. She did not want to bring up the memories.

"I know that. You know that. Zoey isn't sure. She knows I prefer working at the station, doing real police work. She thinks it's because of you. She thinks I want to be close to you."

Sarah relaxed, still uncomfortable with the conversation. "I suppose that's a normal reaction. She's young and insecure. I never thought I would say this about her, but I think she has potential. She just needs to get out from under the Mayor's influence."

"That's the other thing that has her upset. She's sure the Mayor will find out she talked to you. She's afraid the Mayor will fire her."

Sarah nodded. "I can understand that. She's talking against her boss. She's an Administrative Assistant. Exposing information comes with a lot of risks for someone in a position of confidentiality. Getting fired is one of them."

"I've tried to tell her that she is doing the right thing. That she wouldn't be doing it if she didn't know it was the right thing to do." Keith's eyes twinkled. "I even told her to remember your coffee cup, your motto, *make sure you're right then go ahead.*"

"You didn't!" Sarah exclaimed.

Keith's expression changed. "Yeah. She didn't like that very much."

"You think? Men!" Sarah shook her head. "Keith, tell her I said she just needs to hang in there. Everything is going to work out. She's doing the right thing. She just needs to keep her head down. And you - don't force her out of her comfort zone. She's young and still has a lot to learn. She'll do alright if she stays in control."

"That sounds kind of cryptic."

"Maybe so, but she'll understand. It's a woman thing." Sarah knew Zoey was in turmoil because her anchor had become a millstone. The young woman had a choice of releasing the weight or being dragged down with it. No matter the circumstance, it was life-changing to lose a mentor.

"Oh, Zoey did mention …" Keith looked down uncertainly, "didn't want me to mention it … she said on Monday morning early, the Mayor handed her a brown, manila envelope and had her deliver it to the front desk at the Marriot."

"Really?" Sarah perked. "Who was it for?"

"No name. Just a room number. She didn't remember the number. She dropped it at the desk and asked that it be delivered to that room."

"What was in it?"

"It was sealed. She said it was "puffy" and not very heavy."

"When we get back from the funeral, talk to Kimmie again. Find out if she remembers anything about the birthday surprise, especially the salad switch."

"Okay," Keith replied querulously. "But she said she wasn't even sure that happened."

"Something caught her attention. Otherwise, she would not have mentioned it. Press her."

# CHAPTER 32

## Monday 10:00 A.M.

The funeral lasted longer than most. The Devaney Police Chief was invited to present the eulogy. Sarah maintained her composure, relying on anecdotes of John Wyatt's time on the force to paint a picture of a dedicated police officer who loved his family and his city. Sergeant Honeycutt as the senior employee with Devaney PD - and unofficial historian - shared her experiences with John and how his career fit into the history of the Department.

A sound system was added so people outside the United Methodist Church could hear. The crowd outside was huge. Inside, family filled several pews on the right side of the sanctuary. City, County and State dignitaries filled the remainder of the right side of the sanctuary. Devaney Police officers in full uniform were pall bearers and sat in the left front pew. Law enforcement officers, some with spouses, filled the rest of the sanctuary. Civilians and several more law enforcement officers stood outside the church. From her seat inside the church, Sarah had no idea the size of the crowd there to pay respects. If she had known, she might have worried about the procession more than she already did.

It was 11:45 before a Highway Patrol car with strobes flashing led the procession from the funeral home. Two Devaney PD cars blocked traffic to allow the entire procession to fall into line. Sixty-seven law enforcement vehicles with lights flashing joined the procession as it wound its way through Devaney and to the highway that would eventually lead them to the cemetery north of Fort Scott. Sarah was driving her car with Lieutenant McCuskey in the passenger seat. Sergeant Honeycutt settled into the back seat, prepared to nap as they traveled.

The vehicle that was noticeably missing from the procession, at least in Sarah's mind, was the Mayor's. In fact, only one Councilman traveled to the cemetery. The time involved was a lot to ask of working people.

Shortly after noon, Sarah's phone rang. The Bluetooth connection was made. The ID was for State Highway Patrol. Her first thought was that the lead officer had a question or information. It was a State Trooper from a headquarters complex near Topeka.

"Corporal Johansson, how may I help you?" Sarah asked after he identified himself.

"Chief, Captain Anderson assigned a DNA investigation to me. Apparently, you have a case working over there."

"Yes. I didn't expect much this soon."

The Corporal laughed. "Well, it helps when the sample comparison involves someone important. People in the limelight leave DNA everywhere and much of it on record. No court order required."

Sarah grinned in Lieutenant McCuskey's direction, a reward for Taylor's attentiveness and curiosity. "That's good. Does this mean you have an answer already?"

"It does, Chief. The sample you sent me is a familial match to Senator Sheffield. Probably a son."

Sarah felt the warmth of satisfaction spread across her chest. "Would you swear to that in court?"

"With ninety-nine-point-nine-percent certainty. That's about as good as it gets. Your sample comes from the Senator's son."

"Thank you, Corporal. I'll let you know if I need anything more."

"Just call any time. Is this the man who killed your officer?"

"That's better than ninety-nine-point-nine-percent certain," Sarah replied. "Between you, me and jury, I'd say one-hundred-percent."

"Glad I could help. Like I said, just call if you need anything more."

Sarah sighed heavily. She used the Bluetooth to tell Boston. They agreed to interrogate Spencer as soon as they returned to Devaney. She called Liz and asked her to arrange the interrogation time with Grant

Hesseman. It would not happen if Grant did not agree to be present with his client. Liz knew to invite the DA to participate or observe.

It was 5:00 when Sarah arrived in the Police Station parking lot. A stop at Sergeant Honeycutt's house delayed her arrival. At the station, Lieutenant McCuskey looked at Sarah curiously when Sarah did not turn off her car. Sarah explained, "I'm going to see if I can get Cary Beecher to listen to me this time."

"The Councilwoman? I thought Sloan and Mendelson were helping you with the budget."

"They are. This is a personnel issue. Councilwoman Beecher is the HR connection for the Council."

Taylor grinned, "Maybe you can talk her into firing the Mayor?"

Sarah returned the grin. Taylor was unaware of how close she was to the truth. Her phone rang. Grant Hesseman's ID. "Hello, Mr. Hesseman."

"I'm tied up in traffic. It will be at least an hour. You can't talk to my client until I'm present."

"I know that, Mr. Hesseman. We'll see you and your client in an hour."

Sarah called Boston, who was already in the station. Boston told her that he was going home to change clothes. He said he did not want to ruin his uniform by sitting in a small room with a scumbag and his lawyer. Sarah called Councilwoman Beecher. After a few minutes of reluctance, the Councilwoman agreed to meet Sarah at her real estate office. Sarah did not know the woman was a Realtor.

Beecher Realty was owned and operated by Harris and Cary Beecher. Harris was the principal broker. Cary forced a smile and invited Sarah into her office. "Chief, I thought we settled this at the funeral home Saturday."

"Councilwoman, a lot has transpired since Saturday. I think you will want to hear what I have to say." Sarah doubted the woman cared, but she had to say it to the person with the knowledge of processes within the city.

"Even so, I'm not sure what you expect from me."

"Guidance, Councilwoman, guidance. That's what I hope to get from you."

Cary Beecher sat in her desk chair after offering Sarah a seat. She watched Sarah adjust the chair and sit. "Okay. I'm listening."

Sarah carefully laid out what she knew. "As I said Saturday, Mayor Kamen is a blood relative of our murder suspect, Spencer Sheffield. She and Wynn Sheffield are first cousins. That means the Mayor and Spencer are first-cousins-once-removed."

"And I as I told you Saturday, kinship is not a crime. You and I may share common ancestry for all we know. My mother's maiden name was James, blood related to the infamous James Gang family. Should our professional interactions be suspect because of it?"

Sarah ignored the question. She knew her ancestry and did not dwell on the strawman argument. "The issue is, as I said, the Mayor is interfering with an ongoing investigation and indirectly tampering with the jury. I received proof a few hours ago that Arthur Stevens is Spencer Sheffield - as we have asserted. We have direct evidence that Spencer Sheffield, cousin of Mayor Kamen, fired the pistols that killed Officer Wyatt. I know for a fact that she is still directing a Devaney Police Lieutenant, an employee of the Devaney Police Department, to find evidence that Winston Baines, not Spencer Sheffield, is the killer."

"That sounds like a good idea. Investigate the only other potential suspect. Either prove him the killer or leave no doubt that Spencer is the killer. Maybe that is something you should have considered."

Sarah stared at Cary Beecher incredulously. Her mind raced to the possibility the Councilwoman was on board with Jordon Kamen. As Zoey mentioned, sometimes Realtors were used to cover for secret business developments. "Councilwoman, do you think we have not already vetted Winston Baines' alibis? He was the first person we arrested, because of his possession of Spencer Sheffield's vehicle."

"I don't know what you do or don't do," Cary protested. "But the Mayor does have authority over the Police Department. She has the authority to offer directions, give orders to the police."

"Actually, Mrs. Beecher, she does not. She has authority over the Chief of Police, not the rank and file. She has no authority to engage in police work or to direct it."

"It might be valuable to your career if you remember the part about her authority over you," Cary said menacingly. "Pursuing her family tree is poor politics."

Sarah shook her head and held her anger in check. "This is not about politics, Councilwoman. I can assure you that if my cousin, or any other family member, was the primary suspect in a case, I would recuse myself to avoid the appearance of impropriety."

"The Mayor is not the investigator. You are. It doesn't sound like she is stopping your investigation. She's merely pursuing other options."

Sarah calmed herself and asked, "Mrs. Beecher, have you looked into NEO-Energy Sources?"

"No. Why should I?"

"Because I noted Wynn Sheffield's probable connection to NEO-Energy Sources."

"Where the Senator invests his money is none of my business. Why is it yours?"

"Two reasons. He is the cousin of the Mayor of Devaney. Also, because the Mayor of Devaney arranged a meeting between the CEO of NEO-Energy Sources and Terrance Overton, Senior." Sarah believed she was right to assume the person who met with Overton was Carter Laughlin using the alias of Carlton Bates. She waited for a response.

"Chief, again, why is that of interest to me? Politicians invest in businesses all the time. Mayors woo businesses to build in their cities all the time … to bring jobs to their constituents. I expect Mayor Kamen to do that for Devaney. Overton Enterprises is one of the premiere development firms in Devaney. In fact - in the county. Connecting the two makes sense. Worrying about it doesn't."

"It *does not* make sense if the Mayor is making policies that interfere with Overton Enterprises so NEO-Energy Sources can get a site in Devaney that belongs to Overton Enterprises."

Cary Beecher stood up and leaned across her desk. Heatedly she said, "Chief, cities make policies that are advantageous to job creators all the time. Even the State does it. Tax incentives. Utility assistance. Infrastructure." She leaned back, embarrassed by her outburst. "The list goes on. Governments waive everything from zoning restrictions to environmental constraints. It's how the world works. Chief, as I said Saturday, I will not become involved in a feud between you and the Mayor. Work it out - or leave."

Sarah watched the emotions wax and wane on the Councilwoman's face. Until she knew something factual, she could not safely pursue what needed to be pursued. "Councilwoman, it might be of interest to you to know what happened early Sunday morning in the city jail." She watched Cary fold her arms across her chest and challenge Sarah to continue. "At 1:00 A.M., I received a call about a fight between Spencer Sheffield and Winston Baines."

"Sounds to me like an error on your part, putting the two men in the same cell," The Councilwoman snipped.

"One would initially think that, yes," Sarah replied. "But one would not necessarily know that Spencer Sheffield - still lying about his identity - attacked someone in the original cell where he was assigned and was moved to avoid further conflict. One would not know that he and his lawyer convinced the Judge that he should be allowed to stay in the general population rather than be put in a single person cell."

"Are you saying he manipulated the Judge?"

"That's exactly what I'm saying. Spencer wanted to kill Winston, needed to kill Winston, so he could claim he was attacked by the real murderer and had to defend himself."

"That's a stretch, Chief. How could he pull that off by himself?" Cary walked from behind the desk to stand at the side. Her arms uncrossed but still not believing.

Sarah felt the tension in her shoulders relax slightly. It was now or never. "He couldn't. Let me give you a quick timeline. At 12:47, video shows Spencer, AKA Arthur, placing a call on a contraband phone. At 12:48, while everyone else was asleep, he grabbed Winston by the throat in a stranglehold. Fortunately, Winston struggled enough to knock Spencer backward into another prisoner's bunk. That prisoner shoved Spencer away, which loosened his grip. That shove gave Winston the ability to defend himself. Jailers intervened within a few minutes."

"Go on." Cary touched her chin thoughtfully.

"As I said, I received a call from the jail at 1:00. Oddly enough, Judge Varadkar received a call within a minute of that time. His call came from Counsel for Spencer Sheffield. Sheffield's attorney demanded an immediate review of his bond hearing. In the middle of the night," Sarah added for emphasis.

"So, you think the prisoner was calling his lawyer?" Cary's interest was piqued.

"No doubt. Initially, the lawyer told the Judge that Winston was killed in the attack. He was operating on someone else's word. That tells me Spencer intended to kill Winston and then dupe everyone into thinking it was self-defense. The criminal element seems to forget that this is a surveillance world. We have twenty-four-seven video cameras inside the jails and all public areas." Sarah wanted to add something regarding the fact that most of the coverage was to prove the Mayor wrong in her accusations that the police were overzealous when dealing with citizens.

"You have videos of the whole thing?"

"Absolutely. I would not be telling you this if I didn't. Plus, we have phone records from the lawyer, the Judge, the Mayor, the contraband phone, the Jail phone, Lieutenant Glasgow, and me. The lawyer knew about the attack before it happened, and the Mayor heard about it while it was happening – told to her by Spencer Sheffield's lawyer."

"Why?"

"To protect Wynn Sheffield's son."

"Why?"

"To keep the family name clean. Maybe NEO-Energy Sources didn't want an investor who was under scrutiny."

"Companies don't care, as long as it's not a key officer. Is the Senator a key officer?"

"No. Not as far as we can tell. Just an investor. We don't even know how big. But NEO-Energy's shady history tells me they cannot face too much scrutiny by the public eye. I also don't think the Senator could withstand the exposure a deep investigation of his association with NEO-Energy that his son's actions might bring. I believe the Mayor is purposely muddying the waters around Spencer to protect her deal with NEO-Energy and the Senator's reputation."

"It's all so murky," the Councilwoman said worriedly. "But, still, even if the Mayor has acted inappropriately, even illegally, what would you have me do? I can't fire her."

"No. I wouldn't expect that to happen. I would expect her agenda to be delayed until this is settled."

"You mean the budget?"

"That and anything else that could legally bind the city. Councilwoman Beecher, I will tell you that there is a real probability the Mayor will face some legal issues because of her interference into the murder investigation."

"Accessory?"

"I doubt that, but aiding is likely. Maybe more. I am asking you to ask for delays on any city business initiated by the Mayor until this is settled."

"Why me? Why not another Councilmember? Someone more vocal."

"That's exactly why I came to you. That's why you were recommended as someone I could trust. You are the least opinionated. Your reputation is for being cautious, of gathering the facts and evaluating data before you make a decision. I'm offering you facts and the data. If you recommend a delay for the Council meeting, the rest of the Council would accept it as non-political."

Cary Beecher returned to her chair and slowly lowered herself into it. "Do I have to decide now?"

"I don't expect that. The next Council meeting isn't until tomorrow night. I assume the agenda can be changed back to the published schedule at any time between now and then. I know you need to evaluate what I've shared with you. Maybe something more will unfold."

# CHAPTER 33

## Tuesday 12:00 Noon

Sarah spent the morning doing two things. She and Boston completed the fishbone on the whiteboard. After the late evening interrogation with Spencer Sheffield, the man's true nature came to light. He hated his father. The reason he hid behind an alias was so he could do things that would hurt the Sheffield name while maintaining reasonable anonymity. As Spencer Sheffield, he played a part in several burglaries, relying on young people like Buzz and Bear to do the theft. He kept his hands clean to avoid leaving evidence of himself. He lived as Arthur Stevens but told his cohorts in crime his true identity. If caught, there was nothing other than their word to connect him. In his angry mind, he believed he would walk free in the end hidden within his alias, and the notoriety would bleed over onto the family name. As Spencer Sheffield, he dealt drugs on a low scale, low enough that only his name was exposed, but never enough for law enforcement to expend resources to come after him. Doubt. Doubt about the family name was his desired outcome. He moved to Devaney because he heard his father was interested in a project in Devaney. Devaney was just another place to cast a shadow over his father's name, to hurt his father. His attorney, paid for by Wynn Sheffield, frantically tried to disassociate Spencer from the murder. Grant Hesseman sat helplessly in the Interrogation Room as Spencer spewed his hatred.

At its core, Spencer's hatred for his father was a hatred for authority. That hatred drove his almost maniacal desire to kill a police officer, to kill a surrogate for his father. His bitter hatred clouded his judgement. Killing a police officer would not be overlooked like a burglary or a minor drug deal. Anonymity and murder do not mix well. Spencer's sociopathy interfered with his primary goal to create public distrust of his father. He immediately realized that he had to separate himself from the murder. He devised a plan that his less-than-rational mind thought would establish the perfect crime. Winston Baines was supposed to die in a car wreck, in Spencer's car. Because of the physical similarities, Spencer thought no one would question the identity of the deceased driver of the car that was owned by him. Spencer did not expect Winston would be caught before he wrecked. He did not consider the fact the police would be looking for his BMW as rapidly as they did. He did not expect the two teenagers to become frightened and rat on him. Nothing of his plan indicated he was logical.

Sarah knew the case against Spencer was a piece of cake. A few additional bits of evidence would be added before it came to trial, but they would merely be icing on the cake. Conviction was assured. The only thing left to be determined – as far as she was concerned – was the sentence, life in prison or lethal injection. Case closed.

Sarah also worked on the budget. Councilwoman Beecher did not seem to be willing to enter the fray. Either the woman did not believe Sarah, or she believed the city could survive whatever the Mayor did regardless of any potential legal actions against her. Every time Sarah reviewed her budget proposal, her doubts increased. If the Councilwoman was unwilling to delay the process, would she also be unwilling to hear the facts on the budget? Sarah could resolve her concerns about Cary Beecher possible alignment with Jordon Kamen, personally as well as politically. Sloan and Mendelson were only two votes out of nine. According to Bill Keck, Beecher was one of the easy wins. Sarah was afraid she might have driven Cary away by being too strong. Even women were manipulative within the good old boy system.

Keith called, "Chief. I was able to talk with Kimmie – the Server at Dave's." He paused until Sarah made a sound of acknowledgement. "She didn't remember anything else – except one thing." He paused again, for effect. "She found a plastic baggie on the floor beneath the young man's chair."

"Why would a plastic baggie be on the floor?" Sarah mused aloud.

"I wondered that same thing. Then I thought of something. He was probably nervous. If he brought the aconite to the restaurant in a baggie, he had to hurry to not be noticed. Let's assume he had the aconite in the baggie in his jacket side pocket. Most of those have a stitch to hold them shut, so they don't interfere with the drape of the jacket. Maybe he hurriedly pulled out the aconite leaves and shoved the baggie toward his pocket but missed."

"It's a possibility. Too bad we don't have that baggie."

"Ah-ha. But we do. Miss Kimmie noticed it after the table was bussed. She picked it up and shoved it in her pants pocket so she could put it in the trash later. She forgot. The baggie was still there."

"The same pants she wore a week ago? How many times did she wash them?"

"Yes, and none." Keith laughed. "I heard a few excuses for why not, but I didn't care. I have the baggie. I'm on my way to Alicia."

"Good job, Sergeant. I hope there are viable prints on it after she handled it and carried it in her pants pocket." Sarah's hope was that the prints matched someone in the system.

Sarah's phone rattled fifteen minutes after Keith called. It was Assistant ME Stacy Kemper.

"Chief, the leaves you sent me match the pieces I found in Mr. Overton's lungs. It doesn't prove who did it, but I am willing to testify they came from the same source. Where did you find aconite growing in this part of the country?"

"They are pretty blue accent flowers when used in a mixed flowerbed," Sarah replied cryptically.

"*Pretty* dangerous is what I'd call them. Kids could put them in their mouth. That's scary. But I suppose there are a lot of poisonous ornamentals. Most are only lethally poisonous to pets, but they do cause a lot of diarrhea every year."

Sarah walked to the coffee pot. It was empty … and hot. Someone broke the rule. Whoever gets the last cup is supposed to brew a new pot, unless it was after noon, then they were supposed to turn off the pot. She checked her watch and decided to turn off the pot. She would get a bottle of water instead. The vending machines were on the ground floor in two places: in the breakroom for employees and in the lobby for the general public. She needed to stretch her legs anyway.

Mayor Kamen walked through the front door just as Sarah descended the stairs. She saw Sarah and stomped toward her in a rage. "What have you told Lieutenant Glasgow?"

Sarah stopped in her tracks. "I told him Winston Baines is not a murderer and he can stop his investigation." The conversation occurred early in the morning when the Lieutenant arrived for his usual job of snooping under the Mayor's direction. She tried to recall anything else she might have said. The conversation with Lieutenant Glasgow was brief and cordial, lacking tension, a change from previous days.

"That's not what I'm talking about. You told him he doesn't have to follow my orders." Jordon Kamen was loud enough that everyone in the lobby and nearby rooms peeked to see the cause of the disturbance.

"Mayor, I'm not sure how you came to that conclusion, but I'm positive you did not hear anything like that from the Lieutenant."

The Mayor glared at her. "Just because you have proven Arthur Stevens is actually Spencer Sheffield, that doesn't mean he is the murderer. I want to know the truth. Lieutenant Glasgow will get to the truth if you stop your interference into *real* detective work. He works for me ..."

Sarah snapped. Rage rose from the center of her gut and settled in her brain. "YOU want to use your influence to help your cousin. Mayor, step back or I will go to the DA and tell him you are interfering with a criminal investigation. Do you understand?" Sarah's hands were shaking with rage. Every PD employee within hearing moved closer. Sergeant Spader's hand was near her service weapon. The holster was unsnapped.

The Mayor fumed a moment, then wheeled and stormed out of the station. Two uniformed officers followed her and stared out the door. They watched until they were satisfied that she was gone. Sarah smiled appreciatively when they turned to assure her all was well.

Sergeant Spader muttered, "I can't stand that woman!"

Sarah replied to the Sergeant loud enough for everyone to hear, "Don't let the Mayor ruin your day. She's not going to ruin mine."

"Every time I hear her voice in those Press conferences, I throw-up in my throat," Sergeant Spader said, with a crooked grin. "Not pleasant."

Sarah's jaw dropped. "Thank you," she blurted. "Do any of you have a print kit handy?"

Sergeant Spader looked shocked. "Ah ... Yes. We keep one here in the desk. You never know when one will come in handy. Why?"

"Have someone dust the microphone in the Squad Room for prints. Send them to Alicia." She hurried to the Lab to give Alicia instructions for their use.

A few minutes after 3:00, Alicia called Sarah. "That was brilliant, Chief! How did you know there were fingerprints on the microphone that would match some of those on the baggie?"

"Just a hunch, but I had to make sure I was right before I moved ahead. Are they good matches?"

"Yes. I found thirteen points on a thumb print and ten points on an index fingerprint. I can't find the print in the system though. Do you know who it is?"

"I have an idea, but I'll know positively soon enough."

"Good, because there was some vegetable matter in the baggie. Leaves, but they aren't marijuana. I'll test them to see what they are."

"Overnight them to Stacy Kemper. Tell her to compare them to the samples I sent her the other day. Super-duper rush."

Sarah drove to the Courthouse to talk with the DA. She laid out everything she had regarding the Mayor's interference with Spencer Sheffield's murder investigation. As a participant, he was fully aware of the early Sunday morning events. The other data helped highlight the illegality of her actions. His own observations were supported by the evidence Sarah presented.

"This is serious, Chief. If everything checks out, and I don't doubt it from what I've seen, I question whether you should be involved."

"That's why I'm here. I know I'm right, but I don't want to go ahead under the circumstances. Conflict of interest. If ... when ... it comes to her arrest, I don't want my involvement to be her defense."

"My thoughts exactly. It's not easy in these cases. I'm going to involve the Sheriff if that's alright with you."

"I think that is the right thing to do. Either him or the State Police." Sarah was glad the DA's level of concern about interfering with the investigation of Spencer Sheffield was the same as hers. "Mr. Dunn, I also have concerns about any decisions that might be made by the Mayor while this is under investigation."

"I can't address that. The Council is part of the checks and balances, not the District Attorney's Office."

"But, Mr. Dunn, the Council as a whole is not aware of the situation. Only Councilwoman Beecher has heard any of this. A Council Meeting is scheduled for this evening that could result in several long-term decisions, decisions that could impact the city's future."

"I'm sure there is proper redress for any decisions that are suspected to be unduly influence."

"I'm sure there is, but the impact could be costly to the city and damaging to some citizens. It's a risk we should not take."

The DA looked at the information on the list Sarah gave him. "Who did you say has heard some of this?"

"Councilwoman Cary Beecher. She's head of the Personnel Committee."

"Okay. I'll talk to the Sheriff. I'll make sure he's on board. He'll probably come to you for any other evidence you have. I will also talk to the Councilwoman. She will do what she wants to do. I have no influence over city business."

"You have influence, Sir. Maybe no authority, but you do have influence."

Councilwoman Cary Beecher called Sarah an hour before the Council Meeting. "Chief James, this is Councilwoman Beecher. After discussing the circumstances surrounding the inclusion of departmental budgets in tonight's Council Meeting, the Council Parliamentary Committee has recommended that we follow the originally published budget hearing schedules. Your budget presentation will not be required until the regularly scheduled time next month."

"Thank you, Councilwoman Beecher." Sarah felt a burden lift from her mind. She wanted to ask the Councilwoman about the Mayor's reactions to the decision, but she also knew to allow the Councilwoman the dignity of a technical excuse. The result was the same.

# CHAPTER 34

## Wednesday 9:00 A.M.

Sheriff Herriman knocked on Sarah's door. He came up the front stairs and simply waved to Liz as he walked to Sarah's office. He smiled when Sarah looked up from documents on her desk. "How are you this morning?"

Sarah stood and walked around her desk. "Mixed emotions." She shook his hand and motioned toward a chair. "We've still got fresh coffee, if you want a cup."

"That sounds good."

Before either of them could leave Sarah's office for the coffee pot, Liz arrived with two cups of coffee. "Chief, I can pour this into your cup, if it's empty."

Sarah smiled, again unnerved by the attention. "Empty enough. Thank you, Liz."

Liz closed the door as she left.

"Chief, I would have called you last night, but I reckoned you were in that Council Meeting. How did that go?"

"They decide to go with the published schedule. I heard through the grapevine that the Mayor was upset, but ..." Sarah glanced at her phone, "I haven't heard from the Mayor this morning. I guess she's trying to figure out who to blame."

"Either that or she's waiting for the other shoe to drop," the Sheriff said. "And it will." He held the file folder Sarah gave the DA. "Do you have backup copies of the evidence to support this?"

Sarah nodded. "I have a copy of the thumb drive that has videos of several of the Mayor's outbursts in the station. I won't interpret them for you. I'll let you decide. I have the jail house videos, Judge Varadkar's recorded transcript of the emergency bond hearing Saturday night – Sunday morning, and a copy of the phone records of all participants."

The Sheriff was hesitant. "I spent some time with the DA. He kept the copies you gave him. He said he was going to show them to someone on the Council. I'm not sure what he expected me to do if he kept all the evidence. I'd like to see those if you don't mind." He chuckled lightly. "I suppose I'll get one of my Sergeant's to play all of this for me. I'm more of a paper kind of guy."

"I have all of it written on paper." Sarah handed him another folder. "Unfortunately, my notations might influence your thinking."

Sheriff Herriman grinned. "I reckon the Mayor's actions will influence me more than your notes – though I do respect your opinion more than most." He put on his reading glasses and perused the folder's contents. After a few minutes, he closed it and tucked his glasses in his shirt pocket. "Miss Sarah, this may not be enough to convict her of aiding a felon, but it's enough to cause the citizens to demand her removal."

Sarah smiled appreciatively. "I didn't tell the DA everything." She pulled Keith's folder from a desk drawer and placed it in front of her.

"Why not? If you have proof positive, this becomes a felony for sure."

"If you've got time, I'd like to go over something that makes that pale in comparison."

The Sheriff lifted his eyebrows and reached for his glasses. "You've got my attention, regardless of time. What do you have?"

A copy of Keith's hand drawn timeline was the first document in the file. Sarah had blacked out the names and merely used Subject 1, 2, etc. She handed it to the Sheriff. "I'm showing you this to get some feedback. I'm not pawning it off on you."

Keith's hand printed fishbone chart was neat. It was cluttered with ribs and even had a couple of ribs with appendages. The only thing with a question mark was a DNA request pending with the State ME. The Sheriff did not rush. Finally, he removed his glasses and stroked his chin thoughtfully. "I have a feeling this one was hard to unravel. What is aconite?"

"A plant that is used for some home remedies, mostly arthritis, but also heart issues and blood pressure."

Herriman thought a moment and glanced at the timeline without his glasses. "It would seem that you've already decided it caused heart issues, killed Subject 1."

"I think the evidence to support that is conclusive. Here's the Police Lab and the State ME report on the presence of the toxin."

The Sheriff lifted his glasses in front of his eyes and tilted his head to gain focus on the lab reports. "You darkened the name, but Subject 1 apparently ate some of the aconite. They found some in his stomach content … in his vomit." He studied the timeline again, still holding his glasses rather than wearing them. "He ate some in a salad. Subject 6 gave it to him."

"Without giving you the interviews with the names, can you determine which Subject provided the aconite?"

The Sheriff puzzled with the timeline for a few minutes. "Subject 3. Subject 3 if the pending DNA result can be connected to the flowerbed – though it's still circumstantial to a point." He considered his conclusion for a moment then added, "I'm probably not the best person to deduce stuff. That's why I have detectives. I may be a peace officer, but I'm also a politician." He laughed.

Sarah grinned at his self-deprecating humor. "Don't sell yourself short. You reached your conclusion rather quickly."

"Well," the Sheriff tapped his glasses on the timeline, "it's not hard when all the answers are recapped for me."

"Would you arrest Subject 3 based upon what's there?"

"Without the final piece, no. Question Subject 3, yes. Arrest, no. Subject 6 is who I'd arrest. Subject 3 provided the murder weapon. Subject 6 committed the murder."

"Accessory to murder?"

"Subject 3 *and* Subject 5. Subject 5 appears to have had prior knowledge of the murder. Is there a chance the Subjects will flee?"

"Two are not immediately available. Subject 3 isn't going anywhere. As a matter of fact, subject 3 probably doesn't even know we are aware of the murder."

"Fat and happy, huh?"

Sarah smiled wryly, "I'd never describe Subject 3 as fat or happy."

"What's your next move?"

"Wait for the ME. Go to the DA. If he's on board, make the arrests."

"I don't see how he couldn't be on board."

Liz texted Sarah. She would not do that if it was not important. *"City Council on the news."*

Sarah read the text twice. Her brow furrowed with uncertainty. The Council was seldom *on* the news. She stood. "Sheriff, the Council is doing something. Let's go see what it is."

The Sheriff and Sarah stood near Liz's desk and watched Kyren Bailey talking against a backdrop of City Hall. She was in the lobby waiting for someone to approach the podium the Mayor had permanently installed. The placards and signs boasting *"Citizen Friendly"* were on the walls and above every doorway in view of the lobby. Kyren was repeating herself with variations of the same message to fill airtime while she waited. *"The City Council is preparing for a briefing. We are uncertain the subject of the briefing. Our efforts to contact Mayor Kamen have been unsuccessful. Neither of her assistants are answering calls."*

Nine Councilmembers and the City Attorney came from the Council Meeting Room in single file. Councilwoman Beecher led them onto the stage that held the podium.

Kyren intoned, *"The Councilmembers are approaching the microphone. The Mayor is noticeably absent. We're not sure what is happening. We will stay right here until we know."*

Councilwoman Beecher went to the podium and adjusted the microphone. *"Ladies and Gentlemen of the Press. Fellow citizens of the great city of Devaney. The Devaney City Council met in an emergency Executive Session this morning. We are now prepared to vote on the matter discussed and want to do so publicly, as prescribed by law. Because the Executive Session was unplanned and unannounced, we are going to vote here in the lobby of City Hall as soon as the meeting is officially called to order."* She turned to look at the Councilmembers standing in a row behind her. *"Do I hear a motion to call this meeting to order?"*

*"Miss Chair, I move this meeting of the Devaney City Council be called to order."* Councilman Sloan recited his prepared motion.

*"Second,"* said a Councilwoman almost immediately.

*"The motion to call the Devaney City Council meeting to order has been made and seconded. I call for a voice vote. All in favor, say AYE."*

Every Councilmember said "AYE."

*"All opposed, say NAY."*

There were no NAYs.

*"This meeting of the Devaney City Council is called to order. What is the first order of business?"*

Councilman Sloan said, *"The first order of business is to have a rollcall voice vote regarding the immediate suspension of Jordon Kamen as Mayor of Devaney for alleged illegal actions performed under color of law."*

Immediately, at least two Councilmembers voiced "Second."

*"The motion has been made and seconded to have a rollcall voice vote regarding the suspension of Jordon Kamen as Mayor of Devaney. I will call the roll."*

Unanimously, the Council voted to suspend Mayor Kamen. Sarah's eyes were wide open. She was barely breathing.

Councilwoman Beecher then asked, *"Do I hear nominations for interim Mayor?"*

Councilman Sloan spoke. *"Madam Chairperson, I move that there be no interim Mayor nominations. Rather I move that we establish a special election one month from this date so the citizens of Devaney can select their Mayor."*

"Second" was sounded by all the Councilmembers. Another rollcall vote confirmed unanimity.

After asking if there was any other business and hearing none, Councilwoman Beecher asked, *"Do I hear a motion to adjourn this meeting of the Devaney City Council?"* The motion was made, seconded and approved.

Kyren screamed for attention. *"Councilwoman Beecher, what prompted the removal of the Mayor?"*

Councilwoman Beecher looked nervously toward the City Attorney. *"All questions regarding the Mayor's conduct will be addressed by the City Attorney."*

City Attorney Clay Benson stepped to the microphone and cleared his throat. *"The only response I have at this time is that the Mayor interfered with a criminal investigation. As Mayor charged with oversight of the Police Department, she did not maintain her objectivity and allow the Police Department to conduct an investigation. That is all I will answer at this time."* He summarily walked away, and the Councilmembers followed him.

Sheriff Herriman frowned. "I guess the DA didn't need my input after all … unless he wants me to arrest her if he files charges."

Sarah was numb. She was not sure what she had expected to come from the evidence she turned over to the DA, but what just unfolded was not it. At least, not the way it played out in public. She wanted to feel bad for Jordon Kamen. Sarah was sure Jordon would pursue legal recourse to salvage her job and her reputation. She was also sure that Jordon probably did not anticipate what would happen next. Sarah was not completely sure of what would happen next. She faced a tough decision.

# CHAPTER 35

Friday 9:00 A.M.

The Council did not dissolve the Department of Public Outreach. They determined that decision should be made by a duly elected Mayor. Zoey still had her job for the moment, but her fear of losing it was stronger. Councilmembers were only paid for meetings. They all had full time jobs or were retired and could not cover the duties of Mayor effectively. None of the Councilmembers expressed an interest in the job. Even without a person in the position, the Mayor's paperwork had to be shuffled. Zoey and Missy knew how to do that under the watchful eyes of the City Council. Lieutenant Glasgow and Sergeant Locke maintained their offices in City Hall, but they reported directly to the Police Chief. Sarah began working to mend fences for the two men. The first thing she did was share the fact that Sergeant Locke was working another case without concern for the Mayor's influence and Lieutenant Glasgow revealed the depth of the Mayor's interference into the investigation. She resolved to fight with the new Mayor for their reassignment to the Police Department, put them back where they belonged. The contact cards and the hotline would be a separate battle; the concept had merit if not value.

The DNA results for the leaves in the baggie were a match to the aconite plants Sarah sent to the State ME, and to the small bits found in Terrance Overton, Senior's lungs. Sarah looked at the photos she had taken to verify the source of the samples. Everything was in place to go to the DA. She saw nothing that could be challenged regarding the veracity of the evidence or the chain of custody. Her appointment with District Attorney Dunn was scheduled for 11:00. She suspected that he anticipated more evidence against the Mayor for her interference with John's murder investigation.

Sarah was nervous. More than she could ever remember. The magnitude of the visit with the DA was not lost on her. Try as she might, she could not keep her hands from shaking. She thought Jordon Kamen's removal would have given her peace. It should have. Without the overbearing Mayor, she should be free to focus on her job. But the first job she had to do was complete the investigation of Terrance Overton, Senior's death, of his murder. Success or failure, the consequences of the job at hand could not be taken lightly. Sleep was not easy to attain. Sarah was exhausted. She was sure she had lost more weight. She could not hide behind conflict of interest when it came to performing her job.

Bill Keck knocked on her door frame. "Good morning, Chief," he said. "May I come in?"

"Of course, Chief." Bill Keck would always reserve the right to be called Chief as far as Sarah was concerned. The sight of him in her doorway gave her comfort, a moment of confidence that everything would be okay. Among all the changes she had to accept, the one thing that did not change in her life was Bill's belief in her, his support for her. Sarah hoped that would never change. "You're always welcome here. Do you want some coffee?"

"I'm good for now. Too much caffeine gives me the shakes." Bill smiled and said, "I think you might benefit from less coffee and more rest."

Sarah asked self-consciously, "Do I look that bad?"

Bill shook Sarah's hand, grasping it with both of his. "You look exhausted – and nervous. I would think you could rest now, settle into a normal routine. John's murder is solved. His memorial is behind us." He paused, then added, "And the thorn in your side is gone." He sat in one of the guest chairs and smiled broadly. "You know, I like the looks of it from this side."

Sarah stopped halfway into her move to sit. "What?"

"Life is much better from this side of that desk. A lot less stress. For all those years, I didn't even know I was stressed. Not even when some newbie mayor tried to upset my apple cart. But … the stress is always there, newbie mayor or not. You can't escape it. Do you know how I handled it?"

Sarah sagged into the chair, unsure where Bill's conversation was leading. "No."

"I embraced it."

"What does that mean?"

"Stress is not necessarily bad, Sarah. If you embrace it, stress will feel natural on your shoulders. It gives you backbone when you need it. It gives you a reason to wade into the worst situations you can imagine. But ... I have a feeling you are facing something bigger than what you've just gone through. Otherwise, I wouldn't be seeing those worry lines on your face. What is it?"

Sarah felt relief from the Chief's words. He could read people and would trust them when they needed to be trusted. "I knew you could say something that would tie all this together. And you're right. It is bigger - and more tangled." She held up a thick folder. "This is next on my to do list. I've got everything ready for the DA. I've run it by the Sheriff. I'd like to run it by you, check my facts." She handed the Chief her timeline without names and waited until he studied it. She returned it to the folder when he finished and nodded for her to explain. "Did you know Terrance Overton, Senior was murdered?"

"No." Bill Keck was visibly shocked. "I thought it was ruled natural causes, heart attack."

"It was, but Junior didn't believe it. He insisted we investigate." Sarah paused and stared at the folder.

"What made him think it was murder?"

"Senior was in relatively good health. No significant heart disease. Nothing that would predict a heart attack."

"Still not unusual for a man his age to have a heart attack. What did you find?"

"Aconite poisoning. There was aconite in his salad the evening of his death. He was poisoned."

Bill nodded toward the folder. "I take it you know who?"

"Sort of. That's what has me bugged."

"Sort of? Either you do or you don't."

"Yes, I do know who, but there was more than one person involved."

"Someone was the key. Who was that?"

"Someone who will get away with it while everyone else will take the fall."

"So, who is involved?"

"The CEO of a company called NEO-Energy Sources. He used Mayor Kamen to stop Overton Enterprises from developing property in the new annexation. She used her power to invoke her environmental agenda to establish a building moratorium. He and his sycophant and the Mayor were involved."

"Did I hear you say the CEO used the Mayor? It sounds like she was unwittingly involved. Innocent of intentional wrong-doing." Bill leaned back and allowed Sarah to explain.

"That's the problem with all of this. Actually - someone else was using the Mayor. An almost invisible, untouchable participant. The CEO was merely allowing it to happen, encouraging action on the part of the Mayor, anything that would give him what he wanted."

"What did the CEO want?"

"He wanted the Overton site that was located outside the city limits. The Mayor pushed through an emergency annexation. The Mayor imposed her environmental initiatives to stop the Overton Enterprises housing development. She was pushing the Overtons to use the property to build a factory for the NEO-Energy Sources instead of the houses and then lease it to them. As you can imagine, it enraged the Overtons and … well, Terrance Senior was always known as a street fighter. Also, she was going to give tax incentives for them to locate here."

Bill nodded. "So far, it sounds like a good game of hardball. Nothing that could be proven to be illegal. Cities offer tax incentives all the time."

Sarah pulled a document from the folder and held it up demonstratively. "Tax incentives are not illegal but offering taxpayer money to a company for development is. That's where the invisible participant came in. He came in to influence the Mayor."

"She was offering city money to them?" Bill raised up to listen.

"Yes. That's why she wanted to cut departmental budgets."

"How did you find out about something like that? Surely she was smart enough to not leave a paper trail."

Sarah smiled and put the document in the folder. "Sometimes honest people can't stand dishonesty, even if it costs them their jobs. Secretive leaders expect others to do their bidding. Sometimes that involves Post-It Notes and verbal directions, things people think of as disposable, untraceable." She lifted a piece of paper with several yellow notes attached.

"Why did they murder Overton?"

"To shut him up - or to force Overton Enterprises to capitulate. I'm not entirely sure. Overton Senior took the fight to the Mayor. As we all know, he was a fighter, willing to go toe-to-toe. Junior's a tough businessman, but he didn't have to build a business the hard way. He doesn't know how to claw his way through the trenches. That was Senior's forte. The powers-that-be behind NEO-Energy Sources' location in Devaney thought his death by natural causes would stop the fight. Aconite is not normally a *murder* toxin. No one would even suspect its use." Sarah smirked. "They didn't count on our curious Lab Rat. Nothing gets by Alicia."

Bill thought a moment. "From what you've told me ... if the evidence you have supports it, the DA can charge them with murder *and* conspiracy to commit murder. Maybe more. You've done your job. Let the DA do his job. When he issues the warrants, you make the arrests and let the Courts decide. You can't do it all. Don't embrace *that* stress. Let it go."

"That makes sense. I guess I'm stressing because I want to see the conclusion today. I won't rest until I see every one of them behind bars. I'm impatient." Sarah smiled weakly.

"Don't be impatient. You know as well as I do, impatience is the enemy of good police work ... and a major stressor."

"Still, in the back of my mind, I'm afraid I may have missed something. What bothers me most is that I don't have any concrete evidence to connect all of this to the person I believe is behind it. All I have is circumstantial. Mostly a hunch."

Bill leaned across the desk and splayed his hand atop the folder. "Sarah, you have enough evidence to begin the process. Once the charges are filed, the rats will start running. With luck, one of those rats will squeal."

Sarah bobbed her head in thought for a moment. "I suppose you're right."

"Better yet, Sarah, *you're* right. Now – go ahead."

Sarah smiled cynically. "I just have to remember to read the Mayor her Mirandas when I go get her."

Bill chuckled at Sarah's comment. He was aware of Clara Taylor's legal maneuver in Joseph Elsea's defense. "So, one of them *is* the Mayor? I thought Subject 3 might be her." He grinned. "With this behind you, are you still on for golf tomorrow? 7:30 tee-time."

Sarah shook her head and sighed. "I'm sorry, but this is not behind me until I have Jordon Kamen and the others in cuffs. I need to take this to the DA in the morning. He's not going to like it, working on Saturday, but we can't let this linger." She paused and smiled devilishly. "I think I'll have Lieutenant Glasgow and Sergeant Locke help make the arrest." Her topaz eyes softened when she looked at Bill. "Chief, you don't know how much I appreciate your support. I miss having you here."

Bill smiled and leaned back in his chair. "Thank you, but you deserve all the support I can give. You need a break from work, but I understand. The charges need to be filed and warrants issued before the suspects move too far from where they are. You were a highly regarded detective when you worked for me. You are on your way to becoming a highly regarded police chief." He paused a moment in thought, then he asked, "How would you feel about reporting to me again?"

A wash of mixed emotions swam across Sarah's mind. She replied with the only response that came to mind. "Being your Detective would be fine by me. A lot less stress. When will the Council reinstate you as Chief?" Sarah enjoyed the role of Chief, but she was not married to it … yet. From the moment she was placed in the position, she took it as a courtship, or a fling. Not a permanent relationship.

Bill cocked his head back and laughed. "I'm not coming back as Chief. That's yours. You've earned it. I'm thinking about running for mayor – if I have your support."

"Mayor? Yes. I'll support you." Sarah was puzzled. "I thought you liked retirement and the lack of stress."

"Actually, I think I like a little stress. What I *don't* like is watching from the sidelines. Several of the Councilmembers and some businesspeople surprised me with a visit last evening. They encouraged me to run for Mayor. They think Devaney needs some stability in the Mayor's Office. For some odd reason, they think I'm it."

"You have my vote … and every vote in Devaney PD." Sarah's shoulders relaxed.

Printed in the United States
By Bookmasters